The Reluctant Guru of Alphabet City

—A Novel

ABSOLUTELY AMA/ING eBOOKS

Habent Sua Fata Libelli

ABSOLUTELY AMAZING eBOOKS

Manhanset House
Shelter Island Hts., New York 11965-0342

bricktower@aol.com • tech@absolutelyamazingebooks.com
• absolutelyamazingebooks.com

The Absolutely Amazing eBooks colophon is a trademark of
J. T. Colby & Company, Inc.

Library of Congress Cataloging-in-Publication Data
Lentchner, Larry
The Reluctant Guru of Alphabet City.
p. cm.
1. FICTION / Coming of Age. 2. FICTION / Psychological.
3. FICTION / Women.
Fiction, I. Title.
ISBN: 978-1-949504-42-2 Trade Paper

August 2023

The Reluctant Guru of Alphabet City

—A Novel

Larry Lentchner

Also by Larry Lentchner

Onederland
Sexual Survivors—A Novel

Available from
AbsolutelyAmazingEbooks.com

Table of Contents

Acknowledgments

I would like to express my appreciation to Dolores Porcaro for her very needed editing assistance.

This book is dedicated to my father, Emil Lentchner, who grounded me in a life of service and ethics, whether, at the time, I liked it or wanted it, or not.

Part One

Goodness is not a product of malevolency. Nor is the reverse true. However, the unintegrated shadow of the parent will manifest itself in the persona of the child. There it swims in a turbulent sea of conflict and confusion.

1

Esther Shapiro's parents were flabbergasted. Her father, Ben, when confronted with the inescapable fact that his precious daughter was somehow involved with heroin, or, at least it was in her possession, covered his ears. He had an unrealistic hope that this simple act could erase the import of the words, the repellant ones that now echoed in his head. It felt as if he had been told that he hadn't served in the war, or perhaps, that the Chinese had suddenly overtaken Korea, or, maybe, that Manhattan, his birthplace, was still the property of that native, what was their name, tribe. It just didn't make any sense. As he sat in a crowded corner of the subway car, he found himself taking out his wallet and pulling out a photo he had taken of her just before the junior prom, what was it, only five months or so ago. She was such a beautiful girl. Her strawberry blond hair fell casually over that pretty peach dress, the one they had found for her in Orbach's. It outlined a face that he thought embodied a classic sort of beauty. It could have been the face of a woman portrayed on a Roman cameo, like on his cuff links, the fancy ones his Aunt gave him, before Esther was even born. Sure, his mother and sisters were all good looking, and Esther's mother, his wife, Rose, was undeniably attractive, but, somehow, all their combined family features had been mixed together to produce this wonderful, spectacular daughter. In the moment though, the same image that usually fetched warmth to his heart and a smile to his face, brought fear and consternation to his racing mind. His little girl. His baby. In some jail cell? What did they call it on those television shows? A holding cell?

No, this couldn't be, could it? It had to be some hideous mistake. He had been at work, at the office, mind you, when he received a call from the Jamaica police precinct, from some officer, an adolescent relations person, or something like that. Ben had a men's suits wholesale and retail showroom over on East 27th Street. He grabbed his jacket and ran out as soon as he got the call.

Some guy named Robinson. Just this side of rude, if you ask me. He had so bluntly informed Ben that Esther was in their custody. His Esther. He needed to come to the station. ASAP. She was being held for possession of that drug, that heroin. How could that be? Esther was in school. They had walked together to the subway just five hours ago. He had offered to drive her to school, but she said he didn't need to bother, and besides, they could enjoy walking. What a great way to start off a day, it was. Your teen-aged kid actually enjoyed taking a hike with you, her father, to the subway. How many fathers could say that? He had felt so proud all along the way. Right through Midland Parkway, like a parade. At this moment, right now, it didn't feel so hot.

He got out at 179th Street, and began to walk over to where he thought he remembered the police station was. Maybe he should call that lawyer, Weinstein. No, let's find out what's going on first. No need to blabber everything out into the world before you know what's going on. That's when he remembered that he hadn't even called Rose yet. And why hadn't they called her first, instead of him. The nurse at school always called Rose if Esther was sick. Well, he wasn't going to take a bunch of time away from getting there and finding out what the hell was going on. Who knows? Maybe they had called Rose after him. Or maybe Esther just wanted him there. These are impossible things to know. Just get there and find out what the deal is, and then maybe it's just a question of showing them that the whole thing is a stupid snafu or something. If Rose isn't there, he could call her from the station. You don't scare the hell out of your wife unless you really know that something is what it's supposed to be. What they're telling you. He was starting to get mad. These goddamn idiots! If this thing turns out to be some big stupid mistake, they're going to regret it. You can bet the family savings on that!

As Ben got closer to the precinct, he stopped for a few seconds, realizing that he'd better calm down before he walked in. Taking a handkerchief from his pocket, he wiped the beads of sweat from his brow and neck, took a couple of breaths, dabbed his face a couple of times, before replacing the handkerchief in his pocket, straightening the peaks, and only then strode into the station. An officer sat on a high bench, like you'd see in a courtroom. It loomed in front of him. My God, you have to crook your neck up just to ask the guy a question. You just walked through the door and it's like you're already in court, looking up at some judge, like you're being sentenced for something.

"Officer, do you know where I could find Officer Robinson?"

"Turn to your right, down the hall, and fourth door on the left." The guy didn't even look at him! Just kept writing on whatever the hell he was working on, like it's every day you get called into the cop station, and it's so normal you don't even have to acknowledge that somebody's there, right in front of you. It's not like he was asking for an escort. The stationhouse was pretty empty, just a few cops walking here and there, not a lot of other people. Those that were seemed on the seedy side. Well, what do you expect in a precinct house? The Bobbsey Twins? They better be keeping his Esther safe.

The door was open. Well, at least the desks, there were two of them, were normal sized. One of them had a negro gentleman, an officer, behind it. Had to be a sergeant. You could tell by the stripes on his arm. Ben had never seen such a messy desk, papers strewn here and there, everywhere. If someone at work had a desk like this, he'd be history! Guess there has to be a lot of paperwork in policing. But look at it! The room was cluttered with documents and forms everywhere. How the hell did they find anything? And where was Esther? Ben thought she'd be there. Hope they didn't lose her.

"Ahem. Officer Robinson?"

He looked up. "Sorry, I didn't hear you come into the room." Ben thought he could see the cop's eyes sizing him up.

"I'm Mr. Shapiro. You called me," and then added, "About my daughter, Esther."

The policeman put down his glasses and straightened out the papers he had been working on, shaking the bundle a couple of times to line the edges up. He slid a paperclip over the top, and put it all in a brown file folder that seemed to contain a number of such, what would you call it, portfolios, cases?

His face eased into a polite smile. "Ah, pull up a seat, Mr. Shapiro. You made really good time, coming all the way from Manhattan. This has to be really difficult for you."

Ben saw one of those solid old dark mahogany side chairs off to the left of the desk, and drew it over. Sitting down, he saw Officer Robinson pull another casefile from the other side of the desk, and review its contents before looking again at Ben. Guess he could find stuff. He tapped the file a few times on the desk, the last tap accompanied by an almost imperceptible flourish.

"First of all, your daughter, Esther is not here. She's over by the courthouse, you know where it is, over on Queens Boulevard?" Ben nodded. "You can pick her up over there in about an hour. Yes, we are not going to hold her overnight. She'll be going home with you, tonight."

"Thank God," Ben's chest sighed and his body relaxed a scintilla into the chair. "So, this whole thing's just been a stupid mistake?"

"No, Mr. Shapiro, there have been no mistakes. Your daughter is in trouble, but she will be able to go home with you and your wife tonight." Officer Robinson cast his sympathetic smile again, as if it could magically calm Ben down. "Esther was one of about a dozen young people caught up in a sting this morning, over on Jamaica Avenue. She was attempting to buy 5 bags of heroin. Unfortunately for her, the individual who she believed was a drug dealer, was in fact a colleague of mine. Once she paid him and started to leave with the drugs, she was summarily arrested, and brought here for an interview. I interviewed her myself. It was when our talk ended that I called you, and she was transported over to the courthouse."

"But my daughter, my Esther, she's never been in any kind of trouble before." The reality was beginning to sink into Ben's thinking, but it still made no sense to him. Esther was a good girl.

"Yes, Mr. Shapiro. It was because we confirmed that Esther has never run afoul of the law before this instance, that we are trying our best to keep her out of the system."

"I don't understand. I don't understand any of this."

"Well, Mr. Shapiro, we have a program that is administered by an adolescent public council here in Queens. It's designed to help teenagers get help rather than jail. That's what I want to tell you about, and that's what Esther is going to need your help with."

"Anything, Officer. You just tell me what you want, and you can consider it done." What, did he need to make a donation, maybe to the Police Benevolent Association? "I'll do anything for my Esther."

"So, here's the long and short of it. We can release Esther to your parental custody. At the same time her court papers will be put away in a judge's file, upon his approval, and there they will sit for one year. We will expect that Esther will have to get some therapeutic help over that time, and if, after a year has passed, she hasn't got into any more trouble, the judge will tear up the file, and the whole incident will be non-recorded history. If she can turn it around and avoid any legal difficulty, it will be as if it never happened."

"You mean you'll give her another chance?"

"Well, sort of. The key ingredient here is that you need to commit to getting her some therapeutic help, something that will address her drug usage."

"But Officer Robinson, I don't think Esther might ever have done this before. This had to have been some crazy first-time whim of hers. She's a good girl, even if I have to admit that we've noticed that she can be a little but impulsive from time to time, if you know what I mean. Kids these days. Or maybe she was just doing a favor, and getting this horrible stuff for a friend. We've taught Esther that she has to be there for others."

Robinson's face soured a bit, and he said very firmly, "Ben, if I may call you that, Ben, you are going to have to face the fact that your daughter, even if she is a good girl, has been using heroin for quite a while now. Parents don't always know everything about what their kids are doing. She keeps her works, that's a needle and other paraphernalia, in her pocket book, and she has tracks in between her toes. That's where she shoots up."

Ben could have been run over by a big and heavy Mack garbage truck. Keeping needles in her bag? Keeping bags in her bag? Shooting drugs into her feet? Who were we talking about here? Part of Ben wanted to run back to work, argue with Sol about the price of buttons, or something, and forget this nightmare was even happening. But men don't run away from things. He'd learned that, for sure, in the war. Stand up, even when it feels you can't. I can do this. I can do this.

"So, what kind of help do we get her? I mean, this isn't exactly an area I know something about. Where do we go?"

"Well, here's the deal, Ben. You're going to go over to the courthouse, and bring these papers with you." Robinson held up the folder. You're going to take it over to Judge Foley's office, and speak to one of his clerks, a young man named George Stinson. He will ask you to sign some papers for the court record, and he will then direct you to the holding area so that you can pick up your daughter, Esther. Once she is released to your custody, you will both go to see a social worker, a Mrs. Williams. Her office is in the annex, just in back of the courthouse. The two of you will talk to her for a while. She'll provide you with all the necessary answers to what I guess are the million questions running around your head, right now. I've written all these stops on a form that's just inside this packet of papers that you need to give to Stinson."

"Do I bring my wife? Dos she need to be there too?"

"That's up to you, Ben. I called you because that's the choice that Esther made, when I talked with her. But if you feel that Mrs. Shapiro should be there, you should certainly bring her along." And with that, Robinson got out of his chair and stuck out his hand.

Ben understood that he was supposed to leave now, and started to also rise from his chair. "That's it? I should go now, and do all this?"

"Yes, Mr. Shapiro. You need to go get Esther." The officer flashed that less than genuine empathetic smile again. "And good luck, Sir. I hope we don't have to have any other dealings, if you know what I mean."

Ben agreed with that. Oh boy, did he agree with that.

2

Esther noted to herself that the women in the cell were mostly pacing back and forth, idly walking about, bumping elbows and hips along the way. She felt as if she were in an overcrowded fish tank, trapped with a school of scaley goldfish, unconscious, anxious and always in purposeless motion. It wasn't the cell that skeeved her out. It was the sickness that surrounded her, the scratching, the muttering, the overwhelming smell of fear. She settled herself on the back bench, off toward the sidewall, trying to find a place to think, to plan, to figure out if there was any way out of this mess.

Okay. I got popped. Had to happen sooner or later. Anyway you figure it, it's on me. Told myself I wouldn't get hooked, and here I am, drug sick and all, needing to go find it, and not even knowing what the fuck I'm doing. What kind of loser am I? Tony ain't here. That sack of shit, always telling me not to worry. Always telling me that he'd take care of me. Sure, and who's the stupid fart brain who believed him? Like a lamb to slaughter, he just leads me in. Damned if that's ever going to happen again. Use or be used. Use 'em for fun or whatever the fuck else you want, but don't let them take you where you don't know the deal. You got to stay five steps ahead of those suckers, or they'll suck whatever they want out of you, and send you on your not-so-merry way.

Esther kept trying to pull herself out of her loop of self-contempt and anger, with little success. The part of her that had known all along that it had to come to this, that she was turning into a god-damned junkie, needed to point its finger at her and tell her that she should have been listening to her inside voice. As long as you can run the "I told you so's," you can convince yourself that you're not the schmuck you are. You really know better. It was just a temporary moment of insanity, and besides, everybody has some of those idiot times. Especially when you're still growing up, a teenager who's figuring it out. She was making herself feel better by making herself feel worse. Ironically, she thought, because for a while she'd been making herself worse, by making herself feel better.

Okay, slow down. This isn't getting anywhere, your head's just running around in circles. Focus. What do I have to focus on? Dad, Dad's going to be here any minute now. What am I going to tell him? That Robinson guy must have told him everything, anyhow. He wasn't such a bad dude, not like the cop who popped me, anyway. God, did he have to make me take my shoes off and show him my stupid fucking toes? How embarrassing can you get?

Oh Dad, how do I get into this with you. You're the nicest, most naïve man in the universe. It's like you don't even know that Mom and I take advantage of you all the time, and you keep thinking that it's you that have to protect us. I don't want to hurt you, and this is going to burst that big fat bubble of yours, the one that has me being some super goody figment of your velvet imagination. I don't know. Is this what I have to do to get you to see me, and not that comic book Betty who's hanging around with Archie? It's me, Dad. The girl who does drugs and does guys, and never knows whether she's using or being used. That one. Oh, what the fuck am I going to tell you? You don't want to hear that, and I don't know if I want you to hear it or not. Shit, I'm not so sure I want to hear it either.

Maybe I should have had them call Mom. Oh sure, and then I would have had to hear her whining and lecturing and making it all about her, and what she has to put up with. Well, I'm going to hear all that anyway, but later, please later. No, it's better that I had them call him. Let him handle her, or at least deal with her bullshit when she finds out. Sorry, Dad. Better you than me. I mean, you married her.

Okay. What's the worst that can happen. That Robinson guy already told me that I'm not going to jail, at least once Dad gets on board. And it's not like he's going do anything else. As long as I stay away from this shit for a year, there's not even a record. So, what are you getting your skirts all ruffled for, girl? I mean your image is blown to shit. But is that such a big deal? It kind of comes down to Mom and Dad, they're the only ones who are going to know about this. Can't imagine they're going to call up Aunt Phyliss and brag about her perfect little niece getting busted for buying smack. Mom and Dad are the only ones that are going to have to know. I guess they'll just have to get used to the idea that little Esther isn't exactly the pretty picture they've got in that pretty frame in their doting heads. What's that saying, "nobody promised them a rose garden?"

What about school? If they send you to some rehab place, you're going to miss school for a while, and do they have to know why? I mean once the office will know, it's going to get out, and . . . . Wait a minute. If I know Jamaica High, the only kids that don't already know what happened this morning are the cheerleaders who are too busy trying to pull their pompoms out of their ass. Hell, they've been talking about you anyway, ever since Tony became an item in your scrapbook. That douchebag! Why the fuck did I get mixed up with him? Well, you know why, but that's beside the point.

You're going in circles, Esther. Keep Tony out of this. The only thing you have to focus on is how you're going to handle Dad. And the truth is, he's always seeing you the way he wants to, so let's just let him do his deal, and we'll move on to whatever the next chapter this stupid comic book of life brings. That's it. Just let Dad do his worried-thing song and dance about you. He'll take care of it anyway, I guess whatever the way he ends up doing it.

With her ruminations on pause, Esther became aware again of her physical surroundings, this cage that she shared with other unfortunates. Was it getting less crowded in here? Maybe some of these chickens flew the coop? And why the fuck is that one looking at me?

A tall but solid black kid, maybe a year older than Esther, started over her way. Her face wasn't exactly smiling out some welcome wagon greeting to the new kid in town. "You that white girl that's been hangin' around with Tony?" she barked.

"Put that in the past tense. Not the first mistake I ever made, in this young life of mine." Whatever relationship this girl had with Tony, Esther was in no mood to fight for something that was anything but special, anyhow.

The girl's posture changed instantly, and broke out in a grin. Yeah, this girl knew the score about the douchebag. "And, pardon my assumption, but I guess it won't be your last. Some of us are just stubborn fools." Both girls spontaneously laughed, and introduced themselves.

"Hey, I'm Esther. I guess you won the same prize as me in this here heroin raffle."

"Yeah, I'm Betania. I heard they're giving away free vacations at that Bedford resort." Bedford was a women's prison, upstate. "I'd just as soon settle for the silver or bronze prizes. Don't want to be too greedy, here."

"First time you got arrested?" Betania nodded in the affirmative. "Then you're probably eligible for that diversion program, like me. Didn't they tell you about it?"

"Yeah, but I don't know if my mom is coming down to get me. She's at work now, and it ain't easy for her to get away. The cop at the station house said I can stay eligible 'till 5 today, and then all bets are off."

"That's pretty fucked up."

"Well, we'll see what happens." Betania did her best to shrug off her fear. It's never cool to let the world out there know you're pissing in your boots. "What about you? Somebody coming to get you out of this popsicle stand?"

The girls talked for a while. Turned out that they had some mutual friends. Playing "who do you know?" kept them both from self-reflection in the moment, which was a welcome diversion. Even here, in the midst of a miserable holding cell, they could immerse themselves in their adolescent world, and shut out their deeper fears.

"Shapiro! Esther Shapiro!" The turnkey shouted out her name from just outside the cell. "You're outa here, Shapiro. Get whatever stuff you got, and let's get going."

Esther cast one startled look at Betania, flung back into the immediate, mouthed a quick, "good luck," and started toward the now opening bars. She had nothing to carry with her, save her anxiety.

"Follow me, Missy. You got your father waiting for you out in the lobby."

3

Ben had been to see the clerk and signed a number of papers that he didn't know or really care about what he was attesting to. The law clerk had diligently attempted to explain every detail, but Ben kept shushing him off. Who cared what the stupid details were? Weinstein could take care of that stuff, anyway. He just wanted to get Esther out of this hell hole and bring her home. They could worry about the legal mumbo jumbo later, after she was safely ensconced in the dinette, and the whole family could talk about it. Maybe Rose could make a little snack. It was three o'clock already, and who knew if they had given Esther anything to eat. And they still had to go see that social worker, that Williams woman. That couldn't take too long. Could it?

He furtively scanned the lobby, not knowing from what direction his daughter might be coming. What are all these people doing here anyway? The lobby was a swarm of activity, and it was difficult to make out anyone in the crowd. Ben had heard the clerk on the telephone calling down for her. How long could it take? For God's sake, if he called down to Sol to bring up a 44 long, in the Seville pattern, it better not take as much time as this.

Suddenly, off to the right, he saw Esther walking next to some uniformed female officer. Esther was trying her best to pick him out of the crowd. He held up his arm, high in the air and called out,

"Esther! Esther! I'm over here." and started walking in her direction. Esther, in turn, heard him, stopped for a second, showed the corrections officer his upstretched hand, took a deep breath and strode so as to meet him. They stopped next to each other in the middle of the lobby.

"Daddy!"

"Esther. Are you okay, sweetie?"

She immediately got it. His focus was on her well-being, not the behavior which got her here. That's what Esther needed to hear. She would be okay now. She lowered her head while looking up at him, "I'm sorry, Daddy. I'm so sorry. But I got into trouble a while ago, and I didn't know how to tell you, and now I've created this big mess. And you had to miss work. And I don't know what to say. And. . . ."

Ben interrupted her, and took her in his arms. "Honey, we'll worry about all that later. We can talk at home. For now, let's just do what we have to do to get out of this place, and we'll get you home. Where you belong." He let go of her, and turned to the corrections officer. "Miss, do you know the way I can get to the annex, where this Mrs. Williams, the social worker, has her office?"

On the way over to the annex, the transformation of Esther from badass to daddy's girl became complete. She appeared smaller, trunk concave, head down, eyes up, mascara smeared with tears, hand holding, steps shorter. As they sat down in the social worker's office, she clasped his hand in both of hers, keeping her face turned to him, making it clear that this new person would have to interact with the father, not the daughter. He was the adult, she the little girl who misbehaved. A naughty little girl.

Sarah Williams's degrees from CCNY and Hunter were hung on the wall directly behind her desk. Ben noticed the frames. Nice gilt. Next to them were some photos of her family, a large family. It seemed she had a half dozen children, who posed dramatically next to Ms. Williams and a gentleman who Ben assumed was her husband. This Williams woman seemed the penultimate mother, projecting warmth and acceptance in her manner and words. Be careful of people who seem too welcoming, he thought to himself.

"Miss Shapiro, may I call you Esther, dear?" The little girl nodded, and sunk further into her father. "Esther, you seem to have created quite a mess for yourself. How would you characterize the situation you find yourself in?"

Esther looked up. "I don't know. . . I mean, I guess I'm in trouble."

"Well, Honey, I'd like you to try to see this from a different point of view. Too many of the teenagers who pass through my office tend to think of this in the way you just portrayed it. In trouble, as if they were bad, caught doing illegal things and in for a punishment. I'd like to see if you can view this whole situation as I do, a young woman who has just let out a loud and clear call for help. This whole diversion program is designed to offer you help rather than punishment. What do you think of that Esther? Would you like to allow us to find help for you and your situation?"

Ben immediately answered, speaking up for the family. "Of course. We'll do anything you ask of us, and Esther has always received whatever help she might need. Tutors. SAT classes. We will do whatever you think is necessary, here."

"Thank you, Mr. Shapiro. But I was speaking to Esther."

"Well, eh. . . Like Daddy said we will do anything you want us to." She started to whimper. "This is the worst day of my life," she murmured through her tears.

"I'm sure it is, Esther. But tell me, honey, do you agree with me that your actions suggest that you are crying out for help?"

"Oh yes, Mrs, . . . eh, Williams. I know that it would be very important for me to receive some help."

The social worker leaned in, just a little. "And what kind of help do you think you need, Esther? Is there a specific type of assistance that you believe would be useful for you?"

"Well, I'm sure that whatever you suggest would be what I need. . . ., um, whatever you think. I'm just so sorry and lost and confused. . ." Esther just trailed off.

Mrs. Williams turned to Ben, and with a sigh offered, "Your daughter seems to want to leave this all up to the adults. She glanced back at Esther and then returned to the father. "She is trying very hard to be polite and say the right things. From my experience, that's not a very good sign in this situation. I'm not sure that she is ready to take responsibility for her actions. Mr. Shapiro, it's going to be very important that you and your wife impress on her as your family enters this program, that if she is going to create a healthy future for herself, she will need to assume accountability for her life. Your part is to make sure that she begins to act like a grown-up rather than a child who got caught with her hand in the cookie jar. She needs to step up and do her part."

Ben contritely assured this Williams woman that Rose and he would make sure that "Whatever was required by the program would be done. Just you wait and see. We'll step up to the plate. Esther will be a good girl."

Internally, Sarah wanted to scream, shake this girl by her shoulders and slap the father up the side of his head. What this kid probably really needed was 6 months in juvie. How often had she felt like this moment, swimming upstream with her arms tied behind her back? But nothing she was going to say today was going to make any difference, and the program was designed to avoid the court system, so she just better send them on their way. Externally, she acknowledged Ben's promise, "We both hope she can stay out of trouble for a year. I sincerely wish you guys the best of luck."

As they were leaving, she muttered to herself, "and he's going to need it."

4

After Rose was reassured that no one had died, and that Ben was home early because "something had come up about Esther," they all sat down in the dinette, for a "family conference." This was an institution that Ben had established years ago, and he was very proud of doing so. Anyone in the family could call such a meeting to order. No phone calls or other disturbances were allowed, and "we'll talk however long the matter requires." He had picked up the idea in an article he read in the Sunday *Times*, "Increasing Healthy Family Communication." It was always Ben who initiated the meeting, as Rose consistently suffered through it, leaving Esther to have intense practice in rolling her eyes.

"So, Rose," he initiated discussion," I want you to promise me that you are going to stay calm. As I said, a little snag, a complication has come up with Esther, and we all need to chat about it."

Rose, of course, reacted to his request for composure with intense agitation. "What? What's going on here? Oh my God! Did someone hurt you at school? Are you sick? Tell me you're OK, and I don't have to worry. Oh God, my mother always told me that being a mother was the hardest thing of all the hard things. What's wrong, what's wrong?"

She would have gone on if her husband had not interrupted her. "Rosie, would you please calm down and take a breath or two? We won't be able to talk about anything if you're going to get all verklempt."

"So, first he tells me everything's bad, and then he wants me to pretend it's just okeydokey. You're driving me nuts, Ben. What's going on?" Her voice became chopped and louder with each syllable.

"Honey, if you can't settle yourself down, we won't be able to talk about it."

"Oh, for God's sake, if you don't clue me in to what this disaster is all about, I'm just going to get up and go outside, take a walk or something, maybe to China. No. Probably, that's what you want me to do. I'll calm myself down with a long, long walk. Is that what you want, Benny?"

It was a stalemate. Ben had no idea how to get into the issue without driving Rose over the edge, and stalling was just driving her over the edge. When she got like this, he always froze in place, paralyzed. Rose, on the other hand, had to gird herself with anger if she was going to face what was obviously some hideous catastrophe that these two had been keeping from her. She hated when people, especially them, when they thought she couldn't deal with things. I mean, she knew that she was the glue that kept everything together.

Esther, who had been playing little girl lost, keeping out of it, in fact just wanting to go up to her room, finally had enough. She stood up, threw the cookies on the table, and screamed, "Okay already. Here's the deal. I got arrested this morning! Daddy got me out of jail! And the only thing you're good for is arguing. I'm going upstairs!" She pushed her chair to the side, grabbed a cookie, and ran up the stairs, slamming the door behind her as she entered her bedroom.

Ben was in conflict as to which of his women he was supposed to attend. Rose's jaw simply dropped in incredulity. How? How could this be happening to her? In jail? The next thing she was going to hear was that Esther was doing drugs! "Ben," she addressed him, his paralysis preventing him from any response, "Ben, what is she talking about? Arrested? Arrested for what?"

Ben took a long breath. "Okay Rosie," and he decided it would work best if he shared the day's events in the sequence in which they occurred. "So, I was at work this morning, maybe it was about eleven, no it was probably a little later. . ."

"Ben, I don't care what time it was. Just tell me what happened, already."

"So, a little before noon, some Officer Robinson man calls me up from the Jamaica police station, a nice man I would add, a very nice man,. . . and he proceeds to tell me that our Esther. . .and I had to make sure he was talking about *our* Esther, he tells me that Esther was arrested by some sting thing on Jamaica Avenue, and I have to come to the precinct and get her." Ben pauses and checks out Rose's face to see how she's handling it so far. Her jaw is trembling a bit, but otherwise she seems to be okay, although uncharacteristically quiet, so he proceeds. "So, I get my things and get on the train, and I find the station house, you know it's amazing how you can pass something a million times and not be sure where it is, so anyway, I find it and go speak to this Robinson fellow."

He pauses again, reluctant to get into the drug part of things. Rose's impatience begins to boil over. "And? And? Ben, you're going to give me a heart attack if you don't get on with it!"

Ben was afraid that he'd give her a heart attack if he did, but obviously he had to tell her all about it. "So, this Officer Robinson, I have to say, his office was so sloppy, but somehow, he managed to find things, he pulls out a folder about our Esther, and he tells me that she was arrested in this sting thing, for, eh, . . . for trying to buy some. . . heroin. Heroin, Rosie! Our Esther was trying to buy some drugs, some of that heroin stuff!"

Ben pauses, and inspects Rose's facial expression again, looking for clues as to when and how to go on. The trembling in her jaw continues, but now her hands begin to wave and shake. "No! No! That's a mistake. Our Esther would never do that. Why would she buy drugs? It's not like she uses them, or anything like that. No, Ben. They had to have made some mistake."

"That's what I thought, Rosie. That's what I thought. I was sure that they had made some horrible and stupid mistake. Here I had just seen Esther off to school and now they're telling me that she's some kind of drug user. That couldn't be. But then they tell me that they found those needle marks in between her toes! In her feet, mind you,

Rose! Our daughter has been using and shooting drugs, and she's been injecting it into the spaces between her toes." His head falls. The ongoing shock of it all gets stronger than the need to protect his wife.

Rose, for her part, sits without movement in her chair, wordless for a moment or two. Finally, she gets up, turns and walks to the sink. "Ben, I don't know if I can handle this." She looks out the window into the back yard. The back yard is peaceful, and it usually calms her down when she gets upset. "I don't know if I can deal with this," she repeats. "How can she do this to me? How can she do this? What's wrong with her?"

Ben realizes that he'd better get up. If he doesn't do something to calm her down quickly, he might get deserted by both of them. He tentatively rests his hand on her shoulder. "It will be okay, Rose. We'll figure out what to do and it will be okay."

She doesn't respond at all, but keeps her focus on that nice porcelain dwarf that they had found last summer in Vermont, when they had joined Phyliss and her family on that cheddar tasting tour. "Honey, there's more. You have to hear the good part."

She turns. "Good part? How can there be a good part? Her life is ruined. That means my life is ruined. And you're telling me there is a good part?"

"That's what I'm trying to explain. It turns out that this whole thing, the whole megillah, it can go away, be gone, go up in smoke like it never happened."

"And you wait forever to tell me this? What? How? How do we make this whole forsaken thing go away?"

"Let me go and get the papers." He quickly runs over to the breakfront, and returns with the packet from the courthouse in his hands, "Well, it turns out, Rosie, that the folks in charge down at the courthouse, they really don't want teenage girls, I think it was just girls, did he say anything about boys, anyway, they want good kids, who never got into any messes before, they shouldn't have to deal with court or, God forbid, they shouldn't go to jail. So, if Esther can get some help with her problem, and stay out of any trouble for a year, mind you just for one year, then the whole deal is thrown in the basket, erased, like it never happened." Ben gets a little taller, having just delivered Rose some good news, or at least some better news.

"This is true? The whole thing can go away? What do we have to do? It can become just our horrible little secret?"

"They want us to get some help for Esther. They want us to find some kind of way of helping her to get rid of these ideas that who knows who has put into her head."

"You mean therapy?" Rose responded. "They want my daughter to go to therapy, where she'll talk about me, and tell some stranger all about our secrets? You know how she talks about me, Ben. And that's to my face. Imagine what she must be saying to everyone else out there."

"No, Rose. If I remember it right, I think I remember it right, they didn't say it had to be talk therapy. They just said that we need to get her some help with, you know, someone or some place that knows about this whole drug using thing."

"Who knows people like that? Who knows about things like that? This is like I've been transported into some horrible movie and have to know about things like drugs and deprivation and all the degrading things. The next thing you know we'll be like the Rosenberg's, getting fried in some chair for spying, or something."

"I know, Rose. I know. Just keep yourself calm. Look, tomorrow I'll stay home and speak to Dr. Berger, and maybe Rabbi Goldsheid. I figure one of them will either know something, or will know someone who knows something. I'll tell Solly to take care of the store, to fill in for me. I'll make up some kind of excuse. Okay? We'll find a place for our Esther to get some help. You don't worry about it. I'll take care of it. Okay?"

"You just take care of my little girl, Ben. You just take care of her." Rose's composure had fallen off the edge, completely overrun by her agitation. "I have to turn the lights off and go to bed, Benny. I feel a migraine coming on." And, so Ben was left alone in the dinette, both of his girls up in their rooms.

5

Rabbi Samuel Goldsheid was a small man, maybe about five foot five, who more than compensated for his lack of physical size, it was said, with a depth and breadth of knowledge. Rose's father, Morty, had said to Ben, when wedding plans were being finalized for his daughter and her soon-to-be husband, "That Rebbe, Goldsheid, he's got more smarts in that little head of his than Einstein. I don't know how one man can know so much." And Morty wasn't famous for handing out compliments. So, it wasn't surprising that Ben sought out the rabbi's opinion before consulting the family doctor, Berger.

Goldsheid sat in his study, behind his desk, and listened patiently, as Ben laid out his tale of woe, from yesterday's events. No less than three times did he interrupt the narrative to reassure Ben that there was nothing to be ashamed of, that the best of families run into problems with confused and acting out children. Especially the teenagers. Ben did think he noticed a slight hint of, was it shock, when he recounted the" between the toes" piece, but then again, who ever heard of such things?

With the events fully chronicled, the rabbi tilted his chair back a bit, and pointed his pen at his supplicant, saying, "You and your family have been outstanding members of our congregation, Ben. I still remember Esther as she was preparing for her bat mitzvah. Such a bright girl, and pretty too. Just because of this setback I don't want you to think that her future is any less than you thought it two days ago. Esther and you and Rose will get through this, and on the other side of it all you will feel stronger and wiser for it. We go through lonely and sorrowful times in the desert before we reach the land of milk and honey.

"But the matter of what to do now, that still remains. Of course, we must be very careful to follow all the instructions and demands of the court system, but we don't want to blindly fall into some situation in which your beautiful daughter will be forced to further interact with those very children who have influenced her into this antisocial behavior. You don't stop drinking liquor by hanging out in some bar, if you know what I mean. It's hard enough for us to avoid all the negative influences that seem to abound these days, but we certainly don't want this drug use to be supported and reinforced by some other poor children who have been caught in its trap."

"Here is what I would recommend. As luck would have it, last summer, on my yearly study journey in Israel, I was told of a kibbutz, on the frontier, up north, near Nazareth. This kibbutz, bless their hearts, is open to teenagers from all over the world, who may have had, shall we say, a problem or two. They get to live and work on the farm, stay five months, and become true kibbutzim. Wouldn't this be perfect for Esther? She could get away from those horrible drug pushers for almost half a year, develop the vigor and mentality of a pioneer, and become deeply immersed in her Jewish culture, one, I remind you that does not often be visited by drug abuse.

"I know that you and Rose would miss her so very much, but surely such a sacrifice could be made for your daughter to come back healthy in mind and body. And, I might add, I am told it is very affordable. Well, at least in comparison to some of these so-called rehabilitation programs."

The rabbi pulled his chair back toward the desk, and smiled. He was pleased with himself that he knew of such a program. Certainly, this was better than going to that Daytop Village, or G-d knows where, and being mixed with G-d knows who. Sometimes it seemed that life in America was becoming more about avoiding social pitfalls than striving for wholesome goals. This was a good plan. The girl would return all the better for it. Maybe it was even G-d's plan.

Ben thought about what the Rabbi was suggesting. If the court would go along with it, and he couldn't think of any reason they wouldn't, Esther would be in Israel, the Holy Land, and for sure she wouldn't run across any druggies there. No one would have to know why she was there. Rose could just let everyone think that she had been invited into some very special program, an honor. It wasn't open to just any-old person, and it was too good an opportunity for their special child to turn down. And besides, they had talked about going to Israel for so long, and had never gotten around to it. They could visit Esther while she was there. It's like *three* birds with one stone. Talk about turning your lemons into lemonade! My god, this was a grapefruit! The more he rolled the rabbi's recommendation around in his head, the happier Ben was that he'd put the doctor second on the list.

He couldn't wait to go home and tell Rose about the idea. And he imagined that Esther would be happy about it too. Compared with going to some Sigmund Freud follower person, telling all your inside stuff to a stranger, this was much better. Morty, you were right! This Goldsheid knows his stuff.

As it turned out, Ben was half right. Rose was ecstatic at the prospect. "Like any mother I will weep at being away from my baby for what amounts to a half a year, but Israel, Ben, Israel! And we can visit her, so my deprivation won't even be that bad. She'll come back and speak fluent Hebrew. How many mothers can say that about their daughters? Oh, thank God that you went to see Goldsheid! You know my father always spoke so well of him." The horror and shame of her daughter's addiction was being turned into a cause for mitzvah! Transformation needed no better example.

Esther, on the other hand, was a different story. "Daddy, you and Mom have come up with some pretty stupid ideas, but this one absolutely has to be the most idiotic of them all. You're saying you want me to go to some stupid farm a million miles away, in a place where nobody even speaks English, and pretend I'm Farmer Brown or something. No, excuse me. Make that Farmer Ben Looney! Daddy! I won't go! You can't make me. I'd rather go to jail!"

It seemed to Ben that his daughter's first impression was on the negative side. It always did take her a little while to get used to an idea. And besides, she was upset from all the going's on over the last couple of days. Ever since he could remember, she had been sort of on the excitable side. "Esther, Darling. You don't really want to go to jail. And you know, it's not likely that the court is going to agree to send you to Grossinger's. Hey, how many kids your age will be able to say they travelled on their own to Israel, and lived an adventurous life on the frontier? Tell me you won't get any points for that!"

"Daddy, you sound like you're planting a tree on a kibbutz, and turning the dessert into orange fields. I know the deal. We learned all about it in Hebrew school. But I'm not some cedar tree. And I don't even believe in some God thing." She was getting hyperventilated and needed to pause for a breath. "I don't deserve this. Just because I made some stupid teenage date-a-bad-boy mistake and started hanging out with Tony, my life is going to hell. An Israeli hell. Ooh, God, this is all so screwed up. I hate it I hate it!"

"Tony? Who's Tony?" This was someone Ben had never heard about before. Maybe this was the influence that had caused his sweet wine to turn to vinegar. He remembered Morty worrying about his granddaughter when she turned teenager and admonishing Ben, "It always starts with a boy. It always starts with a boy." Truer words were never spoken. More reason to get Esther out of town. "So, Esther, who is this Tony you talk about?"

She'd regretted speaking his name out loud the second she uttered it. "Daddy, don't worry about it. He's just some boy I saw a couple of times. No big deal."

"There's no Tony who lives here by us. Is he somebody you met at school?" Ben knew that they should have sent Esther to private school, and not go to that Jamaica High. But Rose, she wouldn't hear about it. We're not going to spend all that money for something that we already pay taxes for and get for free. She wouldn't even listen to him about all the dangers he had heard about. Now look where we are.

"No, Daddy, he's not from school." She was beginning to get exasperated. "He's just a friend of a friend of a friend. He doesn't even go to school."

"You dated someone who's old enough not to go to school? Did your mother know about this?"

"Ugh, Daddy! Do we have to do this now? He's just a guy I saw a couple of times, and that's that. What, do I have to bring every friend I have home for inspection?"

This seemed like a perfectly reasonable proposition to Ben, but he thought better of saying it. "Esther, is it so wrong for me to want to know your friends?"

She just rolled her eyes and frowned at him. "No, Daddy. It's perfectly fine for you to know my friends. But can we get back to this cockamamie kibbutznik deal. Do I have to start wearing a kerchief and go to schul every Saturday?"

"Esther, this isn't about becoming religious. We are talking about a very practical way to take care of a, let's call it tricky, a tricky situation that you got yourself into. You know, it's not fair for you to act like you're the victim here, as if Mom and me are trying to persecute you. We're just doing our best to find an answer to this problem that you dumped in our laps."

So, there it was. Ben was bordering on conceding the unmistakable fact that this whole mess was Esther's responsibility, a notion that was foreign to the Shapiro household. He had trained both his ladies that it was his job to take on any responsibility that was up for grabs. Could he be regretting this outlook of his? Especially now that other male forces were apparently having influence over his daughter?

"Look, Esther darling, come here." He motioned her to him, and cradled her in his arms. "It's going to be okay. I promise you. You'll go to Israel, hang out in the kibbutz for five months, only five months, Esther. No, you won't become a farmer. There will be plenty of other things you can do there. The brochure the Rabbi gave me said there was even a school. It'll be okay, darling. And we'll come and visit you sometime in the middle of it, so it won't seem so long. And puff! It will be over, and you'll be back home, and going to school again, Jamaica High, and seeing your friends, and this whole stupid horrible nightmare will be behind us. There won't be some hideous blotch on your records, and the next thing we know, you'll be off to college, to the college of your choice, wherever you want to go. So, tell me darling, is that all so bad?"

Esther started to come around. Maybe this was the best way out of this ugly God-forsaken mess. She didn't want to go to one of those rehab places, if she thought about it. Maybe getting away from everything wasn't such a bad idea. And she thought that she remembered hearing some things about Israeli boys that were if nothing else, sort of intriguing. Who knows, maybe she should just go along with the whole stupid idea,

6

Esther sat on the Q-29 bus and reviewed her shopping list. She was off to Israel, could you believe it, in just two days, and had only begun to get all the things that were going to be needed. She and Rose had looked over the suggestions in the pamphlet for "newly arriving kibbutzim," adding a few items that in Rose's words, "every girl should have" in a new setting. Make up, a new bathing suit, a portable iron, one of those new small cameras to send pictures home, maybe an outfit or two. Damn! Esther wanted to get some birth control pills, but you needed a prescription for that, and there was no way she'd be able to come up with a reason and get an appointment that quick. On the positive side of the ledger, she had been given the Gertz card for the day, a rare bequeathment of unreserved trust. When she was about to get off the bus, she realized that Gertz was only a few blocks away from the place on Jamaica Ave where she got busted. Guess that's what Mrs. Tilden, her English teacher, would call irony.

Getting off the bus, she walked the two blocks over to Gertz, and was about to go in when she felt a tap on the shoulder, and a "hey, girl!."

It was Betania, from the holding cell, from just a couple of weeks ago. "Hey, Betania, what's you up to?"

"I guess I'm hanging. I got to be over by the outpatient rehab center in a couple of hours, so I'm just killing time. What about you?"

"Doing some shopping," she hesitated a moment and, "Hey, I got my mother's Gertz card. Want to have some lunch? It's on me." And in they went, the Gertz Café on the top floor. They settled into a booth, ordered some burgers and fries, and shared their post jail happenings.

"My Mom made it to the courthouse just in time," Betania began. "It was a hell of a mess. It was like the four o'clock shift change and nobody wanted to stay overtime. But if it didn't happen that day it wasn't going to happen, and you better believe nobody wants to mess with my mom when she ain't going to give in to their stupidity. So, Mom keeps yelling and pointing to the brochure, and they all keep running their 'yes buts', and I'm just standing around waiting to get the hell out of there. Knew she's gonna make them come around. Like I said, nobody wants to mess with my Momma."

"Well, nobody wants to deal with my mother, but that's a whole different deal." Esther changed topics, wanting to stay away from actually describing her mom. "So, what's it like over at that IOP they got you going to?"

"You know the deal, don't you? Five days a week, all afternoon. You got to piss in the cup three days a week, and then there's a lecture and then you got to sit in group therapy. I guess it's all right. It'd be better if there were more girls there, I mean there's only two of us. Truth is, the guys are just a bunch of drooling morons who keep trying to hit on me. Like, good luck, idiots. But what the hell, it beats sitting in some juvie. Now, girl, you tell me. How come my black ass is sitting in some stupid group here in ugly old Jamaica with a bunch of drooling dope fiends, and you're off on some round-the-world foreign travel trip?"

"Hey. I'm not so sure I wouldn't rather be doing what you got on your dance card. How'd you like to be sent off to some vegetable farm in the middle of the fuckin desert where they don't even speak your language? My parents seem to think I'm going to miraculously change back into the goody-goody they think I am after being in the blessed air of Israel, and hanging out with a bunch of religious farmers."

Betania nodded that she understood. "I don't get it. You'd think these parents of ours, and believe me, your mom and my mom ain't twins, you'd think that they'd stop trying to make us into who they want us to be. I mean, my mom, from everything I hear, she was a hell-raiser herself when she was my age. So how come she don't trust that I'm going to grow the hell up and be okay? She's got to know that everybody wants to party when they can, before the whole adult deal pushes them into their little corners and crevices."

"Was your mom super-shocked when you got popped?"

"No way. She and me have been playing this stupid game for the last while, her goin' through my stuff, looking to find the stuff, me telling her to mind her own business. That sort of thing. Getting arrested just proved to her what she thought she already knew. She just didn't believe that I could fool around and not get strung out. I guess my uncle dying from that OD had something to do with that. It's amazing that parents always believe you're going to do the same stupid deal like somebody else did."

"I don't think my parents had a clue. Actually, let's face it. They don't have much of a clue on anything. I mean, like I came home last month when the sun was coming up. Daddy was mostly all concerned that I needed to get to bed. After all, his little baby needed some sleepy-poo. And Mom was pissed that I had ruined her own precious thirty-seven winks. It's not as if either one of them really wanted to know where the fuck I'd been. And I wasn't about to force it on them. Come to think about it, I was hanging with your god-damned friend, Tony, that asshole. Hardly worth the loss of shut-eye."

"Hey, girl. Don't call him any friend of mine. He's just the player he is, and we both of us, we're the dumb fools who got played. No glory there. No friendship there either."

"Tell me, Betania. What do you think his game really was? Was he just looking to get laid like they all do, or was he up to something else? I can't figure it."

"Sometimes I think you white chicks are a little slow in the head. Damn girl, that boy, he was trying to turn us out. Tony thinks he's just the biggest, baddest, prettiest boy on the block, and he's got it in his head he can use some combination of smack and his looks to get you to go out there and sell your ass for him. That boy don't lack ambition. He's just looking to be some movieland pimp."

Esther mulled this over in her head for a minute. Tony was trying to turn her out? Ooh, that was disgusting. I mean, back in seventh grade when they were studying World History, she had imagined herself as one of the grand courtesans in the French palace, but that was a whole different century and a whole different deal. Courtesans, that had a kind of romantic elegance to it. Royalty eager to throw away their crowns for her! To be part of the intrigue at Versailles, that would be something else. A Jamaica Avenue whore, not so much.

It was definitely time to get away for a while. Away from some scummy schmuck who wanted to use you for his profit, away from some nickel and dime habit, that only suckers and losers employed to pretend they were cool. Hey, for five months, how bad could an Israeli agritourism stay be? Meanwhile, back at the farm. . . .If she had learned anything, Esther figured that there were cool folks and idiots everywhere you went. Hell, she had met Betania in the joint, and she was sort of worth the visit.

"I guess that guy's in love with himself to the max," she finally responded. "Kind of the poster boy for a dickhead."

"Hey, Esther. If I give you my address, could you send me a postcard, or something? I never got any mail from overseas. That would be tre cool."

"You got it, girl." She tore off a piece of the shopping list, gave the paper to Betania who jotted down her address, and the two girls were off, Betania to the outpatient program, Esther to Lingerie. In the moment, they both felt very grown-up.

7

Ben and Esther were in the car, on the way to the airport. Driving down the Van Wyke Expressway, Ben could feel himself tensing up. Was he really taking his little girl to Kennedy to go off by herself and be gone for five months? Rose had stayed home, still in bed. She thought she could feel a migraine coming on, (like it often did if she had to get up at some god-forsaken hour). Besides, the whole thing just felt like way too much for her to bear. Too much.

Ben, to the contrary, loved to be out on the road at this hour, watching the dawn come up on the right side of the road, casting long fuzzy shadows off the buildings on the left. Maybe this whole thing was for the good. Maybe this was the start of a new day for his baby, Esther. Who was it who had said, "the more you expect, the more you can expect to be disappointed?" Well, now it was going to be "the more you expect, the more you can expect to be disappointed, the more you need to move past your setback by doing the hard stuff." That's what they were doing. The hard stuff. Esther just had to grow up a smidgeon and learn to do the hard stuff.

For her part, Esther sat curled up in the passenger seat, her face squirreled away from the receding world. True to form, she needed to tuck away her fear in that little space just behind the solar plexus. You couldn't exactly have always broadcasted to the world how much you wanted to get away from your parents and be done with childhood, and then turn around and admit that it was scary as all hell to leave all that security behind. So, yawn a lot, bury your betraying face in your coat, and angrily declare that it's too damn early, and why did you have to get such an early plane reservation anyway?

"Esther dear, that's the way it is with transatlantic flights. They either leave early in the morning or late at night. Business people, they want to sleep on the plane and get there in the morning. Go figure." He gave her a second to digest that before adding, "I know this whole thing is hard on you, Sweetie. But, you're going to do just fine. Better kibbutznik than beatnik, right?"

A long sonorous and suffering "Daddy, please," was her only response. If she could exaggerate the irritation, it might suppress the urge to get all gooey with him. Annoyance is always a formidable maneuver for avoiding open affection. The only thing more embarrassing than her father had to be her attachment to him.

For the fifth time he asked, "You're sure you have the passport and ticket?" She just picked up her head enough to stare at him with one quizzical eye. "I know, I know. I just need to make sure. I told you about the time your Aunt Phyliss left her ticket in the back seat of the car, and Mom and I drove away, didn't I? And then she tries to turn it around and make it my fault. I didn't ask her enough times, she says. And," he paused for effect, "and if I'd given in to the part of me that wanted to ask her again, you know about that part, she would have told me to nag her sister, not her, that we weren't married. Okay, you want me to shut up now." The more anxious Ben got, the more he went on a bit. He knew it, but stopping was another thing.

Esther went back inside again. The hardest part about this whole thing was that she had no idea what anything was going to be like, over there. You can't have a game plan if you didn't know what game you were going to play. I mean, at Jamaica High you knew the deal. There were black kids and white kids. There were preppies and druggies. There were jocks and there were hippies. What was it going to be like there? Farmers and daveners? Was all the rock and roll going to be in a minor key? Did everybody or anybody get high? Would she fit in, or was this going to be a bunch of long days nights? Kibbutzniks and beatniks, Dad. Right?

Her body felt all right. That achy, painy, fluey drug sick feeling had gone away pretty quickly. Guess she wasn't that strung out. And at least she could eat again. Hell of a way to lose a couple of pounds. Truth be told, Esther was sure as sure can be that she didn't need a stay in some kibbutz to convince her not to go near that shit again. Like Daddy had said last night, nobody learns to stay away from the stove without first getting a little burned. And this was going to turn out to be just a little blister, he was sure of it. She wanted to respond, "So why do I have to go half way around the stupid world if a little band-aid will do the trick?" but she knew better then to voice it. This one wasn't up to Dad. The stupid court had all the say-so here.

They crossed the Belt Parkway and Ben advised Esther to search for the way to El Al. "These crazy signs, I get lost every time I come here. Is it green, or red? It should be blue." Continuing through the maze of road and underpass, Esther did her best to direct him, and miraculously, they arrived at the parking lot near the terminal for the smaller international carriers.

Esther started to get out of the car, but Ben reached out to stop her. "Wait a minute, Sweetie. Wait a minute." She reclosed the door, and turned to see him, finding his eyes clouded with tears.

"Esther, my daughter. Listen a minute to you father. I need you to listen to me." He fidgeted with his key chain, as his voice trembled. "I can't believe I'm sending you off on this journey. I'm not ready for this. I can only hope that you are. Tell me that you can do this, Esther, tell me that you can do this.

"Daddy, I can do this. I'll be fine. C'mon, you know you always worry, and I always turn out to be just fine. Right? Don't I always turn out better than that horror movie you've got in your head?"

Some level of alarm swept through Ben's face, as he digested her diminishing the gravity of the situation. "Esther, we wouldn't be here like this if you always turned out okay." This was as close to an admonishment as Ben could muster. "I need you to tell me you are going to be a good girl, and do the things that the kibbutz tells you to do. I need you to come home in a little bit and be okay, so we can put this whole situation behind us. You'll do this Esther? You'll be a good girl?"

"I'll be a good girl, Daddy. I promise."

8

Ein Harod was intermittently beautiful and horrid. The transformation of a desert, as with a person, does not occur evenly. One could find many panoramas that were worthy of placement on a postcard, only to turn around and find a ghastly Quonset hut dormitory, corroding the view. The splendor of a horizon extending orange grove was interrupted by hastily thrown together storage buildings in what seemed to be part of no earthly plan. It was a hodgepodge of people, places and things, drawn from the wide diaspora; what in America would represent a melting pot, a Jewish melting pot, sans the golden cobblestones. The oranges themselves were a perfect metaphor for the kibbutz. They were an ancient fruit, but a modern miracle. Desolation had been transformed into hope. They were a globe but comprised of sections, each separated by thin walls. The one and the many; Sweet, but tart.

Esther saw only the horrid, as it was all unfamiliar. Once off the bus, she stood in the dusty road and surveyed her new surroundings. She needed a minute to find herself, before finding the "welcome center" that the folder promised. She was hot, tired and scared shitless, and all that had to be hidden inside, only to be projected into her perception of this foreign world about her. Droopy and dreary. That was the word for it, she told herself. Dreary. This had to be a place for

34

sad old people, Oh God, she would never find anything or anybody she wanted to fit in with here. She was looking at a five-month punishment of a life embodied by dreariness. A hollow cost she had to pay. Ooh, that was the worst pun she had ever made. Don't ever, ever, ever say that out loud! The older Esther got, the more she found herself needing to keep her thoughts private. Maybe that was why getting high felt so right, even when you knew it was wrong. Everything was private when you were high.

All right, here goes nothing, she said to herself as she trudged off toward the X in the insert map that marked her welcoming. Imagine her surprise when she pushed through the screen door and spied what had to be the absolutely most gorgeous hunk of a guy she had ever seen. Looked about eighteen-ish, with that James Dean look that was just her classic turn on. So that's what they mean by taking your breath away! And without breath, the words become impossible to speak.

After what seemed like an impossibly long interval, she was finally able to stammer out, "Hi, … uh, … I'm Esther, …. Esther Shapiro."

Damn it! Did he have to smile like that, as if he could so easily recognize her discomfort. And did it have to be a cute smile? Why couldn't they have had some weary old sad guy, the one she had been expecting, some guy like that to be here and greet people?

"Esther, I was hoping this was you." He rose and walked toward her, motioning her to put her bags by the side of his desk. "I'm Edel, Edel Habib. I guess you could call me the 'meeter and greeter' person, here." And did he have to have such an adorable accent? Well, I guess it shouldn't be a big deal surprise that people here spoke English with an accent. She should be thankful someone spoke English at all. But what was it? It didn't sound like all the Yiddishe accents that her grandparents and all their generation had. It was crisper, and didn't sound like, er, well, . . .old.

"Good. You've arrived in time for me to give you my orientation schpeel. Then, I'll show you where you will be sleeping, and it will all take place in time for you to have dinner. You must be hungry after such a long journey."

She tried her best to gather herself. She didn't want to flirt. She didn't want to even insinuate that she liked anything about this place.

But there were so many ways she could play with about being shown to her bed and how hungry she was. Esther! For God's sake, stop it. Cool your ovaries down, girl. "Well,…. thank you, Edel. That would be great."

She sat down and Edel reviewed all the features of the kibbutz, and the orientation which would begin for her after breakfast, the next day. The rest of the week would be spent half-time working on the farm and half-time in the offices. By next week it would be decided which area would suit her and the kibbutz best for her stay. A conversational Hebrew course was open to her on Tuesday and Thursday evenings. He thought that the food was very good, fresh, and she would be happy with it. There were another thirty-five teens in the program, most from the U.S., but some from Europe and Australia. And he went on, explaining all the do's and don'ts, musts and maybes.

Esther heard his voice, mostly as a melody, paying almost no attention to the content of his words. She wanted to know about him, not the stupid kibbutz! Could he tell that she wasn't paying attention? Was he interested? He damn sure was interesting. "Are you from here, or are you one of kids in the program?" she finally inquired. Did she have to say that? You know, for a girl that thinks of yourself as pretty cool, you're acting like a damned idiot! A horny idiot at that!

Edel didn't answer immediately, but stopped and made eye contact, before proceeding. It was that moment in which it became clear to him that this new American girl was attracted to him, and with that revelation he needed to take a more complete inventory of who and what she was. And the package was, how do Americans say it, the package was nice. Sexual tension takes a significant turn once both parties experience that particular energy, at any age. His voice, accent and all, lowered just a bit, and his chair slipped, maybe an inch forward. "Actually, I was born right here on the kibbutz."

"What's it like to grow up on a kibbutz? It's got to be real different from coming up in the US." Okay, I guess that's a neutral question, she thought. Anybody would be interested in that.

"Well, I'm not so sure I'm a good example of a kibbutz kid. My Mom's a Litvak Jew, who emigrated from Russia, but my dad is a Palestinian, whose family has been here for more generations than anybody knows. For them it was a special romantic thing, but for everybody else, not so romantic, or even special. I mean, everybody's cool and everything, but I never get the feeling that anybody really thinks we should be here. I'm that kid that is always looking to find the right fit, you know, looking for the kids that get who I am." Edel's eyes sought hers again, seeking reassurance that he was a good fit with her. Had he needed to get into all that? Too much information! Way too much, you schmuck!

She couldn't imagine anyone not getting who he was and not wanting to fit in with him. "Well, I don't know anything about the kids here, but you seem a perfect fit for this girl." Esther sucked in a breath, as if she wanted to take the words back. Of all the corny lame things she could say. "I mean, you seem like a pretty straight-up guy to me." Hopefully that toned it down a bit. It didn't.

"Well, I'm certainly straight, if that needs any clarification," he offered, making the decision that if they were going to flirt, it might as well be out there in the open. "Would you like me to show you where you will be sleeping?"

So, two kids from opposite sides of the world, both possessing incredible needs for acceptance, set off on a trek to Esther's Quonset hut dormitory. Edel busied himself by gallantly carrying the luggage, while Esther's focus was on avoiding actually touching him. She thought she knew where this was going, but was it? He played tour guide along the way, pointing out this and that, although both of them knew that she couldn't care about any of that, anyhow. As they got close to the dorm, he did his best to be casual about mentioning that "You won't be able to meet anyone inside. Everyone's probably out working and they most likely won't get back until just before dinner."

"Oh, that's such a shame. I wanted so much to meet the girls before getting involved with anything else." She allowed her sarcasm to signal her intent, the time for coquettishness having passed. There better not be anything probable about it.

As they reached the door, Edel glanced about, insuring himself that no one else was headed this way. They went inside, and he immediately reached for something else.

9

Having hastily done the deed, they lay together, intertwined in the single military style cot. Each bed was paired with a small bureau, the many pairs arranged symmetrically in rows, filling a large domed room. The cot's size forced further intimacy, and they clasped each other's body close, if nothing else to avoid falling on the floor. It was in all aspects a clumsy moment, the fervor sated, and now the hovering questions hung in their respective heads. Did I really do this? Oh God, what do I do now? Did I just fuck up big time? No, this feels really good.

She pulled his chin over, so his gaze left the ceiling and was now focused on her. Even at an early age, girls know they have to take over once the lovemaking is done. How do they know that? It's not taught, is it? "Well, you certainly are the best 'meeter and greeter' I've ever run across. Do all the girls get such a complete orientation?"

"Well, only the ones named Esther, whose beauty requires a deep inspection." Was that romantic enough? Or was it stupid and corny? I never know what to say, here. I mean, it's not like you can maintain the connection without words, but words never really cut it. Can you be romantic without being super cliched? "We better get our clothes back on. Somebody could be coming back soon."

"Yeah, I guess I wouldn't want anybody to get the right impression about me," Esther giggled. They both gathered their far-flung clothing from around the floor, dressed, and sat down next to each other on the cot. She rested a hand on his thigh, while he put an arm around her waist. "Seriously Edel, I don't know what it's going to be like for me here, but at least I feel like somebody's on my side. It's pretty scary for me to be somewhere where I don't know anybody, and I don't know the score or even how to play the game."

"Was that a game we just played?"

"No, that's not what I mean. For sure, that was wonderful. But you hear my words and don't get what I'm saying. I'm just happy that I don't feel so alone here, anymore." She paused, getting that she shouldn't be so deep, and decided to change the direction of the conversation. "What do kids do here anyway? I mean, in the movies they showed us in Hebrew school about kibbutz's, the only things they showed outside of farming and heavy-duty meetings, was a bunch of people doing the hora. Is there anything to do here?"

Edel laughed. "That's it. Compulsory hora dancing every night! No, Esther. It's like it is everywhere else. The only difference I guess between here and other places, is that just about everything we do here is with the whole group. We don't have little houses and little living rooms where just a few people watch television together or listen to music, or something. Most everything here is a group activity." He leaned over and whispered in her ear, "Except for a few things that have to be more private, that is."

"Well, I'm glad that some things are private," She tickled his thigh. "Speaking of more private stuff, do kids get high here?"

"It's pretty easy to get some weed. Kind of like everywhere else, I guess. You know, mostly on weekends. Other stuff, not so much. You're not some speed queen, are you?" He seemed ever so slightly concerned. You hear a lot of things about American kids, spoiled and all that.

"No way. I, uh, go in the other direction."

"I heard about some kids that know somebody that can get other stuff, but that's probably not such a hot idea. Israel is kind of weird, different from other places."

"What do you mean?"

"Well, with the situation always going on with the Palestinians, we're always in what amounts to a state of war. For security reasons, you can't go here, and you can't go there. Lucky me, I'll have to go into the army in just another two months. And, the people who do all the shady stuff, you know, like selling hard drugs and stuff, that's all mixed up with national security. The government doesn't really know if you're dealing with just another dealer, or maybe some Arab agent. So, the lines between unlawful, criminal and outright treason can get blurred easily here. You don't want to get into any funny dealings with these Arab guys."

Esther laughed. "Ooh, I thought I just did. Or maybe, just halfway did."

"No, that's not what or who I'm talking about. I may be half Palestinian, but I'm born and raised a Jew, with a Jewish mother." He was a bit irritated. She was making fun about things that weren't very funny. Don't fool with other people's sensitivities. "Esther, I'm just telling you to be careful who you're dealing with."

"Not usually my best trait. But, I guess you already know that." Hey girl, stop being cute. Can't you see he's trying to look out for you. "No, okay Edel. I'll be a good girl."

The truth be told, Esther wanted to get high. Was it a sex thing, or was it a guy thing, but somehow, whenever she got involved physically with a guy, she always looked to get high almost immediately after she uncoupled? Like she needed it. Couldn't figure that one out. Right after you felt so good, why wasn't good good enough? Come again? Was she some kind of pleasure fiend? Didn't feel like that.

"I can see everybody heading back here," Edel said, after looking out the window. He stood and took her hand. "Maybe it's time I should show you the dining area."

"Oh, cool. That would be great." They headed out the door, Edel dropping her hand as they stepped outside.

10

In her first four days in Ein Harod, Esther had become almost compulsive about finding a connection to get herself some smack. It wasn't as if her body was saying she needed it, and she wasn't even sure she wanted it. If anything, it was more like a stubborn identity thing. Maybe I'm a stranger in a strange land, but I'll tell you who I am, you won't tell me. So, whether she wanted it or not, the hunt to prove she could be successful at not doing what was expected of her outweighed any introspective investigation of her motivations or real desires. You know. You want what you want when you want it, and if you don't want it for sure, then you want to want it, and that's close enough to wanting it. You get on a roll, and it takes you where it does.

Just about everyone she asked, and she had asked pretty much everyone she met, confirmed what Edel had told her in the first place. Grass was easy to score, but any of the hard stuff wasn't, except maybe from some mysterious Arab, some guy that they all had heard about, but nobody knew, for sure. It made sense for her to continue asking around, because if everyone had heard the same rumor, then there had to be some truth to it.

The kids here were cool enough. About half of them came from the States, and, yeah, some of them were super religious or Zionists, but a lot were up for an adventure, fed up in one way or another with the usual high school scene back home, and had heard about this weird opportunity. She hadn't met anyone who had her particular circumstances, a legal deal. Hard to say if a lot of them were sent here because they'd done something wrong. Nobody, including her, wanted to talk about that. Sent for the "Israeli forefathers cure"? Nobody was going to own up to it if they were,

To her surprise, the religious kids were sort of okay. They didn't have any big need to convince anybody else to be like them. There was even a couple of sisters from some evangelical Baptist something, not even Jewish, whose parents thought the Holy Land itself, the land, the dirt, would bring their acting out daughters back to the bosom of the church. And those kids were down enough, although Esther thought that they might be lezzie. I mean, that's okay. Live and let live.

Edel and her weren't an official thing, but it seemed like just about everyone got the drift. He had a special kind of rep among the kids, you might say he was an elder statesman, or something like that. He was the oldest, and all, and about to enter the compulsory military service. He served as a conduit to the grown-ups who ran the place, being that he came from the kibbutz, along with his parents. Esther divined that he was really into her. Her mother probably would have said smitten. Of course, once she sensed the depth of his being taken with her, her interest started to dwindle somewhat. I mean, he was still cute and all, but. . . . Why was it like that? It was only a couple of days ago that she was all hot and bothered about him. Damned if she could figure out why she only kept her deal going for guys who either played her, or didn't care that much one way or the other, but if a guy started to fall heavy into her, she went the other way. Well, at least for now he was the only game in town. And a cute game at that!

It was Saturday morning, and a lot of the kids were at sabbath services, and Esther figured it was a good time to head over to the kibbutz "store," a kind of commissary for the youth program where they could charge for an array of basic personal items. She needed stamps to write back home, and she wanted to get that postcard for Betania. There was something about that girl. Esther wished she was here and that was what she intended to write, even if it was a cliche.

She kept twirling the wire rack thing around, hoping to find at least one postcard that wasn't a landscape. There was an absolutely splendid card that featured a tractor. How exciting can you get? She settled for one that was mostly scenery, but included a small shot of her dormitory in the background. She could draw an arrow to show where she was staying. Maybe get two of the cards, one for her parents. Daddy would like that.

From in back of her, she heard a low and heavily accented voice say, "You the girl that's been asking everyone about getting some 'H'? Did I get that right?" His hand was on her shoulder, preventing her from turning around. "You just keep looking at those postcards, girl."

"Um, yeah, I guess that would be me. Who's asking?" Esther was more startled than anything else. This place was like a high school, rumors and gossip flying everywhere. Well, if a monopoly board suddenly appears before you, you might as well throw the dice, Actually, make that appears behind you. "Yeah sure, that's me."

"Meet me at 8 o'clock tonight, at the front gate." He told her how much money to bring, and when she felt the pressure on her shoulder leave, she turned, but he was already gone. Weird as all hell. The store was hardly crowded. How did he manage that? Now, all she had to do was figure out if she was going to go to meet him there. The whole thing felt like a stupid scene in a James Bond spy movie. She had to admit, one of those scenes which never turns out particularly well.

Esther bought the post cards and the stamps, and ambled slowly back to the dormitory. Was this kind of deal safe in this place? The last thing she wanted was to get busted again. Here. In the middle of the promised land. Should she check it out with Edel? No, from what she was beginning to pick up, he probably didn't want to know too much about that side of her. And she didn't want to hear him telling her to be careful, playing like her male protector, and stuff. Yeah, but if she didn't want to hear it, how come she was asking herself?

By the time she got back to the Quonset hut, she had come to a conclusion. What the fuck, enough already. Stop thinking about it! Just do what you're going to do. It's not like worrying about it really makes any difference.

11

A few minutes before eight, Esther was pacing back and forth by the front gate. Funny how she was late for everything, but for trouble she made it a point to be early. No way I'll ever figure me out, she thought. Nothing much was going on. A few adults walked in, looking haggard, returning from work, somewhere else. God knows where, in this empty desert. A lot of dust flew up every time a car or truck went by. The guy in the guard house kept looking at her, she thought suspiciously. What's this kid doing out on the road, anyway? The voice in the back of her head pointed out that it wasn't such a bad question. What the hell are you doing out here, anyway?

By a quarter past she began to think that it was time to call it quits and just hop on back to the dorm and forget this whole stupid deal. She checked out both directions, and was about to hoof it, when a van, one of those little European style vans, pulled up beside her. The side door slid open, and this guy says, "Get in, come inside."

Esther hesitated for a second. She was surprised. She'd assumed that the guy she'd met in the store would be on foot, and not telling her to get her ass in some Tonka Toy van. Well, I guess, when in Rome, ...

Once inside, she immediately was struck by a whiff and a half. It smelled like shit, literally, like shit. This van thing must be used during the day to move animals here and there. There was one guy driving, and another sitting next to her in the back seat. They looked, and for sure smelled, about as clean as the van. God, she was probably going to smell like that too, when she got out. Ugh. Let's just get this over with. The guy who was sitting next to her asked if she had the money. Same voice as the one in back of her when she was buying the postcards. For some reason, that settled her down a bit.

"Yeah, I have the money. You have the stuff?"

"Yes, but can't do exchange out here on the road. Too dangerous. We go to a place a little further down road."

Esther kept one hand in her left pocket, where she had the cash. I mean it's not like they're going to take the Gertz card. She looked back and forth from the guy who was driving to the one sitting next to her. It's hard to read people when you don't know them, I mean, not know them in particular, but know the whole group of them. It felt like they were checking her out, in some way. Was that checking her out like she was checking them out, like for possible danger, or the other kind of up and down? I sure as fuck don't want to deal with any come-ons here. Oh shit, this wasn't going to become one of those deals, was it? For God sakes, she just wanted a little smack to snort. Not some complicated tit for tat, or was it tit for whatever, game. Guys can be such a pain in the ass. Wherever in the world they come from. And, ugh, these two were slimy at that.

The one who had done all the talking, back seat guy, said, "Relax girl, we almost there. We will get you what you want."

As they pulled into a driveway on the left, marked by a low crumbling stone wall, Esther's fears began to surface, big time. The place looked seedy as all hell. It was stone dark, and she was alone with two dirtbags who she didn't know from Adam, and looked like they belonged in some stupid horror movie. What should she do? Okay. Calm down, do the deal, and get the hell out of here.

"You get out now. We are here. We will go inside and you will have your stuff."

Something was telling Esther not to go, but what was the alternative? Driver guy was already out of the van and heading toward the door, and the other guy was sort of lightly pushing her out of the back. "We go, we go." She tentatively put one foot out, and turned to ask, "Why can't we just do the deal right here? There's no one else around."

"We go inside." It was not so much an answer, but a command. What if she just said no, Take me back. It didn't feel like they would pay much attention to that. Esther found the ground with her other foot, stood up, and followed the driver toward the house. This wasn't good. But you know the deal. Whenever you feel afraid, just hold your head erect, whistle that tune. . . . . Doesn't make much difference if they pick up on your fear or not, girl. Just do your best to bluster your way through it. And, maybe they're just being cautious, and you're working yourself up over nothing. Just bluster, buster.

The inside of this place was even grungier than the outside. Dust and grime seemed to cover a bunch of old and thrown together stuff. Aunt Phyliss wouldn't be pleased here. Okay, so it's a shit hole. Just do the deal and get out of here. Bluster baby, bluster. "So, are you going to sell me some smack now, or just take me back to Ein Harod?" she threw out while looking back and forth from one to the other, not knowing which one was the actual dealer.

The driver spoke for the first time. He reached into his pocket, took out what looked like an eight ball, and put it on the table. "We party now."

You gotta be kidding. But his face had no smile on it, and this guy wasn't asking. He had some notion in his head, oh who knows what the fuck he's thinking. "Look Buddy, I'm not here for some social occasion, and there's no way I'm partying with you. Now sell me some of that or let's just get the fuck out of here!"

The son-of-a-bitch just repeated, "We party now," switching the emphasis to "now."

Okay girl, it's time to scramble. Can't be that far back a walk, can it? Didn't seem that long ago when she had been in the car. Esther started for the door. She was immediately blocked by the back seat guy. "Hey, get your hands off me, Mister. I'm done with this. You can keep your shit."

Back seat guy didn't say anything, just took her by her arms and forced her to the single chair next to the table, He pushed her down by her shoulders and compelled her to sit. Driver guy came up close to her face. "You said you wanted party. We party."

"I never said I wanted to party with you. I just wanted to buy a little of this shit. Let me out of here, damn it." She started to struggle to get out of the chair, but back seat guy held her down firmly. And that's when driver guy came up around the table and smacked her hard in the face! "We party now."

There was a finality to that hard slap in the head. Without any verbal process, the realization, knowing she wasn't going to get out of this, slapped her in the head a lot harder than the actual blow. Esther, who could wiggle, tease, think or lie her way out of or into anything and everything, wasn't going to get out of this one. Her mind went strangely still, the ever-present narrative turned off and silent. Her body lost all its tension, the deer in shock and feigning, if not accepting, death. She went into a hazy consciousness, aware and not aware. Some part of her went to her room, back home. Daddy was next to her on the bed, telling her that it was going to be okay. She had some minimal awareness of what was going on right here in this hell-hole, more like she was watching than like anything was happening to her. She watched herself get shot up, stripped, smacked around, fucked and forced to suck the other one off. But it was all visual, something she saw, like some horror porno movie, a hideous TV show, not her, not her body, no sensation, all outside. They did what they wanted, and Esther wasn't there. She was home in Queens with Daddy.

When they were done, they threw her in the rear seat of the van, and drove rapidly down the road, back to the kibbutz gate, where she was pushed naked onto the pavement, even while the car was still moving. Her clothing followed on top of her. The guard by the gate rushed over. She remained mute.

12

Esther just barely started to come out of it in a hospital in Nazareth. For three days, she had been fundamentally in a fugue state, lying in a comatose-like condition, occasionally thrashing about, the agitation displaying itself yet remaining unvoiced. As her consciousness returned, her now open eyes remained unfocused, refusing to recognize this world that had proven itself beyond her ability to control.

Police had been notified that she was stirring. They needed to interview her as soon as possible. The state security system officer assigned had put together the basic facts of the case, but legal decisions clearly needed to be made. This girl was at one and the same time an offender and a victim. She had apparently not only flaunted illegal substance laws, but more importantly had established a relationship with known Arab terrorists. That she had become the object of their terror was disquieting, but ultimately an outcome of her own making.

How this naïve American teenager should be treated by the Israeli criminal justice system was an open question. While she had broken both drug and security statutes, she couldn't be expected to be familiar with the ongoing state of war ever-present in Israeli society, and the legal regulations that this hostile environment required. Any parent, from any culture, would only feel concern and alarm for this disturbed adolescent, but prosecutors everywhere need to insulate themselves from a quasi-parental attitude. Esther's status as a criminal versus a victim was ultimately a stalemate. The political position that Esther's situation warranted was still another matter, and this was more centrally problematic. The matter of relations with the Jewish population in America was hardly insignificant. This was an overindulged and willful teenager that had been sent to the kibbutz in an effort to infuse her with a pioneer mentality, an image that was carefully cultured by the Israeli government. A highly esteemed American Rabbi had referred her. Prosecution was out of the question. Return to the kibbutz was equally a non-starter. The only resolution that made sense to those who were responsible for a politically acceptable outcome, was for her to be returned to her parents, and America, as soon as she was medically transportable. At the end of the day, the girl, and her problematic behaviors, was their issue, not Israel's.

The American embassy had therefore been notified that it would be appreciated if this girl would be transported back to the U.S.A forthwith. She was to be accompanied by an American diplomatic aide, not her parents, as their presence in Nazareth would only complicate an already delicate situation. The embassy made contact with the Department of State, back in D.C., who in turn notified Ben and Rose that their daughter had been injured, and would be coming home in a few days, as soon as she was fit to travel. The parents were advised that Esther had indeed broken some laws, but was not going to be charged with any crime. The girl had been attacked while in the process of an attempt to purchase illegal drugs, but there were to be no legal encumbrances attached to this. Their daughter was in the hospital, for observation; however, she appeared to be in no medical danger. She would likely arrive home before the postcard that she mailed on her way to the gate.

For her part, Esther continued to internalize and stuff her shock, grief and horror throughout her entire hospitalization and conveyance back home. She meekly acknowledged the young woman who was charged with accompanying her, responding to questions and suggestions with simple one-word answers. Her facial posture remained composed and without emotion. Anyone who knew her, would have had a hard time recognizing this robotic persona. The bruises were beginning to heal externally, but the internal damage to her spirit was profound, and lingered.

A federal sheriff's officer met Esther at JFK as she deplaned, and she was whisked through customs, and immediately driven to her home in Hollis. It was a beautiful spring day, in a neighborhood that prided itself on the brilliant red azaleas featured in every home's garden beds. It had been only eleven days since Ben had driven Esther to the airport, for her to begin a new adventure, and change the direction of her life. She returned changed in a manner which no one could have anticipated.

Part Two

1

Esther Shapiro's parents were flabbergasted, again. Maybe less than the last time they were flabbergasted, but flummoxed, nevertheless. She did what? It's one thing for somebody who likes those horrible drugs to try and find them on some South Jamaica street corner, but in Israel? In the holy land? When you're there because you did the same thing here? Esther's smart. How could she be so dumb? For three days they stewed and worried, unable to understand, forced to sit in their house and try to figure the whole mess out. And why couldn't they, or at least Ben, fly over there and bring their daughter back home themselves? Something's going on here. Who was hiding something, and what were they hiding? There were so many more questions than answers, and all they could do was sit around the dinette table and try to conjure up a scenario in their heads that Esther, their Esther, was okay, and that everything would turn out to be fine. Oh, please God, let it just be fine, once she got home.

And it's not as if they could talk to anybody about it. You don't exactly put up a big welcome home sign in the front yard when your kid's being sent home for the second time for being a, how do you say it, a drug user. Could you imagine how Phyliss would just eat this up? And Goldsheid, that stupid old excuse for a rabbi! He was the one who finagled this whole lunatic plan up in the first place. It's not like you'd want to talk to that imposter again. No, they were absolutely alone with each other in the midst of this worrisome prelude to who knows what. They both did their level best to get through this difficult time, remaining in their respective lanes. Ben solicitously attempted to console an inconsolable Rose, while she maintained the familiar dynamic of criticizing him about the form and manner with which he approached her. By staying in their comfort zones, as best as they could, during these trying times, they could count on their relationship to comfort them, while waiting for the forecasted tornado to return.

Neither of them could have possibly predicted what they were about to experience. The nice young woman who had traveled with Esther rang the bell, and while she was busy introducing herself, Esther slipped past them all, without a word, went into the kitchen, and made herself a chocolate milk. Sitting down by the dinette table, sipping her drink, she was impassive, staring at the refrigerator magnets, as if waiting for them to move. When her parents dispensed with the State Department lady and rushed into the kitchen area, all she could say was, "Fox's U-bet is so much better than Hersey's. They didn't have any over there." Ben construed this as a statement that she was glad to be home in her customary surroundings, and replied, "We're glad too that you're home, Sweetie."

This was the tenor that remained in effect for the next two days. Esther slept much of the time, and when awake strode about in a mechanized manner, her affect unemotional and confined to the simple activities of daily living. Ben and Rose didn't know whether they should bring up anything about Israel and the kibbutz and who knows what happened, or just wait for Esther to initiate those discussions. It was maddening. Ben kept reassuring Rose that "she'll be ready when she's ready," but, in fact, he knew by her distance and the far-away look in her eyes, that left alone, she might never be ready. His daughter, Esther, who sparkled through life as if she was Tinkerbell-made-real, had withdrawn into a detached shell, and didn't appear inclined to come out. She was polite. She was helpful, in a superficial sort of way. At the end of every meal, she just rose and gathered the dishes, brought them to the sink and washed them, without her parent's request. Not even the dishwasher, mind you, the sink. She displayed no interest in reaching out to any of her friends, and seemed disinclined to talk about any plans, for school, or anything else. No make-up. She wore an old sweatshirt and some baggy running suit pants, all the time. Rose found herself checking the hamper to make sure she was changing her underwear. It appeared that she did. Well, thank God for small things.

Ben worried a lot about the Court. Clearly, Esther had violated the conditions through which she could avoid dealing with the criminal justice system. Now what? Did the Israeli government and the Queens Country courthouse communicate with each other? Were all the official people going to have to find out about this? Was it was his responsibility to make some kind of report to that social worker lady. A father should tell on his own daughter? His Esther? Not a chance! No way! Maybe when they start serving kasha knishes at the White House, for some fancy-dancy lunch.

Besides, she was in no condition to have to cope with lawyers, and judges and all that. Nobody should have to go to court if they weren't right, and Esther wasn't right. He wracked his brain trying to figure out what was wrong with her, and what he should do about it. She reminded him of those guys he had known from the War, what did they call it, "shellshocked?" It was like they took all the person out of the body, and just left the flesh to walk around and look like a ghost of who they used to be. Ben remembered feeling sorry for those guys, maybe even a little guilty that it happened to them, not him. He had often wondered what happened to them, over the years. What was going to happen to Esther? Was she going to stay like this? Was she going to wake up tomorrow and be the headstrong daughter he knew and loved?

What caused this, anyway? There weren't a bunch of bombs, like over there. She didn't have to see arms and legs flying around, unattached to the bodies they belonged to. I mean, the State Department lady had said that she had been attacked by the drug dealer, that pusher person, and she had a few bruises that were still healing, but was that enough to turn her into a shell of herself? None of it made any sense to him.

What was he supposed to do? Esther was sick. There, he said it. She's sick. Not like the flu or whooping cough, or something like that, but sick in the head., not herself, not his wonderful daughter. But was this some temporary condition that she would just snap out of, or could this be more serious. Rose thought that she was probably just down on herself for being naughty over there, and, anyway, it was probably a few days before her period. "You know how I get just before my friend comes. I don't want to have to deal with anybody then, Ben. Even you. You'll see. She'll get her period and just like that she'll be her usual self. Now stop all your worrying, already. You're driving me crazy1" She then waxed a little philosophical. "Kids! They drive you nuts. First, she's a non-stop impulsive mischief maker, getting into one thing or another, all the time. And it gives you migraines and pushes you to your grave. And then she turns into some zombie-like thing, and you worry yourself sick about that. There's no winning. There's no winning I tell you."

Ben certainly didn't feel like a winner. After a lot of thought, and pacing in the bedroom, it came down to two things, either he was going to call Berger, Dr. Berger, and find out if he had any recommendations about what to do, or he was just going to have to sit down with Esther and talk with her about it, talk it all out, whether she wanted to or not. The problem with Berger was that he always made you come into the office. You could never get him to tell you what to do over the phone. Probably a money thing. You know doctors these days, more concerned about getting their money then helping their sick patients. Should we really believe it's a healthier thing to take the bus all the way over to Utopia Parkway and then have to sit in a waiting room with all kinds of sick people, who knows what they have?

Not that Ben cared about the money. His daughter Esther was priceless, and he would spend anything necessary for her to get better, just get better. After all, hadn't he just spent a fortune sending her over to Israel for what turned out to be a few days more than a week? No, it wasn't about the money. It was those nurses and reception people in Berger's office. They'd blab all over the neighborhood, and Ben couldn't abide with that. His daughter, Esther wasn't going to become the "talk of the town." So, he'd better just knock on her bedroom door and go in to talk to her himself.

Ben stationed himself in front of Esther's door. "Esther, honey? It's Daddy. Is it all right if I come in?"

No answer was forthcoming. He asked again, "Can I come in, Sweetie?" He wasn't sure, but he thought he heard a muffled "sure" come from her room, so he undid the door a little bit and peeked in. Esther was lying in bed, her head thrust into the pillow, legs akimbo. Seeing her fully dressed, in the sweats, of course, he opened the door and gently walked over to the bed. "Make me a little room here, honey. I want we should talk a little bit. Okay?"

Esther nudged herself a little into the center of the mattress, and pulled her legs and arms in toward her chest, loosely in a fetal position. "Sure, Daddy. Let's talk."

"Well, darling, Mom and I, we have noticed since you've been home, that you've been especially, shall we say, quiet. I think that's the right word for it, quiet. You don't seem your usual self. Usually, you're more, shall we say, active. Um, . . . I just wanted to make sure that you're okay, that nothing's making my precious girl unhappy, or . . . troubled."

"I'm okay, Daddy. I'm just tired." She rolled over to face the wall. "I'll come down in a little while."

"Well, I'm glad of that, cutie, but could you just tell me, . . . you seem to be, should I say, ... kind of reserved, yes that's a good word for it, reserved. That's different from who my baby girl usually is, I mean, more often than not, different from your usual self. Do you think so? Is something the matter? You know, you can tell Daddy anything. I just want to make sure that you're okay."

Usually, by now she would have become exasperated and shooed him out of the room. But now, she just repositioned herself again, and stared up at the ceiling. "It's okay, Daddy. I'm okay. Thinking about things, I guess,"

He reached to take her hand, but she withdrew it, hugging herself. "So, what are you thinking about? Anything particular?" Maybe she would talk to him if he wasn't too invasive.

"Kind of everything and nothing, Daddy. I'm just adjusting to what I learned over there, in the kibbutz. You know, sometimes you just learn one solitary thing about life, and it's just one little thing, but it sort of changes everything."

"What's that, Esther? What's this new thing you've learned?"

"I don't know, Daddy. It's kind of a thing, kind of a feeling. It's hard to talk about it."

"Could you just sort of tell me a little bit about it?"

She started to sit up, but seemed to change her mind, and sank back into the pillow. "I guess it's like I realized that I'm not in charge. I'm not in charge of them, I'm not in charge of me, I'm not in charge of stuff, I'm not in charge of anything, and I'm not even in charge of not being in charge. That's all, Daddy. I'm not going to waste all my energy and feelings trying to be in charge anymore." And she rolled over, and faced the wall again.

"But Sweetheart, you're just sixteen, you're not supposed to be in charge of everything. Give yourself some time, Sweetie. Your whole life is in front of you."

Esther just sort of grunted a whatever-you-say "sure," and closed her eyes. "I don't want to talk about it, Daddy. It's okay. I'll see you downstairs in a little bit."

He was dismissed. Dismayed, and dismissed. As Ben walked slowly down the stairs, he thought about how he had always believed that his little girl, his little Esther, could do anything she wanted. She had the smarts, and she had the spirit, and the sky was the limit for his little girl. Now, that all seemed kind of broken.

"Well, she'll grow out of this. Just a setback. Just a stage. She'll come roaring back. God help us. You'll see." But she wouldn't. All transformations are not mind-blowing or inspirational, or desired. Sometimes the permanent acceptance of new insights into the order of things in this universe just plain stinks. It all depends on the perspective of the revelation.

2

Somehow, or other, the New York courts and an Israeli something or other did communicate with each other about Esther's less than stellar experience at Ein Harod. Sarah Williams, that nice social worker lady, had been notified of the circumstances of the Shapiro girl's return to Queens County, and had been asked to interview the family at their home. A determination had to be determined, whether she should be violated, and sent back to family court for sentencing, or allowed to seek a more appropriate treatment. As the worker sat in her car, parked in the Shapiro's azalea lined driveway, she reviewed the case material, and the report which had been sent by the State Department.

"Sometimes it's hard to imagine that white folks could be quite this stupid," she thought to herself as she perused the material. "I guess they figure that their kids are better not be put in the same category as all of the rest of our children that mess up their lives. Send her off to Israel? To some Gad forsaken kibbutz? Hell, why not give her a big old allowance and get her an apartment in Paris? Maybe on the Left Bank. Maybe call it some special cure, the 'French Rehab'. I just don't get these folks. They make enabling into an art form!"

She did her best to check her feelings. "But I can't let my upset with the parents get taken out on the girl. She's not responsible for their idiocy, even if it's turned her into such a major-league sick and spoiled brat. Besides, that poor kid has had enough punishment, from what I'm reading. Talk about a violation! Nothing we could do would be a greater violation than what she's already experienced. I wonder where her head's at now." She returned the materials to her briefcase and headed to the front door, doing her best to maintain that practiced benevolent smile.

The family met with her in the living room. Sarah couldn't help noticing immediately that the girl sat alone, on the ottoman, rather than cuddling up next to her father on the sofa. While her parents were engaged in their buttering up patter, Esther's conversational tone was flat, almost removed from the discussion. Polite. She allowed her mother and father, mostly the father, to carry on the discussion.

"Esther, would you prefer that we talk alone, or would you like your parents to continue to meet with us? Sometimes, at moments like this, we can feel a need for privacy."

"No, that's all right, Ms. Williams. Mom and Daddy can be part of anything we talk about."

"Okay, Esther. Tell me as best as you can how you are recovering from the horrible trauma that you were subjected to. No one, under any circumstances, should have to endure such treatment, whether they opened the door for it or not. How are you doing, my dear?"

Ben and Rose's attention perked. What was she talking about? What had happened to Esther over there, and why didn't they know about it?

But Esther simply replied, "I'm doing as well as anybody would, I guess, Ms. Williams. It seems that things have become quieter up in my brain, though. I'm just glad to be home."

There was none of the false ingratiation that Sarah remembered from their first encounter. Just a matter-of-fact tenor. Her facial expression was flat, limited, like her voice, without emotion. Depressed?

"Would you like me to set you up with an appointment with our sexual assault counselor? My girls tell me she's a really good woman to talk to, and very helpful."

"Wait a minute!" Ben jumped up. "Are you telling us that our Esther has been raped, or assaulted in some sick way, or something like that? Did somebody hurt her like that over there?"

"I'm sorry, Mr. Shapiro. I guess I just assumed that you were advised of this. It never occurred to me that neither Esther nor the government folks would have kept this information from you."

"Is this true Esther? Did some horrible beast of a person assail you like that?" Ben's voice was rising by decibels. And Rose, right next to him, began to shake.

"Please calm down, Daddy," his daughter replied calmly. "It won't help any of us for you to get all excited and everything. And you too, Mom. Mrs. Williams is here to try to help me, and you getting all bent out of shape isn't going to help anybody."

"What, I should act like I don't care when some stranger tells me that my flesh and blood has been desecrated? Are you trying to send me to my grave, young lady? Answer your father's question, Esther. Did somebody force sex on you?" Rose's voice grew into a howl. Her shaking finger was pointed at Esther as she spoke.

Esther hardly reacted. She ever so slightly nodded her head back and forth. "Mom and Daddy. What happened was I tried to buy some drugs, and the people who were supposed to get them for me raped me instead. It's done and over, I can't do anything about what they did, or my stupid mistake, And I don't want to talk about it."

Rose was not capable of letting this go. She was borderline raging. "You don't want to talk about it? So, who are you not to want to talk about what I've got to put up with. I send you to Israel because of all the crap that you pull, and you come home like this. And you don't want to talk about it? I've had it! I've had enough! I can't deal with any us this anymore!"

"Mommy, please."

"Don't you Mommy please me. You don't get to tell me when anything's done and over!"

Maybe it was all the fury that Ben was feeling and unable to direct toward some unknown rapist who had attacked his precious daughter. Maybe it was the powerlessness he damned himself with for being unable to protect her. Maybe it was having to discuss any of this in front of this stranger, even nice as she was, a stranger. But in this momentous moment, Ben stood up and turned to Rose, shaking his fist at her. "Rose, shut the fuck up! For once in your life would you realize for even a second that it isn't always about you! Either you shut your mouth or I'll shut it for you!" His fist remained shaking in the air.

Rose flushed, reddened, and with mouth agape, ran from the room, shouting in back of her, "I can't take it. I can't take it. I'm going to my room," and just like that she was up the stairs, the banister trembling, the bedroom door slamming behind her.

Ben continued to stand, his fist now shaking at the absence of the object of his anger. The room fell silent. Esther stood up from the ottoman, held her father's hand steady for a minute, and said "Well, that was very dramatic." She apologized to the social worker for putting her through what had to be a difficult situation, and then turned to her father. "Daddy, please sit down now. We still have to discuss with Ms. Williams whether I go back to school, or have to go to jail, or what's going to happen with me."

Well, this is certainly one for the books, thought Sarah. I guess we know who the adult in the room is now. Both Ben and Esther were looking at her, anticipating that she would redirect the meeting back to where it belonged. About the only thing that was clear to her was that she wasn't going to send this child back to court for sentencing. Whether it was depression or PTSD or just being knocked up the side of her head, this girl had changed. Let's let the doctors at the IOP over in Richmond Hill deal with figuring out how to help her. It felt a bit, maybe a lot, over her pay grade.

"No, Esther, you're not going to jail. I'd like you to start at the adolescent Intensive Outpatient Program in Richmond Hill, and we'll take it from there. They can tell us if you're ready to go back to school, or not. Off the top of my head, though, I imagine that they'll tell you to return, sometime in the next month or two. Is that okay with you?"

"That will be fine, Ms. Williams," Esther offered. The two of them went over all the details about where and when, while Ben quietly watched. Part of him was relieved that a plan for Esther doing something, anything, was being put in place, and another part was focused on what to say to Rose after this meeting was finally over. He was scared, for sure, but also a little proud of standing up to her. For himself he would never do that, but for Esther?

With all the arrangements made, Ms. Williams stood up to go, but when gathering up her papers, turned again to her client. "Oh, I almost forgot. Esther, given what happened to you in Israel, I'm going to need that you take a complete physical over at Jamaica Hospital. We just need to know that you don't need any further medical attention. Here's the telephone number. You can call them anytime to set up an appointment. As long as it gets done in the next 14 days. Okay?"

"Sure, Ms. Williams. And I want to apologize once more for that whole hullabaloo with my mother. I'm not crazy about admitting it, but she doesn't handle stress or anxiety very well."

"That's all right, Esther. There is nothing for you to apologize for. I'll see myself out, and I'll see you the next time I visit the IOP. Good day, Mr. Shapiro."

Ben waved silently goodbye with his presently non-menacing hand. Mostly, he was acknowledging to himself that now it was his daughter who was apologizing for how Rose couldn't handle her emotions any time she was overwhelmed by life. That had always been his job.

3

"Wow, I can't believe that I checked the mailbox on my way out this morning, and there's a postcard from you. And then I get here, and here you are, voila, like in the flesh!"

"Hi, Betania. How are you doing?"

"I'm okay. Not much different than when we met a couple of weeks ago. But what the hell are you doing here? The last I checked you were supposed to be in Israel. You even showed me where the hell you were sleepin'. What's up, girl?"

"It's a long story, frankly very painful, with a lot of ugly happenings along the way. You mind if I don't go into all the particulars?"

"Hey, you don't owe me any explanations. I'm just glad to see your sorry ass in here."

"Thanks. And double the feeling back to you. It's good for someone to be glad to see me, even if I'm not exactly being what they expect."

Betania looked over her prodigal friend, and she indeed did seem somewhat a sorry ass. Her face seemed like it had been roughed up a while back, and you couldn't quite put your finger on it, but something else was wrong. Like she was just being polite and everything, but not really here. "Esther, I don't need you to lay any of the facts on me, you know I always have my own soap opera goin' on, but are you okay? Just askin'."

"It's all right, Bee, I'm just sort of worn out and leaving the fighting to the fighters."

Whatever that means. "I hear you that." She let it go, seeing that Esther wasn't going to run down that road. "Hey, we got a couple of minutes before we got to pee in the bottle. Want me to show you around the place?"

"Sure, that would be great," Esther responded, and Betania escorted her around the room. The rehab had taken over a building that once housed a Bohacks grocery store, empty for a number of years. It was a large open space, no walls, areas allotted to different functions, but calling out with an echo that there was no privacy to be found here. A nurse's station, what looked like a lecture set up, a circle of folding chairs for group therapy, desks with side chairs where counselors were busy setting up for the day. All very open. Sort of a supermarket for fucked up kids, was the impression running around Esther's head. A variety of adolescents wandering in, more guys than gals. Betania introduced her to them along the way. Nobody showed a high schooly interest in who the new girl was. Just a couple of polite "how ya doin's.."

Esther couldn't help thinking of Edel, back in the kibbutz, and his showing her around. It had been the beginning of her fucking up everything back there. She knew somehow that it would be markedly different if she was just arriving there today. She wouldn't have made a play for him, and no way would she have nailed him. Esther, you were an idiot, asking for trouble every time you turned around. And Edel, the truth is, he could have been a good thing. Sad.

Somebody or other gave out a loud call that it was time for "urines," and everybody headed over to the nurse's station. Esther was pleased to notice that there were a couple of bathrooms, just to the right. "Well, at least there is some degree of privacy," she observed to herself.

Urines collected, the motley group headed over to the group area. Everyone seemed to have some regular place to sit, routines which were established without any particular thought, but unwavering nevertheless. A daily deal for as long as they stayed in the program.

Betania damn near pushed some guy out of his seat to make room for Esther to sit next to her. "Hey, Brian. Move your butt over a bit, would you? I need for my friend to sit next to me."

Settled in, Esther checked out the counselor who was sitting across the circle from her, waiting for the group to lose their restlessness. Harley Davidson tee shirt, jeans, prematurely bald, probably in his mid-forties. From what she could see, he appeared to be assessing her at the same moment. "Okay group, settle down. We have a new member with us today, Esther." He extended a hand in her direction. "Esther, my name is George, and I'm the counselor for this group. Would you mind telling us a little bit about yourself?"

How do you respond in these situations? Do I mind? Esther wanted to say an outright no way. A couple of weeks ago she would have had some smart-ass remark ready, and it would have been out of her mouth before she could control herself. But now, she just honestly replied, "I'm not really comfortable with all this, but here goes. I'm Esther. I was arrested about a month ago for possession of heroin. I guess you could say I had a little bit of a habit, mostly just snorting, skin popped a couple of times. Got to shooting after a while. Probably been the worst month of my life. The one thing I can tell you for sure is I'm done, and not just with the stuff. I mean I'm done with needing to be cool. I'm done with being some teen aged asshole. I'm done with fighting this growing up deal. I guess that's about it. Right now, it feels kinda simple." And she sat down, crossed her arms and legs, and waited.

The counselor noted to himself that this newcomer certainly laid it out concisely. Hard to tell if it was truthful. No feeling though. What was most remarkable was the cold, flat demeanor. Not just a lack of emotion, but also no gestures, kind of physically blank. Mechanical. Something's going on here. Did she belong in this group? Hard to tell. Probably a good idea to get a psych eval. "Welcome to our group, Esther. I don't want to press you to go any further right now. You'll share with us along the way as you get to know us and feel more comfortable." He turned to the rest of the group. "So, what's going on with everybody?"

Esther listened, motionless and mute in her chair. Some girl, Judy, was complaining about her parents, and how they were watching her like a hawk, felt like she was in jail. There was a guy, Tommy, who didn't know how to handle all his old friends, like they were all still doing their thing, and he didn't know where he fit in anymore. Brian, sitting right next to her, wanted to know how long he was going to have to keep coming to this group. It had been eight weeks already, and he wanted to get back to school. To Esther, it felt like some big collective whine. She wondered if the counselor wanted to scream and tell all these winey-asses that they should stop complaining for a minute, and say something, anything constructive. But she didn't. She watched and listened. Just something else, one more thing for her to accept. This was the way it was, and it wasn't her place to challenge or contest it.

At some point she listened to Betania tell Tommy that he needed to assert himself. He needed to tell his friends where he was at, to hell with what they thought. Assertion? She thought not. She had asserted herself into all kinds of shit, and that plain wasn't going to happen anymore.

Later on, in the didactic session, the counselor George, the same one from the group, was talking about peer groups, and how teenagers all felt that they had to have a collective identity. They could use this collective identity as a step, in maturing, as a stop along the way to developing an individual identity. But some kids get stuck at this point, he said, and never went on to become a person on their own. They get all jammed up at trying to fit in with their peer group, and lose their common sense. Like they ever had any, Esther thought. George was saying that being just like everyone in their peer group became more important than being right, or good, or yourself,

Esther agreed with most of what he was laying out. She was never again going to fight to be part of the that collective identity, or even fight to seen as special by some stupid peer group. But she didn't want to fight to try and be herself, either. That seemed to be the hard part for her. With her parents, especially her mom, it was always a fight to just be who you were instead of who Mom wanted you to be. She absolutely couldn't believe Dad fought back at her the other day. That for sure was a first. And look where that got him.

With him it was different. He usually didn't try to force you to do what he wanted, or become who he wanted you to be. He just made it so damn hard to disappoint him. There's a question. How do you get to be who you are, if somebody really loves you? I mean, just because they love you doesn't mean they're not going to have expectations. And then, you're on the fast track to letting them down. But she sure wasn't going to bring any of that stuff here, in the group. Maybe if she got a chance with George, alone. He seemed all right.

Mostly, she just felt so dirty. It was like the slime that came off those fucking perverts hadn't just been shot inside her. It had penetrated her pores. Inside and outside she could feel the filth. And that made her realize how grubby she had been herself, and how it felt like she could take a million showers and never clean all her shit away.

It was weird. She had heard all that stuff about how women should never blame themselves for being raped and attacked by men, but any way you looked at it, she was the one to blame. I mean, yeah, they were creeps and pricks of the first degree, and she hoped that some Israeli soldier gunned them down in a gutter, but she was the one who walked right into their little web. She might as well have said here the fuck I am, why don't you rape the shit out of me. Oh, fuck it, Esther. Don't go down that hole. It's just one more thing that you can't fight. It happened, and you can't take it back. No do-overs. Just stop fighting and see where that takes you for a change.

Some kid she didn't know was yelling now. He was pissed at his brother about something or other, wanted to punch him out, but his father had separated them, and made him go to his room. All these idiots knew was how to fight. She was sure they were going to try to pry all that anger and rage out of her for how and when she was attacked. Absolutely no way, no way in hell. Running her fury would mean those bastards got to her, like they poisoned her with their diseased bodies and minds. Don't care if it's false front or false pride, or false any fucking thing. She wasn't going to be tricked or cajoled into running her rage.

At some point she became aware that George, the counselor, was asking her something.

"Esther, you all right? You seem like you went some place far away."

"No, I'm okay. I was just thinking about something. Please don't ask, I want to keep it private, for now." Maybe she wasn't going to share that much, but she wasn't going to lie about it either.

"That's fine, Esther. It's just your first group, and you'll be ready when you're ready. No rush." He looked at his watch. "And we better stop. We're a couple of minutes overtime, and you guys need time to gather your belongings."

4

Coming home after the IOP was not a pleasantly anticipated event. Daddy wasn't going to be home for another hour and a half, as he had gone back to work as soon as it was settled that his daughter would be going to the rehab in Richmond Hill. Some things can only be put off so long. That meant being home alone with Mom for ninety tension filled minutes. Rose had barely talked with her first and only born, since the day of the social worker's visit. Somehow or other, it was all Esther's fault that Daddy stood up for her, and all her fault that she had been raped, and all her fault anything else that was faulty. Not that she played like Cinderella's stepmother and harped and yelled at her constantly. She just stayed in her room and wouldn't respond if Esther said anything. Came down to the kitchen for a little something, but kept her face turned away. Esther could hear her on the phone, complaining to someone or other about her travails. You know, the poor Rose thing.

It was like coming home to a chest freezer pretending to be a home. It looked all pretty and shiny okay on the outside, but as soon as you walked in, a cold wind hit you from the north. Brrrr. So, Esther would sit down at the dining room table with the journal she had started to keep, a few days after she came home. She had thought of keeping track of her thoughts and feelings when she ran across an old diary from when she had been in fourth of fifth grade. It immediately just made sense to have some place to put all the things she couldn't say. Funny how you can talk to yourself on paper all the things you can't just outright even whisper to yourself. I guess putting it down in the stupid old composition book gives it some air of properness, or something like that. Mom didn't even ask what she was doing while emerging to take her trips to the kitchen. Used to be that she would need to know every stupid detail about anything she saw and didn't know.

The whole situation was just plain weird. Should she cook dinner? Not that she knew what she was doing in the kitchen. But it didn't seem like rocket science. But what would she make? There wasn't anything much in the fridge since Mom had, how would you say it, gone on strike? Daddy had made a big old cheese omelet last night when he got home. Who knew what they were going to eat tonight. And Daddy shouldn't have to cook anyway, when he got home from working all day. That wasn't right, any way you looked at it. So, Esther sat at the dining room table, one train of thought about the immediate discomfort running through her mind, and another more distant stream of contemplated feelings and ideas being penned for her private consideration.

Eventually she heard Daddy by the front door, turned the composition book closed, and went to greet him. Oh, good. He was carrying s couple of bags of Chinese food, and damn, it smelled delicious!

"Hi, Daddy. Let me take those bags. Should I set up some plates in the dinette or the dining room?"

"Wherever you want, Sweetie. Is your mother still in the bedroom?"

"Yeah. No change in that department."

"Okay, set the table for three. I'll be down in a minute."

As she put out the plates and silverware, and the special inlaid chop-sticks Daddy had bought her last year for Chanukah, Esther could hear them dimly from the bedroom.

"Oh, come on down, Rose, please. I got you some sweet and sour pork, with some house special fried rice, just like you like. A little bit of duck sauce for the egg roll. Come on down."

"Ben, you sound like Red Buttons with the 'come on down's'. No. No, my headache's just too much. Maybe you could bring me up a plate."

"Rose, my darling, it will do us good to all sit together and eat dinner. Come on, you can come back upstairs after dinner if you still don't feel well enough to watch television."

"Ben, you're pushing it. You're pushing it. What, you think I don't know you're trying to inveigle me with some sweet and sour sauce and an egg roll? You think I'm stupid? I said I wanted a plate up here. Is that so complicated?"

"But Rose, you've been locked up in the bedroom for almost a week now, This can't go on forever. It's not good for you, Sweetheart."

"So, now you know what's good for me. What's good for me is if I had a husband who stood up for me, not someone who yelled at me in front of a stranger, in front of my daughter, in front of the world. So, all of a sudden you know what's good for me? What's good for me is if I could eat my dinner in peace, right here by my make-up table."

"Okay, if you insist. I'll make you a plate. Maybe I'll find out from Esther about her day at the rehab, and I can tell you all about it after dinner. Or maybe you could just think about coming down for a fortune cookie, after you finish your plate, We always have fun sharing our fortunes. Don't we?"

She just shot him a look, and he gave up and headed down the stairs. "We'll talk later, Honey. We'll talk later."

Esther helped him put together a plate for her mother. She knew better then to ask if she should take it upstairs. He took the tray, turning as he started to go and said, "Start without me. It'll get cold. I'll be right back down in a second."

"No, Daddy. I'd rather wait. If it gets cold, we can put it in the oven," expecting he might be a little while.

He was back fairly quickly, muttering his way along, but changing his air as soon as he hit the last step. "All right then. Let's dig right in. We have a little feast here, a Chinese feast I tell you."

"Daddy, why does she have to be like this?"

"Well, you have to remember, your mother is a very sensitive woman."

Esther put down her chop-sticks and looked at her father quizzically. "What do you mean? Sometimes I can't believe how insensitive she is to you."

Ben smiled. "I don't mean so much that she's sensitive to other people. It's just that she can't take a lot of pressure or stress. You know the way she gets her migraines and cramps." He stopped and took her hand. "Look, Sweetheart, we've all been under a lot of stress and strain for this last couple of months. All of us. Maybe you haven't been at your best, and I have probably been a little grouchy with your mother, and yes, she's difficult to deal with when she gets, shall we say, overloaded. But we're going to bounce back. We always do. You'll see. So, tell me, how's it going over at that rehabilitation place?"

Esther just let it be. She'd talk to her journal about it when he went upstairs and started to entreat her all over again. You can't fight it. Didn't mean she had to join it. So, she smiled without emotion instead.

5

E sther read a magazine, *Popular Mechanics*, in the inner waiting room of the pediatric clinic at Jamaica Hospital. She wasn't really interested in those new rotary engines that Mazda was developing, and hadn't thought much about there being no new advancements in engines since the internal combustion deal, but anything to take her mind off all the poking and prodding they had put her through. They had given her a full physical, external and internal, taken blood, and even more urine, for God's sake. Damn! Those stirrups. No wonder everyone complains about that. And why did she have to go through all this? She was fine. She told them so. Even the bruises had all healed up, and by now, nobody could tell anything had happened. A whole lot of institutional build-up-your-job bull shit! Well, at least she got out of IOP for a day.

The article about heating your house with a swimming pool in the basement was actually pretty interesting. Guess you have to put that in before you build the house on top, can't exactly pick the house up, dig a pool, and then put the house back. But it would be pretty cool if you could.

And why can't I just go home, if they are all finished. No, I have to stick around for the results of the labs. And all the questions. What vaccinations did I get before I went to Israel? Did I ever share needles with anybody? That's gross. Knock it off, Esther, the whole thing's gross. And that one's on you. Her internal voices were suddenly talking up a storm, which made Esther realize that ever since she started keeping a journal, she hadn't heard nearly as much chatter in her head. Interesting.

And where do they get off asking me if I was sexually active with anyone other than the rape? What a lot of nerve. What does that have to do with a physical? It's none of their fucking business, and I'm not going to tell them squat about Edel. I mean, this is going into my records over at the IOP and with that Williams woman. Oh, let's just get this over with so I can go home.

Eventually, the nurse came by and let Esther know that "Dr. Estancia will see you now." As she escorted her back to the examining room, Esther wondered if she was a student nurse. She seemed barely older than herself, and you never could make out what those hat things meant. This one, the hat, seemed different than the others on the nurses nearby. Smaller. Entering the consult room, Esther observed that the doctor wasn't there, but was advised that, "Doctor will be right in. Just have a seat and he'll be right with you."

More time. But just as she was going to lament that she left the Popular Mechanics in the waiting area, it turned out that the nurse was right, and Dr. Estancia strode in carrying her folder. He also carried with him a broad smile, learned while he was a beginning intern, as a means to communicate to his patients that any anxiety they felt about their condition was unwarranted. They would be fine. His smile was particularly wide this afternoon. It only served to create more annoyance with Esther.

"So, Miss Shapiro, we have all your results back, and I'm pleased to inform you that for the most part, you are in excellent health." And he sat there, a young intern who was clearly not totally comfortable proceeding.

"For the most part? What do you mean?"

"Well, there's one thing that the tests picked up that wasn't anticipated."

"Did those bastards give me syphilis or something like that?"

"No, no, Miss Shapiro. Nothing like that. It's just that, eh, . . . , it's just that you're, that you are pregnant. Now, in cases like this, where a woman has been assaulted. . ."

Esther jumped to her feet and cut him off. "I'm what?"

"Now calm down, Miss Shapiro. Yes, I did say what you think I said. It is one hundred percent confirmed that you are pregnant."

The meeting went on for another fifteen minutes or so, but Esther remembered almost none of it, other than the bold fact that she was, in fact, pregnant, no question about it, one hundred percent, bet your bottom bitty on it, that there was a baby growing inside her, and that her life, one more time, would never be the same, again. No, she didn't want anyone to call her folks and speak to them for her. No, she didn't want an appointment with some other social worker. No, she couldn't breathe and could they just let her go, and get the hell out of this whatever this was, hospital or clinic, or whatever.

Once outside, she instinctively made up her mind that she wouldn't take the bus, but would walk home. It was a long walk, a good two hours to Hollis, but she needed the time to think before she got home. This whole deal was fucked up beyond belief. It would've been better if they told her she had syphilis, or the clap, or something. Anything else. Why me? Why do I get to be knocked up when everything in my whole world has been knocked up and down and over and through, and I'm damned if I know which way is which. Well, at least I know my way home, if home is still home, that is. Who knows anything these days. This is all so fucking unfair. I could scream. I could scream it. It's not fucking fair! Shut up, Esther. It is fucking what it is.

The idea that the scum of that scummy Arab prick could have taken hold inside her revolted her beyond comprehension. It was like the rape that just kept raping. She'd been able to force her mind to not be there when it was happening, but she couldn't do that now, this wasn't something that was hurting her from the outside, and she couldn't just turn it off, change the channel, go somewhere else. This was inside, in her, like it was her. She couldn't see it, or feel it, touch it, but now that she knew it was there, she knew she could see it in her mind, and feel it growing. Inside. And it was devastating and beautiful and ugly and magical, and the worst thing that ever happened, but also could have felt good, if only she could get rid of the picture of that horrible face that hung above her before she made the image go away.

Somewhere around when she got to Hillside Avenue, she thought about maybe, just maybe, this hadn't come from the rape. Maybe it was Edel's baby. No, she shouldn't use the word baby. Pregnancy was a condition. Baby was something else, something special. But what if this pregnancy had come from Edel. Did that change anything? In some ways it changed everything, in some ways it changed nothing. Yeah, then it might not be as hideous, but being beautiful was an even bigger problem. If it was beautiful, you can't just get rid of it. If it was the result of some creep of a slug you could just be rid of it and never look back on the whole thing. If it was an outcome of the most gorgeous man she had ever known to exist, that was a harder thing to deny, a tougher deal to push out of existence. She had to push this into existence, or push this out of existence. This is all so fucking unfair. How can anybody make decisions like this, much less, her.

And she had to make the decisions. And she had to make this one now, and it had to be made before she got home. Once she walked through the front door, they were going to try to take the decision from her. And she knew that couldn't, wouldn't happen. Any way you shake it, parents make decisions on the basis of what they need to happen, or for Mom, on the basis of what she wants for herself. No, this had to be Esther's deal, Esther's life, and Esther's choice. Oh God, she could just imagine seeing Daddy's face. How could she do this to him? And she could see Edel's face. If it was his, how could she make this choice ten thousand miles and a world away? This is so damned fucked up!

By the time she got to Midland Parkway, Esther was thinking that maybe this whole thing wasn't about what she wanted, or Mommy wanted, or Daddy wanted, or even what Edel wanted. It sure as shit wasn't about what those rapist sons-of-bitches wanted. Maybe it was about what the world wanted or what the world needed. Oh great, now how are you going to figure out what the world needs? Talk about being stuck on yourself. Esther Shapiro, from Hollis, Queens, a literally fucked up sweet sixteen-year-old little girl who's going to rehab because she's a damned druggie fool, that's the one who's going to miraculously determine what the world needs. Lots of luck, Charlie, or Tony, or whoever.

No, you idiot! Can't you see it? You're not making this choice. Mom or Daddy isn't making this choice. The father, whoever the fuck it is, isn't capable of making this choice. None of you can make the choice because the choice has already been made. The stupid fucking unfair world made this choice when you got pregnant. That's the way it is.

By the time Esther got to 188th Street, it was all pretty clear and settled. Since she had returned home, she had already made the bigger choice to stop fighting and let things be what they needed to be. She was pregnant. She was pregnant because the world, or the universe, or who the hell knows what, needed her to be pregnant, to have a baby. There, she had said it. It was a baby. And whoever its father was, the baby was beautiful, and that was that. She would have it.

6

As Esther walked up the flagstone path leading to the front door, she just assumed that Mom would be upstairs, in the bedroom, as per usual these days. That would leave her with some very necessary time to journal, to write this confusing whirl of uncertainty and total conviction down in one place, a place to hide from anyone else's needs, wants or demands, a place to reacclimate herself to whatever the hell was to come. She had decided to keep this whole pregnancy thing to herself for a while, at least until Mom and Daddy got past this stupid fight which they were perpetuating day after day after day. That should only take a century or two. The War of the Roses was nothing compared to the War of the Shapiro's. Anyway, the last thing she wanted to deal with was their anticipated reaction when they heard about the baby. They were going to go nuts. They were going to go bonkers, bonkers and then some. And besides, if she could delay clueing them in for a couple of months, then it would be too late to do anything about it. She'd kept secrets from them for a lot longer than two months. No big deal.

But even before she got there, the door opened, and there they were, both of them, arms gesticulating all over the place, simultaneously beckoning her in and blocking her way. What the hell was Daddy doing here? He never got home from work before six. And Mom was not only out of her room, but halfway out the front door, shouting for the whole world to hear, "Oh my God, you're home. You're home. We were so worried. Where have you been, Esther, where have you been?"

Startled and confused about how she could be late when she wasn't expected to be home at any particular time, Esther could only reply, "What are you talking about? I just got out from my medical, and I walked home. Um. . .is it all right if I come in?"

Mom's hysterical tone continued unabated. "Of course, of course. Come in, Darling. Go. Go. Sit down in the dinette and I'll make you a chocolate milk." And Daddy just hung out in back of her, with some stupid baffling look on his face, allowing Mom, who he was supposed to be fighting, to lead the charge. Mom, who hadn't given her the time of day for a week and a half, now she was proffering a "nice" chocolate milk. Fox's U-Bet, the great mood stabilizer.

What the fuck? What in all hell is going on?

Somewhere between the front door and the dinette she got it. Those sons of bitches! That stupid student nurse and Dr. what's his name. They called Mom and Daddy! They fucking promised they would respect my privacy, and then they fucking turned around and called my parents and spilled the whole deal before I even got home. And Daddy comes rushing home, again, and all their fighting is forgiven and forgotten, and they get all worked up. Now I don't even get to let it all sink in and settle, for even a little bit. Those miserable bastards! In the moment all Esther wanted to do was run back to the hospital and punch the stupid student nurse in the face.

Trying her best to at least act calm, she slowly took of her jacket, and sipped from the milk glass which had been placed in from of her. It was one of those gas station give-a-way glasses you got for filling up. Mom loved getting a whole set. Funny how you notice the small things when you don't want to look at the bigger picture. So, she just sat there for a couple of minutes, sip by sip by sip, stalling for time to figure out what in all hell to say, while her parents continued to hover, also not ready to initiate any real talking. "Thanks, Mom. This chocolate milk really hits the spot."

Eventually, she put the empty gas station glass down on the table with some authority, turned to her folks, who were just watching her from the other side of the table, and said, "I guess they called you up from the clinic."

"Well of course they did, Sweetheart. You shouldn't be left to deal with this all by yourself." This was Daddy.

"Daddy, they promised me. They promised me that it was my right to deal with this all by myself, in my own time. They told me one thing and then just did the exact opposite as soon as I left the room. Daddy, that's not right and it's not fair."

"Oh, stop being ridiculous Esther. You're sixteen years old and they're going to call your parents," Rose immediately snapped. "So now you know that we know, and that's that. You can't expect some city hospital to do anything other than spill the milk, or beans or whatever people spill. I mean, you're a kid, for God sakes"

"Mommy's right, Honey. Until you're officially an adult, they are required to tell us. Their mistake was not in calling us, but in telling you that they wouldn't. They shouldn't have done that." Ben did his best to calm the waters.

Esther took three or four settling breaths. "Okay, Daddy. I guess they told you. So, what do you want to talk about?" Hell, if we're going to do this now, I'm sure not taking the lead.

Rose jumped right in. "What do you mean what do we want to talk about. You're pregnant! You're pregnant!"

"Yes, Mom. I'm pregnant. Actually, they told me about that before they told you, Imagine. So yes, we all know I'm pregnant. And what do you want to talk about?"

"What do we want to talk about? What do you think? Our little girl is pregnant and she wants to know what we want to talk about?"

"Mom, again, we all know I'm pregnant. I apparently took the test. They informed me I was pregnant. Then they went around my back and told you guys. Then I walked home, and the next thing I know is the two of you are all bent out of shape and yelling at me. Now, is there something in particular you want to talk about, about that?"

Ben interjected. "Honey, what Mom is trying to bring up is the question of what we are going to do about it."

"Right now, Daddy, all I want to do about it is let it sink in, and take my time figuring out where I go from here. It kind of feels like it was only a couple of weeks ago you were driving me to the airport to go over to Israel, and that was a pretty big change in my life, and now I'm sitting with you guys in our dinette, and I'm pregnant, and you and Mom want me to know stuff that I don't know now. I mean, what do I want to do? Well, the usual thing that happens when you're pregnant is you wait a while, get bigger, and then you have a baby. Right?"

"But Esther, you're sixteen years old. You can't have a baby. You haven't even gone to college yet!" Rose was escalating again.

"Mom, I obviously can, even if we all wish that wasn't true."

"Esther, you know what I mean." she was back to shouting again, "It is out of the question. I won't allow my sixteen-year-old daughter to become a mother. I won't allow it! I won't allow it!"

"Esther, Sweetheart. All Mom is saying is that she doesn't want your life to be ruined because some horrible man in Israel attacked you. She wants what I want. You should finish up your high school years, go to college, and then you can find some nice young man and get married, and that would all be wonderful, and if you want to have a baby then, you can have a baby. But now is not the time. Now is not the time."

"Daddy, if it wasn't the time, it wouldn't have happened."

"What, there are no mistakes?" Ben was troubled by his daughter's response. "People don't make mistakes? Even God doesn't make mistakes? Mistakes happen all over the place. The best we can do is to try our best to fix them when we can."

"You mean it would be a mistake for me to be a mother? It would be a mistake for you and Mom to be Grandparents?"

"Not now, Esther. It would be a mistake for all that to happen now, when you are so young and you didn't plan for it to happen."

"You know Daddy, before all this happened, I used to think I was pretty good at planning. But if I think about it, with all my scheming and plotting and planning, that's what got me here, in this room with you guys, talking about me being pregnant. I planned it one way, and it turned out to happen just like to was supposed to, I guess. I mean, you told me Daddy, you told me that you wanted to be a dentist, but then you had to go to Korea, and when you came home you met Mom, and then you had me, so what good did all your planning do? In the meantime, it worked out for you, from what I can see."

"That's different, Honey. We were grown-ups. And even then, it was hard. I don't want it to be so hard for you. I want that all our hard work should make it easier for you."

"I get what you're saying, Daddy. I think that's very true. From what I can see, you do everything you can, all the time, to make things easier for Mom and me. It even feels like that's the way you think about love. Like if you love somebody, you always do your best to make things easier for them. But Daddy, I can't speak for Mom, but with me, while I loved you for making it easy for me, it also made it harder. I became one of those kids who thought that she should automatically get everything she wanted, and get it easy, without working for it, at that. C'mon Daddy, you know I've been a stupid spoiled-ass bitchy brat. It took me getting hurt and damn near killed for me to see that. Please, please Daddy, stop trying to make everything easy for me. Maybe I can even grow up and become a person as nice and loving as you. Let me deal with all the stuff life brings my way, the hard stuff, the easy stuff, and I guess, yes, this baby stuff."

Ben was flummoxed. On the one hand, he felt like his daughter was criticizing him. She was pointing out, correctly mind you, that he really needed to change his most fundamental character trait. On the other hand, he was brimming with pride that his daughter had suddenly matured into some grown up woman, who was wiser and stronger than he could ever had hoped she could be. His little Esther, she wasn't so little.

But all that didn't mean that even a grown-up Esther should be stuck with a baby. Sixteen. No husband. He was at a loss for words. How could he tell her about how impossible this notion was that she was considering, without making it sound like he doubted her abilities and strengths? Even if she wasn't his little girl anymore, it still felt like becoming a mommy could break her spirit, the spirit that was what he had always most loved about his very special girl.

"Esther, could you at least look at the other side, for a minute at least?"

'What Daddy? You want I should think about an abortion?"

Rose immediately interjected. "Don't use that word! They call it "termination of pregnancy'."

"Mom, whatever you call it, it's the same thing. It's a medical deal in which they stop me from being pregnant, they take this baby's existence away. Yeah, I know that abortion's legal now, but that doesn't mean it's what I want to do. For other girls, maybe it's right, but for me, it feels like going against life, my life, the baby's life, even your life, Mom. It's the way life goes, Mom. You don't go get a baby at Gertz, when it feels like you want one. It just happens, Mom. It just happens."

"Daddy didn't say you should have that termination. He just asked if you could think about it. Is that such a horrible thing, to think about the rest of your life for a day or two before you jump in the water?" Rose had become a bit more composed.

"Esther, we would never demand that you do such a thing." Ben added. "That wouldn't be right. It wouldn't be fair. But we'd like you to just mull it over a little bit. That seems reasonable to me. And I want you to also think about that you're not the only one who will be affected here. Mommy's life and my life would be changed a whole lot too. I'm not saying for the better or the worse, but our lives would sure be different. Is it selfish for me to ask you to think about that also?"

"No Daddy. That wouldn't be selfish." For the umpteenth time in just a few weeks, the time to admit that she didn't want to fight had come to pass, again. "Okay. Okay. I'm not promising anything, and I don't think I'm going to change my mind. But I'll think it over for a couple of days. All right?"

7

Wednesday

I don't even know how to start to write about all this. I just looked back at what I wrote yesterday, and it feels like that was some other life, like maybe if I looked at my diary from when I was in 4th grade. Everything's upside down and turned around. I know the facts, but can they really be true? I'm pregnant. What the fuck, it was only a couple of weeks ago I was trying to figure out if I wanted to tell Tony to get lost or not, and now I'm supposed to have a baby by who the hell knows who.

It's horrible. It's wonderful. It's everything in between. Am I really pregnant? It doesn't feel any different. My tits feel a little sore, but maybe I just need a new bra. That doesn't happen so fast, does it? I guess I should ask Mom. Jesus, I can't believe I'm talking about talking to Mom, of all people, about how does it feel to be knocked up? That'll be one crazy conversation. But who else? She's the only one I can think of. Not exactly something to bring up with Aunt Phyliss.

Okay. Pull yourself together girl. You're all over the place. You told them that you'd think about it. Think about what? Getting an abortion? That just feels all wrong. Somehow or other all this weird stuff came together and I'm arrested, and they get this nutso idea I should go to Israel, and then there's Edel, and then that rape happens, and then I'm kicked out and sent back here. Like how could all that stuff happen without it supposed to be going somewhere, without it having, like a purpose? How are you going to fight that?

You know what's even weirder. If I knew for sure it was Edel's baby, I think I'd still want to have it, but maybe not as strong. That's really weird. I mean getting together with him was something I wanted. Wanted? Shit, I made damn sure it happened. Maybe, if I was in control then, it makes sense to be in control now. Like that makes it my decision to make, whatever works best for me. But that other thing, when the assholes did me, that was a whole different deal. I mean no one was in control. Not me, for sure, and you can't tell me that those out-of-control crazy fuckers were in control. How could they be in control of me if they weren't in control of themselves? So, if none of us were, that only leaves life. I mean, I didn't die. I lived. Life was in control, and who the hell am I to tell life that she's all wrong?

I meant what I said to Daddy. Any way you shake it, he took care of me too much. And I became a taker too much, and not a giver. It's time for me to take care of somebody else. You know, that's also weird. Like if you become a wife or something, and take care of a husband, there's not so much to do in the deal. I mean, he's already a grown up on his own. Like Edel, I never met a more put together and competent person in my life, and he's only eighteen for God sakes. But a baby? They're the real deal in taking care of people. They're so helpless. And needy. It's a one-way street. Am I up to all that? Well, I better be, because there doesn't seem to be any way around it. An abortion is not on the table. It's not going to happen.

I wonder what they're gonna say in group at the IOP. Those asshole guys, I can just hear them now, making smartass remarks. I wish there were more girls there. Maybe enough to have a group of our own. Maybe I'll talk to Betania and not bother with the group. And George. Maybe I'll talk to him.

Enough for now. I'm too tired and I don't even know if I'm making any sense. Me and Junior gonna go to sleep. Hey, that's funny. Me and Junior!

8

R ose had been lying on her side, facing the bureau, but rolled over and tugged at Ben's shoulder. "Benny, you awake?"

Ben shot up, startled, from a deep sleep. "What? What's going on? Are you okay?"

"It's fine, Benny." She rubbed his shoulder in the same spot she had just tweaked as he settled down to the pillow. "I couldn't sleep. I've been lying here for hours going over and over this Esther situation."

"Rose, my dear," as he looked at the alarm clock, "you couldn't have been up for hours. We've only been in bed for half an hour."

"Well, it felt like longer," justifying her action. She hesitated a few seconds, but then returned to her need for him to be awake with her. "What are we going to do, Ben? We can't force her. They won't let us do that, even if we are her parents, will they?"

"No, Rosie. If Esther insists on carrying this baby, that's her right, even at her age."

"But what then? What are we supposed to do then? She just goes to the hospital and has this baby, and she brings it home, lah dee dah, and we're supposed to raise it?"

"No, if Esther decides on having this baby, she'll have to be the mother and do the caring for it. And like I've always noticed, mothers seem to rise up to the task, they just step up and into the job. Motherhood, it makes girls think of someone other than themselves. At least, that's what I've always seen, that's been my experience."

"Sure Ben, sure. She'll step up to the task. Like she promised she would take care of that stupid guinea pig? She promised and I had to do all the caring."

"Rose, she was nine years old. Don't get me wrong. I don't want her to have this baby any more than you do, but if she follows through with the pregnancy, she will have to be responsible for its upbringing. Like I say, she will have to step up."

"What, she's going to move out and get an apartment? With what? Our daughter is going to have to go on welfare?"

"No, Rosie, our daughter, our Esther, she's not going on welfare. If she has the baby, and I'll grant you that's a big if, if she has the baby, they'll both live here. We both know we're not going to abandon our Esther; we're not going to force her to live God knows where."

"Easy for you to say, Ben. You'd just get up and go to work, exactly like you do now. I'd be the one who has to take care of it. I'd be the one who suffers all the consequences."

"What are you talking about, Rose. You love babies. I've never seen you happier than when we brought her home, the first few years with our Esther. Am I wrong, Rose? Am I wrong?"

Ben was far from wrong. Rose Shapiro loved little babies. She would pinch their cheeks, and tweak their thighs, and giggle with anyone's neonate, like there was no tomorrow. When it came to infants, Rose lost herself in the cradle of love. Babies never challenged you, they just responded with glee to your presence. Babies loved you back, and you became their whole world. You were always wanted, and always beautiful, and always special, as long as you showed them how special they were. Loving babies was a human contract that Rose could understand and abide. It was only when they became older, like everyone else, that Rose had to fight for her personal space and place.

"You think I'm good with babies, Ben?"

"Do I think that there's ice cream in Good Humor trucks? Do I think that the stars are in the sky? Rose, you're the best with babies that I've ever known in my whole life. And that includes my own mother, Rosie, may she rest in peace. With babies, Rose, you're the best."

Rose thought this over for a little time, before responding to his accolades. "So, you think I'd be a good grandmother, Ben?"

"Rose, there couldn't be anyone better. And it's not like we didn't always want to have grandchildren. It's just earlier than we thought it would be. Just a little bit earlier than we thought."

An image of herself holding a grandchild gradually pervaded Rose's consciousness. She felt it's softness in her arms, it's warmth in her chest and its smile disabled any resistance to its presence. The fragrance of its newness wafted through her head, bringing back the past. She remembered the absolute feelings of pride and completion when she let her own mother hold Esther for the first time, fresh out of the hospital. Just for a moment Mom, just for a moment. I can't bear letting go of her for any longer.

Almost instantly, for Rose, the nightmare was transformed into a reverie. She could sleep soundly with a nascent image rolling through her consciousness.

For Ben, he was now wide awake. This wasn't going to be easy. He knew his daughter. He knew his Esther. She wasn't going to change her mind. Yes, she had become more sensible since coming back from Israel, but you could tell she had also lost her impulsivity. Now, when she spoke an opinion, there was conviction in her voice and in her heart. And this was a good thing, conviction. She didn't flip-flop about everything right off the top of her head, reacting instead of responding. He liked this about the "new" Esther that had returned home. But he wasn't so sure he liked the idea of her having a baby. For him, if it was just for him, one more face to love and one more mouth to feed, that was a mitzva. If God was going to give you another baby to love with the time to watch it grow and become a person all on its own, well that was just delicious. But for Esther, his Esther, what would this mean? Would she even finish high school, much less college? Who was going to want to marry someone, even someone as pretty and smart as his Esther, if it was some package deal with someone else's baby? The required generational mission that Ben had been assigned from his parents, and their parents, that each generation should increase their wherewithal and use those resources to serve the world better, would his Esther be able to accomplish this if she had a child? Maybe the child would have to accomplish this for her, or maybe for him, or maybe for his parents. Always in the desert, always moving to the promised land. So how many lifetimes does it take to meet your promise? How many generations? Ben didn't like to admit that he was getting tired of what sometimes felt like a long and difficult trek. Maybe he'd feel better in the morning. Eventually he went to sleep, a little bit.

9

With all the participants having left for the day, Sarah Williams and George Bleyer met to discuss Sarah's client roster, the ones who attended the IOP. A weekly meeting, it served to keep the Court informed on progress or recidivism, all too often identifying the latter. For many of these teenagers, who hadn't fully developed a "drug of choice," who were new to the game, drug abuse was a faddish happening. And fads are always a core piece of adolescent motivations, even if the new craze has significant danger attached to it. At times the danger only adds to the attraction. From tuinals to reds, from cough syrups to cocaine, the kids might abandon one high while simultaneously testing another, with no particular pattern to be observed, just chasing whatever the next high they met along the road. For both George and Sarah, it was a frustrating and disheartening job to see these kids fall back into addiction with all its concomitant dangers. There had been a couple of OD's in the program this year. They feared that the success rate of the combined programs was not going to be sufficient for the program to be renewed. Wasn't it amazing how politicians demanded statistics demonstrating success for mental health facilities, while at the same time allowing their own august bodies to go years without passing significant legislation?

The Reluctant Guru Of Alphabet City

Esther Shapiro was one of the few bright spots in this dreary perspective. She had attended every day of her six months in the IOP without exception, other than excused medical absences. Each and every submitted urine had come back with negative results. She participated in group as well as could be expected, given the dissimilarity of her situation with her peers. Her father had even volunteered to procure new clothing donations, not only for clients, but for any member of their families. The suits he brought from his store were a godsend in helping both kids and fathers finding jobs. But it was the family dynamic which most intrigued Sarah about the Shapiro's. She found herself needing to prattle on about it, to be certain that it was indeed true.

"I'll tell you George, when I first met that bunch, I wouldn't have given even the remotest odds of that girl making it. I don't think that in the twenty something years I've been doing this that I've seen a more enabled kid. Those parents of hers fawned over her like she was the second coming, and she just acted like it was all supposed to be bestowed on her, no matter how shabbily she behaved. I mean, it was an absolutely classical codependent family system. There was no way that either of those parents could maintain an identity of their own independent from their daughter, and they were killing her with their saccharine and misplaced love. Trust me George, that kid didn't stand a chance and was just using her smarts to set herself up for one disaster after another. Esther was, pure and simple, just a spoiled and angry brat, and she sure enough hadn't begun to make any moves to individuate.

"And then, throw in that lunatic plan to send her to Israel. Who on Earth rewards a kid with an outlandishly expensive trip after she gets herself arrested for buying heroin? It's almost paradoxically funny that the worst of choices and saddest of outcomes became that girl's redemption. It's as if the horror of being alone and helpless and hideously raped seems to have turned her around, in some positive manner. And then, can you believe, she gets pregnant of top of it all. My God! So, tell me, how can it be that she emerges from that malevolent and harmful cocoon as an adult, individuated, and relatively strong? And to throw impossible on top of improbable, her turnabout forces the family system to adapt. Enabling is no longer a viable dynamic. It's like she is the adult who is leading her folks out of the wilderness. I tell you George, I didn't give them half a chance, and now they're all just moseying through a tough situation with thoughtfulness and grace. So, help me, it's a miracle, if ever I've seen one."

"Seems to me that it's just part of the reason we chose to work in this god-forsaken field," George responded. "You can never tell when a piss poor prognosis turns out okay. You tell me, Sarah. Do you think we and this program we run was ultimately responsible for her getting it together?" he wryly responded to her amazement. "Sometimes I wonder if it's just plain circumstance that makes these kids go one way or the other."

"I understand why you might drift in that direction. I get that you could see it that way. But the bottom line is that even in those situations where our therapeutic modalities aren't the primary source of the improvement, we still provide the arena where the different behaviors take root and become reinforced. Heck, just learning the vocabulary of recovery is important. Finding peers and creating systems to support a healthy lifestyle is essential, especially with these kids. As much as I scratch my head and wonder where Esther got it from, I still think this program of ours was helpful in her learning how to express it, especially to herself."

George returned to the decision at hand. "So, what do you want to do with her? She's been here for seven months now. Do we maintain her in the program until the baby is born, or should we discharge her and refer to aftercare now? It seems kind of arbitrary to maintain her in the program until she goes term." He proceeded to add with a smile, "Although I've got to say, having her in the group is great birth control for the other kids."

"I think we should let her go. If nothing else, taking the bus every day to get here has to be difficult for her. Her pregnancy is getting to the point where mobility is becoming problematic. I'll start the paperwork, and why don't you let her know in group tomorrow."

Sarah felt some solid satisfaction on her own bus ride home. "It's good when these old bones of mine get to feel like we're doing something good, every once in a while," she mused. "Just wish it happened more often. It gets old struggling uphill most of the time."

Part Three

1

Throughout her pregnancy, most of Esther's thoughts had been focused on self-examination. While most of the kids in the IOP's group therapy were centered on maintaining and enhancing their image, Esther seemed intent on breaking hers down. She was admired by her peers for her ability to stand up for herself and her thoughts without any defensive bluster, despite knowing what she made obvious, that she was just barely tolerating them. They didn't know that she just barely tolerated herself.

Group and her journal were the two means for her to accomplish her goals of insight and growth. In following a path of strenuous introspection, Esther, early on, had assessed herself as seriously flawed. The group may have seen her as well put together, and the counselors may have assessed her as working on a strong recovery, but Esther judged herself as impaired. It felt to her that she had no core. She had spent her seventeen years in service only to an empty self, which now felt filled only by the presence of the child that was growing inside. The critical voice that constantly played the role of self-inquisitor pointed out that while she admired people like Edel and George and even Daddy, people who seemed to have purpose, she felt herself to be vacuous. No wonder she had been willing to put poisonous chemicals and indifferent dicks inside her body. Anything to try to fill the experienced void.

But recognizing the condition didn't bring satisfaction. Aware of deficiency, she was left to accept that only by dedicating herself to life could she ever hope to find a meaningful path. Somewhere along the way, if she was vigilant, she could hope to find a direction that she experienced as congruent with a self she owned. And for now, that meant binding herself to a goal of raising a daughter who would contrast with her. Her child would be full. She would have purpose. She would know mission. For now, her daughter's mission was Esther's mission. There was no doubt in her mind that she would give birth to a girl. While acknowledging that her certainty as to her child's gender was irrational, Esther clung to this belief. She couldn't let go of the idea that her pregnancy had purpose, and that this purpose was in some poorly defined way a response to her being raped, a response which demanded a female child to heal the wound. She would have a girl!

And she was correct! Aziza Miriam Shapiro was born on the Monday before Thanksgiving. Esther was attracted to the name Aziza because it was used in both Jewish and Arab cultures, connoting the traits of beloved and powerful. She wanted her child's name to reflect both of its cultural roots. Her daughter was like Edel, no matter if he was the father or not, descending from the tribes of both Abrahamic traditions. Her middle name, Miriam, was in memory of her maternal grandmother, Rose's Mom. Altogether, to Esther, her daughter's name represented a full spectrum of the facets of her ancestry, while signifying the self-resiliency she wished to instill in her offspring. As a mother, Esther wanted her girl to be admired and loved, while also being seen as someone not to be messed with. Having observable power. Aziza should represent a step beyond her own journey, brief as that passage had been, to date. Esther had travelled from insecure control to acceptance. Her daughter would not just accurately acknowledge and accept the way the world was, but would grasp life with a steadfast sense of mission, and possess the confidence to see it through. No small ambition for a seventeen-year-old single mother.

From her very first breath, Aziza was extraordinarily beautiful. She possessed a full head of jet-black hair, with large blue-green Berber eyes that even in their initial moments drew you into the depths of her soul. She seemed an old soul, with lifetimes of wisdom inherent in her nascent gaze. There was a knowing that appeared to emanate from her, even in these earliest of moments, a sense that this person had lived many lives and knew of the mysteries the world. She was well formed, of mind and body, from her inception. She did not cry when entering this world. Rather, when presented to Aziza, she just looked around, as if appraising the companions with whom she would travel on this new journey. Content with what she saw, Aziza snuggled into her mother's arms, and slept.

Even then, there was a grace to her. On the afternoon of her birth, while still in the hospital, Esther held out her newborn to Rose, who ecstatically met her granddaughter with eager hands. "She is perfect, Esther. She makes my heart sing," she shared, before turning all of her attention to the baby. She walked around the room a while, and softly sang a Yiddish lullaby she hadn't thought about for forty-odd years. There were no complaints. No complaints about the child, or her daughter, or her husband, or even the hospital and its staff. Rose felt wholly content, perhaps for the first time since she had held Esther in the exact same manner.

Esther and Rose had grown closer as they awaited the baby's arrival. Esther dropped her irritation and embarrassment toward her mother, while Rose ceased being angry at this traitorous girl who had stolen her husband's attention. A fresh bond was established by the pregnancy. Ben was no longer the object to be fought for, as he became the security that supported them both. It became common for him to come home and find them in the spare room that was being converted to a nursery, chattering about the soon-to-be addition, sharing "woman-talk." It brought relief and tears to his eyes. He no longer felt like a referee in his home.

For his part, Ben was overwhelmed with pride. He sat in the straight-backed hospital side chair, leaving the more comfortable one for Rose, and watched his family with delight. He was still getting accustomed to his "girls" getting along, and could sit back and observe them all day long. The baby's birth, and his wife and daughter enjoying each other, validated all his efforts. Working hard was easy if you had something that was worth working for. He had secretly wished for a boy, but knowing his daughter's wishes, had kept this to himself, and was glad that her hopes had been realized. But most of all, Ben was thunderstruck by the appearance of his new granddaughter. All of the newborns in his family had looked like "Gerber" babies, bald and chubby and cute. This new member of his brood was different and dazzling! The contrast between her pale skin and ebony hair created almost an exotic quality to her. She wasn't cute or sweet or adorable, all those baby words. She was stunning. Sure. Rose and Esther, and his mother before them, had all been attractive. Aziza was stunning!

Ben also was pleased with the name, Aziza. It fit the child. There was something distinctive and alluring about it. Usually, Ben preferred simple Old Testament names. But his granddaughter commanded something that stood out from others, that signified what he imagined to be her compelling destiny. It was as if all his hopes and dreams for Esther had been magnified by a factor of ten in the child she now brought to the family. Life was good. Life was moving in the right direction. Life confirmed itself. Yes, maybe life sometimes had some dips, everything can't keep going up all the time, but at the end of the day, life was good.

Lost in his philosophizing, Ben looked up and was startled to see that Rabbi Goldsheid had entered the room.

"Ben, Rose, how good to see you. I had a bris just down the hall, and was happy to see that you were all here," he addressed the room, neglecting to recognize the mother or child.

"Why, Rabbi, it's so good to see you," Rose greeted him. "How nice of you to step in."

He must be coming to see the fruits of his advice, Ben thought to himself, keeping his ironic smile inside. "Yes, Rebi, it's good to see you."

"Isn't it a mitzvah to see our families grow," Goldsheid volunteered.

Ben noted to himself that Rabbis always asked questions so as to make statements, and made statements to gain information. He was testing the waters to see how the Shapiro's, Ben and Rose, felt about the new addition. "Yes, we are certainly blessed, don't you think?" Counter the non-inquiry inquiry with a statement question. That's the Talmudic way.

Taking Ben's smile as a sign that his congregants welcomed their new grandchild, after all, these were tricky situations, Goldsheid proceeded. "Then, I guess you will be looking to have a naming, a *simchat bat*?"

Always looking for business, Ben thought. Always looking for business. "Are you asking us, Rabbi? You think maybe the mother of our blessing has some say in all this?" Make him deal with Esther, even if her "situation" makes him uncomfortable. Which situation? Being unwed, or having no money?

"Well, hmm, I thought, well, I guess maybe you are right." He turned to the bed and baby for the first time. "Esther, my dear. Congratulations. You look well, my dear."

"Do you really think so? I must look better then I feel," she responded. "You know, Rabbi, this birthing deal, it takes a lot out of you."

"I'm sure, Esther. I'm sure."

"So, you want to know if we will be having a naming, Rabbi?"

"Well, yes, Esther. It would seem appropriate, and a way to welcome this new bundle of joy into our community."

"I understand and agree, Rabbi Goldsheid. But, I wonder, do you know an Imam who could preside with you at the ceremony? I'm not sure who the biological father is, you know. It could be my boyfriend, or it could be one of the rapists, but either way, the baby is at least one quarter Palestinian. And being that we don't know if my beautiful daughter was conceived from love, or hate, or lust, or control, it just feels like it would be better if we covered all bases. Don't you think?"

Poor Rabbi Goldsheid, was all Ben could think. Serves the schlemiel right.

2

My (Our) Beginnings

I know that when my mother brought me home from the hospital, she thought it to be a new beginning for her, a time for her to become more attuned with life, to initiate a sensibility that was absent from her life before her pregnancy with me. She has told me as much. For my grandfather, Ben, it was also a new beginning. He had a fresh dream to toil for, another personal mission to help cause to pass. Grandfather was never one to think of himself as the person who could deliver goodness to this world. Rather, he envisaged himself as the enabler of the goodness that would be embodied by those he served. To Grandfather, enabling was a noble effort, with little or no ego attachment. For my grandmother, Rose, it was a new beginning of her return to loving. There were neither conditions nor complications to her love for me. Even for my father, who never knew anything of my existence, it was still a new beginning. Despite his lack of awareness about the consequences of his actions, and despite the evils inherent in his behaviors, he had achieved something good.

Without intention, he had caused the potential for goodness to exist.

For me, it was just the next step of my journey, nothing new, a continuation of a path that had been interrupted by my previous death. This leg of my race was new, of course, but for the energy that is me, death had been but a layover between connected journeys. A new body, a new mind, a new time, yet a weathered soul, well entrenched, poised to continue my purpose for being. The most profound miracle of birth is not the creation of another life, although that is in itself miraculous. But for the intention, the karma, to remain intact with a totally new human being living her life, now that is truly a miracle. The baton gets passed between legs of the race, although there is no contact that we know about between the runners. Pretty remarkable! Beyond cool!

Many people have talked at length about the white light that appeared to envelop them in their near-death experiences. There have been many spiritual speculations about this deathly aura. More recently, scientists have noted that in the process of death there is a release from the pineal gland that generates abundant energy, and explains the burst of energy that incongruently accompanies our expiry. What has received less attention is the pineal "burst" that appears to be present at birth. The immense white energy field that attends death is also a dynamic at birth. It seems clear to me that these are not separate events. What we call the "white light" would appear to be the energy field that taxis us from one life to another. An unrequested Uber, if you will.

When we think of our lives as having a beginning, middle and end, we tend to use this as a model for most everything that we experience. Our tasks, our relationships, our ambitions, and on, are all seen to fall within this linear paradigm. We come into being. We do our thing. We cease to be. Our life is the middle, cradled in between our beginning and end. It all seems senseless, unless we create some existential meaning that justifies the embodiment of vital energy into a temporal form. Each of us may only be a flicker, but in that spark, we hope for purpose, and trust that by merging with the energy of others who share our missions, we can be useful, that there is meaning to our "middling" life.

We extend our need for the paradigm of Beginning-Middle-End to our relationship with everything else. Scientists join philosophers in searching for the beginning of the universe. We wonder if this All and Everything will end. We glory in the birth of new relationships and despair at their ends. In everything we do and accomplish, we seek to justify our beginning, before we meet our end. It becomes sinful if our middle does not validate our coming-to-be. Life becomes work, trying so hard to defend our existence. We judge ourselves and are critical of others in our pursuit of meaning, and experience alienation and guilt as we suffer from varying degrees of inadequacy. The Beginning-Middle-End paradigm sucks the soul out of us, and replaces it with a need for self-justification.

All because we are convinced that our birth was our beginning! Most of us had our introduction to philosophy take place when as a child we were confronted with the query. "Which came first, the chicken or the egg?" It was important to decipher which was the beginning and which was the middle, even as it was scrambling our brains. While Plato had long advised us that "chicken-ness" supersedes the components of its cycle, we adamantly required that there be a beginning. At least chickens, as far as I know, don't strive to justify their existence. They just cross the road.

So, the cycle of energy that I presently experience as Aziza, began this leg of my journey in a hospital in Queens. While that's as far back as I can go in sharing my story, let's not think of it as my beginning. And the you that is reading about my life, didn't start in the hospital you were born. If we let go of the Beginning-Middle-End paradigm, we can appreciate that we've been twirling in the currents of universal energy for infinite durations, forward and back. Yet, the paradox is that this particular leg is finite and does have a beginning, middle and end. Our life is infinite and finite, all at the same time. If I ponder this for a while, I am led to the conclusion that it makes sense to be ego driven and ego-less in equal measure. The trick is to know when to be which.

As your guru, I probably shouldn't be sharing this. Most folks expect their gurus to be ego-less all the time. They are supposed to have had a beginning as an unremarkable blip of energy with unused potential, experienced a transformative moment in which they were "born again," and catapulted into a sainted consciousness in which they selflessly helped others to replicate their experience. Double beginnings allowed them, and hopefully their followers, to have an everlasting middle without end. I'm sorry, but this fairy tale isn't true, for me, and I assume for other gurus. My consciousness cycles from being ego-less to ego-driven continuously, hopefully in tune with the moment of time and place. When I eat my dinner, my ego seeks to be pleased by the taste, and wants to be present for the experience. When we meditate together, I am hopefully not-there in my presence. When I write this message to you, there is hopefully a blend of the two.

I, like you, need to have an ego that has the ability to intentionally disappear for the moments that are sacred, and to do its present duty in the moments that are secular. And I need to keep in mind all the time, that the cycle is the flow in which all of the components of my consciousness exist. In that flow, beginnings are endings, endings are beginnings and all of everything is middles of the whole. If I am to serve you, there must be a self to share, but it needs to be a self that can disappear within the joining. This is like any other love. We join to be one, but must exist as "just-me" to do the joining. And in that love, each new day can be part of an ongoing wave of joining and parting and joining anew.

My love, my desire to join with other energies, existed in all the cycles before my birth. My love for you existed before we met, before either of us were born. The love that is we, exists when we are joined and when we are apart. Beginnings, middles and ends are sometimes real, sometimes an illusion, but ultimately irrelevant.

3

Esther flourished as a mother. As she nursed Aziza, there was simultaneously an awareness of giving nourishment to her daughter, and a meditative centering on self. For the first time in her life, she experienced balance. The more she gave of herself, the more she had of herself. Her time for introspection moved from journaling to these intimate moments with her daughter. Her need to question her bearings and motivations lessened, and she became more focused on accomplishing her personal goals, even while tending to a newborn. And given the support system which Ben and Rose provided, Esther's external evolution soon matched the internal growth which had been evident ever since her return from Israel.

Passing the High School Equivalency test while still pregnant, Esther began to attend Queens College, just a few weeks after birthing Aziza. She took to this with a zeal and dedication which had never been present before. Not surprisingly, she opted to prepare for a career in social work. Her academic achievement began to reflect the potential which she had always possessed, but had never attained.

Esther's days were long. She was up and tending to the baby a little before six, the same time that Ben rose and started to get ready for his Manhattan trek. Daddy and his two girls immensely enjoyed this early time in the kitchen, he lingering over his coffee, while she nursed Aziza. These were the best moments of Ben's daily routine, the time that made all the other efforts worthwhile. Esther knew this, and never failed to greet the day with her father. It was as close as she could get to repaying him for the unrelenting support he gave to her and his granddaughter. They talked about the courses Esther was taking, Ben absorbing the material eagerly. In his youth, he had not been able to go to college, needing to contribute to the family finances as soon as he was finished with high school. He found a job in the garment district, and had been there ever since, except for his time in the service. Now, he felt as if he was secreting himself on her academic shoulder, in college together, a personalized auditing program for him. How lucky could a man get, to be having breakfast with his daughter and granddaughter, watching their growth on a daily basis, and harvesting the classroom lessons he had missed along the way. How lucky could a man get?

When Daddy left, Esther would take a few hours to study before Rose awoke. Studying consisted of reading her text books aloud to Aziza, who lay in her portable rocker, cooing and smiling to Introduction to Western Civilization, sleeping through English 101, seeming to barely tolerate Introduction to Statistics. Esther seemed sure that Aziza appreciated Sociology the most of all the coursework. Imagine. Only three months old, and a fan of Durkheim. Esther herself was solidly into "Soc." She felt comfortable with the assumption of a social rather than individual perspective. It was congruent with her growing conviction that she needed to open herself up the multiple communities of which she was a part, and Sociology seemed like a roadmap to accomplish this.

Somewhere between eight and nine, Rose would wander in and announce that it was her time for the baby. Clear out and leave a little girl and her grandmother alone! Esther quickly showered and ran out to catch the bus to the college. She only had a three-and-a-half-hour window to be back for Aziza's next feeding, just enough time for a couple of classes and maybe a quick stop in the library. It was a tight schedule, but easy for Esther to maintain, because it felt purposeful.

There were times when difficulties arose, as would life present special circumstances, the events that demanded priority over the delicate balance of the daily agenda. Like when Aziza came down with enteritis and Esther refused to leave her side until her digestive system righted itself, or just before Aziza's first birthday, when there was a minor kitchen fire. Not a lot of damage, but enough that the Shapiro family needed to live with Ben's sister for a week, while repairs were completed. Rose would tend to catastrophize in these moments, but Esther would remain calm and adapt, secure in her certainty that Aziza's future was already written, if not revealed.

Aziza's infancy was flying by, as it often does for parents. There didn't seem enough time to document all the developmental changes as they occurred, or to photograph and capture all of what seemed exceptional moments along the way. Rose would sometimes complain that there weren't enough pictures, and Ben would respond that every moment in the company of his granddaughter was permanently embedded in his mind. "It's like when we saw the Grand Canyon, Rose. Even now I can close my eyes and still see it. Somethings you never forget. Or when I first set my sights on you. You know, it's still a beautiful and permanent picture in my mind. You never forget the truly beautiful things, I tell you." And Aziza was, of course, the most beautiful thing that he had ever seen.

Ben wished that he could freeze time in this first year of his granddaughter's life, in the same manner that he could freeze images in his mental frame. He couldn't stop from thinking how these blessed moments had grown out of the worst of times. Was it always like this? Was there some natural flip-flop of good and bad, joy and pain, horror and glee? Did bad necessarily evolve into good? Ben hoped that Esther would take a philosophy class next semester. Maybe then he could answer these troubling thoughts. Maybe then.

Mother and both grandparents talked to Aziza constantly. Rose was versed in baby-talk, rhymes and song. Love was expressed with long vowels and rounded melodies, interspersed with giggles and tickles. Ben repetitively advised his granddaughter of her beauty, wisdom and nascent abilities. "Aziza, the sparkle in your eyes diminishes the sun. You will shine and bring warmth and goodness to this world. Warmth and goodness to this world, I tell you." And Aziza delighted in his accolades. She could feel the warmth and goodness of his love, the tone of his words enveloping her as an incantation of her present and future adoration.

Esther, on the other hand, carried on conversations with her daughter as if she were fully adult. From simple small talk about the events of the day, to sharing the frustrations and joys of living, to questioning the moral and ethical implications of potential choices that loomed large in the future, the dialogue was sustained. Esther experienced Aziza as having a natural inborn wisdom, an old soul who could understand, even if she couldn't yet communicate. Her daughter was a reflection of her own drive for knowledge and knowing, an emerging alter-ego, with whom she could find the comfort, colloquy and insight she hadn't known she had. Ben would hear them chattering away in the next room, Esther with words, Aziza with babble, and would strain to catch it all. "You know," he would tell Rose, "Esther has learned the language that Aziza speaks. She understands, I tell you. When I hear them talking to each other, it reminds me of sitting by the stream and listening to the water flow over the stones. It's calming, and I always seem to learn what I need to know when I do this. I always learn what I need to know." Rose would pat his neck and assure him that this was true. "These days," she would say, "listening to the people we love is the most valuable gift in this life we lead." Whether there was some proper meaning to their communication was unimportant. "Listening is like tasting. You don't agree or argue with the words. You just enjoy."

On all fronts, throughout her infancy, Aziza was held and comforted with not only love, but respect. All aspects of her seemed to command it. The grace and beauty of her form, the brilliance in her knowing eyes, the equanimity that she emanated, all combined to suggest a considerable presence. Many years later, Esther identified this respect as the most valuable gift she had given her daughter in the early years. "It is easy to love our children. And this love, of course is essential to their becoming people that in turn can love. But too often, we fail to respect our children, throughout all of their childhood, thinking that juveniles have less value than adults. But just as children who are not loved will think of themselves as unlovable, children who are not respected will think of themselves as unrespectable. Without self-respect, the child's potential will rarely manifest itself in adulthood."

4

On Respect

I am often asked how it is possible to experience gratitude for every twist and turn of our path, for every person with whom we have interacted, with every action we have witnessed. How can that gratitude be sustained when there is at least as much evil as good, as least as much pain as joy, at least as much failure as success, as much loss as there is gain? We seek to live in a good world, a just world, a world which reflects our belief in the golden rule. We form a primitive belief that if we do unto others as we would have them do unto us, that the world will respond by doing unto us justly and fairly. And when the world doesn't meet our expectations, when life isn't fair, we feel some implicit contract has been broken. We did right, and still we were treated wrong.

Some of us become angry at life itself and decry an existence which doesn't seem to follow a moral code. They either lash out or lash in, acting out their rage against the nature of it all, or hurting themselves for continuing to choose to be part of an inequitable world. They want to bang their bodies against the firmament and shout out like a tantruming child that "It's not fair! It's not fair!" The Universe, in many of these instances, becomes seen as a parent, who disregards the obligation to raise its child well.

We want life to be transactional. If we live right, life should do right by us. In much the same way that many of us anthropomorphize our conception of a divine power, we want the cosmos to be a good fellow and play nice. And when it doesn't work out that way, we'd like to punish the offender for not following our rules, fair rules. If we could, we'd tell this universe to go to hell, and go find another creation to live in.

In short, we lack respect. All relationships require a grounding in respect. And this starts with respect for the conditions of existence. We don't have to like the ways and means of the world, but we would do well to respect that which literally supports us, generated us, and gave us the ability to appreciate and evaluate our own existence. Rather than being transactional, our relationship with the universe requires acceptance.

Respect literally means to look again. It is a process. We perceive something to be. We react to its presence, given our history and inclinations. But then we look again, and give that something its due. When we do this, we value it for what it is, not what we want it to be. We see it as part of something else, rather than a stand-alone item. The value for everything is to be found in its own requisites for life, not ours. In this second glance we strive to perceive Everything's inherent value, whether or not we appreciate it ourselves. In this second appraisal, we become unicentric rather that egocentric.

When I engage in the process of being respectful, gratitude follows, in all aspects of my life. But this is more than an attitude that I simply adopt, a scarf to be put over my head. It requires an everyday discipline. I am a human being, and as such, I have negative responses to all kinds of stuff, all the time. I don't like the mosquito bite or the animal that fashioned it. I experience that the person who rudely bumped into me in aisle four of the supermarket is an inconsiderate and self-absorbed jerk. I hate it when politicians appear to care nothing about those that they should represent, and only care to perpetuate their cushy positions and power.

However, on second glance, the mosquito occupies a needed position in the biological ecosystem, an ecosystem which ultimately supports me. I can respect this, give it value and appreciate that I am part of the cycles of life. When I place myself into the mind of the person who jarred me at the store, I can imagine myriad scenarios in which his harried and single purposed actions were warranted and necessary. I know that there are times in life to be self-centered, paradoxically often in the cause of being other-centered. Even the politician who appears without ethics, can be respected as representing the dark side of our culture so well. I am aware that as a society we would not strive to improve our system of governance, if we weren't aware that there need to be government institutions to stave off and protect us from malevolence. Governance is a dialectal process and requires a dark side to its politics, for eventual social progress to occur.

When we talk about the "work" necessary to further and maintain our relationships, we are really talking about maintaining the discipline of respect. Our natural tendencies to be egocentric in our dealings with the other will lead to conflict. Only by engaging in the process of respect will we come out the other side with conflict resolution and rededication to care, consideration and/or love. It is our appreciation of the other's point of view which allows us to get beyond our own limited vision. Only with our second glance, our respect, do we get there.

Part of this discipline is learning to respect not only what is present, but what is not present. I am often asked by others in our community how to deepen their meditation. My response is to learn to respect the silence. We have all been taught to pay attention to what is there. Often, what is absent is more valuable. Purity requires that we get down to the essence of anything. By respecting what is not there, we rid ourselves of the fluff, the impurity which can obscure that which we seek to know or experience.

If life is a constant process of learning who we are, what we represent, and becoming knowledgeable about our relationship with the All and Everything, then we had better respect ourselves, all aspects of the universe and the winding path that guides through it all.

5

Usually, Esther was on and off the Queens College campus at a quick pace, running to get to her classes, only to turn around and race for the bus to get back to Aziza. Sometimes a hurried visit to the library was needed, in and out of the stacks, check out the book, and dart to the bus stop. When classmates inquired if she wanted to join a study group, or have a cup of coffee after class, she would let them know that she'd love to, but had to get home to her daughter. It was true. The campus social interaction was all around her, but for all intents and purposes, Esther's social life was nil. She had nothing in common with her old high school friends, nor did they identify with her and her life path. Betania had relapsed, and at least for now, Esther had made the decision to stay at a distance. The single time Betania had come by the house to visit with the baby, had left Esther with a deep sadness. Watching her friend wobbling in the hallway, long sleeved on a warm Spring day, and denying that she was using, brought on a melancholic mood, which it took days for Esther to purge. She told herself that their friendship could someday return, but for now it would have to be kept at a distance.

Today was to be different. Aziza needed a well visit to the pediatrician, and Rose had volunteered, well, maybe demanded, to take her. "For the first time in two years," Esther reflected, "I can take my time, stroll around the campus, and maybe even have some lunch in the cafeteria. Yahwee kazowee, I've hit the jackpot today!" She laughed at herself, appreciating how what once would have been so ordinary, felt like such a big deal. As much as she valued her coursework and the knowledge that came from her studies, she had to admit that she was somewhat jealous of all of her peers who took their college-life for granted. Wandering around the student center felt like being abroad, in some foreign city, watching people from a different culture engaging in their everyday undertakings, but at a distance and feeling like a stranger in a strange land.

The choice between the cinnamon roll and the pecan pie had been difficult. While either would have been a special treat, a celebration of the day's liberty, ultimately the cinnamon roll won out. Beyond being gooey, you could peel it out slowly, and savor both the roll and the moment for an extended while. She found an empty table by a window overlooking a view of the busy quad, and busied herself in her indulgence.

"Hey, Esther, is it okay if I join you?"

It was Lian, the girl who had sat next to her in Sociology of Religion. They had chatted in the way that students do when enjoying a class together, but had never seen each other outside the classroom, what with Esther always having to run off. She liked Lian, and was pleased to see her.

"Of course, Lian. Grab a seat. It's great to see you."

"I feel privileged. The mystery girl who slyly sneaks on and off campus is sitting here making love to a cinnamon roll, and I get to spend some time and be in some culinary menage with her."

"Mystery girl?"

"You have no idea, do you, how you're the topic of conversation in the social science groupie crowd? Who is that masked girl, and does she really have silver bullets? And how does she always get the A's?" Lian excitedly dropped into her seat, and began to throw down her BLT and milkshake with a ferocity. Esther had often been amused at the energy which this tiny Asian body exuded. Just sitting next to her in class, one absorbed an animating energy surge. She had regretted that class was their only contact.

"No, I guess I never thought of myself giving off any particular impression. And is it really that noticeable how much I'm enjoying this glutinous delight?"

"Well, actually, yes. From across the way, you seemed the very image of the stereotyped oversexed woman who had finally been able to land the man she was hunting for months. Enthralled and enthralling. But enough about pastry and sex! Let's be clear. I've wanted to get to know you for two whole semesters, so let's hear it. Who the heck is Esther, anyway?"

If Esther had thought Lian emitted a lot of energy in class, the intensity was ramped up a ton-and-a-half out of the classroom. Sharing became irresistible. "And what would you like to know, oh, inscrutable one?"

"Just everything. Who you are, and where you're from, and what you do, and where you hang. Just that stuff," she said and pushed her empty paper plate to the side, leaning in to hear the scoop.

"Well, if I'm going to be honest, who I am is finding out about who the hell I am. I mean, I can tell you that I still live with my folks in Hollis, and that I have the most amazing, beautiful and brilliant two plus year-old daughter the world has ever seen, but the rest of me seems to be a whole lot of discard that I've let go of a while back. Like I've got a world view these days, but not so much an inside view." She paused a second. "Wow, I guess I just went on a bit, although you did ask."

"I get it. You're one of those self-analyzing types, always picking around inside wondering what you'll find in that overstuffed attic you call your mind. Not me, I try my best to be a shallow empty-headed blondie. Now, that ain't so easy for a Chinese chick. I mean, not only is the hair color wrong, but we're supposed to be really heavy on the introspection. Hey, even you just called me 'inscrutable'. Seems to me I'd rather be scrutable. Or at least, screwable."

"You're so full of it. Remember, I've seen you in class. Don't pull that dumb-ass blond on me."

"Ah, so. I guess you'll have to decipher which one is the act and which one is the genuine deal. Will the real Lian please stand up?

"Isn't it enough that I have to figure me out? I've got to extend the process to you?"

Simultaneously, they both broke out in a grin, whereupon seeing the others' smile, it moved to laughter. It was perfectly apparent that these two shared a sense of humor that wasn't often or easily mirrored. "Hey, I like you. Want to come over my place tomorrow, and meet my reality in person?" Esther offered. "You just reminded me. I need a friend."

6

Lian Li and her two years older brother, Shen, lived in a basement apartment on Colden Street in Flushing. It was a sturdy six floor pre-war building, with a spacious decorated lobby, unseen and ignored, but appreciated by the tenants on their way to the elevator or mailboxes. The basement apartment had been originally intended for a long ago building super, but as his family had grown, he required a larger space, and since then, he, and a line of successors, had been ensconced in one of the rare three-bedroom units on the third floor. The entrance to the Lee's one-bedroom railroad flat was just off the sidewalk, in the path to the rear courtyard. Lian had placed a dozen or so planters near the door to their apartment, filling the portal with an array of brilliant flowers. No matter how dark she met the day, the vibrant colors were an immediate reminder, as she stepped out into the morning, that a mirthful persona was a prerequisite for breathing the outside air. For Lian, this outward exuberance was a necessity, similar to the way that other women required cosmetics. You don't leave home without it. Years ago, when she first set foot in an American school, she knew the image she had to adapt. The journey that her mother had taken was expected to produce happiness for her children, and she would not betray the sacrifice by appearing fearful, sad or threatened.

Their father, Li Zheng, had been an influential aide to President Liu Shaoqi. A linguist, he had been responsible for the ongoing program to homogenize the peoples' language from many to one, or at least a few. China was to become efficient, reflecting the power of a collective voice. For over a decade, Zheng's efforts were valued, and he was prized as one of the architects of the emerging society. But in the chaos and disorder that became known to the world as the Cultural Revolution, one ordinary day he simply disappeared. He went to work on a routine morning, but he never returned, and there was never a mention of him again. Publicly, it was as if he never existed. Government colleagues, once friends, were themselves either on the outs or in the ins, and completely avoided communication or even contact with the family they previously visited and spoke of as friends.

Zheng's wife, Genji, had no time to be disillusioned or angry at a betrayal by friends or nation. She made contact with an English professor of linguistics who had come to study with Zheng just a year before, and he was able to entreat his government to secrete the family in Hong Kong. From there, the American government interceded, hoping that Gengi might be useful in giving context to their understanding of China's upheaval. They offered citizenship to the Li family. Shen was ten, Lian was eight. Their father had previously given them some rudimentary lessons in English and French, and in preparation for a new American life, the children were immersed by their mother in English. In a span of barely eleven weeks, New York became their new adopted home.

Genji was herself a statistician, and she had little trouble finding a position with the Metropolitan Transportation Authority, tracking the subways and busses, diligently striving to achieve the ever-in-progress goal of making trains run on time. In many ways, life was good for the newly emigrated family, although their personal cultural revolution was grueling. Although she thrived economically, Genji could never fully accept or appreciate the character of her neighbors and co-workers, or the ethos of this new society. She experienced Americans as frivolous and irresponsible. While she wished that her children would integrate well into their new interpersonal surroundings, she hoped that she would be able to inculcate in them the values that she and Zheng had been raised with. Hurrying home from work, she expected that household chores would be accomplished, food would be prepped for dinner, and homework would have been initiated. She ran a tight ship.

Shen took well to her parenting. He was that child who performed to all expectations, whether the directives emanated from teachers, coaches or Mom. The additional two years in China made a significant difference between his and Lian's acceptance of their mother's parenting style. He was a serious boy, intent on meeting his responsibilities. It wasn't that he performed to please the adult world, but rather he experienced that he had roles to fulfill, and felt accountable to himself to do well. He was a good student. Learning was exciting to him, but the excitement was always in second place, trailing the responsibility to be successful in his duties. He was reserved. He showed his love by actions, not words or gestures. Only in athletics, in which he excelled, did Shen have access to an emotional release. In high school he played both football and baseball, and by his senior year was captain of both teams. His admission to Columbia was assured by the combination of grades and athletic accomplishment.

Lian was a whole different matter, at least by appearances. Seemingly driven by an emotional exuberance, she swirled through life with a lively energy. She was the yin to Shen's yang. No matter how stern and reproachful Genji treated her Americanized daughter, the mold was set. There was an unspoken understanding between the mother and daughter that allowed all the teenager's transgressions to be accepted, as much as they were unwelcome. Underneath the external façade was a young woman who fiercely represented the family values. Her superficiality was just that, superficial. Beneath her veneer lay a bedrock of traits taken from both her parents. She was as dedicated to the community at large as her father, and to her family as her mother, in spite of the valley girl disguise.

Ten years after bringing her children out of China, Genji died suddenly from an aneurism. It had been an uneventful early July day. At her desk at work, pouring over a complex spreadsheet, the statistician simply collapsed and became a statistic. She was forty-nine, her children 20 and 18. For a second time, the children experienced a parent taken from them instantly, with no opportunity to even say good-bye. The loss was profound. Shen took it stoically, intent on reckoning the changes to his roles and responsibilities. He clearly needed to be present for Lian, to support her to the completion of her college attendance, however long that might be. He needed to finish his own academic pursuits at Columbia, and move on to a graduate business degree. He carefully analyzed their financial condition, given the modest life insurance Genji had left them and the social security benefits they would receive. They would be able to live in one of the cheaper two-bedroom apartments in Flushing, if they each found a part-time job. Prior to her death, their mother had insisted that they concentrate on their studies, and wouldn't hear of either of them working. It would be tight, but they could spread the insurance out for the seven or eight-year period needed for them to finish what they needed to complete for their foundation.

Lian's response predictably followed a different path. She was consumed with a far-ranging guilt that she had not shown her mother sufficient gratitude for the strength of purpose Genji had utilized in leading them out of a social and cultural wilderness. She fell into a depression, and became largely mute, expressionless and isolated herself in her mother's bedroom. The bubbly teenager vanished, replaced by a despondent woman who rarely communicated more than pain. The decade of loss caught up with her, and she lacked the defenses to ward away the guilt spewing demons that haunted her, while they in turn warded off the incomprehensible terror that lay below. She was indifferent to any of the food that Shen offered, and paid him no attention when he shared with her information about the apartments that he had scouted. She just didn't care, about anything.

Toward the end of the summer, a few weeks before he was scheduled to return to Columbia and Lian to begin Queens College, Shen began to fall apart himself. His frustration with moving their lives forward after their mother's death, was exaggerated by his sister's inability to get beyond her grief. No matter how he entreated, sympathized, identified and empathized, she was incapable of emotionally leaving the bedroom or expressing even a modicum of desire for getting on with life. As much as he needed to be the rock who would carry on their mother's intentions, he was not strong enough to make it happen. He felt weak, missing something, some essential ingredient to his character that could make what was needed manifest. Ineptitude was something unfamiliar and unacceptable to Shen. Whether in his studies, or athletics, or any worthwhile pursuit, he had always been confident he could reach inside and find the abilities necessary to "make it happen." But now, his sister's cooperation was necessary, if they were to pull through this together, and she was stuck in her psychological paralysis, no matter what approach he adopted. He wasn't strong enough. He wasn't persuasive enough. He was missing some necessary ingredient, didn't know what it was, and for the first time in his life he was lost.

On the afternoon upon returning from scouting the Colden Street apartment, Shen went to the bedroom and told his sister about its size and price and location, and how it was exactly what they needed. In two short weeks their lease on the Bayside home was up, requiring them to move somewhere. Moreover, school was starting for both of them concurrent with the requisite move. Damn it! The shit was hitting the fan, something needed to be done, and all she would do was curl up in her tears, nod her head, and bury herself in the blankets. Shen left the bedroom, breathing heavily. He found himself shaking violently, and could no longer forestall his collapse. An undulating wail escaped his chest, and he found himself grabbing hold of anything and everything that was near enough to grab, throwing it all in any direction, hitting out at anything solid, intent on destruction of any structure. The walls to his being had collapsed, and all that was left was a need to wreck and raze anything in arm's reach.

Lian ran out from the bedroom, screaming, "What the hell is going on? Stop this! What on earth are you doing, Shen?"

"I can't fucking do it! I'm not strong enough! Don't you see?"

"See what Shen?"

"Can't you see that I can't be Mom and do it all? I'm not strong enough for the both of us." His rage spent, he allowed the tears to fall. An avalanche of pain gushed forth. "Lian, I need you. I need you."

She contemplated being needed. Being needed had never been part of the equation. That had been her missing piece. As dedicated as she had been to the family, she had never conceived of herself as substantial enough to be needed. Loyal, sure. Cute, of course. Fun, the one who brought her father's weary face to smile. But, significant enough to be needed? If Shen suffered from being insufficient to carry out his mother's ability to do it all on her own, Lian had been shaped by her mother's architecture to be less than sufficient, being the object of her mother's need to satisfy others. In her mourning, she had given Shen the best that she had to offer, her neediness. That he needed a partner had never crossed her mind.

She grabbed hold of him, and could feel some part of her, perhaps the energy that had been wildly dispersed, solidifying in him. Her clasp, her embrace, was itself a powerful and meaningful action. It was needed. She was needed. The reasons for shrouding herself in her impotent tears vanished in their clench. For Shen to be Shen, she would need to be Lian, a sister, a sibling, a partner, a colleague.

An incongruous smile crossed her face, and as she drew away from him, she put her hands on her hips, replicating a stance their mother had often taken. "So, why didn't you say so, you big jerk? So, tell me again about the apartment."

7

B en so enjoyed Esther having Lian come by the house here and there for an evening, which was happening with more regularity. It was even better when she was accompanied by her brother. He and Shen would bring the chess board to the dining room table, while the girls worked together preparing dinner, just a few feet away. His home was full with three generations, alive with a feeling he had almost given up for lost just a couple of years ago. From the corner of his eye, he watched Rose, presiding over the food prep, laughing at Lian's quips and clowning, allowing herself to be part of the girl-play. Rose seemed somehow younger when Lian was around. And Aziza, well she loved her Aunt Lian fervently, this grown-up who ran and played with her as if she were a preschooler herself.

Shen's seriousness was appreciated as much as his sister's spontaneity. He tended to treat Ben as if he were an admired patriarch who ruled over his realm, even as Ben experienced his role to be there for the women who made all the important and unimportant decisions of life. But the respect that was given to him was welcomed, an acknowledgment of Ben's efforts and dedication. Ben wasn't too proud to deny that he needed affirmation. He was aware that Shen held back in their chess games, that this young man was twice the player that Ben could even strive to be. But he felt that his own game was improving, under the tutelage of this youngster who pretended that it was an honor to play with him. Each time that Ben would finally be forced to concede, he would lean over the table and remark, "There you've gone and done it again. You're a wizard, Shen. I don't know how you do it. I tell you, you're a wizard," pretending to himself that there could have been another outcome.

Sometimes they left the chessboard in the closet and talked about Shen's M.B.A. coursework at Columbia. For Ben, this was the ice cream on top of the apple pie. First, he had the privilege of sharing all of Esther's studies, and now here was Shen, willing to spend hours detailing all of his professors' insights. But this was different then his morning talks with Esther. His daughter's studies were all spanking brand new for Ben. Business, now business was something that Ben had been involved with for close to four decades. And now, he finally had some educated person to talk with about it. Sure, he could talk with Morty about how business was doing. But with Shen, the conversation was on a different plane, about theory and process. And this bright young man was actually interested in hearing about his experiences in the garment district, and how the realities of the past thirty years reflected the theories they threw back and forth. This was bliss. Utter bliss. Ben felt elevated. If Esther taught him about hunting and gathering, and the role of males throughout social history, with Shen he could feel that he had actually done right by the hunt, that he had had gathered well. You know, it feels pretty darn good when you can hold your own kibbitzing with an Ivy League boychik like Shen.

Over on the girl's side of the kitchen, it was all about Aziza. Lian couldn't quite grok how a soon to be five-year-old could possibly be so brilliant and profound. How many times had she recounted to one person or another about the time that she had been playing tag with Aziza, and the girl had stopped for a moment and said to her pursuer, "You chase me, Aunt Lian, and it's fun. But you don't have to chase all the time, when the game is over. Sometimes it feels good to be tagged. I like it when you tag me, and we get to hug."

Aziza was innately confident about her ability to be in charge. "Now, you sit here," she would tell Lian, "And you over here," to her grandmother, "And you can sit me on your lap," to her mom. "Now isn't that just right? Okay, Grandma. Tell us again about the first time you ate a cupcake and got the icing all over your face." The adults around her were at the same time her audience, her teachers, her students, her peers. She adored connecting, fitting in, with people, concepts or this infinite universe she encountered every day. She once told Esther, "Mommy, I don't think I'm growing up. I think I'm growing out. Is that okay, Mommy, to grow out instead of up?"

"Why do you think you are growing out, instead of up," Esther asked.

"Because going up is like when you took me to the top of that great big building. You could see a lot from there, but we had to go up in that stupid elevator. I felt stuck in there. When you go out, everything opens up, and you can go wherever you want, and you're never stuck in just one place. I like out more than up."

"But the moon is up. And I love you up to the moon and back."

"I know, Mommy. But don't be silly. The moon's not up. The moon moves around." And that was that.

Betania had come back into Esther's life, and was another member of Aziza's coterie. For better or worse, she was five months pregnant, and following in her friend's footsteps, had completely cleaned up her act once she made the decision to have the baby. She wasn't sure, one way or the other, if she was going to continue seeing the baby's daddy, and had no idea what she was going to do to support herself and her child, but was resolute that she was going to stay clean and sober. Ben, being the enabler he was, gave her a job in his company as a packer, but that would only work until the baby was born. Being around Esther and her family, gave Betania a level of belief that she would be able to make it through the muddle that lay in front of her. After all, if Esther had been able to prosper with all the shit she had been dealing with, well, maybe it could work for her.

When Lian and Betania visited together, Esther couldn't help but observe a level of competition between the two Aunts for Aziza's attention. It never got to the point where either would outright ask, who the "favorite" Aunt was, but each of them would come up with ideas for "alone time" in the other's presence. "Let's take a walk over to the park, and give Mom a chance to catch up with Aunt Betania," or "Hey Aziza! Let's see if we can search out some salamanders. Don't you just love them salamanders?" Being the only adult with Aziza seemed to be some special honor. There were times, she even found herself jealous that her two friends were getting the benefit of more Aziza smiles than herself.

Esther and Lian were both finishing their last semester, and were to be graduated in June. With Aziza off to kindergarten in the Fall, Esther felt that she could start an MSW program, even if it meant going full time. Mom would be there when Aziza came home. Daddy had insisted that tuition, even to NYU wouldn't be a problem, and her grades were good enough to at least obtain a partial scholarship. Could you believe it? Starting grad school to become a social worker? It was all so perfect for her. Esther had stayed in touch with Sarah Williams, who tracked her prior client's progress with continued amazement. She shared that in her opinion NYU and Hunter were the two best MSW programs in the city. Esther would apply for both, and best of all, Lian was planning to do the same. They'd be able to travel their graduate study road together.

Most nights, Esther would lie down with Aziza and read her a story. It was different from their morning readings, no textbooks, whatever Aziza wanted to hear. One evening, Esther brought the Hunter College handbook to Aziza's room. "Want to hear about all the courses that Mommy can take in September?"

The first course on the list was Introduction to Social Work, and after hearing the course description Aziza asked, "What's social work, Mommy?"

"That's the job that Mommy wants to learn."

"I know that. But what do people do when they have that job?"

"Well, a social worker helps people, helps them figure out how to have the best life for themselves, and helps them to succeed at getting that best life, once they know what that life is."

"I thought that's what parents and grandparents do."

Esther had thought her description had been adequate, but clearly it wasn't. "Sometimes life is confusing, and sometimes bad things happen, even to good people. Social workers try to help people correct and improve the conditions that are making them unhappy."

"So, social workers fix the mistakes that God makes?"

Where did that come from? Esther had never had any discussions with Aziza about religion or a God-head. "That's a pretty complicated topic for just before bed-time, Honey. Let's find some time for that tomorrow."

8

On Universal Intentionality

In our spiritual pursuits, "Why" is often a frequent question. We spend our everyday life on this planet seeking to understand the forces that influence our outcomes, past, present and future. First and foremost, our mind is built for survival, and our continued existence relies on our being able to understand not just our environmental conditions, but the causes that make it so. Knowing the "Whys" gives us what we need to remedy adverse conditions, and therefore to continue, to grow, to thrive, to pursue that which gives pleasure, to avoid pain. Understanding "Why" also feels a requisite for opening up to acceptance. For example, if we don't know why someone no longer loves us, it is difficult to accept that this loss has happened. Similarly, if we don't know why a rule was established, it is hard to follow. Being inquisitive about the "Whys" is a measure of our basic intelligence, valued and therefore a requisite for our teachings, from our earliest days.

So, it is not surprising that we seek to know the "Whys" of the universe. Why does evil exist in this world? Why do bad things happen to good people? Why would God allow people to suffer and die needlessly? Why was the universe created in the first place? The questions go on and on, in infinite regression. Every answer to every question can be subject to another inquiry as to "Why," as the parent of any four-year-old will testify. We look for some ultimate answer to it all, but even if we could go back and understand "why" the big bang happened, we would be asking why the forces that generated the universe to came together in the manner that they did, did. There is always another understanding that lays under the understanding that we discover.

Thus, we are forced to acknowledge that there are limits to our understanding, that we can never understand it all, either personally or as a whole. As much as we rely on science to explain everything, even science is subject to infinite inquiry, and has its limits. Sooner or later the parent has to tell the inquiring four-year-old, "because that's the way it is." This becomes the first lesson in acceptance without understanding. Acceptance with understanding makes things easier. If we know that a loved one died from a disease, it hurts, we mourn, and with difficulty, we accept the loss. But if there appears to be no known causation of the death, acceptance is significantly more challenging. Over history, one of the motivations to believe in a god has been to allow us to accept what we don't understand. We create a category in our mind of that which I can't understand, which only god knows why, and this allows us to accept what has happened and move on in our life.

Although many of us attribute god to be or to have a universal consciousness, we conceptualize that godly or universal consciousness is like ours. Even if is unknown to us, god has a reason "why." In short, we come to believe in a universal intentionality, that the All-and-Everything has purpose, has meaning, that the cosmos knows what it is doing and why it is doing it. We look up at the night sky, observe the infinite, and expect that there are answers in between the stars. They are beyond our reach, but somehow, there is an ultimate purpose to it all.

With this conceptualization of god, we create a godhead that is all knowing, who possesses the answers that we lack, and whose purpose becomes to parent us, because with understanding beyond our capability, that god must surely be meant to take care of us. You created us, for whatever reasons you did, now take care of what you created. We relegate ourselves to be the four-year-old asking our god to give us understanding, and secretly are disappointed and angry when our parent, our god, denies us the understanding we naturally seek.

Is it possible for us to accept that there is no ultimate "why," that there is no penultimate universal intentionality? Einstein couldn't. He wouldn't accept a universe in which his god was just throwing the dice. As brilliant as he was, Einstein lacked the ability to quiet his mind, specifically the part that requires a "why." His perception of the universe lacked unconditional acceptance; it lacked the central ingredient of love.

When we love the universe, we accept the All-and-Everything unconditionally. We accept that "why" is a relevant question only in our phenomenological experience, but that it has no consequence beyond the limits of our lives. As with the four-year-old, "why" is answered by "because." Being is its own cause. I am because I am, and the universe is because it is. I can explore my roots on earthly levels, and find answers, but my purposes and meanings, these I have to provide on my own. I can explore my understanding of a universal consciousness, a creator of the All-and-Everything, but will have to accept that this god has no need to explain itself, and the question of universal intentionality is moot.

When we let go of needing to get to a "why," our communion with the universe changes. Simultaneously, we let go of needing a spiritual parent to guide us through that which we don't understand, We can simply love all that is, the All, and the Everything, with unconditional acceptance. We can pray or commune without words, without questions, without seeking impossible and irrelevant answers. We can merge with it all without fear. We can live with providing our own meaning to life and the universe, and die without knowing what comes next, and why it has to be that way. We can be and let be.

9

Esther found graduate school to be everything she had hoped for, and then some. She had made the decision to go to Hunter, feeling that the NYU tuition was more than the family could afford. Ben did his best to dissuade her. He insisted that she attend the school that would best serve her, whatever the cost. Nothing was too good for his daughter. Nothing. But Esther put her foot down. She would not be made to feel like an entitled and enabled princess, as much as her father needed her to be just that. "Daddy, we're not talking about whether or not I can afford a pair of shoes. The difference in tuition is enough to buy a car and put a deposit on a house. And Hunter is more than comparable with NYU. It's settled!"

The students she met at Hunter were a very homogeneous lot, all tending to be idealistic, socially aware and introspective. Committed to social and cultural change on both a micro and macro level, they created a campus atmosphere that was challenging on both intellectual and personal levels. There was a general acceptance that everybody's private history and personality derivatives were open for public discussion, in the name of preparing to be free of unwanted personal issues which could potentially hamper their effectiveness as change agents. Whether in the classroom or the lounge, questions and intrusions into private matters, which would ordinarily be deemed rude throughout the general culture, here they were an ordinary happening.

Esther often felt like she was back in group therapy at the IOP, except with bright and stimulating peers. And, the professors.! Eminent scholars, well known and well published, they didn't create a distance between themselves and their students. Rather they appreciated their leadership role as a part of what felt like an egalitarian community, and consistently seemed to desire to learn from their students.

Lian had joined her at Hunter, sitting next to her in most classes, much as they had studied together as undergraduates, and was, well Lian! Her capacity to turn on a dime from declarative and serious to flighty and frivolous was appreciated by everyone. Lian seemed to instinctively know when to delve and when to let it go. There were times, especially in seminar settings, when she could be unyielding in her demand for a shared resolution to any particular issue. On other occasions she would interrupt fellow students engaged in an unproductive debate, interjecting an unexpected absurdity, and bring the intellectual sophistry to a needed end. Always with a smile, always with that little unvoiced giggle. Lian was universally loved.

In their second year, Lian chose a field placement working with the immigrant population, that perpetually regenerating group in New York, at the moment, flowing from Eastern Europe, Central America, Asia and the Middle East. Lian identified with these folks, and was determined to help them have an easier transition to America than her family had experienced. Not surprisingly, Esther opted to work with at-risk adolescent girls. It felt to her like a decision that had been made seven years earlier, in the holding cell, by the Queens County Courthouse. She could still see the eyes of her fellow cellmates, scared, defiant, hopeless and helpless. As much as she appreciated the efforts of Mrs. Williams and her colleagues who served those that had been arrested, Esther wanted to devote herself more to the prevention side of the effort, intervening with kids before they became involved with the criminal justice system. She felt that families were becoming more and more dysfunctional, as society strived to adapt to the economics which required two parents to work, changing gender roles, and the increasing disparity between rich and poor. To Esther, it felt that this generation of adolescent girls were pressured to reflect the advances of the women's movement, but deprived of the resources necessary to reach that potential. Filled with hormones, ambivalence and inner turmoil, uncertain about getting beyond their mother's horizons, these girls were acting out and exhibiting more and more social and psychological problems. Female addiction was on the rise. Eating disorders and cutting were becoming commonplace. Crime statistics in general were rising, even for the youthful female population. Esther indisputably knew she needed to be engaged.

As she began to work twenty hours a week at her South Jamaica placement, the schedule was tighter and found Esther rushing frenetically from home to school to placement to home again, barely ahead of an appointment here, or a deadline there. While Aziza was now in school full time, and was naturally a very independent child, Esther felt that she needed to put some limits to Rose's supportive role, and be there for her daughter herself. Mom wasn't getting any younger, and had always had emotional and physical limitations. Lately, she had observed many of the same conflicts she historically had with her mother flaring up between Mom and Aziza. As the child grew older and had a more clearly defined personality, her grandmother couldn't help herself from challenging the budding independence and burgeoning belief systems. Rose had always enjoyed the most perfect of relationships with infants and toddlers. However, as they became more autonomous, Rose experienced herself as less needed. This was a familiar loss, a void that had always been difficult for her to fill. Her lifelong theme of losing significance and love was provoked again. With her role poorly defined, Rose couldn't help herself from being irritated with the people she looked to for confirmation of her worth.

Watching the two of them in the kitchen, with Mom insisting that Aziza was too young to toast her Pop Tarts by herself, and Aziza pouting, wanting to show off how she could be self-sufficient and make her own after-school snack, brought Esther back to all the ridiculous battles that had been warred twenty years earlier. As much as she relied on her mother to be there for Aziza while she was away, it was becoming evident that her presence was needed, as much as she could possibly carve out. And not just in the service and protection of her daughter. Mom was beginning to show some physical strain from caring for her granddaughter, even if she denied it. Ultimately, the responsibility was hers, even if it wasn't clear which generation she was protecting.

The dysfunctional triangle of her parents and herself could have emerged anew, but Esther knew this time around to keep Daddy out of it. Loving Mom as much as he did, he could never comprehend that she could still feel abandoned. And by Aziza, no less.

The solution to this confounding issue fell into her lap out of the blue. One Saturday evening Betania was visiting for the weekend. Her son, Bobby, now two years old, had been put to sleep in Aziza's room. Aziza adored her "cousin," and was thrilled that she could teach him all about dinosaurs after breakfast the following morning. She had lined up her dinosaur books and figurines before going to bed, establishing a lesson plan she would employ. "Teachers need to be organized," she told Mom, "Just like putting out your clothes on a school night."

Betania and Esther were relaxing in the living room, identifying with each other about the difficulties of their perpetually dash to catch up with their tail, caring for responsibilities at work and as a parent. Rose had felt a cold, or something, coming on, and had decided to watch some television in the bedroom. Ben went out and picked up the early edition of the *NY Times*, and was now pouring over the crossword puzzle by the dining room table. It had forever been his weekly goal to finish the puzzle in less than 75 minutes. Of course, when he did, he proclaimed that this week it was too easy.

Betania related, "I know I sound exactly like my mother, but right now it just feels so damn good to take a little time to do absolutely nothing, to simply hang out with a good friend. I can hear Momma now, swushing me out of the room, saying 'Just let me be a minute, Girl. I got some catchin' up with myself to do.'" Betania's mom had recently moved down to North Carolina, to be with her brother. She had always wanted to return to her birthplace, and now that Betania was clean and working for a couple of years, it felt safe for her to go. Her daughter would somehow eke it out and make ends meet, once she took over the lease on the rent-controlled apartment they had lived in since Betania was a little girl herself.

"Tell me about it, Girlfriend. Even a shower is starting to feel like a luxury. Hell, I don't think I've had the time to shave my legs in god-knows how long. Not that there's any great need for that these days, mind you."

"Let's face it. Time for ourselves, time for some guy, time for any damn thing went right out the window when we had our kids. I mean, I ain't complainin', and I love the hell out of that little boy upstairs, but it stopped bein' easy right about the same time we started to do the right thing. Ain't that something. Well, at least you're not spinning your wheels like me, goin' nowhere quick. At least you're goin' to school and getting somewhere for yourself."

"Yeah, but let's not hang out at this pity party too long. You know, we made those decisions all by ourselves to take the hard route. Just paying our dues for past mistakes. We're both catching up, Betania. Let's not pretend that we thought it was going to happen in a minute."

"I hear you, and make no mistakes about it, you're catchin' up. Not so sure about me."

Ben put down his pencil and called from the dining room, "Anybody know a seven-letter word for 'whining'?"

"Very funny Daddy. Very funny."

Ben left the unfinished puzzle in the dining room and joined the girls. "Seriously, you know I'm proud as punch about both of you. And I get that you're both struggling to keep it all together. Maybe I can do something to help here. Maybe I can help a bissel ."

"Daddy, you're already doing a lot. For both of us. I know I can't think of any way I could have achieved anything if it weren't for your support."

"And that goes for me too, Mr. Shapiro. Without your help I'd be in some sorry state."

"Well, just hear me out, girls. Suppose you, Betania, stopped working with me in the city, and instead moved in here, and helped out with everything that needs to be done around here. I mean, we all know Rose is having a hard time keeping up with everything, and you, Esther, you're running a marathon every day, and if we had a full-time housekeeper, you all could slow down a step. I mean, it's no big thing for me to transfer your salary from one job to the other. And then, if you're living here without rent, you could save enough to put together what you need for your next step. As far as I'm concerned, it sort of takes care of all my girls. All of you, including Mommy and Aziza."

"Are you serious, Mr. Shapiro? I mean that would be just plain spectacular."

"Serious as some union guy in the garment district about wages.

I just figure it would be easier on everybody. Maybe even me, if it helps keep Mom in a better mood."

"Hey Daddy, do you know some umpteen-letter word for the most wonderful Dad in the world? Because I do!"

Betania moved in a few weeks later, at the end of the month. It was a little cramped. With only three bedrooms. Bobby and Aziza had to share, as did their mothers. Having Bobby in her room lost some of its luster, once it was an everyday happening. But having Aunt Betania around all the time more than made up for it, and Grandma became so involved with Bobby, that she wasn't pestering Aziza anymore about every little thing.

Rose's headaches disappeared again instantly. She'd never had a little boy to look after before, and Bobby became her new darling. "You know, Ben, boys are really different than girls."

"Rosie, my love. I think we knew this before."

"No, I'm serious. Benny. I mean Aziza is probably the brightest little girl I've ever known, and I'm not saying that because she is our own grandchild, but Bobby is so much different then Aziza was at that age. Or even Esther. He's always fixing to take things apart and put them back together again. That little bubbeleh is a born engineer, I tell you."

"Our little brown bubbeleh, a good boy, a good boy. I'm glad you're happy with this new arrangement of ours, Rose. You being happy, that makes me happy."

"I know, I know. Now who's talking about things we already know."

10

Rose loved to play Candyland with Bobby. They would sit by the dinette table in the kitchen and play for hours. Not surprisingly, Rose made it a habit to cheat, so as let Bobby win. No matter how many times Betania objected to the ruse, letting Rose know that "It isn't goin' to help my boy succeed in this life if he thinks he's always goin' to win," Rose simply delighted in his delight, and continued to stack the deck. When she wasn't playing outside, Aziza would sit and watch the game play out, but never commented, even if her sense of fairness was being tested. She would peer at the board intently, but remain adrift, lost in her thoughts.

One evening when they were alone, Aziza asked her mom," Did Grandma always let you win when you were a little girl?"

Esther thought back, "To tell you the truth, I don't remember if we played Candyland, but Grandma believes that her little ones are the best of the best, at everything, and wants them to believe it also. You know how she is always telling you how you're the brightest and the most beautiful girl she's ever known, and how you're going to succeed at everything you ever try for? She certainly did that with me also."

"But how can I be the brightest and the prettiest, if you're also the smartest and the most beautiful? That doesn't make any sense."

"Well, Grandma doesn't always care about making sense. She needs to feel like being a mommy and a grandma is worthwhile. It confirms that she is accomplishing good stuff in her life. And believing that she raised me and you, and even Bobby to be special, that gives her that feeling. You know, we all like to feel like we do good and special things in life."

Aziza looked bemused. Finally, she blurted, "I don't think I like Candyland."

"Why's that, Honey? You always used to enjoy playing it with Grandma yourself."

"Well, Candyland is all sweet and stuff, and makes you feel like you're a winner, when all you did was throw the dice. It makes it seem like everything's all about luck."

"And do you think luck plays a big part in people's lives?"

"Well sure, like how lucky I am to be growing up here, and always having good food and you and Grandpa and Grandma around to take care of me. But, when I think about it, that's just fluky. I didn't do anything to have it so easy. And like Grandpa's always saying, think about all the children all over the world who don't have it like me. That's really bad luck for them. And the girls that you work with and try to help. Was it just bad luck that their lives are kind of crummy?"

"That's a complicated question you're asking. Both things are true. On the one hand most of the girls I work with were born into difficult circumstances. Many of them were poor, and others had, let's say, not-so-good parents. But it's also true that most of them made some very bad decisions on their own, and if they don't learn their lessons from their mistakes, and start to become more responsible, then their bad luck will never turn around."

"So, you're saying that it's like water is H2O, one part this and another part that. Takes two things to make another, it's both bad luck and also their own fault."

"Sure, just like when you win at something, or succeed, it's both good luck and your skills, or abilities, and let's not forget, your effort."

Aziza went inside again, pensive. Eventually she asked, "Mommy, could I make up a board game, sort of like Candyland, but different?"

"That would be great, Sweetie. Of course, you can. I think we have all the supplies you might need."

"Thanks, Mom." And then she added, "I sure am lucky I have you!"

For the next couple of days Aziza was mostly in her room. Rose tried everything she could to coax her out, but the girl was committed to creating an alternative to Candyland. She even turned down some latkes for an afternoon snack. "Save them for me, Grandma. I'll have them for dinner. Please, would you?" On the second day she asked for construction paper and colored card stock and some glue, but not that gooey white stuff. By the time the weekend came around, she asked that everybody gather with her in the dining room, for the unveiling of her new game.

Aziza had dressed up for this grand opening, and was wearing the new outfit Grandma had bought her last weekend. She carefully positioned everyone around the table, before bringing out the game components from a pillow case. "Ladies and Gentleman. I present you with 'The Way of Life', a new game from Aziza Shapiro," and began to place the board, cards and pieces in their proper place on the table.

The game board showed a winding road, much like Candyland, with many stops along the way. She had colored in a landscape background, with an assortment of animals portrayed in a meadow-like setting. There was an outline for two sets of cards, which she carefully placed, keeping the stacks neat and tidy. One end of the path was marked "Starts." The other side read "Ends." Aziza took out four pieces, borrowed from another game, and put them just off the board near the beginning of the "Way."

"So, everybody, pay attention now. Here is the starting point. If you have the highest roll of the dice, you get to pick your piece first and then move it eight stops ahead. If you get the second highest roll, you're going to start six stops ahead. And so on and so on. The person who got the crummy roll gets to pick last, and starts at the back. That's because we all know that some people are lucky and start out life way ahead of everyone else, and other people start out a lot behind.

"Everybody gets to take turns and roll the dice and move their piece the number that they roll, like in all the other games. But, if they land on one of the red spots, then they pick up one of the 'Get It Right' cards, and depending on if they answer the question correctly, they move an extra three steps forward or three steps back. If they land on one of the blue spots, they pick up a 'Luck' card, and move forward or back just because the card says so. Sometimes somebody can pick up an accident card from the luck pile, and then they die, and have to take their piece off the board. Then they have to wait until the next time the game gets played. Anyway, whoever gets to the End first, wins."

"That's it, everybody. Do you like my game?"

None of the grown-ups knew what to say, until Rose eventually ventured, "A lot of this game doesn't seem fair, Aziza, with some people starting way ahead of the others."

"Well, Grandma, remember when you took me to my friend Iris's birthday party, and I complained I got the smallest piece of cake. You're the one that told me that sometimes you get a big piece, and sometimes you get cheated, and the right thing for me to do was to smile and be glad I got something. You were right. The cake still tasted good, even if it was kind of tiny. Like that stupid brother of hers, Theo, said, 'Who says life has to be fair'."

11

On Karma

Many of us think of karma as synonymous with fate. They imagine that our path is somehow predestined. Some people postulate that the events and actions of a previous lifetime cause consequence in our present existence, a kind of punishment or reward system in which the universe, or a critical god, adjudicates a final sentence from a lofty bench on high. Karma becomes payback. This notion often mollifies injured people who feel helpless to carry out the revenge they desire on those who did them wrong, that chickens will come home to roost eventually. They want to feel that the tables will eventually be turned, even if it doesn't happen in this lifetime. Others, who believe that they were cheated of their due, can project into their yet-to-come being and be assured that they will be eventually be compensated for their efforts or their goodness. Justice may not always reign in the present, but fairness will rule over time.

Resentment and spite seem to be the ultimate source of this definition of karma. It is indicative of a heart grown hard; a spirit harmed which discards the joys of living in the now. My life may suck, even if I am a good person, but eventually I'll be paid back, with interest. It's an inter-lifetime Cinderella story in which a late but godly prince of energy places a well-fitting slipper on a future deserving foot. The maiden who had been impotent in her lifetime, is rescued and empowered in her next.

The greatest fault of this perception of karma as a predestiny is that it takes the suspense out of the drama of life. If our outcomes are fated in this lifetime, we become robotic entities, programmed to do what we do and achieve what we achieve. God the Programmer colludes with social systems and genetic expression to leave the individual without free will or choice. This is a life of spiritual slavery, in which we don't even have an opportunity to confront our enslaver, as the master hides in the past. When we fail to recognize the benefits of doubt and uncertainty, we lose our capacity for mystery, romance, adventure, daring and play. We become the bride of an arranged marriage, forced into a relationship with life in which love is replaced by duty.

We all journey through our lives and lifetimes on a path that never stops. We can imagine that we take a break, have a vacation or a retreat from life, but the truth is that our path continues to unfold whether we are conscious and aware of the movement or not. Our path consists of an endless series of loci, a string of pearls that stretches out into the future, infinitely reaching toward a conclusion that always remains ahead of us. Yet, though our path is infinite and unending, we live in the moment. Each instant of our life has an integrity of its own. There is a present moment, even if that instant is gone by the time that we become aware of it. And it is in that instant, in the intersection of past and future, that the magic of life happens, that karma transpires. Karma is the magical interaction of the antecedent direction of our path with the distinctive moment of the now. While the direction of our path has been previously established by the myriad moments of the past, this only establishes a momentum, an intention, which will react with the present, giving direction to the next. Karma is the space between the moments, where all the direction is gained, much like the synapses are the space between the neurons, where all the thought is created.

Karma resolves a basic paradox of life. We must live our life in the now yet we must also live our life as a journey. With karma in mind, we approach every moment aware of our intention, yet open to change. We can have a sense of our mission, a knowledge of our purpose, and still find new determinants along the way. We evolve. We explore. We learn. Life is additive, accumulating the experiences of the past, while achieving new tendencies and meanings as we go. We can never be trapped in the ennui of an existential morass when we know that our relationship with the All and Everything is never static. Both the universe and ourselves are recreated continually. The Creation is invented anew in every instant.

We need to value the drama of life, and appreciate the necessity for suspense. Most of us learned that if we turned the pages to the final chapter of a book because we wanted to know the outcome prematurely, that we were making an ill-advised mistake. We ruined our reading experience by our intolerance of suspense. Patience is required when living life as an art. The plot needs to thicken, the form needs to emerge, the rhythm needs to lead us to song. A well lived life requires the stamina to ride our anxiety about outcomes to its conclusion. Unknowing needn't generate stress or angst. The next stop of our journey may yield a pleasure or pain, a loss or a gain, a success or a failure. It may remain steady at the helm or swerve in a whole new direction. The trick is to welcome the new scene, the new act, the new twist of theme, and be aware that the next moment is nigh. We continue to collaborate with our path to create new art. That is the way.

Karma is also the foundation for experiencing the rare moments we alternately call spiritual bliss, satori or enlightenment. Existing in between the instants, karma is what holds together the entire string of pearls. The bliss is born in those extraordinary instants when our consciousness experiences the entire path as a unified whole and we comprehend that every single loci is connected with every other. In those instants, when our path is revealed to have no wasted moments, every cell of our body, ever moment of life, every action and reaction, become an indispensable part of the creation of a perfect being. In that time, the puzzle is complete; it all fits together. This then becomes the moment that we experience the perfection of the All and Everything, in which All is connected to Everything, and Everything is found in the All. It is blinding and revealing. It is the momentary moment we can grasp the infinite.

12

Shen walked the half mile from the campsite to the river. The earthen path, strewn with mulch, completed its windy journey at a small clearing, well shaded by a full canopy of maples. The Delaware River flowed placidly through this stretch of woodland, and the rafters drifted by, enjoying a few leisurely moments before urgency would overtake them again when the rapids approached. Shen wondered how often campers like himself sought to get away from the dither back at the campsite, and found refuge at this spot. It was peaceful, even if he wasn't. He sat on a large stone, and lost himself in the languid current.

He and Lian had joined Esther and Betania, and the kids, for a long weekend holiday, up near the Water Gap in northern New Jersey. They had rented a voluminous tent, large enough to hold the complete crew and their sleeping bags. Bobby and Aziza were enthralled, both with the thrill of an outside "bedroom" in which most of their favorite people slept and played together, and the delight in meeting scores of other children who teemed across the campground. "Best friends for a weekend" met, played, promised to be pen pals forever, and shared attitudes and life stories from faraway places. Like Canada, and Michigan, and even Utah. They were in and out and in of the tent, drawn by the excitement that was held outside and inside.

Shen rarely had get-a-way time. Months before finishing his MBA at Columbia, he had been sought out and hired by a large investment firm, and upon graduating had joined the lot of young traders working massive hours on end. Money had now become plentiful, but not the time to spend or enjoy it. This was, however, no difficulty for a young man locked in to investing in his life, and securing the aspirations created by his parents. The loss of the casual social life which most of his colleagues at work boasted and grumbled over was not a problem for Shen. His furtive love for Esther was.

Usually, he could obscure and deny his feelings towards her. He could strive to be able to involve himself with other conversations on the far side of the room, or leave the room altogether, removing himself from his impulses to declare himself, to touch, to hold, to display outside what he felt inside. He reviled himself as deceitful. He had hidden his ardor for years, for any number of reasons. She was his sister's friend, and somehow the family-like atmosphere left him with a feeling that his adoration was somehow incestuous. Esther never dated, and had never indicated in any way that she might be interested in pursuing a relationship with any guy, much less him. As much as he wanted to impulsively shout out to her his devotion, impulsivity was contradictory to everything that Shen was about. The longer he remained silent, the more impossible it became to break the silence.

But laying right next to her all night in their respective sleeping bags, had felt more then he could bear. His mind had been insistent on driving through every stop sign, and he didn't want to apply the brakes. But his hands had felt paralyzed, while filled with discontent for the prudent part of him that precluded touch. Awake most of the night, as soon as the sun rose, he had to get away. From her? From himself? He left the tent, traveling any way that his feet and his anxiety took him. His escape brought him down to the river, skipping stones across the water, wishing he had either the audacity or the stupidity to be able to blurt out his hidden affection. Even if, as he was certain, she was to confirm that she wasn't interested in him in that kind of way, at least he would be freed from his emotional imprisonment. If only just for one day he could share Lian's ability to leap into anything and everything. As many times as he had criticized her for being impetuous, he envied her impulsivity and the courage it reflected.

There was a rustle of branch and stone behind him. "What are you doing down here? Don't you want to have breakfast with the rest of us."

It was Esther. She had been woken by his rustling, and followed him outside, thinking he was just stretching his body to greet the day. She called out to him when he started to walk away, but he didn't hear her, apparently lost in his thoughts.

"Oh, I just needed a minute to catch up with my thoughts." As she casually plunked down next to him, he didn't dare look her way. "Didn't sleep well last night. My mind kept going and going, racing around the track, scrambling in all directions." This was as close to the truth as he could risk.

"Me too," she almost whispered. There was a weighty pause, before Esther took his chin and forcibly turned him to face her. "Shen, I haven't been very kind to you. I'm very sorry."

"What do you mean? You've never been anything but caring." Where was she going with this?

"Shen, I never should have allowed our sleeping bags to be next to each other last night. Honestly, we both know that."

He took her hand away and turned, so as to keep his gaze on the river. "I hope my tossing around all night didn't keep you up," avoiding the issue of whatever it was that both of them knew.

Esther's patience was exhausted. "Shen, for god's sake, would you just for a minute stop pretending you're a man lacking even the slightest degree of self-awareness. It's not as if either of us hasn't felt this sexual tension that's been hovering between us for ages. Damn it to hell! Who knows? Maybe I slept next to you last night just so I could bring it all to a head. I'm tired of bottling myself up, and watching you bumbling and fumbling around me. Maybe I set up this whole damn weekend, just to break the ridiculous unease that we've both been living with. Enough already!"

Now he truly felt like a fool. "Has it really been that obvious?"

"How long have we known each other? Seven or eight years. You've been my closest male friend for all that time, and for the past year you totally ghost me? I didn't have to be a genius, like you, to put it together."

He continued to stare down the river, paralyzed with ambivalence. One part screamed internally. How could he be such a jerk? Even she was perplexed at how a bright person could be so stupid. His other half was relieved. It was out. In the open, after all this time. He wanted to turn and hold her, to embrace her. It was as if his ability to speak went dumb, caught between the two poles. And then, just as he was starting to panic, she abruptly threw up her hands and stood up, ready to leave.

"Shen, I can't…"

Totally out of character, disregarding the fears that still flowed through his body, he jumped up and took hold of her. "Please don't go. I know I'm not very good at this, but please don't go." Without thinking about it, he kissed her, intensely, urgently. She responded with an equal urgency, and their bodies remained clinched, unable to let go.

Esther pulled back her head, but not her body, needing to speak but unwilling to unravel their arms. "I've wanted you to do that for so long."

"You never gave me the slightest hint." They pulled apart, but remained holding both hands. "I've loved you for so long." His grip remained strong, even as his torso began to tremble.

"That feeling is mutual, Shen. And it has been, for a while," and she broke off one hand and put it to his chest. "Hey, calm this body of yours down a bit. Let's sit here for a few minutes. I've got some confessing of my own to do."

They returned to the stone, but in a very different space. "No Esther, you did nothing wrong. It was me who should have been able to approach you truthfully. I've been such a coward."

"Please stop reassuring me. This isn't about either of us doing anything wrong, and I've got to get this out. It's not like there are any rules, even if kids think there are. You've just been being who you are, Shen, and I've known and respected that. However, there are somethings you've got to know about me. Ever since I had Aziza, there was no way in Hell that I was going to allow myself to even think about a relationship. Shit, before I became pregnant with her, I was the queen of flirting. You wouldn't have stood a chance if I'd known you back then. Trust me, you would have known exactly what I wanted.

"But Aziza wasn't conceived in a relationship. I was viciously raped, when I was in Israel. And after her birth, between raising her and going to school, and keeping up the crazy pace I've been on, I think I conveniently avoided the aftermath, the lingering horror of it all, the PTSD, whatever you want to call it. The real truth is, as long as I could avoid any romantic or sexual relationship with any guy, I didn't have to deal with the leftover trauma, the residue of a nightmare. When I couldn't help becoming aware of your interest, your feelings, my denial of my trauma started to fall apart. That's when I discovered that I as much as I wanted you, there was also an awareness of all the fear and rage and helplessness which had been buried inside me for years.

"Shen, I'm scarred and I'm scared. Just thinking about going further then a kiss brings up a ton of anxiety. There was a rightness to your holding back, even if there was no way you could know about it. I am, we are, going to have to take this very slow."

"Not a problem." He smiled. "You know, for a guy that raced in the dashes in High School, I'm surprisingly good at taking things slow. But I guess you know that already. I've made that way too obvious. What I can promise you, is that you will never experience any pressure coming from me. For sure, I will stop being the fool who hides what he's feeling, and doesn't communicate his love. But I won't pressure. That's a promise.

"When you speak of past influences, it makes me think of my first days in America. More than anything else, I was bewildered by the way that boys and girls interacted here, how brazen they seemed to be, especially about sex. I'm certainly not comparing my level of distress to the hideousness you went through, but it helps me to understand my awkwardness. Yes, going slow, that works for me too."

When they returned to the campsite, holding hands, Betania and Lian were busy doling out the cereal to the kids, and had a pot of coffee percolating on the fire. Lian looked over at their intertwined hands, grinned, and commented to her friend, "Well, would you look at that. It's about fucking time!"

13

Esther's worry that the family was not going to take to this new relationship well mostly turned out to be reactive. Her fears were rooted back in her adolescence, when her folks didn't appreciate her seeing any boys, much less the inappropriate guys she went out of her way to choose. Ben's response couldn't have been more to the contrary. He was overjoyed.

"Esther, my dearest, if it was me that was choosing some man for you, this is what I would pick, a man like Shen. Someone exactly like Shen. This is a good match. You know, yes, I know you know, there are so many reasons why men and women get together, some of them good, some of them bad. But at the end of the day the only thing that matters is they have to be a good match; they need to see the world from the same window. Those values that your sociologist people talk about, they have to match up. Shen, he fits with you, and your thinking, like a glove. Like a glove, I tell you. And, if you don't mind me saying, he's a pretty good fit with the rest of our family."

Ben's response wasn't really the one she imagined had the potential to be negative. If Daddy was anything, he was supportive. But he had gone so far beyond support in the expression of his delight. For Ben, Shen was a more than welcome addition. It was Rose's approval which had taken her back a bit.

"To be absolutely honest, Esther, I've been waiting for this day to come, and hoping it would never happen. I mean, don't get me wrong, I've always wanted to see you happy, and married, and living a good life. What mother wouldn't want that? And I knew that sooner or later you were going to start getting interested in men again. So, who wouldn't? But I worried. I worried that you would bring some gonif around, some shlepper who didn't fit in here, with our family, who belonged somewhere else. I mean, Darling, you'd have to agree that your picker with the male animal hasn't been too hot.

"And then you go and bring home a guy who's already a perfect fit in our home, in our family. Oh, this is wonderful. I don't have to worry about losing you, or losing Aziza, or having some stupid fights with you about some stupid boyfriend or husband. I mean, maybe Rabbi Goldsheid wouldn't be yelling his praises about this development, Shen being Chinese and all that, but what does that idiot know? After all, think about that lunatic daughter-in-law his son married. You know that's not going to amount to anything good."

Mom and Daddy were in the "okay" column. That left Aziza. Should she talk to her alone, mother to daughter, or bring Shen into the conversation. It's not like Shen was some stranger who Aziza was just meeting after her mom had been dating him for months. She had known Shen most of her life. After talking it over with Shen, the two of them decided to that it would be best to have all three of them in the dialogue. They all sat on the bed in her room.

"Aziza, you've probably noticed that Shen and I have been spending a lot of time together, just on our own," Esther tip-toed into the conversation.

"Yeah, you've been leaving Aunt Lian out a lot. Are you guys mad at her or something?"

"Not at all. Your Aunt Lian and I are still the best of friends, and Shen loves his sister almost as much as I love you. We haven't been leaving her out or avoiding her, we have just wanted to be alone with each other more."

"How come? You always used to talk about 'adult time', that it was time for me and Bobby to go to bed, and then the whole bunch of you guys would stay up. You know, both of you, and Aunt Betania, and Aunt Lian. What? Do you have a 'secret club' now?"

"No secrets," Shen introjected. "Mom and I are trying to tell you that our feelings for each other have changed in a different way, a loving way. Mom and I have fallen in love, Aziza. It's exactly because we don't want there to be any secrets that we're sharing this with you now."

Aziza crawled up into her mother's lap, something she hadn't done in a few years. "So, you and Uncle Shen are boyfriend and girlfriend now?" And then she launched into a thousand questions. "Are you going to get married? Can I be the flower girl? Where are we all going to sleep? There's not enough room for you, Uncle Shen, and Mommy and Aunt Betania to all sleep in Mom's room. And do I still call you Uncle Shen. Should I call you Daddy> You know, I've never had a father before…."

"Slow down, Kiddo. Yes, Shen and I have been talking about getting married, not today or tomorrow, but not too far away. And I don't know if it's going to be a big party, or just us family, but either way you will be part of it, and if you want to be a flower girl, then that's what you will be."

"And you can call me anything you feel comfortable with, anything you want. No, that's not true, you can't call me Dennis, or Howard or some name that's not mine. Aziza, I know that you've never had a dad before, although Grandpa Ben has always been there for you in a Daddy sort of way. Let's just see how it goes. If it turns out that you want me to be your father, then I will be very happy, frankly overjoyed about it."

"Okay, that's it. I'll be the flower girl and you'll be the Daddy," She jumped down. "I'm going to go tell Grandma. She's probably going to have something to say about all this. She always does."

Mom and the newly minted Daddy watched her running through the hall and down the stairs. They had spent days fretting about the complex dynamics and the potential emotions that Aziza might experience, and it turned out that there were only two necessities. She needed to be the flower girl, and she needed to have a father. With these conditions met, she would leave the rest to them.

It was a relief to include the household in their romance. Since the camping trip back in the summer, Esther had needed Shen to accept that their involvement be kept from her parents and Aziza.

Only when she felt herself confident that the relationship would be lasting, would she allow the rest of her family to be privy. She had thoroughly avoided any level of dating after Aziza was born. As she had shared with him, there were sexual issues which felt like an insurmountable barrier to any relationship. The aftereffects of the rape left her repelled by even the thought of sexual contact. As much as she desired Shen, and it wasn't as if there hadn't been enjoyable experience in the past, she could feel the walls go up as soon as the most rudimentary physical contacts were exchanged. She often wondered if she could be as patient and understanding as Shen was, if their roles were reversed. For sure, she found it difficult to be patient with herself. She didn't want to just love this man, she wanted to satisfy him, look after his needs, and join with him on all levels. She loved him partly because he was different from just about every man she had ever met, but the traumatized part of her lumped him in with all of the miscreants of his gender.

The turn in their coupling had come a few months earlier, when they were laying together one morning, over at Shen and Lian's place, in Flushing. They enjoyed spending the night together, talking, cuddling, away from the commotion of the larger grouping at Hollis, even if it meant they had to encounter their stymied physicality. Esther's parents had become accustomed to her sleeping over at Lian's, and were happy to look after Aziza and give Esther a break. Shen was always patient, as he had promised, and never pushed, poked or prodded. Esther was particularly frustrated upon getting up that day, with herself, and the situation.

"Shen, every time we sleep together, I keep waiting, anticipating, looking toward to the point when I can welcome you into me, join with you, make love with you. I don't get it. I feel more secure, safer with you, then I have ever felt with anyone. And still, here we are, here I am. If I even think of giving you the green light, I can feel all of my body tightening up. It's like a rigid clamp that immobilizes my muscles. I've got to be the picture girl for 'up tight', and I don't mean that just figuratively. Sometimes I think I should I be telling you to disregard my tension, and just take me? Is that what I need to get by this? If it was just me, I'd declare myself a lost cause, but I won't give up on us. Damn it! As much as I try, I just can't get through this by myself."

Shen was slow to respond. The last thing he wanted to do was to disrespect her anxiety, even if he was given permission. That wasn't him, and the part of her that was locked in fear wasn't the one that was speaking, anyway. Instinctively, he knew that would be disaster. You don't have to be Sigmund Freud to know that nobody gets over a rape by asking to flat-out be taken. Fighting fire with fire didn't apply here. He turned toward her, stroking her shoulder and said, "I'm not the one of us who has any great psychological insight or knowledge. Remember me? I'm just the financial guy in this relationship. But it seems to me that your frustration is giving you some bad advice.

"Esther, you're a take charge, assertive woman. I think that you were not only hurt and wounded and horrified by what happened, but also outraged that you were unable to protect yourself, that you couldn't be you, and were forced to be a victim. That had to have enraged you, at them, at yourself, at the entire world for turning your sense of who you were upside down. And now, all that anger seems to be directed at punishing yourself, like you were, what do Americans say, grounding yourself, depriving yourself of any sexual or loving pleasure. No, the last thing I want to do is to try to push through and disrespect all that. The Esther I want to make love to is that assertive, aggressive, take-charge woman you are. And if that means that right now you have to do all the initiating, and deciding, and directing, that's okay. It will all balance out in time. But for now, stop worrying about how you are going to react to me. You keep picturing our lovemaking as you responding to my advances, and that doesn't have to be the case. I'm not a guy that has a problem with you being 'in charge'."

Esther immediately knew he was spot on. Her conception of sex had changed when she was attacked. Prior to the rape, Esther had tended to be aggressive, both physically and emotionally. Whoever that girl was seemed to have vanished when she was assaulted and stripped of any defense. Now she clung to a totally defensive posture. She closed her eyes and imagined herself embracing the attitude she had left behind, obscured by fear and resistance. Maybe guilt? The thought occurred to her that it was as if she had been hiding out in someone else's body, and now, as she envisioned how it used to be, she could feel herself reentering herself. For the first time in years, she could experience her physicality. She could allow herself to appreciate her strength, and give herself permission to hold, to grasp, to be free to achieve her intention. It had been wise for her to give up control in most areas of her life. But hell no, not in this one. If anyone was going to be the "taker," it would be her.

She made sure their relationship was consummated that morning, and most days thereafter.

14

Certifiably happy about the impending marriage, Aziza wasn't so sure about moving. Even at ten, she had to admit that whatever expectations she harbored that they would continue to live with her grandparents were unreasonable. Unwinding 15 skeins of yarn and tying the ends together, she had accurately measured it out. Her new bed was going to be exactly 253 feet from her present bedroom. That wasn't so bad, was it? Shen had bought the house directly across the street, and everybody was going to have more room. Aunt Lian would move into the new place with Shen and Mommy. And the best thing about it all was that she would have her own room, all to herself! Even Bobby and Aunt Betania would get their own rooms. This was all pretty neat, but it was leaving the familiar behind. Would it feel right? Would she still be able to have cinnamon toast with Grandma, when she came home from school? New was a good thing for toys and clothes and stuff, and maybe sometimes friends, but changing everyday life seemed different. Even if it was just across the street.

She had talked with Grandpa about her apprehensions. He listened carefully to her concerns and then asked, "So what are you really worried about? Aziza, I hear you being all verklempt about moving to the new house, but I'm not hearing anything specific that you're not so comfortable about. You like that you're going to have your very own bedroom, all to yourself. You like that Mommy and Shen are getting married. Who knows, maybe you'll even have a baby brother or sister someday. You like all that. So, what are you really losing sleep over?

"Tell you what. Why don't you see if you can make a list of the things that you think you might not be so happy about, and then we could look at it together. Maybe there's lots of them, maybe just a few. You go make the list, sweetheart, and then we'll talk about it together. We'll discuss it, the two of us."

Aziza returned in a couple of hours with her list in hand. "Here it is, Grandpa," as she handed it over, somewhat sheepishly.

He read it out loud.

1- *Can I come over here right after school just like I always do now?*

2- *Can I paint my new room any color I want?*

3- *We'll have to get a new phone number. Will my friends remember it so they can call me up?*

4- *Does Shen really want to be my Daddy, and is he going to turn out to be real strict when he does?*

5- *Grandpa, are you okay with Shen becoming my Daddy? This is sort of a change for you too.*

6- *This whole list is stupid! I'm just making stuff up because I have this sort of feeling of being scared, and I want it to be something clear and plain. I don't like it when I'm scared and don't know what's really frightening me.*

Ben lingered on the list after reading, and then smiled. "So, what this is really all about, is you feel like you should be a fortune teller, and know what's happening before it happens? Maybe I should get you a crystal ball for your birthday?"

"No, Grandpa, it's not like I want to know everything about everything. But aren't you always telling me to look both ways before I cross the street?"

"Sure. And you should do that. You should always look both ways. You know why? It's because you already know that there are cars that speed down the streets, and a lot of people who are driving those cars don't look and be so careful. You should be careful because everyone else isn't always careful enough. You already know that. So, is there something you know about living across the street, something that you should be scared of?"

"But that's the whole problem. I don't know. It's all going to be a new thing."

"Well, let's see. Do you know that Grandma is always going to want to see you when you come home from school? That she always is going to want to have something special for you?"

"Well, yeah, but…."

"And do you already know that Mommy wants you to have your own way, when you're being reasonable, and not getting in anybody else's way?"

"Sure. Mommy says all the time that she wants me to be in charge of my life as long as I don't mess up other people's lives."

"And I know that you know that I love you, and will always want you to be happy, and loved by other people as much I do. So, it seems you know a lot. And what you know appears to be pretty much in the good column."

"But what about all the stuff that I don't know about? I can't figure out everything, Grandpa."

"That's right, honey. You can't predict everything before it happens. You can think hard, and study hard, and learn everything that can be learned about what you expect your future to be. And after that, it's all about the adventure of exploring and living with what comes next. You like adventure, don't you?"

"You think moving across the street is going to be a new adventure?"

"Sure, we don't know what will happen, but it will be an adventure, as we live and find out. And when you move out of that house and go to college, that's going to be an adventure too. And when you're all done with college, and move into your first place on your own, that's going to be a new exploration also. That's what I'm trying to tell you, sweetheart. This whole life of ours is an adventure. Sometimes it turns out great. Sometimes, not so much. Sometimes in between. Ups and down and trips and falls and getting up again, but just remember what your grandpa told you. You learn everything you can, and then you make the adventure happen. Learn everything you can, good and bad, and then be the brave girl you are."

"You think I'm brave, Grampa?"

"Yes, I do. You had to be brave to realize that you were a little scared, and come ask me about it. Lots of people aren't brave enough to admit that they're scared. You had to be really brave to take all of Grandma's wool, to measure out how far from here to there. It seems to me the you've been brave ever since you were a little baby."

"I guess being brave isn't always about the big things, the things that everybody cheers about. It sounds like you have to be brave about all the little things. And the medium stuff too."

"You just discovered something that a lot of people never figure out. Being brave is all about the little things, and that's what gets you to the big things. Aziza, you're both brave and smart."

"I don't know about that, Grandpa, but I'll try."

15

On The Courage To Live

I remember when in my freshman year of college, I first learned about cephalo-caudal development, the process that takes place in our first nine months of life through which we learn about our physical body. It astounded me that there was a time when I had no awareness as to where the different parts of my body were, how they moved, what they could do, and how they interacted with everything else out there. I had always felt that knowing about and experiencing my body was a given, a knowledge I had been born with, a preestablished condition. And then I discovered that even my senses had also been required to be learned. Sure, the nervous system worked from the start, but the brain had to learn how to interpret all those messages which it received. Seeing, feeling, smelling and all the rest had been beyond my capability at birth. That was the moment I understood the hidden significance of our being born as a blank slate, a tabula rosa.

The great evolutionary advantage that we human beings have over other animals on this planet has been our ability to learn. Therefore, we do not rely on instinct, which would get us going faster, but also undermine the process of our learning and understanding of who we are and our relationship to our environment. So, it appears that at the onset of our consciousness, we knew nothing of who or what we were, nor anything that constituted the world in which we were residing. We were assaulted with stimuli which we lacked the capability to interpret or understand. Extreme trauma was our first ever experience. Because of our tabula rosa, our initial encounter with life instilled our first, and perhaps our foulest or most malevolent lesson, the fear of the unknown. This fear lays underneath every learning that has followed. No matter how much we learn, no matter how much sagacity we possess, there will always be more that is unknown than known, and the future will always be scary unpredictable.

If fear is a component of our bedrock, must it keep us estranged from the world about us, alienated from our own future? If life entails the ongoing learning of who we are and our relationship to the All and Everything, must we fight ourselves and our predilection to fear every step of the way? This is true only if we lack the courage to turn the next page, to be curious about what will crop up around the next bend of the road, to experience life as an adventure. People ask me, "What is the purpose of fear if it opposes love?" I encourage them to appreciate the balance of love and fear, as they would do well to appreciate all the basic balances. Without a balance of gravity and dark energy, the universe would collapse. Without a balance of the tedious and the extraordinary, life would have no drama. Without a balance of body and mind, we would be constantly ill. Each side of the fulcrum ultimately supports its opposite.

Fear protects us. We avoid that which might threaten our survival because we experience fear. Fear can also paralyze us, render us immobile and subject to attack. As we become more accepting of the balance of fear and love, we know when to practice fight or flight, and when to choose adventure and exploration. An essential component of living a full life is knowing when each respective road is to be followed. When is it appropriate to flee? When is it fitting to be courageous? When do we play it safe? When do we walk on the wild side?

The answers are found in the origins of our embedded fear of the unknown. The process was designed to support our ability to learn. When we have learned knowledge that supports the fear, we would be wise to give integrity to our trepidation. Even here, we need to be clear that we are not generalizing a negative learning about a specific situation or person onto an entire class. If the fear is simply apprehension about the unknown, then we would be equally wise to choose the courageous path.

Life requires courage, if it is to be lived. The courage to experience the infinite possibilities of what may happen in the next moment. The courage to extend ourselves beyond what we already believe about ourselves. The courage to love folks that are different from ourselves. The courage to allow our minds to be free from inner constraint. The courage to allow our self to disappear as we join with what we are part of. The courage to find our missions and pursue our destiny.

Many of us fear life even more than death, because it is the known unknown. Surrounded by a culture that proclaims a world of worry and danger, people hide inside a cocooned existence. Their path becomes short, lacking color or drama. Their love becomes tepid. They can even learn that it is better to protect their children from living.

Every religion has a creation story, in which an energized godhead generated the All and Everything out of nothingness. Beyond the infinite power and glory of this original fabrication of a universe, I like to contemplate the courage it took to generate a universe which was dynamic, in which good and evil, fear and love, matter and energy, space and time, and on, could all interact and produce the drama of life. Our gods had the courage to produce a vibrating, oscillating interactive world, in which order could be found by working through the chaos. I dedicate myself to following their valiant footsteps and having the courage to live in the world that they created.

16

Plans for the wedding needed to be made. Esther and Shen were both clear that they wished it to be a low key, low expense event. As much as Ben was willing to "spend it all" on his daughter's nuptials, and Rose had visions of "some fancy catering joint, like the one for the Rothstein's kid, remember Ben, just last year," the bride and groom were adamant. They would have the wedding in their new back yard, under a tent. Shen had no family other than Lian, and Aunt Phyliss and her brood were about all, on the Shapiro's side of the family, that Ben could tolerate. Most of the invitees were friends of Shen and Esther from their respective jobs, twenty-five or so. Betania and Lian would be the bridesmaids, and, of course, there was no question but that Aziza would be the flower girl. Shen asked Ben to be his best man, and walk both he and Esther down the aisle, together. Predictably, this brought Ben to tears. Esther chose to wear the white suit she had purchased for her MSW graduation. Spending a fortune on some "stupid gown" was out of the question.

She was also insistent that she would do all the cooking herself, with Lian, her mom and Betania helping. Over a month's time the new chest freezer in the basement was loaded with trays of foods that were known to signify good fortune, lentils, longevity noodles, black eyed peas and greens, and kasha varnishkes. The fried chicken and orange salad would have to be prepared just before the event. Rose knew of "that new bakery, the one over in Fresh Meadows," that she had heard made super cakes. All the tables, chairs and serving trays were easily obtained, from the same outfit from which the tent was to be rented. But Rose put her foot down when it came to Esther's wish that they avoid having to clean up china and silverware, and just use plastic. "I'll not have my daughter's wedding and her beautiful food besmirched with such a thing! Esther, you use plastic and I'm not coming! It's either the plastic or me, your mother!" And that was that. The rental company could provide more than enough china.

The one issue that remained to be disentangled was who would preside at the wedding and actually marry them. The family sat in the "old house" dining room, hoping to find a solution which would work for everyone. Esther was clear that Rabbi Goldsheid was "the last person on this planet I would want to marry me," and her father agreed with her. "I can't even think about that ganef, that idiot, without remembering the whole Israel fiasco. He's a ganef, that idiot, a ganef, I tell you."

But who? Shen had no particular religious affiliation, and Esther's identification with Judaism was cultural, not religious. Ben and Rose had always supported the local synagogue, but attendance at services was reserved for High Holy Days, well, at least sometimes, and then, only if they could get a ticket.

Rose agreed that Goldsheid "just wasn't the right fit, although there is some positive history, I might add," but wasn't comfortable with some "politician" justice of the peace, even if Ben did have a connection to that Mayor in Elmont, "you know, the one that helped Sol with that DWI thing."

"I'm not going to have my daughter married by some crooked ticket fixer. That's bad luck, I tell you. No way do we do that."

Shen eventually pointed out that "it seems that none of us have a personal connection to a cleric who we would all be comfortable with. Maybe we need to explore finding a Unitarian minister, or someone like that,"

Aziza had been listening to the conversation from the kitchen, and piped in. "I don't get it. What's the connection betwen religion and getting married? Is a wedding a religious thing? I mean, I know that a lot of people get married in churches and synagogues, but why?

It's a family thing, not a god thing."

The adults were silent for a minute, before Esther finally responded. "You bring up an important question, Honey, but one that we should probably talk about when we have more time to delve into it. Let's just say for now, that religion has been associated with presiding over rites of passage, like weddings, births, becoming adult, and on, for as long as history has been written. But your question makes me think that maybe that's the real issue we're talking about here. Neither Shen nor I are comfortable with most religions, and getting some government agent seems like a cop-out. Who's left? It's not like we can marry ourselves, at least legally. Isn't that what we're dealing with?"

"Wait a minute!" It was Ben. "Rose, do you remember your cousin Emil? You know, that egg-head son of Bernie and Betsy? I think he became a CPA, or something like that. Got married and moved to California. Well anyway, didn't he belong to that, what-do-you call-it, that Ethical Culture Society, that kind of non-religion religion, if you know what I mean. I think that we might want to contact someone from there, someone from that Society."

The solution was at hand. Shen reached out to the Brooklyn Society of Ethical Culture, and found that there were Leaders, who followed their title and served the leadership function for services and rituals, and who were fully licensed by New York State to perform marriages. He was given a list of Leaders who lived in Queens. By the end of the afternoon, Leader Henry Posert was booked. Esther and Shen would meet with him to design the ceremony and create the vows. Before dinner, when they were alone, Esther noted to Shen that "the whole conversation reminds me that I've given no religious education or training to Aziza whatsoever. There's something very wrong about that. It's like I've avoided the subject completely as far as she's concerned, and that leaves her without any basic understanding of a pretty important part of her identity."

"From what you have told me," Shen interjected, "the Hebrew School training you received left you feeling like religion was a lake filled with hypocrites and scammers. It's understandable that you wouldn't want Aziza to swim in those waters."

"Yes, but that doesn't justify avoiding the issue altogether. I'm just saying that like it or not, organized religion is an important slice of society, and I'm not preparing her to deal with it if I keep her ignorant. Besides, while I may not be a believer, Judaism is a big part of my identity, and Aziza's complicated identity is something she's going to have to deal with as she becomes more sophisticated as to her roots."

"So, what do you want to do?"

"I know I don't want to enroll her in any specific religion training. They're all sales jobs, intended to indoctrinate, and that's the last thing she needs. How about for the next couple of months we take some weekend time and visit services at different churches, synagogues, temples and mosques, the three of us, and just explore, talk about and see what she and, even us, are impressed by. You know, this could be a good learning experience for all three of us. What do you think?"

"That would be fine, and come to think of it, fun, but only if we bring a positive attitude to it. You know, I was brought up with the notion that religion was the enemy of the people, the opiate of the masses. It would be easy for me to visit one service after another, finding fault and fraudulency at each stop. That can't be our intention. Can we agree to approach each visit with an eye toward finding goodness, even if in some situations it may be encased by an intermittently malevolent institution?"

"Hey, can we agree to approaching all life, and its institutions, with exactly that attitude? I certainly hope so. It feels like we could both fall into the trap of being tainted by the hurts and deceptions of our pasts. We don't need to go there, and we certainly don't want to pass a negative attitude on to all of our children. Sure, let's make a habit of focusing on the goodness."

"All of our children? Plural? Esther, are you implying something here, or am I interpreting something you weren't intending to say?"

She took a long breath. "Well, ..."

17

Aziza implored that she be allowed to accompany them to meet Leader Posert. She reasoned with her mother that after visits to Buddhist, Catholic, Methodist and two denominations of Jewish services, that an Ethical Culture authority would be important to meet, even if they weren't going to a service. "Mom, I promise that I'll butt out when you and Shen talk about the marriage and your vows. I can even go wait in the car. Please? Please? I just want to see what a no god religion is all about."

Esther found herself fascinated by her daughter's response to her introduction to the world of religion. They had traversed a motley assortment of religions in the last month. Remembering her own petulant and persistent resistance when her parents had sent her to Hebrew school, she wondered how it was that Aziza was responding so differently. Perhaps it had something to do with exploration rather than indoctrination. The process of self-identification needs to be experiential, she reasoned. When our personhood feels dictated, there can hardly be an inner resonance. The only proper reply when being told who you are is rebellion, or at least that had always been her own response.

She was quite proud of Aziza's observational skills, evident in the questions she asked after each new religious encounter. For an eleven-year-old to notice the lack of a choir and the spartan decoration of a conservative Jewish sanctuary, and appreciate the sustained mourning of the 2nd Temple, was impressive. She asked a myriad of questions about relationships, noting how differently the respective clerics related to their congregants, and zeroed in on the nature of the link between priest and receiver during communion. "Is he really acting like a parent, who is feeding his child? I mean, like when he was giving his sermon, he called everybody there his 'children.' Do all religions act so 'parenty'? I mean, you tell me I have to decide when I'm grown up what I want to be, if anything, but most of the places we've visited seem to treat their followers like they were kids. Except for that Buddhist priest. He even talked to me like an adult, when we chatted after the service. I liked him then, but didn't understand a lot of what he was talking about during the service. It was sort of like going to the synagogue, with all those foreign words. Why don't they all just speak the same language that the people who go there speak all the time?

"Come to think about it, is the priest or minister or rabbi or whatever acting like everybody's parent because he thinks God is sort of a parent, just for the whole universe? I mean, it seems like each one of these religions had some kind of story about how their god started everything. You know, Mom, you were around before me, and then you made me, so you're my parent, and these religions all talk about a god that was around before everything else, and then made everything into what it is, and is sort of like a parent to everything. But who said that the universe and everything had to have a god make it. Maybe it made itself."

It was good that Aziza was asking these questions and making these observations, although both she and Shen felt unable to answer many of them. There would be a lifetime to search for answers, even if she was the impatient pre-teen she was. Esther worried about Aziza becoming adolescent. She was already starting to move through puberty. Would she transition into a senseless sensibility, and lose her curiosity behind a veil of know-it-all dismissiveness? Oh, there were times she wished her daughter wasn't so damn beautiful. Good looks hadn't served her well when she was a teen. Right now, Aziza loved when folks noticed and paid attention to her precociousness, and seemed not to care when attention was paid to her physicality, her attractiveness. She nonreacted to compliments about her appearance as if she hadn't heard them, like they were nonsense. Would that change when her hormones kicked in? Esther looked back at her own teenage years with horror and regret, recognizing that had she not become aware of the power of her sexual appearance, she would have focused on other, better sources of power. It was a theme she saw over and over again with the girls she engaged with at work. It felt like the advantage that ultimately disables women, more often than not. Hopefully, Aziza will maintain the priorities she seems to be expressing now, she mused.

Henry Posert had agreed to meet them at his home, in Kew Gardens, so they wouldn't have to drive all the way to Brooklyn. It was a modest Tudor bungalow, on a windy street. His wife met them at the door, and escorted them to Henry's study. Leader Posert was a tall man, a full head over Shen, trim, with short blond hair and wire rim glasses. He was reading at his desk, but immediately rose and greeted them cordially when they entered. "Shen, Esther, how glad to meet you. And who is this that you've brought with you?"

"This is my daughter, Aziza," Esther responded. "She has been studying a wide range of religions, and insisted that she be given the opportunity to find out about The Ethical Culture Society."

"How exciting," Posert replied. "Most usually, people don't seek us out until they are adults and grow frustrated in their attempts to find a spiritual base in which they can feel comfortable. Tell me Aziza, what is it that you would most want to know about Ethical Culture?"

"Like I was telling Mom and Shen, I wondered what a no-god religion could be all about." She stepped forward to engage with the leader.

"Come and find a chair," he said, motioning to the three chairs that surrounded his desk, sitting down himself. Aziza chose the middle chair, directly facing him. Posert continued, "It's more that we don't have a godhead than a god, if you can understand what that implies, Aziza. We see ethics as a requirement for continued existence in this universe, and strive to understand the complexities of ethical considerations in the societies and cultures in which we live. In this respect, ethics itself is our god, that which creates goodness and wisdom. Do you get a feel for what I am saying, Aziza?"

"Sort of. You're saying that God is not some wise old bearded guy that lives in the heavens, but more like guidelines for living well in this world. Like the ten commandments weren't the word of God, but that the commandments themselves were God, or at least godly."

"That's a very good way of saying it, young lady." He turned to Esther, "You have a very special daughter. She captures the nature of who we are very well. But perhaps we should get down to the business at hand. How may I assist you in your upcoming marriage?"

Arrangements for the wedding were easily established. Both Shen and Esther found Henry, as he preferred to be addressed, a delightful and sagacious man, and hoped that this relationship which they were forming would go beyond his presiding at their wedding. They had been discussing the content of their vows ever since they decided to marry, and Henry agreed that their declarations to each other appeared to suit who they were and the marriage they intended to live. He would be delighted to be part of their ceremony. He also suggested that Aziza's role extend beyond her flower girl duties, and that as a vital member of the newly forming family, "She too should get to talk a bit about the role she wanted to play. It is easy to focus on the relationship of the wedding couple and not realize how impactful a marriage is for the children. I have a feeling that this wise young lady I have just met will have some important contributions to this ceremony."

"Mom does say that I'm always putting my two cents in everything. Yeah, I'd like to do that. Is it OK with you guys?"

Shen responded before Esther could break through her smile with words. "It would be more than OK, kiddo. Your two cents is a hundred dollars to Mom and me."

18

The weather on the day of the wedding couldn't have been more perfect. Gainsborough cumulus clouds reigned over a clear autumn day, making the tent all but superfluous. A hundred pots of chrysanthemums had been preordered from a local nursery, and showered the back yard with their colorful display, way beyond anything that a florist might have created. Esther had laid out the folding seats in the back yard in two concentric circles, surrounding a flowery chuppah which she and Shen had made together in the garage. "I don't want this to feel like a proscenium stage, a dramatic production with us here and an audience there," she had said to Henry. "Besides, circles are more representative of what marriage should be all about, like rings, never-ending and suggesting fulfillment. I don't want there to be any right angles in our life. They suggest opposition and lack the sense of waves or the arc of time."

The smaller inner circle was reserved for family, and the closest of friends. The outer circle seated associates and colleagues and acquaintances. Esther and Shen stood by each other's side under a chuppah, Leader Posert in front of them, with the flower girl, Aziza, just off to the right. Posert seemed to grow even taller as he proclaimed, "We are gathered here today to share in the wedding celebration of Esther and Shen. As a leader of the Ethical Culture

Society, I find myself honored to preside in their joining together. I find it a blessing that I have had the opportunity to meet folks who care so much about representing the best of what humanity can offer. Look around you and note how carefully this couple have dedicated this wedding to peace and beauty and love, not just their love, but love as an active, powerful human force. It speaks well to who they are, their families, and their future as a couple. They appear to me to be committed to serving their communities with their considerable talents. They pride themselves as being the product of family and culture, extending back untold generations, yet hope to bring fresh and vital insight into the family traditions they will be creating for themselves and their children. I experience them to be a thoughtful, conscious and loving couple. I truly celebrate their love which I have been privileged to be near and connect to." He paused and then asked, "Esther, would you like to share with us the wedding vows you are declaring today?"

She turned to her intended, took his hand in hers, and brought it to his cheek. "Shen, it is my clear intention to be the best partner with you that I am capable of being. I will seek to be loyal, positioning our union with the highest of my priorities. I will consistently strive to resolve our differences in a manner through which we understand and respect each other's points of view, and seek to find common responses to our conflicts. I will make every effort to care for, protect and cherish your mind, body and soul, from this day forward, for the rest of my life. I will look to learn with you, to support your missions in life, and to share my callings and passions with you. I will do my utmost to protect, maintain and build our love, knowing that our union is a foundation piece for each of us individually, our family, and the many communities to which we belong. May our love be a force which is freeing to ourselves and those that we love."

"And you Shen. Would you share your vows with us?"

He continued to hold her hand, but drew it to his chest. "I promised my mother, shortly after she brought us to America, that I would never betray my father's sense of righteousness. She felt that she needed, in his absence, to remind me that my life was dedicated to principles that are an outgrowth of many generations of our family. As part of that process, she needed to be reassured that for both my sister, Lian, and myself, we would seek a life partner whose world view was consistent with our origins. I remember her holding up her finger to my face and saying, in Mandarin, 'I don't care if she is ugly, or poor, but she must be a match for your character.' How lucky am I that I have found you Esther, whose sensibilities are in agreement with hers, and, remarkably, you are so beautiful, as well.

"I promise you today that I will also endeavor, every day, to be the best partner that I am capable of being, no matter what my mood or what the tenor of that day might be. I promise to give more energy to listening to you than to speaking to you. I vow to follow you when you lead, and to lead you when you follow, but mostly to walk our path of life side by side. I will always seek to care for and protect you and our family from all the dangers that life may manufacture. I will support your strengths and your undertakings, and look to include you in mine. I will treat our love with the care, respect and energy which it deserves. I promise all of this, from this day forward, for the rest of my days."

Henry took both of their hands and clasped them in his. "Your union is strong, and your vows are moving. I'm sure I speak for all of us when I say that this marriage which you have just defined validates our beliefs in love and the potential for 'coupledom'. But there is one more member of this family, and this new union, who is willing and wanting to share her feelings and intentions with us today. Aziza, would you please address us all?"

Aziza stepped forward in between her mom and Shen, who turned toward her. Ben, and most everyone who knew her well, found themselves surprisingly startled, observing a girl who had suddenly blurred the line between girl and woman. It was a transformative moment. She stood tall and proud, secure in addressing the gathering without notes.

"I'm so fortunate to be able to be a part of this wedding. When my Mom and my Dad, yes Shen, I'm going to call you Dad, get used to it! Anyway, when Mom and Dad, and Mr. Posert asked me if I wanted to say something for this wedding today, I wasn't so sure about it. After all, weddings are supposed to be about the bride and groom, and not the kid. But when I thought about it, Mr. Posert was right, my family was changing, with Shen coming into it, and I was a part of that change, and not just in the ways that it would have an effect on me. I mean, each of us is going to cause things to be different as much as the situation will cause us to experience things differently. And I guess that includes Grandma and Grandpa and Aunt Lian too. So, it kind of makes sense for me to include my promises, my vows about this whole new family we're setting up today.

"It looks like I'm going to have less attention from Mom, with Shen, I mean Dad, coming into the picture. But then again, I'm going to be gaining a lot more attention from him. It's okay. I promise that I'm going to trust that the plusses and minuses all work out, and I'm not going to become one of those whiney kids who always wants more just because things have changed. You know, the ones who want it like it was, but also want all the good stuff from what's new. Besides, you all are going to have to get used to the idea that I'm not going to be around as much as I always have been when I was younger. And I guess you all know that I'm going to have a brother or sister pretty soon, so I'm going to have to be good with sharing family with the new baby also.

"But what I really want to promise, is that I will never forget how lucky I am to have the family that I have. I'm fortunate in many ways, but the family I was born into is at the top of the list, and now, it's all only increasing. I hope I can live up to who we are. I guess most of you know my grandpa, Ben. He's the best. I mean, he doesn't have a whole lot of degrees, but I think he knows more than most anybody I know, even if he's always repeating himself when he tells you what you need to know, but he's the kindest most loving person I know. And, Mom, she takes after him, cut out of the same cloth, to use Grandpa's phrase, if you ask me. And it's not surprising that she's marrying Shen, because he's sort of like Grandpa also. Mom picked a good one, just like Grandma did.

"So, what I'm really saying is, this family of mine is really good at this love thing, and I'm making a vow that I'm going to try to be as good at loving as the rest of the family."

As Henry had the bride and groom kiss each other and declared that they were now officially married, Ben found himself once more lost in tears. The span of the last dozen or so years, from when all that difficulty with Esther happened, to now, when things were as perfect as they could ever be, the entire timeline flashed forward, and joy simply filled his heart. He remembered his father talking to him on the day he married Rose. "There are going to be good days, Benny, and there are going to be bad days. Good times, bad times. Just keep doing your best, your very best, mind you, and there will be a lot more of the good days than bad days." Dad was right. Just keep doing your best. Somehow or other it will somehow work out.

He turned to Rose, to share this wonderful moment in their lives. But something wasn't right. Something was terribly wrong. Her face seemed locked, staring ahead, but with a flustered expression, and a few drops of drool running down her chin. At one and the same time her side near to him went tense, and she collapsed into him. Shielding her from falling, he yelled out, "Rose, what's wrong?", but she didn't answer, as the guest in back of them helped ease her to the ground. "Esther! Esther! Call 911! Mommy needs help!"

There was a rush of commotion and a guest from Esther's work, a doctor, came and took her pulse, shook his head, and began to pump her chest, desperate to try and bring life back to her. For fifteen minutes he worked on Rose's still body, while the horrified assemblage looked on in shock, helpless to change the moment back to the fullness of joy that was now totally vanished. Eventually, he shook his head again, and stood, turning to Esther and sharing, "I'm sorry. There's nothing more to do. She's gone."

19

Ben insisted that they hold the shiva in his house, and not across the street. "Your house should hold the joy, not the sorrow. That is for me. It's bad enough that Mommy died in the middle of a blessing, but somehow or other, we have to keep our joys and our sorrows separate. They shouldn't bleed into each other." He didn't want to hear about life holding pleasure and pain as part of the two sides of experience. "Duality, schmuality!" He intended to bear as much of the sting by himself, and to shield Esther and Aziza from living in her death. "Sure. Sure. They love her and mourn her like I do, but they don't need to spend all their time smack in the middle of their grief. Just maybe I can help them all get away from it for some minutes here and there." In mourning, Ben needed to be Ben, and find some way to direct his energy to making it better for them. That's what his marriage had been all about, and it was the only way he could salvage himself.

Aziza wandered through both sides of the street. Grandma and Grandpa's house was full of people, in and out, and back again. While she knew a lot of them, there were many she had no idea who they were, or how they were connected to Grandma. She watched all the foodstuffs piling up on the dining room table, the one Grandma was always telling everyone to keep their stuff off of. The casseroles and fruit baskets just reminded her of all the food that had gone uneaten at the wedding. She wasn't hungry and couldn't imagine ever eating again. Did grownups all drown their sorrows in kugels and babkas? There were these two "receptions" side by side, and none of it made any sense to her. Many of the same people who cried at the wedding, during the ceremony, not when Grandma died, many of these same people were laughing and talking business at the shiva. She heard people talking about "celebrating Rose's life," and couldn't get how they could jump from the immediacy of the death to some big old cheery overview of the life that had been lost. Nobody talked about the cemetery and the horror of watching the box with Grandma in it, going into the ground.

On the other side of the street, it was just as confusing. Mommy cried constantly at home, but as soon as she crossed the street she acted like a hostess at a party. Shen hovered about Mom, which was good, because she wanted to help Mom herself, but had no idea how to do that. Aunt Lian seemed at a loss about how to act in a situation where she couldn't make jokes or try to lighten things up. Mostly, Aziza felt alone, something that she had never felt before. This was quite new. All of these people were walking around on both sides of the street, but they weren't relating to her and she had no idea about how to relate to them. She felt guilty that she wanted Grandpa and Shen to console her, and not just Mom, even though she knew that Mom needed their attention more than she did. She gasped when she wondered what it would feel like if she lost her mother, and that felt like a very selfish thought. Especially just a few days after she had told everybody that she wasn't going to be one of those selfish and self-centered kids.

At some point she realized that it felt like no one, especially the adults, knew enough about death to deal with it. They said all these empty sayings and comforting baloney to each other, but it all seemed like such an act, like let's get this whole thing in back of us by playacting a ritual. One that they could revisit, and replay the tape, every time somebody else died. In a moment of insight she wished was untrue, Aziza realized that adulthood was really an illusion, made up for people to pretend that they weren't children who didn't know what they thought they should know, and didn't have the powers they wanted to have.

Henry Posert might be someone to talk to. She needed someone. While she hadn't known him for a long time, it felt like he was a person she could look to for some clarity, if not comfort. He knew about this stuff, and it felt like he understood her. Aziza knew that Posert had been to the shiva a number of times, and was relieved when she saw his car outside. He had to be somewhere inside. She found him talking to Aunt Lian, in the dining room. They were in the middle of a conversation, so she stood near, waiting for an opportunity to pull him aside, if possible.

"Hi, Sweetie," Lian saw and addressed her, "do you need me for anything?"

"Actually, I was hoping to speak to Mr. Posert, for a minute. But I don't want to butt into your conversation."

"No, we're good. Just sharing some thoughts about China and religion, and a whole lot of seemingly important stuff, or nonsense, depending on your point of view. He's all yours, kiddo." She left and walked into the living room.

"It's good to see your, Aziza. What can I do for you?"

"I don't want to be a nuisance, Mr. Posert. But there were a few things I wanted to talk with you about. Would you mind if we talked on the back porch? I think we'd probably be able to be alone there."

"Aziza, I've been thinking a lot about you these past couple of days, and frankly, I've been concerned. This has got to be an incredibly difficult experience for you. I would be very happy to have a chat with you."

They wound their way through the crowded kitchen, and found some solitude on the screened-in porch. A couple of all-weather chairs looked out on the back yard, and Aziza found one of them, with Posert following. They looked out on the garden, whose foliage was just past the cusp of changing to fall colors. The lawn was blanketed with oranges and yellows, the beautiful beginning of the end that was to come. It took a minute for Aziza to initiate their conversation, and Posert was patient, knowing she needed to gather her thoughts.

Eventually she ventured, "I've been thinking a lot about death, I mean not just Grandma's death, and a lot of my thoughts seem to go in circles and confuse me."

"Well, that puts you in very good company, Aziza. Many of the world's greatest thinkers have said something of that kind. What in particular about death and dying seems to befuddle you? It's a pretty big topic."

"I just keep thinking about the moment of death. I mean, one second Grandma is there, and then poof, in the next moment she's not. It doesn't make any sense to me how life could suddenly just not be there. The body is there. The tissue is there. What went away? I mean, I know Grandma had a stroke, and that her brain, I guess, got flooded with blood. I understand the medical end of things. Maybe I'm not asking about death at all. Maybe I need to have a better understanding of what life is, before I can understand what the loss of life means."

Henry paused for a moment before he answered. He thought to himself that children have the ability to get to the heart of things, unlike adults who have learned how to avoid and obfuscate. Eventually, he rolled into responding to her. "You are a wise girl, Aziza. You ask the important questions, even if they are the difficult questions. Here's what I can tell you. We human beings have been searching for an understanding of what constitutes life, for as long as we have had the ability to reflect on our existence. That's why the ancients came up with a notion of 'soul', an essence of life which couldn't be seen, but could be thought of as unique to every being. Many religions and philosophers have thought that the soul goes on, long after the body is gone. Biologists have long speculated that life began when all the right chemicals were in place and some special energy came along, often thought to be lightening, and sparked life into existence. While that gives life a start, for the planet as a whole, it doesn't address the issue of individual life. More lately, some neurobiologists have talked about a particular small gland in the brain, the pineal gland, and think about some energy that comes and goes from that tiny gland as being what brings life to a body, and what takes it away in its absence.

"However, any way we look at it, nobody knows, not in religion, not in science, not in philosophy, no one knows for sure the nature of the energy that ultimately constitutes life. They may have beliefs, but not for sure, for certain, knowledge. There is one thing that we do know for sure, that energy can never be destroyed. It can be transformed, but never destroyed. So, what I can tell you is that in the moment of death, the moment that you're thinking about, there is some kind of transformation of the energy of life, whatever the nature of that energy is. Some folks think of that transformation as going to heaven. Some folks think of that transformation as reincarnation, being transformed into another life form. Some folks think of the energy moving from one universe to another. But nobody knows for sure exactly what the life energy is or how it transforms."

"So, when somebody dies, is their energy transformed in a way that they're still them?", Aziza asked. "I mean, like when water is boiled and goes up as steam into the air, it mixes with all the other water in the air, it just makes more humidity. Can we tell if the energy, or soul, or whatever it is, gets spread out into everything, or does it keep its own specialness?"

"Again, you get to the heart of the matter, Aziza. Does the energy that is being transformed after death maintain its integrity? That's one of the big questions that a lot of serious people debate, but no one can know for sure. I wish I could give you an answer, but I can't."

"I guess you'd have to be dead to know, but then you wouldn't be able to tell me anyhow," Aziza mused.

"Well, let me tell you what I am capable of relating to you. Aziza. You and your grandma loved each other. And that means while you were both still here on this planet Earth, you shared your Earthly energies with each other. She became a part of you and you became a part of her. Loving means the sharing of who we are with someone else, and once shared, that energy is a part of you that cannot be taken away. Grandma may have died, but some of her energy will reside in you forever."

Aziza contemplated this. "But does that mean that some of my energy died with her, that some of my energy became transformed with hers?"

Posert smiled, appreciating the moment when he was learning from a child. "I've never thought of it like that, but I think you have to be right. Some part of you has been transformed with her, some way, somewhere, somehow."

"This energy stuff is really confusing. I keep going back and forth about how much I want to think about it, you know, death and energy and life and stuff, or how much I would feel better pretending it doesn't matter. I mean, I've been listening to a lot of the adults inside, and the way they blow the whole thing off, and then they say a lot of silly stuff to avoid thinking about the hard stuff, and it really annoys me. But are they, maybe, better off, not thinking about things that sometimes can't be answered anyway?"

Once again Henry admired how a barely adolescent girl could have such insight. "I think you are asking a larger question, Aziza. Some people think ignorance and denial are bliss. They want to go about their lives and not contemplate issues that don't have immediate or comfortable answers. They want to feel secure in their lives, and feel that the big questions will leave them unsettled, or afraid. Luckily, other people have the courage to look at and question all the unanswerables, knowing that this is the only way to eventually get to the higher truths. For those of us like you, who naturally question most everything, it would be difficult to avoid and hide behind ignorance. Perhaps this is a blessing, although it leaves you uncomfortable or troubled at times."

"Grandpa talks about the courage to live. Maybe this is part of what he means."

"I would think so. Your Grandpa strikes me as tangibly wise. Hopefully his wisdom will help him get through a difficult time, right now."

Aziza went inside for moment or so before asking, "Mr. Posert, is it fear then that makes so many people believe in some daddy-like god, some supernatural person who will help them avoid thinking about the questions that make them nervous? It's kinda weird that grownups end up being so much more afraid of everything then kids. You'd think it would be the other way around."

"You'd think so, you'd think so. Just make sure you follow your Grandpa's advice and hold onto your courage. You're a brave girl Aziza."

"You and Mommy and Grandpa keep telling me that. I'm not so sure."

20

On Staying A Child

Many people divide life into stages. Such as "child vs. adult." Subsequently there is usually a further division of those stages into substages, like "infant, toddler, pre-teen and adolescent" and "young adult, adult, middle-ager and geriatric." Through this process of the segmentation of a life, they suggest that life is cumulative, that we achieve various life skills at each age, and then move on to new life challenges in the next stage, armed with previous learnings. There is value to this segmentation. For example, children shouldn't have to deal with earning a living, or sexuality, before an appropriate time. We would hope that these issues don't arrive until adulthood, when minds and bodies are better prepared and able to engage in a healthy manner.

However, this segmentation or chopping up of our lifespans can also have a deleterious effect, if applied to attitudes. When we assign specific attitudes to one life stage and imply that it is only relevant to that time of life, a considerable loss can take place. To posit loss of an attitude in subsequent stages goes against the notion of life skills and learnings being cumulative. For example, we expect and appreciate that children are curious, enquiring and seeking to gain an understanding about their relationship to the universe in which they find themselves. Yet, upon reaching "adulthood," many of us find these attitudes to be anachronisms, better left to adolescent years or even younger. These folks fear that continued exploration into the understanding of who we are, what the universe is, and the possible relationships between the two would interfere with pragmatic responsibilities. They believe that childhood should have given them a base for an understanding of self and world, and that now that they are all grown up it, is the time to accomplish, to provide, to make one's mark on the world. Questioning one's footing could interfere with this new life stage. They don't want to be "childish." They consider the lingering of bewildered and questioning attitudes as naive, or possibly even weak. These matters are supposed to be done with, and whatever could not be answered in childhood, becomes assigned to a category of "unanswerable by humans," the territory of faith, beliefs and religion. It is fascinating that at the same time that people abandon a spiritual attitude of their own, they assign it to gods and institutions, an outsourcing of their spirituality. That is to say that as soon as they become adult in the worldly sense, assuming adult responsibilities, they become children in the spiritual sense, abandoning their adult responsibilities.

The essential question here is what is meant by "unanswerable"? Are issues that cannot be answered in the immediate to be forever left in such a category? Some would have it so, despite history telling us that over time the incomprehensible can turn and achieve a transformative clarity, and relationships that were undecipherable can become solved. This brings to mind the unnecessary conflicts between that which previously was assigned to faith, and knowledge that is gained at a later time. History is replete with such battles. How could our planet revolve around the Sun when we once believed that the Earth is the center of the universe? How can evolution have taken place over millions of years when we once believed that God made everything in one week? These conflicts arise because of an insistence that what is unanswerable and accepted on faith remain so at a future date. When rigid belief systems replace the child's mindset of exploration, much is lost for both the individual and the society.

What if we abandoned the category of "unanswerable by humans," and replaced it by "what we currently have no clue about" or "without a working hypothesis"? What if we accepted that what we think is axiomatic is basically what appears to be now? What if we maintained our child's sensibility of everything being forever new and subject to investigative scrutiny after we gained our majority? The child needn't be the "father of the man," but can exist side by side with his successor. Wonder and awe are not the enemy of pragmatism. The perpetuation of wonder and awe is necessary for spirituality to remain strong in our hearts and minds as we progress through all life stages.

If we are able in this respect to maintain the attitude of a child, we will undoubtably experience various levels of cognitive dissonance along the way. Every time we run across a conflict between what we thought to be true and a new and different learning, we will probably experience such a dissonant anxiety. However, if we maintain our childish attitude, we can experience a delight in life presenting us with a new dialectic, and therefore, a new opportunity for resolution. In adulthood as in childhood, it is the application of wonder to a dialectic conflict that yields the joy when a new vision bursts out of the nether. This is the heart of mystical thinking. This is the source of the ongoing spirit.

Popular psychology asks us to care for our "inner child." That is wise advice. While doing this, I would additionally implore you to allow your inner child to care for the adult you. If you can maintain the attitude of your child, you will bring vigor to your marriage, as you realize new facets of your partner every day. You will welcome conflicts because you know they carry the opportunity to bring new resolutions and advances in your family life.

If you can maintain the attitude of your child, you will achieve greater success in your work as you discover both new problems and new solutions. You will welcome the moments of daydreaming as opportunities to break free from the binds of assumptions.

If you can maintain the attitude of your child, your relationship with the All and Everything will grow stronger over time. Communion or prayer will be an opportunity for curiosity and exploration. Your spiritual vision will grow wider and will deepen.

Welcome what feels unanswerable with wonder!

Part Four

1

One would have thought that Aziza would be exceedingly popular in High School. Her beauty was unequaled. As she moved past puberty, the very pretty girl was transformed into that rare person who truly took people's breath away at a single glance. Her long jet-black straight hair contrasted with her warm ivory skin. Piercing blue eyes reflected the brilliance of mind they stood before. Everything about her was sharp, yet softened as the parts came together with a hard-to-define grace. As is common with young women whose physical presence is stunning, Aziza did nothing to accentuate her appearance. If anything, she did her best to downplay it. She never wore make up, and tended to conceal her body, which had become statuesque, under drab and droopy clothing, so that unwanted attention might be minimized. But her willowy movements gave away the secret behind the cloth. As did the natural ability to laugh, cry, or experience any emotion with outward abandon. Folks who are uncommonly beautiful don't fathom becoming embarrassed by how their image might be judged, even when they have lost their composure. At some point, a high school friend commented to her, without rancor, "I hate you. You even laugh beautifully."

It isn't that Aziza was unpopular. She just had no interest in competing for anyone's attention or friendship. An excellent student, in all honors classes, she didn't want to hang out exclusively with the "preppies," even if she enjoyed some of their company some of the time. Being with any group exclusively didn't sit well with her. Aziza wanted to feel free to enjoy the company of anyone and everyone, and didn't like being filed away in a folder with any one group. She found her friends here and there, and while known and recognized by most everyone in her school, she avoided being labeled and constrained by the usual adolescent groupings. It wasn't her style to have some entrenched peer driven style. While the overall impression that most students had of her was positive, there was an undercurrent of resentment for what was fairly obvious, that she didn't care much either way about their approval or acceptance. Some kids identified her as "stuck up, thinks she's too good for us." The truth was, Aziza just wasn't into comparing herself to anyone. She knew instinctively that all personal comparisons were invalid.

If anything, she was the unofficial leader of the non-group group. The smallest of the teen groups in the school, it was comprised of Aziza and her three closest friends. They were a motley group, who had little in common other than being bright and ferociously averse to adolescent cliques. Even if most of their literary tastes didn't jibe with each other, they all located "Stranger In A Strange Land" and "Catcher In The Rye" at the center of their fictional universe. These four kids "groked" each other."

Billy "Moose" Evans lived up to his nickname. At six foot four and 275 pounds, he dwarfed Aziza wherever they went, and they traveled together often. Approached by the football coach to join the team a couple of times, Moose declined with a mocking smile. "Coach Strong, I'm pretty sure you don't want me on your team. I'm probably the clumsiest oaf in the totality of this great city of New York. I'd be stomping all over my teammates, and missing the guys on the other team. Besides, I'm a pacifist through and through, and frankly don't get off on sports at all. Doesn't sound like a super pick up for you, does it?" Moose's self-assessment of his coordination, or rather the lack of it, was basically accurate. But what he lacked in physical dexterity, he had in abundance in his mental proficiency. In his science and math classes, he was that kid who was only called on in class when no one else raised their hand. It was a foregone conclusion that he had the answer. He was expected by his engineer father to follow in his footsteps, and Moose did entertain the possibility, but his love of science fiction drew him to Astro-physics, or maybe human factors engineering.

Moose's social bearings were less predictable. His personality was more passive than aggressive, but there was another side. Mostly he was submissive, that big guy who would defer to other people's assertions, even if he knew better. But when it came to issues that really mattered to him, watch out! The big mouse turned into a lion in a flash. He'd yank cigarettes out of people's mouths, and tell them to stop killing themselves. He was on to the climate crisis long before it was a "cause," and called out energy transgressions wherever and with whoever he ran across them. When the high school, a building constructed in the 50's, installed air-conditioning, he was the lone objector, marching by himself in front of the school's entrance in August, with a large placard proclaiming, "IT'S NOT COOL TO WASTE ENERGY! WE'RE NOT WIMPS!" Actually, it was while conducting this protest, in between his sophomore and junior years, that he and Aziza became friends. She was the only student who, upon hearing about this sole objector to everyone's comfort zone, went to see him on his solitary picket line. She just needed to find out what he and it was all about.

Alex Mendez, lived around the corner from Aziza, and while they had known each other since they were toddlers in the playground, didn't become friends until high school, right around the same time that Alex uncloseted himself. About as small as Moose was large, Alex was all about the arts. He fancied opera with the zest that most of his peers reserved for the Rolling Stones. Most of the time he could be seen walking around with his sketch-pad, the small game hunter stalking for things of beauty. He was openly gay, and actually welcomed the moments when he might be verbally abused, seeming to enjoy calling out the idiots that thought they were taunting him. Of course, if the derision was accompanied with a physical threat, he was glad to have Moose around. He had a lot of smart-ass in him, and was often just this side of putting himself in one danger or the other. Aziza worried that he would someday put his life in jeopardy by his brashness with fools, but he wasn't deterred. He just responded by advising her that "Your looks have a greater potential for assault than my flippancy. And you don't even go out of your way for attention, like some of us morons do."

The last member of the non-group group was Alicia Walters, a precocious Goth poet of sorts. Alicia's lamented that "true bohemianism" was over, that the baton had been mistakenly passed to a "hippy" generation, which had lost the depth of character of the beatniks who preceded them. Her idols were Jack Kerouac and Anais Nin. She longed to be anywhere but in Queens, always in her head planning her life in Paris, Haight Ashbury or Tangiers. Tall, but delicate in frame, she wore rings on all but one of her fingers, reserving the right to flip someone off without adornment. She made a point of her earrings never matching. Her hair was consistently changing, black to blond to green, as Alicia demanded of herself that her anonymity be seen.

While philosophically opposed to sports and competition, she religiously watched roller derby whenever she could on television, rooting for her team, the Brooklyn Red Devils, who could kick ass with the best. "No, it's not a sport," she would declare. "It's regulated violence, and I love it!" A vegetarian, her diet consisted of her three essential food groups, vegetables, Snickers Bars and weed. Behind all the affectation was a sweet girl, kind and generous to her friends, easily hurt, and ready to put on her sneakers, run and hide at the slightest hint of rejection. Aziza was the only female peer she had grown to trust.

When they could, the group liked to hang out in Aziza's basement. Her parents were pretty cool, for parents. They didn't react to stuff the way their own parents did, especially Esther, Aziza's mom. She worked with kids in East Harlem, and knew what was what with this generation. Sometimes, Alicia would come by to see Aziza, and instead proceed to spend hours with Esther, Lian and Betania. They became a kind of triumvirate surrogate mothering team for her. Alicia's relationship with her own mother had degenerated into a constant battle, in which her mother consistently argued about what her daughter looked like, and how she was a poor reflection of the family. Her daughter's appearance was experienced as a rejection by her parents, no matter how many times Alicia tried to communicate that this was her "own deal," and that she wasn't acting out the rebel, with or without cause. Lian had the ability to make Alicia laugh, even when she was steaming mad. Lian had that way of making your most ludicrous argumentations seem funny, even to yourself. They would sit for hours in the kitchen, the moms giving Alicia a space to complain and vent her spleen, eventually getting the teenager to accept what she really wanted, a surrender on her own terms.

Moose, on the other hand, was a devotee of Shen. The conversation here didn't differ much from his talks with his own father, but he could trust that Shen didn't come from a place of self-interest, wasn't motivated by a parental need to steer his child in one direction or the other. One of the things that Moose had observed recently was the way adults always seemed to have hidden agendas with kids his age, were always utilizing covert communication to maneuver them in the direction they wanted. Whenever he felt this, he became irritated, turned in and tuned off. But Shen, while as quick-witted as Moose's dad, never exhibited a scent of manipulative quality. He was just simply interested in who you were. The two would often walk around the garden, sometimes in Cunningham Park, lost in science and technology.

And, of course, everyone loved playing with Roulan, Aziza's baby sister, who had just celebrated her third birthday. Getting a babysitter was never difficult for Esther and Shen whenever they would get a rare night out, and neither Ben nor Aziza was able to fill the role. The list of available teens who adored taking care of her was endless.

In the years after Rose's passing, the communal nature of the Shapiro "compound" grew in numbers, with Aziza's friends joining the mix. The two houses on either side of 197th Street, exuded a vibrant and exiting energy, a diverse and inclusive feel, that attracted a multigenerational camaraderie. For everyone, it just felt over-the-top good to be acknowledged and accepted without predefinition.

2

Aziza's family was the first in the area to have a home computer. Shen had brought home a Macintosh, confident that it would be an aide in handling the family's finances, and hoping that Aziza would gain a facility for computerization. He was certain this would be a benefit for her education. When they went to Radio Shack to browse the various programs that could be used for keeping records, they were all amazed at the range of programs available for purchase. Home decoration, cake decoration, garden planting schemes, games of all sorts and, of course, Microsoft Word. They came home with an assortment of new electronic goodies, and for a while, the competition to use the computer replaced the old arguments about what show to watch on the boob tube. Esther began using the word processor to write all her process report for the agency, and now kept all her client records in screen folders. Shen found that he could not only keep financial records for the home, but could do probability studies without travelling to work. Even Roulan began to insist that she wanted to play Lemonade Stand and Reader Rabbit. Esther and Shen had a conversation about buying a second computer, maybe a Tandy, but found it hard to justify the expense. That issue was resolved when Ben, who had recently retired, settled the matter and purchased a Mac for his own home He secretly wanted it to be an inducement for the kids to hang out at his house. And maybe he could keep up with the times by learning a few things or two, himself. Maybe he could do that.

For Aziza, the computer created a major inflection point in her adolescence. At first, she was continually seated at one of the computers or the other, sometimes learning to program or playing Tetris, but mostly she was writing. Word processing allowed her to release all the obsessive thoughts that had been incessantly swirling around her mind for years, to give them flow, to gain direction, and to find meaning and clarity. It was different than throwing your ideas to paper. It felt to her like her thoughts could evolve, right there in front of her. The frequent talks she had with Henry took on a new direction, as she began to print out a page or two of her ramblings and ruminations, throw them in an envelope and post them so he would receive her missive in a day or two. Invariably, he would reply back to her within a week, responding to her ideas, praising her precocious insight and suggesting some philosophical or theosophical directions which she hadn't considered. He had become something of a philosophical/spiritual mentor over the past two years.

A regular progression began to unfold which lasted most of Aziza's junior and senior years in high school. She would have conversations with her friends, mostly Alicia and Alex, full of adolescent angst and social commentary, which in turn would prompt Aziza to spend hours at the computer trying to work out one more of the unfathomable unanswerable issues the world presented. At some point an insight would germinate out of somewhere within {or was it without} her, and she would rush to get it out of her head and on paper. She'd print it and read her musings over a few times, ultimately either throwing it out, feeling it offered no sense at all, or, if it continued to positively resonate, she would mail it to Henry.

"Thank God, or whatever, for Leader Posert," she would often ponder. "Somehow or other he leads me through this wilderness in which I perpetually find myself. Am I the only freak who feels compelled to wrestle with all this, I don't know what to call it, ..., all this cosmic shit? How nice it would be to worry about a prom dress or a football game, or something normal. Even Alicia, freaky as she is, has her roller derby. Well then, I guess I should also thank that Russian, Pajitnov for bequeathing me Tetris!"

Often, with her mind racing around in circles, going nowhere, the next thought eluding her, a feasible solution just beyond cognition, she would turn to the falling pieces for relief. The correct placement of the next dropping Tetrinimo into the complex matrix gave Aziza a sense of completion, sorely needed after tussling with her internal enigmatic puzzles. Sure, there was always another falling shape to deal with, and eventually the tide became overpowering, but along the way order could be brought to chaos, and her mind would still. There was satisfaction. An experience of a sense of closure would fill her, if only for a fleeting moment.

Like so many others of her peers, she began to spend more time with the game. She used it before writing to calm herself down. It served the function of taking a little break here and there, whether from writing or from homework. Tetris became her steadying mechanism, her turn-to device in all manners of life for calming herself, for self-soothing, for tamping down the waves of obsession. In some ways it was better than pot. Hell, it was even legal. But at the point when she found herself waking in the middle of the night, with shapes falling into perfect apertures in her dream, Aziza began to worry. She remembered a conversation with her mom about the differences between addiction and dependency, and this sure felt like she was becoming all too mentally reliant on that click which went off in her head when the shapes converged and disappeared.

The next morning, Aziza approached Esther, and asked if they could talk. "Mom," she began, "I know this sounds kind of lunatic, but I think I'm becoming addicted, or maybe dependent to Tetris," and she proceeded to share the way it seemed to be taking over her thoughts and time. "I really got freaked out this morning when it was invading my dreams. I mean, that space is supposed to be reserved for symbols of fear and rejection and sex and stuff, not colored shapes falling from space."

Esther successfully hid her amusement. At exactly the age when she herself had become addicted to heroin, her daughter feared becoming strung out on a computer game. Not that there wasn't an issue here, but at least life wasn't paying her back for the struggles she had put her parents through. "Well, you know that it's a distraction and a self-soothing mechanism. Do you think that Tetris is the problem, or is the issue really some level of stress or anxiety which needs to be calmed?"

"I don't know. I mean I wouldn't call it anxiety. It's just that sometimes I feel I need to focus, and the thoughts that I need are just the other side of somewhere I can't reach. If I think about it, it's more frustration than stress or anxiety."

"So, we're really talking about frustration. What if you can't resolve all the world's remaining theosophical conundrums before your seventeenth birthday? Seriously, honey, what's driving this rush of yours? Give yourself time to read and learn. Isn't this the time in your life to be discovering more questions than answers?"

"I guess I know that. But, once I get on some train of thought, it's awfully hard to disembark. Sometimes I call it an obsession, but other times if feels more like a calling, I guess.'

"Well then, maybe the distraction of Tetris isn't such a bad thing. It is giving you some time to breath in between your wrangling with ideas, and it seems important to you to follow what you term a calling." She motioned for Aziza to come by her, and embraced her. "Of course, maybe if you allowed yourself to be a teenager and got obsessed with sex, drugs and rock n' roll, you wouldn't be getting so dependent on some mindless computer game." They both laughed.

"Sorry Mom. That was your thing, from what you've told me. Not to be a disappointment, but I'm just too nerdy. Must be like Grandpa says, it skips a generation."

"And I've got no complaints about that. Good for that!"

3

On The Value Of Distraction

When we were children, most of us were frustrated when we found that we couldn't be in two places at the same time. We wanted to be outside playing with our friends, but wanted simultaneously to be home in the kitchen, able to sneak a goodie from the cookie jar. We wished we could enjoy sleeping in bed but concurrently be downstairs listening to the grown-up's conversation. We felt burdened that we couldn't jointly go to school and also be seated with the clowns at the circus. It wasn't fair. The world was immense, with billions of events happening in every microsecond, and it felt like we were missing out on most of it because we were stuck in one place at a time.

Our minds would wander, wondering what it was all about elsewhere. Okay, I can't be all the places I want to be, but I can wonder about them, imagine them, dream about what it's like. Imagination could take us to all the places that physics denied. We could live in a reality while escaping to a fantasy, and nobody else needed to know about our mental absence.

In time, this process extended to action as well as place. We wanted to be able to do two or more things at the same time. If I'm swimming, I can't be hiking. Why not? Why do I have to choose between this and that? Why am I limited so much? Maybe I can walk and chew gum, but I want to simultaneously climb trees and make popcorn and hit a home run. Acceptance of being ambivalent and learning to be patient didn't really cut it, as much as our parents assured us that there would be plenty of time for everything. We all knew these parental platitudes weren't really true.

Our restrictions in time and place and action led us to worry, as anxiety became part of our experience. While I'm stuck here, I can't fix the problem I know is going on there. The limitations imposed by universal laws left us feeling helpless, unable to leap tall buildings in a single bound, or to beam up from place to place, or be superheroes, who were capable of deactivating natural law. So, we realized we had to figure out all these seemingly impossible issues on a pragmatic level, while imagining another world in which it could all be just the way we wanted it to be.

For the great majority of us our minds became a whirligig, a dust devil of thoughts, feelings and desires. Our brains became clutter-boxes of yesterday's thoughts, coupled with today's, the racing too quick to process them all. No wonder we wanted to "shut the damn thing off!" There was too much going on in our mentality to problem solve our everyday concerns, much less cogitate clearly about higher order thinking. Being intelligent didn't suffice to overcome the challenge. While having greater intellectual power allowed one to handle more traffic of mind, this same attribute created more issues to ponder. Intelligence giveth and intelligence taketh away.

So, when we are told to "Be here now!", to erase the board, to allow ourselves a space of "no think," most of us can only envisage a new superhero, Clarified-man, who would be capable of such a feat. When people are being taught to meditate and told to "clear their minds," most folks, if they are being honest, feel like they are being told to climb Mount Everest in their sandals. Yes, we know and appreciate that if we are to commune with the All and Everything, we must let go of all the trivial nonsense that disallows our mental reach into the infinite, but the task seems impossible. We have no idea how to turn the damned thing off, short of trauma to the head or chemical intervention, neither of which is particularly desirable.

Yet, we are told about plenty of people who are capable of such accomplishment of mind. Not mind over matter, but mind over mind. How is this possible? They must be sainted, or savants of some type. What do they know that we don't? Is it magic? Actually, the last on this list is closest to the truth. The practice of magic involves sleight of hand. The dexterity of the magician intentionally misdirects our perception, distracting us from reality while steering us to illusion. The key to magic is distraction.

The key to achieving the desired empty mind is also distraction, but of another kind. The aim is not, as with magic, to be fooled into an illusion, but to have sufficient mental space to comprehend a "higher reality." Luckily, the evolutionary path has given us the biochemical mechanics to achieve such a calculated distraction, and leave us "emptyheaded." The neurotransmitters and endorphins in our synapses have the ability to calm our minds, and create a state of "wellbeing." This is a natural mental state which occurs in all organisms that have a sufficiently developed brain. In a biosphere of predator and prey, animals must be able to distinguish when they are "safe," and the chemical activity in their synapses can create this state of mind. When the conditions of a harmless environment are perceived, the appropriate neurotransmitters are released and the animal can rest, and feed, letting go of a hyperalert status. Their brains can rest.

Human beings have the additional ability to generate this biochemical process independent of environmental conditions. Listening to soothing music, especially if it is in a 4/4 time signature, can do the distracting trick. The repetitive rhythm, along with the melodic tune, especially when untethered to lyrics, can release serotonin and dopamine, and leave the individual in a mental state oblivious to time, place or thought. The person is distracted from the events of the day, and is able to "lose him or herself" in the song. The more familiar and adored the music, the more powerful is the release from unwanted thought or emotion. But accomplishing this mentality is not limited to quiet and removed activities. Athletes talk about being lost in the "zone." A baseball player can be free from all thought while in the batter's box, despite being surrounded by 70,000 fans screaming their hopes and fears. He simply needs to know how to distract himself, and therefore not be distracted.

When one's breathing is timed with the rhythm, this further deepens the state. An intentionally generated rolling easy breath is always helpful in this deepening. Adding a visual rhythm which alternates between a single point and the widest possible vision, further enhances the process. We call these events hypnotic trances and they are commonplace throughout our days, most folks experiencing them 10 to 12 moments throughout their waking hours. When they are self-induced, we call them self-hypnosis or meditation.

The beginning of the "distracting" process usually starts with the breath, establishing a rhythm to take us into a calm. Often a mantra is used. There is nothing inherently meaningful about the mantra, but the repetition creates the necessary rhythm, a "music of the mind" if you will. Mandalas can be effective in generating a visual rhythm of focus. For the practiced meditator, as the neurotransmitters begin the process of clearing away anything other than simple thoughts of wellbeing, a familiar space is reached, and it is easy to simply slide into the nothingness. The well-practiced devotee can even become familiar enough with the state to enter with the first breath, creating the opportunity for what is sometimes called active meditation or walking hypnosis.

These inducements to distracted wellbeing are not restricted only to the path of spiritual attainment. Most of us have many self-soothing habits and comforting experiences which serve a similar purpose through our every-days. We are often unconscious about the behavior or its intention, but it works, slowing our minds, and allowing us to be in the moment. An embrace, which in other moments might stimulate an awakening, can, in other moments, stimulate a quieting. A memory, which at one time could have been exciting, can alternately cause us to be lost in reverie. Stroking a beard, or one's brow, or twiddling of thumbs can be a self-soothing mechanism to calm the mind and allow for the racing to slow.

Allow yourself to be intentionally distracted from your lives, for a moment, for an hour, for enough time to be sufficiently with(in) yourself to be outside yourself. If you wish to be in communion with universal energy, you will need to temporarily distract yourself from your personal concerns and your personal mythology. Take this vacation from life as you know it, not by touring far-a-way places, or your aunt in Chicago, but by reaching inside yourself to get beyond yourself. Go inside to get outside.

Utilize the magic to enter the mystery.

4

The four friends travelled throughout the city on weekends, delighting in its cultural and social offerings. Saturdays tended to be their day for exploration, the subway taking them one afternoon to the Cloisters, another to the MOMA, still another just to meander about the Fifth Avenue Library. Museums, historical sights, Broadway matinees, when they could afford the tickets, the Bronx Zoo, the Coney Island Aquarium, it was all a city-wide playground, stimulating one thread or another of their awakening. Shen, of all the adults, most encouraged their wanderings. He recalled fondly when he had first arrived in the U.S., when he made similar treks about his adopted city. "My mother insisted I visit all the cultural institutions so as to orient myself to this new world, and my new life. But in taking in the culture of New York, I discovered a plethora of new wonders, which in turn expanded my world view. Ideas, perspectives, beauty, it was all there for the taking."

Each of the quadrumvirate had their personal perspective to satisfy in their joint journeys. Moose was always focusing on the architecture of it all. In looking at things, be they buildings or objects, he always needed to deconstruct and reconstruct, demanding of himself that he know just how it was that things came together to form a larger whole. Alicia sought inspiration. As angry and outraged as she was with the society in which she felt trapped, she was always on the lookout for symbols of kindness and devotion, the antidote to her contempt. If her persona declared her to be a wrathful rebel, her poetry betrayed the image, leaking out her internal enthusiasm for a family of man, her inner loving Dickinson. New York City was her muse.

For Alex, it was all about beauty and style. Walking between exhibition rooms at the Met, he was constantly torn between the masterpieces on the walls and the stylish clothing of the folks that he walked among. Sometimes, while watching a drama, he found the play distracting him from taking in the costumes and the sets. Once, as the four were leaving an Albee play, he commented to Aziza, "What I love about his characters is that they can do contemptible with so much panache!"

Aziza's attention was similar to Moose's, but on the human, not physical, architecture. She was drawn to the struggles of people, and how they rose or fell in the aftermath of their exertions. Her favorite museum was the Immigrant Museum on the Lower East Side, where she could imagine her great grand-parents arrival in the new world, and their insights about freedom from poverty and starvation. A trip to the Apollo, to her, went beyond the music, demanding of herself that she experience some sense of the vitality of people who others would call under classed. Where did this vital life-force come from? Underneath it all she was searching to know about this singular spirit that appeared to drive folks of such diverse backgrounds and histories. She successfully pushed the group to come with her to religious services in a mosque off Atlantic Avenue in Brooklyn, to St. Patricks Cathedral in Manhattan, to a Baptist church in Harlem, to a storefront Pentecostal observance in Corona. How did heart, and soul, and spirit and psyche come together? Every daytrip gave her some thread of insight, which she pondered and played out on the page for the next few days, after returning home.

But whatever the destination of the foursome was during the day, the "Village" marked the completion of the day in the evening. From the orthodox bohemia of Greenwich Village off Washington Square, to the eclectic East Village of Second Avenue and the Fillmore, to the melting pot of Alphabet City, like the multitudes of teenagers before and after them, they sought and found a living district for alternate identity. It represented a pulsating nation for the non-group group. Evolving from the Bohemian to the Avant Garde, to the Beatnik to the Hippie, this had been tribal land, and the totems were everywhere. Most of the older coffee houses might be gone, and the hip scenes were all moving to the east, but there were still informal poetry readings over on 8th Street, and the bars on Avenue A usually didn't card them, especially if Aziza led the way in. A midnight ride home on the Independent Line would leave them off at 179th Street, a bus ride away from Aziza's house, where they'd all stay over. It was always a cool day.

One night, arriving back in Hollis in the wee hours of a June evening, none of them could sleep. Amped from their journey de jour, they sat in Aziza's finished basement and sorted through the day. They had just returned from a poetry reading at the 92nd Street Y. Alicia's excitement about becoming part of a half century of literary tradition was contagious. Auden, Eliot, Frost, Hughes, Thomas, so many of the greats had stood right there, had been reading, at one time or another, just a few feet away from the space they currently occupied! Literary time travel had been achieved! And then there had been a quick stop at the Black Horse, Dylan Thomas's old stomping ground. Does it get any better than that?

"Hey, guys," this was Alex. "I know this sounds like I'm some corny high school cheerleader, but today was one of the best days of my life. I don't want to think that graduation is less than a year away and we're going to be split up in college towns all over the country."

"Who says it has to be like that?" Moose interjected. "Last time I looked, we have many of the best damn schools right here in the City, and if we're honest, the simple truth is all of us have the SAT's and grades to get into any college we want. Any reason why we can't all hang together for another four years? Where do we all want to go anyway? Me, I'd be fine with Cooper Union."

"F.I.T.'s been my first option forever," Alex declared.

"Columbia's at the top of my list," enjoined Alicia. "Even if it makes my folks happy."

Aziza smiled. "You guys all know that I've always wanted to go to NYU." She paused. "So, is it settled? Do we all pledge to go to school in the city?"

"And we could get an apartment together, maybe down in Alphabet City," added Alicia. "With four of us together, it would be cheaper than each of us separate in a dorm. And face it, dorms are so high school."

It was soon agreed, and a pact was established. The Four Corners would remain intact!

5

Aziza and Esther were putting the kitchen back together after supper. Esther washed while Aziza dried, as was their routine, a moment each of them valued through the week, a time to be alone with each other for a few minutes and catch up.

"It's not that I have any objections to the four of you rooming together," Esther asserted. "I just don't want you, or really any of you, to be isolated from all the other students at your respective schools. One of the great benefits of going to college, especially at large universities like NYU and Columbia, is that you get to interact with a global student body, kids who come from every corner of the world. It seems to me that as much education happens in the dorms as in the classrooms."

"Mom, I'm going to see all those kids in my classes, in the cafeteria, all over. I mean, sure I would meet a few more in the dorms, but part of the reason I want to be on a city campus, is the value of the city itself. Talk about isolation! Staying just within the college community can be even more restrictive. Hell Mom, you never set foot in a dormitory, and it seems to me you did just fine. I don't know anyone who has a broader and more diverse social network than Dad and you."

"Ziz, I just don't want you to crimp your experience. And my college experience is hardly the best model for you. I limited myself and my outlook in too many ways to count. Just promise me that you're not going to let college become an extension of your high school years. I've seen so many bright and capable kids narrow their focus when they get to college. Just at the time when their minds should be expanding, they seem to contract their purpose, worrying more about some future job, or who they're dating, than a world of ideas they're getting introduced to. Careers, friends, relationships, these are all important parts of life, but they can also bog you down and be a trap."

"And what is the likelihood that your daughter, that would be me, is going to forsake the world of ideas for social or practical purposes? Aren't you always telling me to get out of my head and be a teenager?"

Esther pitched the towel on the counter. "Okay. Okay, I'm just trying to get you to be where you're at when you're there. You know, if you're in high school, be a high schooler. If you're in college, why not be a coed? I just don't want you to look back later and regret that you missed out on the moment."

"Mom, it was you that taught me that what I do needs to emanate from who I am. Besides, when I think about it, I'm a pretty age-appropriate person. Which reminds me, uh, do you think you could set up an appointment for me with the gynecologist?"

"Well, that was an interesting segue! I guess, er. . . . sure. I can do that." A few clumsy seconds passed. "Are you seeing someone? I didn't know that you were dating."

Aziza was quick to respond. "No. I would tell you if I was seeing anybody. It's more like I want to be prepared for if and when I might get involved. That's what you always have always told me that I should do, isn't it?"

In truth, Aziza was being less than fully honest about where she was at. Sexuality had been an area that left her confused and conflicted. She had never been even slightly interested in any of the boys she knew at school. With the exception of Moose, and Alex who was gay, she had almost nothing in common with any of them, and thought most of them to be, frankly, infantile. And the way these flirtatious boys, who were foreign to everything she stood for, were constantly hitting on her and playing their adolescent peacock games, left her feeling something in between amusement and rancor. Which isn't to say that she was unaware of her attractiveness and the effects it had on guys. She often wished her looks away, not wanting to be bothered by unwanted attention.

As the daughter of an unwed 17-year old, she was very aware of needing limits and boundaries in all things sexual, and less than comfortable with the power and control that appeared to be at her disposal, if she desired it. She didn't like that there were some parts of her that valued her beauty, and the influence it had on others. It felt to her almost like a handicap. Being attractive was ego-inflating, and for someone who was dedicated to be as egoless as possible, she found herself in a struggle with herself. The whole subject was an unwanted conflict that she did her best to avoid.

But, as she moved beyond the familiar haunts of her neighborhood, and travelled more about a cosmopolitan city, she had become aware that her outward appearance allowed her to interact with interesting people on a different and deeper level than her three friends. Clergymen, curators, poets or just new acquaintances, everyone seemed more drawn to her and allowed her greater access, and it was perfectly clear that like it or not this had something to do with her sexual persona. She didn't flaunt or flirt. It was simply organic to the natural human social process. People, of both genders, are drawn to attractive people. This disturbed her, but at the same time, she couldn't deny that she enjoyed feeling more significant.

She couldn't talk about it. To anyone. It would sound conceited and entitled. And even if she got past that, she would only hear feedback that this was the way the world worked, and if it gave her an advantage, so be it. Which was true, but left her feeling disadvantaged by the advantage.

Until, one remarkable night when she experienced an unfamiliar desire within herself. Sexuality had always been an external dynamic in which others were drawn to her, not the other way around. As a teen who tended to intellectualize most everything, she felt almost stunned by a visceral response in her body. It was disjointing.

It was on the day that the quadrumvirate was visiting a storefront church in Corona, another weekend day, another daytrip journey, another place of worship she had encouraged them to share. There was always more to learn about the ways in which the human spirit evidenced itself. They sat with Ricardo Huertas, the pastor, who had been so kind to give them an audience, to explain to them the precepts and principles of his congregation. Reverend Huertas was an interesting man, more down to earth than most of the clerics they had visited. His son, Eduardo, came by and interrupted them for a moment, just to relay a message from his mother, and smiled at Aziza, a simple everyday smile, precipitating an inner response previously unfelt. They barely spoke. In fact, Aziza was unsure later if they had spoken at all. But she thought of him, most every day, for the following week. What was it about his smile which had engaged her so? His eyes had been so dark and piercing, yet they seemed, when she tried to remember them, to signal a delight. In meeting her? Was that just his look, or had he felt the same vivid sensation as she? It was ridiculous. Why was she obsessing about someone she barely knew.? He was just the son of an interesting man she had met for an instant, for a moment. For God's sake, stop it!

And then he called. He had asked his father for her number. They talked for over an hour, and it was only when she agreed to meet him on Saturday for a cup of coffee in Flushing, that they had been able to hang up and let go of the conversation. They seemed to mirror each other in so many ways. He was a first-year student at St. Johns, not sure whether he wanted to major in Philosophy or Religion. It appeared to her that he reflected every facet of her interests, and as they talked there was this synergy, in which they both found themselves expressing insights they did not know they knew. He was some combination of shy and emboldened, that hit just the right place for her.

She told Alicia that she wouldn't be able to hang with the group on Saturday, avoiding telling her why. Her folks assumed when she went out that morning that it was another weekend jaunt for the foursome. Why was she being so secretive? Why did it feel like she needed to keep this feeling she had inside all to herself? It didn't make much sense to her as she got on the bus to Main Street, walking as if she was on autopilot. Perhaps most troubling, why did she have this lunatic intuition that this day, this lunch, was going to be momentous?

When they sat in the outside dining area of the Doorpost Café, it became okay, well more than okay. Yes, she liked him. She really liked him. It felt good that he was so damn beautiful, and for the first time she liked that she complimented this beauty of his. They were a fit on so many levels, and even if along the way he made it perfectly clear that his interest in her wasn't purely about intellect and world view, it felt good to be wanted. She noticed others noticing them, and found that she could enjoy people identifying them as a couple. Later, when she did confide in Alicia, she said "We arrived each of us by ourselves, but left as a couple," causing Alicia to groan out an "Oh my God, how plebian corny get you get?"

As she finished the dishes, Aziza knew she had to correct her mistruth. There was nothing to hide or be ashamed of. "Actually, Mom, I've recently started to see somebody," and she proceeded to tell Esther about Eddie.

6

On Love And Transformation

Love is a state of being. Love is a state of being in which we are drawn to and become one with another, and in so doing recreate ourselves as part of a new, larger whole. As our boundaries dissolve to accommodate the merger, our selves will never be the same. Love is progressively transformational. The more we love, the more we become unified with the All and Everything. When we love, our selves expand. As we look into the eyes of our beloved, we see mirrored a self which we could not have known or expected before being part of this new higher order. Through love, we are able to access our fullest potential.

Despite all these benefits, there are many who fear love. They focus on their loss of a perceived self, because they don't conceptualize themselves as living life on a path, as continually undergoing growth, change and transformation. They would prefer a stable persona, lacking karma, without direction. They buy into a notion that upon reaching adulthood, one should attempt to remain as static as possible. The anticipation of love, for them, equates to a foreboding of what they see as damage.

We are fortunate that we have social and sexual needs and drives that move us toward love thereby motivating us to overcome our fear. Evolution has served the spiritual path well. Our evolved biological self encourages us to go beyond the isolation, the restriction, of our bodies. External pheromones and internal hormones call us to move toward union with others. While we cannot ever fully know another, we are driven to grasp the fullness of those we love, as a limit that we can approach, despite it being unreachable. Even in a specific union, love is progressive; it grows with time and mutual experience. We learn more and more about the other as time and love allow. Love becomes the ultimate dialectal process, in which the respective selves are constantly recreated into new forms, requiring corresponding modification in the other, and on. Only when fear outweighs the natural drives, can this process stagnate or regress.

Attraction is the mechanism through which our social and sexual drives manifest themselves. We like to think that we are aware of those attributes which cause us to be attracted to someone else, even if the process is often subconscious or chemical in nature. Our histories and conditioning allow us to be more comfortable with attraction to people with various social labels, physical characteristics, or personalities. This comfort is a product of what is learned and familiar to us. If we wished to remain stationary on our path we would always seek such comfort. Frequently, it is the attractions that are ambiguously discomforting and exciting that signify a love which potentially might move us further along on our path, and assist in bringing us to our next transformation. We might also be hurt, rejected or scorned, with little experience of gain. All roads do not lead to where we want to go. Life, and love don't move constantly on an ever upward journey. The ups and downs, the wave of life, the suspense inherent in the consequence of approaching another, this is the stuff of romance. When we dedicate ourselves to love, we accept and appreciate that the outcomes will represent a wide array of emotions, some decidedly unpleasurable.

There is a degree of sexuality in any love, be it lover, brother, sister, friend or foe. But there is likewise a component of humanity, community, family, commonality, dissimilarity, or empathy in our attractions to every love. With the continued acquisition of self-knowledge, we are able to integrate new and wonderous associations into our lives, without creating personal or social conflict in our selves or the others that we love. Sexuality doesn't need to dominate or override our array of attractions. It can be said that we each of us have a community of those that we love, and we do our best when we tend to our sound community relations.

Love is enduring. No matter that contact with the other may end, through choice, circumstance or death, once we have merged with another, they have become a part of who we are. Once loved, always together, even when it doesn't feel that way. We can lose touch with what is inside, when we seek it outside. Love is not only progressive, but also cumulative. We continue to grow along the way with every love we incorporate, and there cannot be a loss. There may be hurt or pain resultant from the ending of a relationship, but we don't lose that which has become a part of us. Sometimes we need to seek ways to accommodate that which the departed gave to us, without identifying those parts as them. As people come and go in our lives, we would do well to take time out, to reflect, to meditate and to allow ourself time for reintegration. Learning to love oneself is not a onetime action. As we learn and grow and love, we are transformed, and from time to time we need to get reacquainted with ourselves, to take stock of who we have become and what it means for our purpose and missions in life, to love ourselves again.

We cannot deeply love without deeply knowing the other. It is easy to assume that the other is who we think they are, either a projection of who we need them to be, or perhaps the persona they project, hiding themselves behind the veil. Because we may have learned to fear the process of love, we need to learn to question our honesty in our presentation of self, and to encourage our loves to do the same. We also need to be aware that we most of us have a personal mythology, a story that we have made up for ourselves about who we are and what has happened to us along the way. If we conceptualize the other as part of our story, if we cast them in a needed role in our personal mythology, then we are likely to miss who they actually are, and only love an empty projection of who we need them to be. When one of us do this, it is unfortunate. When both of us do this, it can be catastrophic. With two overlapping mythologies, love is an illusion for both, and neither is sufficiently in touch with the other to learn or gain anything. As the truth is revealed, both parties will tend to regress further into their mythology, turning resentful. How dare you become someone who conflicts with who I need you to be! There is little gain and much pain is such an unloving relationship.

Knowing the other is the labor of love. Our conditioning can direct us toward assumptions about who the other is, based on our history, our mythology or the level of our need for them to be who we need them to be. The more we love someone, the more we would be served by acknowledging that there is always more to learn about who the other is. We need to allow ourselves to be surprised and intrigued at facets we didn't know were there, rather than feeling misled and possibly disgruntled when the other is different from our expectations. As we learn more and accept more, our love will grow and we will individually expand. Striving to know the other leads to unexpected growth in self. Love doesn't become stale. We become stale when we think we know all there is to know about our love.

Where love exists, fear cannot. Where fear exists, love cannot. Each of us is but a part of the organism we know as humanity. Each of us is but a part of the organism we know as the Earth. Each of us is an essential part of the All and Everything, and as such, we are called on to love, accommodate, integrate and transform. We love, therefore we are. I love, therefore I am.

7

As much as Aziza wished it was otherwise, her relationship with Eddie had an influence on other parts of her life. While she was determined that the quadrumvirate would maintain itself just as it was, and despite her insisting that Eddie accept that she needed time, a lot of time, with her friends, difficulties arose. Alicia was particularly put off, and no matter how much time and energy Aziza invested in reassuring her friend that nothing had changed, there was a jealousy that couldn't be overcome. Somehow, Alicia experienced a loss of attention and closeness, just because Aziza would speak about Eddie or relate what they had done together. The rest of the group had no bearing on Alicia's need for exclusivity, but an outsider did.

Moose liked Eddie well enough, he said, but often sniped that he wasn't radical enough, that he accepted too much, and was naïve when he thought that the necessary sought social changes could be achieved from inside established institutions. The two of them would often debate one issue or another, and Moose would usually stake out the more uncompromising position, insinuating that Eddie was a "liberal without a cause." Eddie invariably held back on his retort, not wanting to upset Aziza, which Moose would take as a victory of sorts. Aziza would shake her head and silently call the whole interchange a bullshit example of male braggadocio, frustrating Eddie, who was doing his

a benefit. In contrast, at first Shen seemed to become overly paternal and protective, intruding himself more into her plans and wanting to know more about where she was going, how they were getting there, and such. For sure, Aziza thought, this was no gain.

Interestingly, that changed after a night when the four of them all went to the movies together, and stopped at a diner on the way home for some coffee and dessert. Eddie insisted on picking up the tab, and voila, the mistrust faded. Aziza couldn't help herself from laughing about it with Mom a week or two later.

"Male rites of passage are really weird, Mom. Like twenty-two dollars and fifteen cents somehow makes Eddie more acceptable?"

"Well, I guess the ways we women size each other up is just as unfathomable to guys," Esther responded. "I distinctly remember your Grandfather warming up to Shen and I getting together when he realized that Shen had saved enough to buy this house. It's not a money thing. The money is just a symbol that the hunting and gathering and protecting isn't something they'll have to keep worrying about. It's safe to pass it on to the next guy."

"Whether we need it or not. I mean, it's clear that Dad fully appreciates and respects you as his peer, but that doesn't stop his need to protect you, does it?"

"No more than our need to protect them in a motherly manner does, whether they need it or not. Don't get too hung up on gender roles, Honey. You'll always be able to feel the difference between a dick's need to dominate and a man's need to provide. Trust your gut on that one." Wow. Mom could be blunt when she wanted.

Roulan was perhaps more in love with Eddie than Aziza. She demanded his full attention whenever he was near. All week she needed to know if she could count on Eddie coming by on the weekend. Once there, it was a continuous "Please. please, please, will you read to me? Play with me? Come outside in the backyard and push the swing for me." Aziza tried to run interference, but it wasn't necessary. Eddie didn't have any siblings, and took to Roulan's enthusiasm immediately.

As the school year began to edge closer to graduation, Esther encouraged Aziza to go to the prom. "I know it's corny, and it feels like you would be acquiescing to a silly and expensive tradition that each generation foists on the next, but I've got to tell you, I wish I had the opportunity to go when I was your age. I missed out on all those end of high school events, and the truth is, they give a sense of closure to your teenage years. Having you as early as I did, I missed the transition."

"I don't know, Mom. I can't see myself preening in front of the crowd and showing off Eddie. It's all so ridiculously competitive."

"Just because the motivations of others are confounding, doesn't mean that your participation has to follow suit. Frankly, in most everything I do, my motivations differ from those around me. Get used to it. You don't have to avoid the fun things that society affords just because your world view is different. Have fun. Be you. And dance."

With some trepidation, Aziza agreed to ask Eddie if he wanted to go. No limos. No after prom blow-out drunken parties. Eddie added, no tux. Actually, he had been to his own prom, last year, and had anticipated that they would go together, this year. He added, "I can't wait to see you in a prom dress. You always dress down. I've got to admit that even if it makes me a sexist asshole, I want to show everyone that my girl is the most beautiful one in the room. Is it horrible that I take so much pride in how gorgeous you are?" Aziza didn't respond.

When mother and daughter went shopping for the dress, Aziza was fully cognizant that it was the first time she was deliberately honoring her appearance, not concealing it. As she tried on different gowns and looked into the mirror at three different stores, it was unlike any self-appraisal she had ever performed. The experience bordered on being traumatic. Searching for insight, she asked herself, "Why do we attempt to give our houses the best possible appearance? It doesn't have to be because we want to be a show off. Pride doesn't have to be false-pride. Perhaps it gives others an indication of who we are, in truth, and hopefully makes our friends feel welcome. Some people need to make the outside look different from the inside. I can try to create the external as a match with the internal." She kept going back to the word honor. "I'm not trying to make myself into something that I'm not. I'm just honoring the body that holds me." That got her through it, although she needed to repeat her insight a number of times, as if it were a mantra.

On prom night, as everyone was gathered to take pictures, Ben proudly announced "I never thought I would get to see perfection in my life. But here it is, in front of me, and in the form of my granddaughter, mind you. This is perfection, right here in this room, right here in this family, perfection." Nobody disagreed.

8

On Revelation

There are many descriptions of spiritual revelation happening in the burst of a moment, in a flash of light, a split second of time in which everything is turned upside down, never to be the same. Life reveals itself to be what it is, and all the illusions disappear as eternity is condensed into an instant. I have no reason to dispute these accounts of an exploding reveal of the Way. Famous saints, and seekers and sinners have all made declarations to this effect, a single moment in which a new transcendent path was suddenly disclosed. However, I would strongly advise those who search for a spiritual pathway to do the work, rather than await a cataclysmic moment. If one is always on the look for a flashing neon sign, one is likely to miss the message embedded in the landscape. If such a wondrous moment awaits you, let it take you by surprise.

In many areas of life, we can be tempted to hope for instantaneous benefit. A hit on a zillion dollar lottery! A glance across the room in which eyes meet and a true love is born. A thunderbolt of insight which solves a seemingly unfathomable problem. And it isn't as if these rare moments don't happen. We read about them all the time. Somebody has to win the lottery! But as we wade through the vicissitudes of life, most of us have learned that disciplined effort is what most usually gains the desired prize. If we wait on the corner for the rocket ship, we will most likely miss the bus. We have been advised, and we have learned through experience, that there are no "short-cuts" to knowledge or perfection, but some little part of us still hopes that the genie will visit us as we sleep.

There is some divergence in the yogic traditions as to the nature of shakti pad, the stage of awakening. While all embrace the patient practice of prayer and meditation, there are some that also give a guru the ability to instantly give shakti pad to a devotee. It is not my intention to challenge the veracity of such gifts. It is my intention to remind us that on the occasions when these sacred moments occur, whether through a guru's involvement or through life events, they are moments when a myriad of independent discernments come together to make a new and superseding understanding. It may be experienced that it happened in a flash, while actually a single new comprehension brought a thousand stored understandings together, and suddenly all the pieces were in their perfect place. It's not the straw that broke the camel's back, but the single brick that completes the road.

Mandalas wordlessly teach us the relationship between the parts and the whole, as we go back and forth from the Every thing to the All there is. What is it what changes our focus from all the independent components to a unified vision? It can be a quirk of the moment, or it can be a history of going from parts to wholes and back again in our observations. At times it can be a guru's intention. Whatever it is that precipitates the flood, the more we practice, the more we become facile in perceiving ever larger wholes. Eventually, we can incorporate Every thing into the All and Everything. The ability ultimately comes with time and effort.

All of us are born with a need to understand our phenomenological universe. With some it mostly manifests in learning about the interpersonal universe. In some it manifests in learning about the physical universe. When we were toddlers, we wanted to know everything about everything, but as our paths unfolded, we became specialized in our need to understand. From Astronomy to Zoology, from glamour to politics, from stamp collecting to body building, we studied and learned different pieces of the infinite puzzle, and within each of the specialized areas there were "aha!" moments in which disparate parts came together. For those of us who return to the child's need to understand it all, a fool's need some would say, every moment of our life, every learning of our life, every love in our life, it is all necessary to imply or infer the missing piece or pieces and complete the whole. This is the momentous moment of revelation. This is the moment when it feels as if everything comes together and suddenly the senseless makes sense, and all emotion is condensed into a feeling of awe. It is the ultimate "aha" moment, comprised of all the "aha" moments which preceded the paroxysm.

Be patient. Nudge yourself forward and allow the process to swell. Trust that there will be a miraculous moment when it will all come together, but know that the timing of the apex is unpredictable and that the dam will break at precisely the right moment. Follow your inclinations about areas of interest, and watch yourself see ever and ever larger landscapes. Find out what's on the other side of all the mountains you come upon. Eventually you'll get to the dark side of the moon.

9

On Living In Your Body

Chicken or egg? Body or mind? We are tempted to ponder "who's on first?" and "who got there first?" even though we already know that there cannot be egg without chicken, chicken without egg, mind without body or body without mind. Our linear mind has un unrelenting need to go back in time and find an antecedent to everything. What came before the universe? Who was I before I was me? The linear mind creates a paradigm that left unchecked can imprison us in a world of illusory answers to obsessive illusions. However, we are of this time and of this planet, and we are best served by accepting that psyche and soma are a unity that cannot be separated. I am my body as equally as I am my mind.

But what of the relationship between the two, these twin components of our being? If we allow our minds to become locked in an object relationship with our bodies, we will become divorced from our physical manifestation. We will fall into the traps of body comparisons, body shame, and sexual dysfunction. Thinking about our body as if it was separate from the self that is observing itself, is like being ensnared in a carnival maze in which all perception is distorted. Each mirror further distorts the others misrepresentation.

Bodies were meant to be experienced from the inside out. Bodies were meant to be experienced subjectively. Bodies were not meant to be thought about critically, judged as if there was an ultimate corporeal ratings scale. Bodies were meant to be lived in, appreciated and honored.

If we live in our bodies, from the inside out, and consciously honor our form, our ego will accept its housing without catering to or fearing social commentary. Energy will not be wasted on false vanity. We will cease false comparisons of our physical form with others, choosing substance over appearance. If we honor our bodies, we are more likely to be honorable with others.

Soon enough our bodies will vanish and we will go into that good night, and enter into the universal mystery. Will we have honored our physical incarnation while the opportunity was there? Will the value with which we regarded our body have been sufficient to maintain its health and endurance? Did the esteem with which we held our body allow us to be both comfortable and confident in our own skin? Did we allow our bodies to experience our life, or did we falsely protect our bodies with an anesthetic armor, locking us in an intellectual penitentiary? Will we find ourself asking if we utilized our bodies as a mechanism of love or fear?

The universe is composed of matter and energy, the ultimate and definitional dualism of the All and Everything. This is reflected as a microcosm with our body and mind. Be honorable. Be unified. Be your part of the All.

10

Aziza's graduation party was in full swing, on the third June weekend after the actual commencement. She had asked her folks to postpone it for a week, so that her friends could be part of the gathering. Actually, when her parents had advised her that they wanted to throw a party to celebrate her completion of high school, she had replied "I really wish you wouldn't."

"Why not, "Esther intreated. "You've certainly earned it, and it gives us a chance to express our pride in you. What's so bad about that?"

"You know I don't like calling attention to myself. Do we really have to do this? It's just so,… so…such a 'look at me, ain't I grand' thing to do. Guys, I mean it's just high school. No big deal."

"Well, maybe it is a big deal to some of us," Shen countered, unusually for him, somewhat harshly. This was rare, but he felt he needed to represent the larger family. "Aziza, sometimes your humility can cause you to be oblivious to other peoples' love of you. Part of loving is be receptive to other people's need to love you, even when it feels awkward or uncomfortable."

"Like your grandfather," Esther added. "He missed the opportunity to do this with me, and it would mean a lot to him."

"You know, Mom, you've used that one a bunch of times before."

"But it's not just your grandfather," Shen declared. There are a lot of us who have been part of your journey for the past eighteen years. Betania and Lian, obviously your mother, and, well, frankly me. It's not just a rite of passage for you alone. Can't you see that your achievement is part and parcel of the dreams and aspirations for the rest of us?"

Aziza knew he was right, and was embarrassed. Another example of egoless being ego-full, she reflected. Damn all those paradoxes, anyway! "Okay, Okay. I get it! We'll have the party."

And so, it was settled. The party would be indoors. Nobody in the family was up for an outdoor event, given the memory of Rose's death. Some things don't fade away, as much as we'd like them to. Lian and her husband, Marty, insisted on being on charge of all the decorations. He was a set designer, who had just staged 'Sweet Charity' on Broadway. The two of them went all out for the event, combining his expertise and her wit. The basement, to which Aziza was denied entrance for three weeks, was transformed into a Star Wars set. Each of the Quadrumvirate was portrayed on wall boards, clad in Empire uniforms with mortarboards, leading the world into a far-off future. Of course, Princess Aziza, glowing scepter in hand, fronted the charge.

Neighbors, friends and family mingled up and downstairs. The parents of Alicia, Bill (he had decided that Moose wasn't a fit anymore), and Alex had all been invited, and accepted. Alex brought his new boyfriend, the first time he had publicly come out with his parents present. Nobody seemed to notice. This was a surprise only to Alex. Eddie's folks were also at hand. It was a motley assortment of people, reflecting the multifaceted relationships of Aziza and her family. But they all interacted smoothly, with natural groups forming. Ricardo Huertas and Henry Posert found each other immediately and were in deep conversation underneath the portrait of Alicia climbing into her jet. Ben stood in the center of the room, intent on embarrassing Aziza with story upon story of her prodigious accomplishments at various ages. "This granddaughter of mine, she's going to amount to something, I tell you. She's going to amount to something." Shen and Bill's father, had never met before, but found they had a lot of similar interests. What were the chances of one of Aziza's friend's parents being a student of Chinese history?

Aziza took to the role of hostess, travelling with Eddie from group to group, careful to acknowledge everyone. Shen's admonishment had been taken to heart, and she now saw the event as an opportunity to thank all the people who had been present for her throughout her life. She had reflected on and become comfortable with recognizing the many people who had contributed to her raising. And she didn't mind showing off Eddie, even if, perhaps because, it caused him some social discomfort. They were enjoying each other, and the celebration.

Later in the afternoon, when some of the guests were just beginning to leave, Henry asked Aziza if he could meet with her privately. They went upstairs and sat on the back porch. He carried with him a present, which he had chosen not to place on the "starship" table, designed for gifts. He had something of a solemn air about him.

When she unwrapped the gift, she found a gilded looseleaf folder, with every musing she had sent him over the years, bound and collected. She was astounded that he had kept them, much less organized and assembled them into a more or less volume. In the very front, Henry had written her a message.

Dear Aziza,

I have had many students, but none like you. I have known many searchers, but none like you. Over the years I have felt so privileged to receive from you your musings and insights. I have witnessed your understandings grow from precocious intuition to comprehensive discernment. To have played some small role in that growth is a source of great pride for me. It has been like a piano teacher watching Mozart grow from prodigy to composer.

You don't know how rare and perceptive you are. To you, it seems like your need to delve into the spiritual framework of this world is just ordinary, everyday teenage stuff, or an obsessive neurosis. It isn't. Your drive for transcendent and religious understanding is apparently only matched by your resolve to push through the impenetrable. You are gifted way beyond the level that your humility allows you to appreciate.

I can't pretend to know where all this will take you, as you move out into the world as an adult. While I don't wish to burden you with weighty expectations, we both know that with the blessing of ability there is also responsibility. Responsibility to use it, and to use it well. Please feel free to continue to draw from me whatever help I can be in supporting you, whatever the direction you take.

The best gift I can give you on this momentous day is to return the gift you have given me over the past few years. I have kept all these thoughts and musings of yours, because I knew that you would not. Thus, I have been able to see them as the beginning of a body of work, not separate and independent contemplations. I believe that you will continue to take all this forward, even if there isn't clarity yet as to where it will lead. I know that you are sufficiently wise and determined to follow your path where it will lead you.

Safe travels.

Your always loving Uncle Henry

His gift and words left her dumbfounded and somewhat teary. As usual, he was patient, and gave her the room and time she required to gather her thoughts. She ran her thumb through the pages, her pages, as she sought the words to express her feeling. Eventually, she put the binder down and hugged him close, "Uncle Henry, you just blow me away. I'm struggling to respond because of the range of feelings that you provoke in me. You have always encouraged me to dig deeper, even when other people who love me have wanted me to lighten up. That's been a big help for me not to feel so weird and different.

"I can't believe you have kept all this, much less put it all together. How lucky am I that Mom and Dad found you when they got married. But do I really I deserve all these praises?   You're laying it on kind of heavy, Henry. Don't you think?"

"Not at all, Aziza. My guess is that I'm just the first of a lot of teachers or professors who will recognize that you are one-of-a-kind. You'd better get used to that. Hey, if I told you that you have amazing handwriting skills, which by the way you don't, but if you did and I said so, would you be so quick to question? It seems to me that somebody had to tell Picasso when he was young that he had over the top artistic abilities, or he might never have been so daring. I'm just trying to give you some feedback to help you know what's in you."

"But Uncle Henry, what if I end up just wanting to be some ordinary person with some ordinary husband and a couple of ordinary kids? Does this responsibility you speak of mean I have to pursue some graduate degree in philosophy or religion?"

"I spoke of responsibility, Aziza, not obligation. You will have to follow your own path, not one that I or your parents or your soon to be professors might map out for you."

"Sometimes I feel that I want to do it all, to study and learn everything and be everything, even if I know that that's stupid. On other days I desire nothing other than hiding out in my room with a box of Good and Plenty's. But, at the end of the day, there's just so much out there and I guess I'm selfish enough to want to understand the big picture issues. I don't know. How does anybody ever single out what they are going to do with their lives?"

"What we do needs to emanate from who we are. You know that. This is the time in life when you should double down on learning the guts of who you are. Maybe you don't need to worry about what you're going to do with it right now. As you gain knowledge about what's out there, let it instruct you about what's inside. When I give you the feedback I do, it's to point out the considerable power that you hold within you. You will direct the power where you do, when the time is right.

"And by the way, kiddo, you have other responsibilities too. Like laughing and loving and dancing and playing. That's all part of learning about who you are."

Aziza chose this moment to wipe away the tears and to laugh as instructed. "You mean it's also my responsibility to be irresponsible from time to time?"

"Well, the Byrds told you there was a time for everything under the sun."

"Look who's getting biblical." They laughed and hugged again. "I think I'd better get back to the party. I need to be able to thank everyone before they leave. And thank you again, Uncle Henry."

But before returning to the basement, Aziza stopped first at her room, stowing away her gift from Henry in her night table. Next to her journal and the pressed corsage from Eddie for prom night.

11

On Our Ever-Changing Self

At any point in our lives, we possess both a world view and an image of our self. Neither of these is static. The events in the world about us, a kaleidoscope of happenings, constantly alter our perspectives, which in turn transform our sensibility of our own being. Similarly, when we experience a shift or transformation of our self, the eyes with which we look out on the world are dramatically changed. Time and tide interactively push and pull our persona and our vision of the world about us on a continuous basis.

We need to strive to maintain our personal mythology free from our ego's need for constancy, not just to be true to our mutable self, but also to avoid distorting our perception of the swirling events and people around us. The planet wasn't created to be a set for our movie, even if or when such a delusion would allow us to be less anxious. While we don't want the history of the world to be a study in chaos theory, and we look for and struggle to create order out of disorder, deep down we know that change is the only constant, and the history of the world can best be studied through the lens of chaos theory.

Our path can be viewed as our accumulated self, travelling in everchanging directions, with the winds of the world rushing by in irregular streams. Our Karma is the product of the magic within the moment, all of the mayhem interacting to create the next definitive step. The steady stream of these moments, the loci, comprise the atomic structure of Time. While our lifetimes are finite, time is infinite. In our limited time on this planet, we can be cautious in our steps, fearing the repercussions of the next karmatic moment, or we can boldly stride into a chaotic unknown, gaining a wider and deeper self as we wander. Each step along the way has the potential to gain wisdom, if we remain focused and vigilant for congruence, even as the turmoil swims around us.

While we are free to move or not to move, and also to move in whatever direction we choose, it is our wisdom which will help us in choosing the steps which resonate with the accumulated self. We hopefully learn to channel our efforts toward a rightness of fit in our choices, always advancing our knowledge of who we are. The more we know who we are, the more we are able to gain more knowledge about who we are. The more we know who we are, we can learn about new aspects of ourselves, new facets of our complex being. Thus, our Self becomes at one and the same time the constant and the variant. It isn't that we change. We add. We adapt. We transform. We sometimes discover whole new continents of our being. At other times, the alteration is minor. In either case, the essential need revolves about the issue of our accepting life's reworking of who we are.

Just when I've learned to love me, I find that I need to learn to love me all over again. Just when I've learned about what feels to be my purpose and mission, I need to redirect my efforts toward new bearings. Just when I've learned my borders, my limits, and my boundaries, I require a reset of my perimeters. It can feel like I'm always struggling to keep up with my present form, and then figure out my new presentation of self to share with others. Will I still be accepted? Will I still be liked? Will I still be loved? It is safe to be who I am evolving to be?

We tend to divide our life into broad chapters, usually identified as the periods preceding or subsequent to momentous events or transformations. Pre or post when I got married. As soon as I became a parent. Before or after I felt financially secure. Once I had that first mystical experience. After I read Sartre. But within each chapter there are more subtle alterations to our self. Being self-aware is remaining as open to both the obvious and nebulous newness within us, as we are to the changes about us.

Part of this self-awareness is recognizing those facets of ourselves which remain constant, no matter the extent of our transformations or alterations. Over time, even as we accept change, we appreciate what appears to be a core constancy. We learn to recognize this as our character, our ethos, consisting of those immutable principles which guide us to our larger purposes and missions in life. As the contrast between what is always reworking and what remains constant becomes more evident, our life becomes easier to navigate, and we can gain more trust in our karma. Knowing that there is an inner core allows us to accept the alterations to our self without anxiety, shame or confusion. Every chapter, all the plot lines, all the diverse renderings of self, become unified. All the karmic moments are joined and the totality of our path, that golden thread that defines our meaning within the All and Everything, is revealed.

Part Five

1

The long-held plans for the Quadrumvirate had come true! They moved into the four-story walk-up at 387 East 10th Street on the first of September, giving them all a week or so to get settled before their respective schools began their first semester. In Alphabet City, between Avenues C and D, the building boasted a proximity to a women's shelter, reserved for newly recently released convicts, a ten and a half block walk to the 4th Street stop of the Independent subway, a plethora of bars, and some of the coolest bodegas and bakeries in the five boroughs. Not exactly tree lined, but it was only a short walk from Tompkins Square Park, idyllic in the daytime, a junkie's garden after dark. New York City had, for a week, been smack in the middle of a heat wave, and the hydrant immediately in front of their stoop was wide open and spouting, allowing the neighborhood kids to dance in its water and cool their dancing bodies. Shiny wet little bodies ran circles around the hydrant oblivious to the adult hustle and bustle that surrounded them. This left the furtive attempts to navigate the furniture and boxes from the rented truck around the water stream without bumping into the children to be no easy task. Early in the afternoon, the roommates' eager exhilaration surpassed any fatigue. After a couple of hours and a dozen or so trips up the front steps and four windy staircases, toting heavy loads, the energy levels collapsed, even if their excitement remained hidden inside their charley-horsed forms.

It was a building that had been home to immigrant families for over a hundred years. The cyclic waves of Irish, Italian, Greek, Jewish and more recently Ukrainian migrants had remained a steady stream for over a century. Lately the neighborhood had taken on some of the overflow of the East Village, which itself had grown as a run-off from Greenwich Village proper, a generation earlier. The iconic New York bohemian community, second only to Paris, would last a generation in a given area, drawing artsy adolescents from the suburbs, and creating an ultra-cool atmosphere to its environs. As the teens grew into their own generation of prosperous adults, they materially returned to their rebellious roots. A market was created for higher class housing units, for those now grown hipsters, who craved proximity to their remembered stomping grounds. Consequently, the true artists, the committed avant-garde who produced the aura, would get priced out and have to move over a bunch of avenues. Three generations later, the process couldn't go any further, as the next stop was the streaming waters of the East River. In the moment, the neighborhood was a diverse mix of students, artists, East Europeans and Latinos, each subcommunity thriving, separate and joined, key components of an intense community. For Aziza and her crew, it was exhilarating to be away from the neatly groomed gardens of Hollis, and in the concrete vibrancy of E. 10th Street, in the heart of Alphabet City.

A railroad flat, it had four rooms, back-to-back to back. A peeling entrance door led into the eat-in kitchen, which overlooked the depths of the back alley. Early '50s appliances begged to be cleaned, surrounded by stained cabinetry that held the lurking omnipresent roaches. A living room, which had cradled many lives, was soon to be converted to a study area. This was followed by two bedrooms. It had been decided that the women would sleep in the front bedroom, overlooking the street, so the men shouldn't have to pass through their sleeping quarters on the way to their own. The furnishings were a rag-tag collection of basement furniture, collected from all of their parent's homes. None of it quite fit together with any thematic nature, rendering it "student chic." But it was homey, and once the move-in was completed, they collapsed on the color-clashing soft furniture with tired bodies and energized smiles. It was home, and they were home, albeit too tired to even contemplate who was going to take the truck rental back to Queens, and who would venture to get some take-out for supper.

"Give me your tired, your poor, your befuddled masses," Bill mused. "This is the veritable moment we join the exhausted, poverty stricken but happy student class."

"So, we've instantly moved on from our Queens middle-class origins with one Hertz truck and four flights of stairs?" retorted Alex. "How rapid is our descent!"

"Please, no socio-political inanities today, guys. I'm just too tired." This was Alicia. "Can we just gather up some coin and get a pizza? I don't know about you guys, but I'm famished."

Recognizing a need for unwanted but needed action, Aziza rose up, shook herself off to gather some energy, and took charge. "Okay, I'm going to bring back the truck. Why don't you guys set up the kitchen while I'm gone, and time out the pizza party for an hour from now, when I should be back. I'll pick up the pie on my way from the subway."

On her way back to Manhattan, in the subway car, she stretched her long legs out from the seat and bent backwards, to relieve her lower spine, which had begun to cramp. By the morning she would be having aches and pains for two. But the day was almost completed, and it was satisfying. Her new life had begun! She was out in the world, in Alphabet City with her friends, and eagerly awaiting the start of a different level of learning as a student at NYU.

Sometimes Aziza thought of herself as the ultimate question machine, producing a dozen why's and how's for every answer gained. Loose ends never seemed to get knotted, but reached out like tentacles, yearning for a "solvation." She hoped these soon to be attended classes in philosophy, religion and literature would begin to bring some closure to her charging thoughts, but simultaneously feared they would only complicate the process more, bringing her to deeper chasms of uncertainty about the nature of things. Why did she have to torture herself so, needing to poke and prod at the invisible and the unanswerable? Would it be so terrible to just be another coed, a college student, satisfied with starting a new adventure, having good friends, enjoying her relationships with a good guy like Eddie, and leave it at that? Why did she always have to push the universe's envelope?

Her life had always been secure. Her mother, Shen and her grandfather consistently supported her with a solid foundation, providing for all her essential needs and most of her wants. She had never wanted for anything or lacked any of the basics. She had been lucky enough to be housed in a strong, healthy and attractive body. She had never suffered from any social distress or disastrous events. Why then did she have this compulsion to look past the security of her life's condition and repeatedly challenge what seemed impenetrable? There was this elusive anxiety about the large questions that left her insecure, needy and, she had to admit, almost desperate for more satisfying answers, even if they always, in turn, led to more questioning. The more she knew, the less she knew. Oh, fuck it, could there be a more hackneyed phrase, she demanded of herself. Now I'm insatiably requiring why's about my why's, Let's just walk back to the apartment and eat some pizza. Pizza you can always count on. You're hungry, you eat it, it's done. No matter how many sections it was sliced into.

As she walked through Cooper Square, carrying two pizza boxes, she again slipped back to her inquisitory core as found herself contemplating the spinning cube statue. She'd passed it a zillion times before, never giving it much thought. But now she perceived herself as the cube, a form that didn't match its base, on edge, spinning but somehow stuck. It felt good to be weighty, but being locked in place and overwhelmed by gravity, was another matter. She needed to get beyond her spinning in place cross-examination of everything in particular. She needed direction, some drive that would take her toward some specific target, a path that had some firmament, not just handfuls of stones bouncing around tangentially in their own merry way. Show me the way to be home.

A beggar sat by the cube, half asleep but holding a sign, reading "Help me feed my children. Please." The fortyish woman seemed somnolent, or maybe she was on the nod. Balancing the pizza with her left hand, Aziza emptied her pockets of change with the right, and placed the coins in the almost empty bowl set to the side of the panhandler. Maybe her plight was true. Maybe not. But it felt good to pay attention to someone else's predicament and get away from her own pain-in-the-ass whiney-ass ruminations. The sound of the coin in the bowl seemed to stir the woman's consciousness, "Thanks, Dear. Now, you go and do your parents proud this semester." Clearly, a vagrant who knew her patrons. Had she once been a student herself? Was she a spinning cube sitting next to the spinning cube? Was this where no direction led?

Yet again, Aziza pushed back on her cogitations as her growling stomach led her back to pizza. Thank God for pizza. Pizza offers direction, even if triangular. She quickened her step, all questions now reduced to pondering the quality of the toppings from the new pizzeria she had found.

2

The semester began. Predictably, Alicia loved two of her five professors, hated most all of her fellow students and thought of her long subway ride uptown as an opportunity to practice her roller derby skills. Bill found himself gleefully immersed in theoretical physics while horrified by Cooper Union's environmental practices. Alex settled himself excitedly into both his fashion studies and the Village's gay scene. Whatever ambivalences the roommates had about their university milieus, the apartment and Alphabet City continued to meet all of their positive expectations.

Aziza quickly found herself identified by most of her professors as that student who reminded them why they chose an academic life and teaching, way back when. She not only thirsted for their lecture material, but always had her own take on what they presented, challenging them to take their lecture notes a little further. The process that had begun with her interaction with Henry blossomed in her coursework at NYU. The gilded loose-leaf folder he had gifted her grew bulkier every week, as she rushed home to reconsider and rework her reflections. These treatises on Everything and All, her homework for and to herself, represented an avenue in which she hoped she would find her path, a way through the wilderness of questioning and confusion. Aziza longed that the thirst would someday be sated. It felt as if resolution was always just on the other side of a new lecture, one which would bring a key concept, a new perspective. But as she integrated the new and the old, the dialectic always created another area of inquiry, another empty hole that needed to be filled.

As much as she was enthralled by her school work, she simultaneously found it to be insufferable. The never-ending search produced a low key but buzzing anxiety within her body. She sometimes feared that her need to know was becoming an unhealthy compulsion. Would it literally drive her crazy? On a warn Indian-summer evening she lay cuddled with Eddie in his Brooklyn apartment, hoping that being wrapped in his arms could miraculously release the tension throughout her body and allow her to unwind. She had urgently anticipated making love with him and letting herself and her ruminations dissolve away in the flow. But her stiff and achy body just couldn't go there. Dissatisfied with her body's defiance and fearing she was disappointing him, she turned and asked, "How is it, Eddie, that we take much of the same course work, and have such different responses? You seem to revel in a great intellectual courtyard which you turn into your own private playground of spiritual gymnastics. You play with it all, come to conclusions and leave the process comforted by concepts that strengthen the foundations of your principles and world view.

"I enter the process at the same point but am quickly trapped in an infinite miry quicksand. Every time I begin to have some minimal feeling of firmament underneath me, it shoots me out into the vastness again, without any sense of position or direction. It's like I'm stuck in a subway car that never lets me off. The views through the window at every stop are scintillating, but it goes on and on, without a terminus, or end to the journey. It's like a rush hour to nowhere."

He stroked her hair. "Ziz, I wish I was able to somehow convince you to get off your Sisyphean ride, and settle for a restful neighborhood of ideas and beliefs. But unlike me, you're this pure searcher, a frontiersman who never settles down, needing to travel over the next mountain range and explore the next unknown. Maybe it's different for me because I was brought up in my father's church, was groomed in a system of beliefs and values that grounded me in a supportive community. I look for ideas and concepts that have some potential to be comforting and give direction, perhaps to a future congregation, if I follow my father's path. I don't seek ultimate truth. I settle for what works in the here and the now, not in the all and everything."

"Oh, Eddie, I envy you, even if in the next minute I want to pull you into my way of thinking. So, you think that this endless and never sated journey of mine goes back to an origin without a starting point, the lack of a launching pad to push off from? You're probably on target. There's some truth there. You know, I still have an aversion to religion. To me, they all come down to systems of beliefs and practices which dictate peoples' attitude toward their universe. By directing their behaviors and limiting the needed questioning they deprive their believers of an individuated and intimate experience of spirit. Sure, I have to acknowledge the security it affords its members. But for me, I have this personal aversion that I can't get beyond. As much as I'm jealous of the contentment that lots of folks feel, for me, it would be a trap."

He sighed and held her eyes in his own. "You're the Lone Ranger, honey. You want to solve the mystery, help people feel better about themselves in the little town they live in, but then, with a hearty cry of Hi Ho Silver, you're off to the town, just over the horizon. That sucker never gets to settle down and have a life. I mean, he's got his Tonto, and I guess that would be me, someone to keep him grounded, hold his kite string. But at the end of the day, eventually, the Ranger always heads out into the lonely desert to explore some difficult new mystery. I don't want to change you, Kemosabe. I love you how you are. But I wish you could give your poor mind a rest sometimes."

"Trust me Tonto, I want that more than you can imagine. How many times a day do I find myself wanting to tell my brain to just fucking shut down for a while." She sat up in bed, considering a thought. "You know, if only I had been brought up in some specific religion, I could go through a process of rebelling against it, and after railing about its stupidity I could replace it with a version 2.0, tailored to my current worldview, and be satisfied. The content would change a little, but the overall limitations would remain just as they were."

"And what would be so bad about that? Isn't that how religions, and as a matter of fact, most institutions, evolve?"

"But would I continue to evolve, or would I settle into a different kind of quicksand. I really don't want to shut my mind down, even when I think I do. It forces me to continue to evolve. You know, something that I really respect about my parents is that despite having to overcome heavy duty trauma when they were young, they never let themselves allow the relief from their ordeals to cause them to get stuck in a security trap. They kept moving toward new challenges."

"Your folks are very special, and I agree, they've maintained a progressive attitude. But they also know how to kick back and relax, and enjoy the life they've built."

"Do you think they did at 19? Maybe I suffer from some petulant and immature impatience with wanting to be there already, wherever there is. Maybe I just need to learn to trust that the train will come into the station right on schedule, like Henry and Mom and Grandpa tell me it will."

"That's something that my father tells me a lot. 'Slow down, Eduardo. Slow down. You've got lots of time to live your life,'" he mimicked his dad.

Aziza poked him in his side. "Well, that's when he's telling you not to get so serious about me. You should take your time and play the field before picking out some particular girl."

"C'mon Aziza. You know he likes you."

"He does. But he worries that I'm going to get you mired in responsibilities which will keep you from what he foresees for your future. Hey, my folks absolutely adore you, but they still tell me how concerned they are that we're taking things too fast." She lay back down again, took his head in her hands and kissed him. "And talking about taking things too fast, how about we slow this evening down and stop all this infernal talking. It occurs to me that my body seems to have lost its tension, Tonto."

"That works for me, Kemosabe. I always thought your body was essentially sensible."

"Oh that's what you appreciate about my body."

"Oh yes, my dear. It's always been about your physical sensibility."

3

On Encountering the Spiritual Brat

Those of us who are caught in the sacred snare of spiritual inquiry go through times when we tie ourselves up in gordian knots, endlessly pursuing some resolution to our interminable questioning about the nature of things. These are the times we reach for the stars and find that our arms don't reach and our hands can't grasp a desired but elusive truth. Some long ago learned imperative to persevere, to try harder to understand, pushes us to pursue a tenuous understanding that teases us with bits of realization while remaining beyond our apperception. Our brain aches as it attempts to squeeze out a something from nothing.

Unfortunately, meditative techniques don't always bring a sorely needed relief. Our minds can be so cluttered with unwanted thoughts that crave their contents to be cleared out, wanting only to be empty headed. But instead, it can feel more like a laser sharp focus is encountering an impenetrable barrier. This frustrates us literally beyond belief. It can feel like we have regressed to toddlerhood, and we want to throw a tantrum, demanding to have what is unfairly disallowed. But we're not a toddlers, and there is no parent to rail against. Life's limitations are just saying "no, not now, not yet!" and we hate that. I like to term this our "inner spiritual brat," who arrogantly wants to know more than her maturity entitles her to comprehend. The brat wants it all NOW!, and has no appreciation that she is not ready for it. Perhaps there are missing elements that she will eventually learn in time. Perhaps she has not developed a sufficient emotional capacity to embrace what could be challenging. Perhaps there is a cognitive dissonance which must be first resolved. Whatever the reason, a resolving edification is not going to happen in the right now, as much as she wants it straightaway.

There is such a thing as spiritual maturity. Our comings and goings and growings in everyday worldly matters can allow our minds to ripen and develop on multiple levels. There is no such thing as a spiritual path that is separate from our biographical or biological path. The division of the "heavens and the earth" is an illusion born of segmentation. We move through our lives as a unified being at the pace that we do, not necessarily the pace that we want. How then can we manage the times when our spiritual brat is complaining that it needs to know more, especially when the wanted storehouse of illumination is apparently closeted? Can we shed our questioning for some time and allow ourselves to be at least temporarily ponderless?

At such times we are often told to be patient. We may be advised that the train will come into the station at just the right time, not according to our needs or our expectations. But we tend to greet these cliched adages with equal measures of acceptance and exasperation. The brat still wants what it wants when it wants it, and abhors hearing that the time will come when it comes, if it comes.

Patience is a product of experience. When a life situation has cycled before, we grow confident that it will maintain itself in the future. How long did it take until we became convinced that the waves would continue to come to the shore, and that the light of the day would follow the dark of the night? Newlyweds can be overcome with fear when they have their first significant fight, but grow confident over time that there is a rising and falling pattern in their relationship, because a wave of intimacy is driven by the force of their union. When the perception of our path is based on a cyclical rather than linear paradigm, we grow more confident that everything doesn't have to be what we want it to be right now. The brat recedes when she appreciates that the loss of the now is impermanent. This time will recycle and come again, transformed by the events that occur between now and then. There is no guarantee that successive waves will accomplish what we wish would occur now. But there is direction. There is movement. While we are always incomplete as long as we are alive, the ongoing drama of living augments us with every twist and turn. I can stretch and reach for the Golden Ring, and if my hand can't reach and I fail, I can try again with the next go round of the carousel. Until then, I can do and play and love and ponder everything else, with some part of me staying vigilant for the return of the opportunity to reach out again for the ring.

Sometimes the spiritual brat doesn't hit out against its limitations, but holds its breath and pretends she doesn't care. She becomes tempted to forego all future spiritual inquiry, and assert that "none of this really matters" and her advancement would be better served by attending to terrestrial concerns. Such an inwardly directed tantrum can evolve into a dark night of the soul, which may or may not ever be resolved. While all people don't require a conscious pursuit of metaphysical experience, for those who do, the denial of a need for contact with the Universal, empowers an unconscious drive to thwart the conscious repressing self. Self-sabotage and self-harming can be resultant. Having no object to hit out at, the brat turns on herself.

Maybe tomorrow will be the day we resolve the issue that plagues us. Maybe next month or next year. Perhaps in our next life. There is wisdom in the confidence that all things return, that we always get another shot at the ring, even if we're not in charge of the circumference of the merry-go-round. The train will come into the station right on time, just not our time.

4

The Quadrumvirate regularly hung out at The Thatched Rooster, a pub on Avenue B, just off 9th Street. Most of the bars in Alphabet City were hard drinking shot and chaser joints, but The Rooster catered to a different crowd. Stylistically somewhere between an English Public House and an American coffee house, students, artists and assorted Village characters gathered over an assortment of 54 domestic and imported beers and ales, cappuccino and espresso, sandwiches, brownies, pastries and scones. Dart boards, air hockey and foosball tables were set up in the rear, with tournament results hung on the back walls. Announcements about local events, gallery openings and concerts, interspersed with personal and sales classifieds were to be found on two huge corkboards, on either side of a wide mahogany bar. Almost nobody was carded, if one didn't count the invading suburban teenagers on weekends. It was a comfortable neighborhood scene for the community of artists, writers and students, the perfect local watering hole for after class and evening outings, if papers or exams weren't if the offing.

Alicia had secured a part-time waitressing job at the Rooster midway through the first semester, partly to be close to all the action, partly to be nearer to the poet/bartender, Arthur. He was the embodiment of all she desired in a guy. His lanky body displayed a cavalcade of tattooed images, matching his rambling iambic patter, with which he chatted up his patrons at the bar. Holding an iconic reputation though-out most of the area's bohemian scene, he was perhaps more of a draw to the Rooster than the beer he served. Alicia was smitten, and found, to her amazement and pleasure, that her feelings were reciprocated. Her edge became smoothed a bit. She spent less and less time at the apartment, between her classes at Columbia, the job and occasionally staying by Arthur's place. Not that Aziza was particularly bothered. Alicia's absence created more alone time for her in the bedroom, sometimes for herself, sometimes with Eddie. Travelling out to Eddie's place in Brooklyn all the time was sometimes a drag.

Aziza and Eddie started to garner a celebrity status themselves in the pub. They were that cool attractive couple who were into religion, theology, mysticism and all that otherworldly stuff. They would stop by the Rooster for a beer or two, usually on a weekend night, and inevitably a cluster of folks they knew and didn't know would gather around their table and the conversation would proceed to center about spiritual matters. The atheists needed a foil to debate with and the Jungians wanted to explore an array of archetypal allegories. It was fun most of the time, and sometimes stimulating. Aziza could let go of her strenuous questioning, and play lightheartedly with ideas and notions put forth by strangers. Eddie took it bit more seriously, with some sense of serving the needs of the folks who spontaneously congregated around them. They would hang for a couple of hours, with Aziza eventually imploring Eddie that they needed to head back to one of their apartments. As much as it was enjoyable, at some point it became bothersome, at least to Aziza. She didn't like feeling that she needed to give people easy answers to complex questions that required more rigorous examination. As the night wore on, she could feel like they were demanding of her, even as she knew that it was all just Saturday night intellectual swagger and frivolity. On those nights, she would begin to recoil inwardly, and grow quiet.

On the way back to his place, on the subway, Eddie complained "Why the need to rush out? We don't have anything going on tomorrow."

"Ed, it was enough. Did you hear that guy, the one who was insisting that until there was a satisfactory universal definition of God there would never be any peace in this world?"

"Well, it's not like he hasn't any truth there. In some ways all wars are about the clash of religions."

"That's not the point. He really wanted our table to step up to the plate and end all wars, arriving at some universal insight into the nature of God, while cogitating over some brownies and a surfeit of brewskis at the Rooster. Don't you find that even a little bit oppressive? It's like a mockery of the things we devote ourselves to." She paused. "And before you tell me to lighten up, could I remind you that you're the one who says that we need to take everyone seriously, that everyone you meet in life is a potential congregant, whether they know it or not."

"All right, you're right. I'll admit it was a tad over the top. And how about that friend of Arthur's, the one who insisted that the ritualized recitation of mantras was the only path to communion with a higher power? In Hindi, of course. I'm surprised that didn't light up your "save me from idiots" board."

She lightened up, for a moment, and moved to sarcasm. "Well, right on, brother. After all, if we seek the peace that passeth understanding, we must speak in tongues or languages that are beyond our understanding. For God sakes, what on Earth is that all about? I'll never understand why it makes it better for some folks to try to commune in a language they don't come close to comprehending. I feel like I'm ten, and in the synagogue, and I can't get why they all need to talk in Hebrew."

"Honey, it's not so complicated. It comes down to people being over the moon for anything and everything exotic. Think about it. Fashion, perfume, hell, even sex, they're all more appealing to the majority of people if they're wrapped in some bizarre or exotic package. Isn't that just human nature?"

"I get it for things and adornments. We want what we don't have, and we want it even more if our friends and neighbors and countrymen don't have it either. We want to be unique and different, as long as we can characterize it as stylishly fitting in. Mysterious but not odd. But extending that to prayer? Spiritual union? Can people really feel like they're relating when they can't even relate to the words they speak?"

"You are assuming that people want a relationship with their God. That ain't necessarily so, to coin a phrase. Maybe, it's escape they really desire, and getting away from their usual linguistic world becomes an asset to them. Whether it's speaking in an idiom they don't know, or taking a drug that relieves them of any sense of self. You know the deal. Spiritual intimacy can be safely sought on an expensive holiday in Machu Pichu, but never in your own backyard. Escape is what a whole ton of people are looking for. They're not interested in finding out who they are or their relationship with the universe."

"You're right, but that's so damned sad." She momentarily hesitated. "Oh Eddie, are we the weird ones, taking this all so seriously? Sometimes I think I would have been better off being born in the metaphysical age."

He smiled. "Your devotion to the thinking process of metaphysics would have been more accepted then, Ziz, but I'm afraid you would have been burned at the stake for the content of your convictions, if you dared to speak about it. And that would have made me very sad. To coin another phrase, I've grown accustomed to you face." He hesitated and then continued. "No, I don't think we're the weird ones, if our friends at the Rooster are any judge of that. The truth is you seem to have garnered some oversized celebrity at the Rooster. And that's not just because you're so damn beautiful, although it probably helps. They absolutely flock around you, wanting to hear your thoughts."

"Eddie, they flock around three breasted women and sword swallowers in the side shows! That's why they call it a freak show."

"No, Honey. You're no side show. You've been the main event for me ever since the first time I saw you in Dad's church. And for them, the fact that you are not only attractive but can take their thoughts to a different level is what brings them to our table. Maybe you need to take yourself as seriously as the rest of us mere mortals do."

"Unfortunately, it appears I take myself and my mentation too seriously. We both know I've got a serious compulsion to question everything and totally frustrate myself with the paucity of answers I get in return." She stood up even before they approached their stop, a physical movement meant to change the mood. "I'm sorry, Ed. I don't want to ruin tonight. I'm being a royal pain in the ass, and dragging you into my discontent. Let's talk about something else, and get off this train of thought. Pun intended."

"Uh, yeah. Sure. How about them Mets?" he sarcastically exclaimed.

Aziza punched him in the arm, as they left the subway car, smiling. "Surely you realize that it is my destiny to be an Angels fan. The essential question is how many Angels can you fit on home plate at a time. I mean Who's on first, and God's playing shortstop, and let's just shut up and walk."

5

On The Cosmic Joke

Spiritual seekers tend to be serious people. Whether by constitution or learning, they ponder, they think long and hard and heavy about matters that many of their peers would find a ridiculous waste of time and energy. Pondering can be a very exasperating mental process, vexing at best, maddening at worst. It could almost be called a mental disorder, this obsessive need to understand the nature and meaning of the All and Everything. It could certainly be deemed arrogant to strive to unlock the secrets of the universe. We searchers are disposed to suffer our spiritual inclination, a depressing condition in which we seem to be Sisyphusian creatures, constantly in an uphill struggle to divine what is impossible for a mortal being to fully grasp.

This certainly was the case for me in the formative period of my spiritual journey, and I suspect this to be true for the majority of saints, gurus and prophets. Yes, there have been some who experienced enlightenment in a flash of inspiration although they had never considered the pursuit of a spiritual life before. And there have been some who were led to become spiritual guides after a life of sin and degradation, waking from their mortification with a driven need to atone. But for those of us who can trace our seeking to know the unknowable back to our early childhoods, the path was mostly harrowing, punctuated by intermittent moments of joy, when a fulfilling insight occurred. Looking back, how thankful we are now for those relieving instants, as they offered encouragement for us to continue the difficult trek.

I remember the exact moment when I realized that enlightenment needn't be so heavily wedged in the doldrums, and in fact that it was light. I had been presented with a laughing buddha, a figurine that was a model for the creation of a larger sculpture. I was alone, sitting in my dining room, with the buddha in front of me on the table. It was a wonderful piece. The artist had created an image through which I could almost feel a harmonic of the buddha's mirth extending into my body and consciousness. But as much as I was amused and appreciated the artistry and immediate emotional experience it extended, I had never understood why laughing buddhas were a "thing." My obsessive nature was, if truth be told, reflexively offended by the mingling of merriment with the sober search in which I was engaged. Spirituality was a solemn activity. It was heart rendering and it was humanistic. But funny? I couldn't get my head around the centuries of spiritual figures who I had read and studied, who figured prominently in my mind and I adored, and who had extolled the virtue of laughing buddhas and talked about the cosmic joke. What joke? What's so funny?

Keeping the buddha in front of my gaze, I decided to role play a dialogue with him. I asked him aloud, glad there was no one else in the room to hear me openly talking to a figurine, "What is so funny? What is it that seems to cause you so much glee?"

And through some part of me, he answered. "At the moment, it is you that is so funny, the way you take everything in your life so seriously. You are hilarious." And his laughter increased, almost to the point of convulsions.

I was offended. "You are mocking me. You are making fun of who I am and the purpose I have in life. Your laughter makes me feel disrespected."

Incredibly, he laughed even more. "You poor girl," he said, "you have no idea how funny it is that you take yourself so seriously. You don't have a clue how hilarious it is that you take life so seriously." And he continued to roar.

"Stop making fun of me," I demanded.

He stopped laughing and became more composed. "But I am having fun with you. Here we are, in your dining room, playing the game of life. Is it not fun?"

And the only thing I could say was, "No, life is serious business, and I need to take it seriously."

At which point he burst into even deeper heaves of laughter, and I couldn't help but join him, as I realized how ridiculous what I had just said was. The thought that I could be ridiculous had occurred to me many times before, but this was the first time I was able to laugh at myself without reproach, to see me as the ludicrous comic book character that I could sometimes be. I kept repeating, almost as a faux mantra, that life was a serious business and I had to take it seriously, and with each repetition the realization of how absurd a notion this was grew funnier and funnier and I laughed heartier and heartier. I couldn't tell which was more absurd, the seriousness I attached to life or myself, the one who had devoted much of my life to such a silly notion. My eyes began to water and my abdomen started to ache, my laughter was so hard. At some point, as the hysteria began to subside, I began to wonder how it could be that I had not seen the obvious, when it had been staring me in the face all those years. How I had tormented myself with frustration and felt inadequate to get beyond my limited understanding? How had I missed the humor of the slapstick spiritual quest throwing not-so-humble pie in my face while the carousel of life turned around and around?

As if he had heard my inner voice, the laughing buddha answered, "But you were not ready to appreciate the cosmic joke. Your ego was still too attached to being the great explorer, even when couched as the humble seeker. As much as you knew that there was value in the search for meaning, you forgot what you knew as a child, that first there was value in the celebration of life."

My friends, allow yourself to enjoy the magical absurdity of the All and Everything without losing contact with the awe.

Allow yourself to "lighten up" and relieve yourself of experiencing existence as a burden, a burden born of the necessity to produce meaning and mission and purpose.

Allow yourself to understand that all comedy is about the recognition of our flaws and our faults and our preposterous pompousness. We laugh at ourselves because the only other choice is to cry. Part of the serious work of letting go of our ego is allowing ourself to look in the mirror and giggle when we see ourselves engaged with the comedy of life.

Laughter is cleansing. When the mental board is crammed with an overabundance of thought, laughter is the great eraser, clearing and cleansing and relieving the mind.

Doors can alternately be seen as a barrier which locks us in, or an opening which sets us free. Laughter can be that "get out of jail" card which wondrously opens the door and sets us free.

6

"So, you guys will be getting to the Rooster about eight thirty or so?" Alicia asked, before leaving for work.

"Somewhere in that neighborhood" Aziza responded. It was her 19th birthday and Mom, Grandpa and Henry, and of course, Eddie, were all driving into the city for a celebratory dinner. Roulan was having an overnight with Aunt Lian, her favorite person in the world, which overjoyed her. A happy evening for both of them. Shen, unfortunately out of town on business, had already called, upset that he couldn't share the day with her. The plan was to meet up for dinner at the 2nd Avenue Deli, and then head over to the Thatched Rooster, where Alex and Bill would catch up with the party.

"Good. I shouldn't have any trouble reserving a table that early in the evening." Alicia broke into a wide smile. "And I've got an extra special birthday surprise for you, Roomie."

"So, help me, if you bring out a cake and do the Happy Birthday chant with Arthur and the crew, I'll rip your clothes to smithereens and throw them all out the back window."

"Aren't you getting testy, for a Guru, no less," Alicia teased. Somewhere along the way, one of Aziza's coteries at the Rooster had dubbed her The Guru of Alphabet City, much to Aziza's irritation. It had been one of those nights when at least a dozen had clustered around Eddie and Aziza's table, engaging in a range of spiritual banter and discussion. While the appellation had been spoken with a sarcastic tone to it, by an ardent and antagonistic missionary Born Again, the name had exasperatingly stuck among all the regulars. Even if others didn't use it with a mocking or derisive attitude, it was still beyond-belief annoying. Aziza had never liked being in any kind of spotlight. Whether the attention was positive or negative was immaterial. So of course, Alicia loved kidding her about it, even though, perhaps because, she looked up to Aziza in so many ways. "Simmer down, my Guru, as far as I know, there's no cake in your future."

"Then what's all this about a surprise? And would you knock off the guru business, please?"

"Well, it wouldn't qualify as a surprise if I told you now, would it? And you know, I think you're going to like it." She checked herself. "Or, at least I hope you're going to like it. It's not like I'll ever figure out what gurus really like, I mean, if they like anything. Anyway, I'm out of here. Arthur will kill me if I'm late again." She gathered up her work apron and was out the door before Aziza could throw a shoe at her.

Aziza, herself, was concerned about getting on her way in time to meet the family. With visions of pastrami dancing in her head, she set off for the 2nd Avenue Deli. It was a warm Saturday evening in early May, and she worried that the crowd of people at the iconic delicatessen would be as oversized as the sandwiches, Sure enough, as she approached the deli, there was Mom, Eddie, Grandpa and Henry waiting in a line that stretched out onto the sidewalk. But it moved quickly, and they were seated in less than ten minutes.

As they waited for their dinner, Ben jumped into the sour pickles and tomatoes which were always present on the fading Formica tables. "Ah, a pickled tomato like this, I haven't had such a pleasure in years, in years I tell you. Did you know, my precious Aziza, that your grandmother and I used to come here when your mother was just a little girl. This was our big night out! She'd get a babysitter, and I'd leave work early, and we'd meet here for something special." He waved his finger at the table. "You know, there used to be a lot of good kosher delis in the city, some even out in Queens, like that place Charney's on Union Turnpike, but the 2nd Avenue Deli, that was always the best. Always the best."

"But Grandpa, how about Katz's or the Carnegie. Some folks say they're better." Aziza loved to goad him into talking about the old times.

"Yes, my darling, there are always people who argue about whether it's the 2nd Avenue, or Katz's or the Carnegie. Just like Mays. Mantle or Snider." He shook his finger at the table again. "But the real answer was always and always will be, the 2nd Avenue Deli," he paused, "and Willie Mays, of course." He held his newly delivered kasha knish high in the air. "The food of the gods, I tell you. The food of the gods."

"Mom, did they take you here as a kid?"

"For my birthday, a couple of times. That's why I suggested we eat here tonight. I can still remember your grandfather trying to explain to me why it was called an egg cream when there wasn't any egg in it. He went on and on, and on, until Mom finally got exasperated and shouted out 'Because that's the way it is! Now, both of you keep quiet and eat your damn sandwiches.'"

"My Rose, she never did appreciate the intricacies of things. She liked to keep things simple. My girls," he looked back and forth at both of them, "my beautiful girls, you must get the trait of picking everything apart from my side of the family."

"So, I should blame you, Grandpa, for my obsessional nature?"

"No. Aziza," Henry interjected, "I'm afraid that may have something to do with my influence. Feels more like interactive conditioning than a genetic inheritance. Sorry about that."

"Nature vs. Nurture," Eddie summarized. "I've got to say, there's a whole lot of nurturing gathered at this table." He reached out with his glass of cream soda. "Here's to you Grandpa Ben. It seems to me that you set in motion all the love and nurturing that has served Aziza so well in her nineteen years."

Ben turned toward Esther. "So why is this boy still trying so hard to earn points with our family? You'd think he'd know by now that we like him." Turning back to Eddie, "Of course, liking you won't help you at all if you ever hurt my precious Aziza. Anyone who's good at nurturing has another side, Eddie. Hurt the people they nurture and you find out about their other side, You find out fast, I tell you."

Aziza started to protest, "Grandpa!" But Eddie immediately cut her off. "No, Ziz, it's all right. I know exactly where your grandfather is coming from. If anyone ever intentionally hurt you, I'd react in exactly the same manner. Some things don't fall in the turn the other cheek category."

"Can I remind you macho men that my daughter, Aziza, has shown us all that she isn't someone who requires your tough guy protection. Frankly," she directed her attention toward Aziza," you're just about the strongest person I know, and I don't say that because you're my daughter. What you call your obsessional nature makes you think and double think before you act. You're a thorough thinker, somebody who pays attention to the details, who needs to see both the details and the larger picture. That's what makes you strong."

"She's right, Ziz. What you sometimes think of as problematic, is actually a source of strength," added Eddie.

"Doesn't always feel like that from the inside out," Aziza pushed back.

Henry decided he needed to reinforce the message. "Aziza, none of us want to make this celebration weighty, but I want to point out that it is easy to mistake a strength of your character as a psychological deficit. Yes, thorough thinking, as your mother calls it, can be tedious, and sometimes painful, when your brain is demanding answers that remain elusive. But you have a resolute nature to your mentation, and that's an admirable character strength. You don't run away from issues. You persevere in the face of difficulty. Going over and over something is psychologically obsessional only if the whole process is symbolic in the first place. Because symbolic questions are ultimately rhetorical. You, on the other hand, are someone who is willing to take on the hard questions."

"Hey, guys, enough." Aziza gestured for them to stop. "I appreciate that you all love me, and I couldn't dream of a support system that could be more robust than all of you have always been. Can we just leave it there. Today is a day when I want to thank all of you for being there for me, even when I'm being ridiculous, and even when I don't know if my stubbornness is in the service of a good cause or a neurotic need. It doesn't make any difference. You are the people who are my foundation, either way, and I thank you."

The table turned still. Eventually it was Ben who broke the silence. "So, Aziza, my dear," he said as he picked up a half sour and held it vertically, "imagine this pickle like it was a candle with a big flame on it. You should blow it out. You should blow it out."

"Wait here," added Eddie, as he placed a second pickle next to Ben's. Soon Esther and Henry augmented the two and created a half-sour garlic bouquet.

"Happy Birthday, Aziza, Now, blow those pickles out! Show your grandfather how much breath you've got."

7

The Thatched Rooster was bursting out of its seams when they arrived, but Alicia had managed to reserve a big table, which Alex and Bill were holding for the rest of the party. As Aziza and her family sat down, there was a shuffling of some of the regulars, moving their chairs from other tables, anticipating another evening of discussion and debate with their "Guru."

Eddie motioned to Esther, "You'll notice that your daughter's adoring fans are all gathering. So, help me, I think some of them just hang out here hoping that she'll show up and give them the opportunity to share their newly conceived insight of the week."

A little bit taken back by what felt to her like a swarm, she asked, "They do this all the time you guys come here?" She surveyed the intentionally peculiar, if not bizarre personas surrounding them, and remembered her own days, long ago, when she haunted the Village, and grinned. "Some things never change, but what exactly do they want of you?"

He lowered his voice so only Esther could hear. "Well, it's all variations on challenging, asserting or cultivating beliefs. Most of them have some proselytizing agenda which Aziza's presence gives them space to advocate. Some are questioners, some searchers, some disciples of the ordinary or the unorthodox. Mostly, they're an affectionate and respectful group of folks who are tuned into spiritual matters."

Eddie turned toward the outer circle and raised his voice so they could hear him over the din. "Hey guys, it's Aziza's birthday today, and this is her family. Could you give us a little space?"

Some of the assemblage deferentially moved away, while others leaned in with birthday wishes and greetings, but shortly, the crowd thinned out and allowed the family to be with their celebrant. As they dispersed, Aziza visibly relaxed.

"These people, they're pushy, Aziza. What do they want of you?" asked her grandfather.

"It's okay, Grandpa. You know how all those people used to come to you over and over and need you to tell them what kind of suits would make them look good? Even when you already had told them the last time. It's sort of like that," Aziza responded.

"My granddaughter, she's a maven. But don't let them pester you, don't let them drive you verklempt. Don't you let them drive you nuts like they did to Morty, back at the showroom. They made him quit and go sell washing machines. Washing machines, I tell you."

"No, Grandpa, it's okay. I'm not like Morty. I've learned how to keep boundaries and know when it's time to leave."

"Look who's talking, Daddy. You're the one who never knew how to say no to anybody. Time, money, advice, you've always been there for whoever, wherever." He just waved his hand, so he didn't have to verbally deny Esther's truth.

Alicia brought an assortment of pastries and cheesecake to the table. The other waitress, Marilyn, followed, carrying the cappuccinos, espressos and beers. When everybody was served, Alicia asked her coworker if she could cover her for five minutes. "I need to give my roomie something." She grabbed an unused chair from a neighboring table. Bill and Henry moved over a bit, and she nudged her way in.

"Hey, everybody. I'm just going to take a few minutes here and then I'll get out of your way and let you be with the birthday girl. But I promised Aziza a surprise tonight, and I don't want to disappoint." She focused on her roommate. "Ziz, I don't know if you know how much I admire you. Yeah, I'm pretty cool myself, and I always put on a show that I have my shit together even when what I look like says otherwise. You know I've always liked the incongruous thing."

"Don't we all," Bill threw in.

"No, Bill, Aziza's not like the rest of us. She's not growing into it, like we are. She's always been there. I don't know how, but she's always had it together, from the time that I met her, back when, in high school. And don't go denying it, Ziz, 'cause it's true.

"So, a couple of weeks ago I started to read your journal thing-a-ma-gee-bee, whatever you call it. I don't know if it was supposed to be private or not, and maybe I should have asked permission, but you weren't there, and curiosity got the better of me. I'd been watching you going back and forth to that looseleaf, putting in stuff and taking stuff out, and you always had this serious but serene look on your face. I simply had to know what was in there. So, I sat down that afternoon and started to read it. You were over at Eddie's and were going to spend the weekend there. I'm sorry, but I guess I'm just too nosey.

"I mean, it just kind of bowled me over. It was like all the things you wanted to know but were just too cool to admit that they mattered. Who knew I cared about spiritual shit? I certainly didn't. I used to be waiting on tables here and looking over at you and your groupies, and I'd wonder what it was all about. It was sort of funny that they all called you their guru, but it wasn't like I paid a lot of attention to what all of you were saying. And then I'm sitting in our room reading, and I realized they're pretty right on about your guruhood.

"So, I'm reading your thing 'On Awakening', and, so help me, I started to shake and tremble. There was some energy being released, and at first it scared the shit out of me, but then when it subsided, and I reread what you wrote, and it all made sense, it all came together. Maybe this guru thing was no joke.

"So, after I calmed down, I had this feeling that I had to do something about it, that it was selfish for me to sneak read your writings, and then keep them all for myself. So, I decided, and maybe it wasn't my right to decide, ... ," she trailed off, looking at Aziza for some sign of approval or disapproval, "I decided to print out a copy of the piece that moved me so, and post it here, on the bulletin board. After all, it's like your groupies can't get enough of you, and I knew they'd be thrilled about it."

"You what?" Aziza glared at her roommate.

"Well, I asked Alex to make an artistic surround for it, which he was okay with and did, and we titled it *Lessons From The Guru of Alphabet City*. Yeah, sorry Alex. I drew you into my conspiracy, but you did do a super job. And Arthur, he had no problem at all posting it. I mean, what he said was that we post the damn results for the dart league, and the guru table every weekend is a bigger draw."

"But I'm afraid it doesn't end there, Roomie. Arthur and I kind of thought people would be interested in going up to the board and reading it, and then running it around their heads before bringing it back to you, when you and Eddie were here. But instead, they all started to insist that they wanted copies for themselves, and you know Arthur, and how he is about money, so he says 'Sure, but that'll cost you a couple of bucks.' And they all say 'sure', and the next thing we know I'm running down to the print shop down the block and getting a big box of copies for Arthur to keep behind the bar. He's been selling them all week."

She reached into her apron, where she kept her bank, and pulled out an envelope. "So, here's two hundred and fifty-six dollars. I know Arthur's taken a cut for the house, but the rest is all yours. Umm. . . .surprise! I told you there'd be a surprise."

8

On Awakening

To be a seeker implies an inclination to find elusive truths, to solve the shadowy mysteries, to broaden narrow perspectives. Those of us who are seekers hope to experience our paths having moments of revelation along the way, when our inclinations are met and we get to see the world through new eyes. We experience this as an awakening. It is as if we were previously asleep, and now that we are awake, we realize that a broader level of consciousness has been achieved.

Sometimes, between our involvement in the urgency of everyday comings and goings of life and our previously programmed expectations about how awakenings might emerge, we miss the very moment we have sought. We "sleep" through our awakening. Our conscious mind remains unaware of the connections that the unconscious has made or the new paradigms that were suggested by the world around us. It's easy to get lost in the "stuff" of our routines and fail to see what is hidden in plain sight. All the components of a new lens with which to view the world can be laid out before us, but we can still neglect to assemble the parts into a complete picture.

However, if we have practiced the discipline of being a seeker, we can trust the unconscious to eventually reveal what the conscious mind has been too preoccupied to notice. Simply because we didn't recognize the awakening when it occurred, doesn't mean that the event didn't happen. It's just that we have unintendedly pressed the snooze alarm, and we will rouse a little later. Insights and understandings, some of them potentially paradigm shifting, may lay underneath the surface of our apperception, waiting for release.

Some other perceptual episode, related or unconnected, will eventually loosen the stored awakening, and it will rise to the surface. It will seem as if it came from nowhere, a lightning strike that came out of the blue. Without warning, it can feel as if the world is turned upside down, and nothing is as it was before. In truth, this "spontaneous" eruption, this rude awakening, was stowed away for later use, and came to light at the moment when it could most fully be grasped and utilized. It can feel as if the heavens have opened and some higher power is speaking to us, revealing what we need to know. History is replete with moments when prophets have experienced such flashes of Truth. We should not fear such moments, but anticipate and welcome them as touchstones of our journey.

The wise seeker, on the one hand, actively rummages through every nook and cranny for a more complete knowledge of the Mystery. On the other hand, the searcher welcomes all the baffling moments, when it seems that the chorus of mind has been joined by a new voice, and the background tone has changed. In meditation and musings, the seeker not only opens herself to an infinite universe out there, but also an immeasurable internal consciousness that only knows some of what it knows. It is not uncommon for the seeker to emerge from her meditation and feel as if some divinity is dictating a message.

Awakenings can happen at any moment, expected outcomes of a questing mind, or shooting stars in a tranquil sky. They transfix us and become the inflexion points of our life, those times when direction turns without any steering on our part. Be both patient and vigilant for their arrival. Do not seek to hasten or force the process with drugs or traumatic behaviors. Knocking your head against the wall might paradoxically feel good, but will never make you wiser or lead you to any useful spiritual knowledge. Staying vigilant entails paying attention to as much of your phenomenological field as possible, keeping your eyes, ears and heart open. When something new appears to be out of place, know that it is your expectation that is out of place, and rearrange your configuration so that the new component finds its place in a fresh montage. The smallest detail can transform what appears to be a colossal ageless truth. Conversely, we can easily overlook the largest factors when they seem obvious and habitual.

You may tend to identify these awakenings with changes in the external events in your life. "When I began my relationship with a new love." "When I moved to Colorado." "When I first began to run a mile before breakfast." But while these changes in your life may have been simultaneous with your awakening, or even precipitated it, keep your attention on what has been awakened. Yield to your new understanding and it will allow your path to flow without getting caught in the reeds.

Awakenings can be exhilarating and dazzling. Often, we can begin to review and replan our lives when we are awakened and full of the rush of the accompanying transformation. We imagine what life will be like while seeing with our new eyes and thinking with our nascent paradigms. We set out for new destinations, and establish new goals.

Never invest so totally in the most recent inflexion that you come to believe that the process is done. There will likely be more awakenings, more transformations, more inflection points. Be spiritually adaptive, always ready to ride the next wave.

Your being is an essential though miniscule embodiment of energy, a single drop of water, in an oceanic expanse of energy. If you stay alert and active there will be many awakenings. Dance with the waves, dive to the depths and travel with the currents. If you fall asleep on a raft atop the ocean, there will still be many awakenings. You will be able to surrender to the waves, the depths and the currents. You are both the drop and the ocean itself. All of your awakenings reveal another aspect of the relationship between the you and the You.

9

Aziza couldn't decide what disturbed her the most, the posting of her piece on the Rooster's bulletin board, or that people were actually paying for copies. She thought of her writings as personal, a private working through of the spiritual issues that plagued her, and demanded answers. Even in those pieces where she directly addressed other searchers, she meant it to be a dialogue between herself and an invented other, in which the discourse might challenge herself to coalesce ideas which needed to come together. Who was she to be telling anyone else how to think, how to live or how to find the peace she didn't possess herself? And who were they to dub her a guru and make her feel responsible for her personal voice guiding them toward practices she could only hypothesize about? Sure, she liked to throw around ideas and speculations and insights with Eddie, or Henry, some of the folks at the Rooster, or hell, even Alicia, if she wanted to join in. But putting her out there as if she was some damned guru?

And what was she supposed to do with the money? Just put it in her purse as if she had somehow earned it? It didn't feel right. Accepting the cash seemed like she was conceding herself to have some swami-ish wisdom which others should seek out and purchase. How egotistical could you be? On the other hand, she hadn't any way to give it back to the people who had laid out their two bucks. And what would she say to them, anyway? Stop paying attention (or money) to what I say? You're foolish for listening to my musings and thinking they're something special? Should she donate the money to some charity? If she was honest with herself, she did like having some extra cash around, even if she didn't like how it came to her. And it wasn't like she had done something wrong or immoral to get it.

When she asked Henry about how to handle it all, he simply advised that if her words had some value to people who were struggling with spiritual issues, then it was so, they had the value implied by the purchase. It wasn't for her to determine the value of her words or thoughts. Anne Frank had meant her diary to be personal, but look at the worth it has had to millions of people. And she was just a barely pubescent kid. If beauty is in the eye of the beholder, then wisdom may be in the purview of the disciple.

Eddie had a different and pragmatic take on it. He pointed out that she had been wondering what to do for a summer job, and if there were folks who wanted to pay her for her spiritual insights, then maybe it was an opportunity to devote time and energy to honing and organizing her thoughts and musings more thoroughly.

His father had asked him to deliver a sermon or two over the summer to his congregation, both to change things up a bit and to give Eddie a feeling for pastoral work. And Aziza hadn't thought that to be problematic, or egotistical or unethical. If she thought about it why was this different for her? Why not choose a topic each week, either something new or something previously composed that she wanted to rework or edit, and put it out there on the Rooster's bulletin board? It was a win-win. Instead of waiting tables in some restaurant or bar like Alicia, she could be doing what she loved the most. And for the people who paid a couple of bucks for what she posted, it could only help, it wasn't as if it was going to harm them. If they felt it was a help, then it was a help. That wasn't for her to decide.

C'mon Ziz, don't make this thing into such a big deal. As far as Eddie was concerned, it was harmless. Could she at least acknowledge that this was an opportunity for an earnest student to make a little cash while doing what she loved. If she wanted, he would speak to Arthur and work out an arrangement about how much he was charging and the amount the Thatched Rooster should keep for itself. If it was going to happen, it probably should be formalized.

The more Aziza thought about it, the more she began to see some validity to Eddie's point of view, even if she was emotionally perturbed about it. The Quadrumvirate had signed a yearly lease and that meant they had to come up with rent over the summer. To ask her parents to support her in the months she wasn't in school wasn't close to acceptable, even if they were okay with it. And she didn't really feature working some minimum wage job that didn't accomplish much more than a paycheck. If she just gave one little piece to the Rooster each week, it would give her the chance instead to spend the summer continuing to study more and delve into the philosophical drifts that moved her. And she had to admit that, for the most part, she did enjoy the back and forth with the folks at the Rooster, even if it became demanding some of the time. If that wasn't the case, then she would have stopped hanging out there on the weekends. Maybe it wasn't the fun that most kids her age pursued, but for her, it was, well usually, a fun and interesting ride.

Oh hell, it was even cool. Yeah, being cool wasn't what motivated her, she didn't have some deep need to be hip. But was there anything wrong in enjoying some cool aura if it was foisted upon you? The truth was that there was something funny about the designation of The Guru of Alphabet City. Sort of like "tergiversation." She had absolutely always loved that word. Contradicting herself and going in opposite directions at the same time. Who knows? Maybe, that was a sort of definition of who she ultimately was.

And if she got off her high horse, at the end of the day, Eddie was probably right. If she had something to say and people wanted to pay a couple of bucks for it, then why the hell not give them what they wanted? Like he said, it's a win-win. Maybe a win-win-win. They profit. I profit. And the whole thing's kind of cool, to boot. And it's not like anything much is going to come of it. Just pray that none of my professors somehow catch up with any of this. That would be true mortification.

10

In the agreement that Eddie worked through, Arthur wanted a new treatise to be posted every Wednesday. This would leave a couple of days for copies to be bought and mindsets to percolate before the weekend. The very nature of the Thatched Rooster clientele was changing. Fridays were now bringing in a whole different crew, people who wanted to throw around, discuss and debate religious and spiritual issues. Who knew there were so many people who were into this kind of thing? Arthur just shook his head and laughed. "Takes all kinds, but if that's what they're looking for, a hangout for the alternative devout, then that's what they'll get." He was amazed that the attraction to the Rooster was even beginning to extend beyond Aziza and her "guruhood." A crowd was even starting to amble in after church on Sundays, filling in a timeslot which had been for all intents and purposes barren of customers, when New Yorkers typically stayed home with their bagels and the Sunday *Times*. Sure, it was still a hip bunch, but a whole different brand of hip.

Over the summer, Alicia already was working five full shifts a week, including Friday and Saturday nights, and didn't want to add Sunday morning to her worktime. Alex eagerly grabbed up the emergent shift. He had a summer gig interning at Time/Life, but the remuneration for that was more about prestige than capital, and he welcomed the opportunity to bring in some serious cash. More and more, it seemed like the Quadrumvirate was taking over the Rooster. Only Bill, who had picked up a summer job with the Port Authority as a vacation replacement toll collector, was left out of the mix. But he would stop by for a beer after work, sadly announcing to anyone who would hear, "Can you believe I'm collecting money for the establishment? Three dollars at a time."

It was a typically hot and humid August in New York. Without any air conditioning, the apartment felt even more oppressive than the steaming sidewalks. In the front room, Aziza tried to drown out the noise from the horde of kids playing in the splash from the hydrant, escaping from their hothouse buildings. However, this was not the kind of weather where you wanted to close the front windows! It was hard to think, much less concentrate, and she considered heading out to Hollis and spending a few days with her parents, maybe just until the heat wave was over. At least she and Alicia had picked up a fan. It didn't lower the room temperature, but it moved the hot air around, giving some minimal relief. Then again, it was one more noise, added to the already deafening din created by the open windows. Aziza had her hair up to keep her neck from getting sweatier than it was, a losing battle, and her mood sank, as she couldn't think, much less write.

The bell rang, and she got up to answer the door, half relieved to have a reason to remove herself from her frustration, and half annoyed that someone or something had a reason to impose on her worktime. Who the hell could it be? Everybody she knew was at work. The image of a pair of Jehovah Witnesses lurking on the other side of the door, leaflets in hand, came to her mind, and set off a cringing shudder through her body. Just what I don't need, that's for sure.

Instead, when she opened the door, she was presented with a woman she didn't know, thirtyish, wearing a white peasant blouse and matching harem pants, and toting a notebook and a small black recording device in her right hand. The stranger tried hard to posture a smile, despite being a bit out of breath from walking the stairs. She transferred her equipment to her left hand, extending the right.

"Hi, there. Are you Aziza Shapiro?"

Aziza nodded, and clumsily shook the preferred hand.

"I'm Claire Ethanger, from the *Village Voice*. Do you have a couple of minutes?"

"I guess that depends on what you need me for. I'm pretty busy at the moment. What's this all about."

"I'm sorry for just barging in on you, but we didn't have a phone number for you. I got your address from Arthur, over at the Rooster, and I thought I'd leave a note, if you weren't in. If you could be so kind as to let me inside, I'd be glad to explain."

Aziza realized she was still blocking the door, and moved back into the kitchen. "Huh, I guess." She cleared a couple of coffee mugs and plates from the table, putting them in the sink, and motioned for the woman to have a seat. "So, what can I do for you, Ms. Ethanger?"

"Please call me Claire," she tendered. "As I said, I'm a reporter for the *Voice*, and we'd like to do a piece on you."

This was making no sense at all to Aziza. Why on earth would the *Village Voice* have any interest in her? "Excuse me. Are you sure you have the right person? I can't imagine any reason why you'd want to do that."

"Well then, you must not be aware of the stir you've created. There's a lot of buzz going around about the Guru of Alphabet City. I've had at least five tips from my sources that I'd better interview you, that everyone east of 6th Avenue is talking about you, and wants to know about who you are, and what you're really all about."

Aziza took a breath, reminding herself inwardly to tell Eddie that she never should have listened to him, and that this whole thing was preposterous. "Claire, I don't know who your sources are, but frankly, I can't believe there's much of a 'stir', as you call it, about me. Yeah sure, I guess my boyfriend and myself hang at the Rooster sometimes and we like to talk about and get into a bunch of spiritual discussions. And some friends of mine convinced me to post the Guru thing. God, I hate that title. But the whole thing's not such a big deal, and I can't imagine that anyone would really want to read about it, read about me."

"Aziza, knowing what readers want to hear about is my business, and trust me, they do want to hear about you." She paused, and then changed perspectives. "Look, the whole purpose of *The Voice* is to keep track of the pulse in Greenwich Village and report on new happenings and emerging influences, long before the major media gets a hold of them. There's a long history of cultural movements which started in the Village, way back from Mark Twain and Edgar Allan Poe to Bob Dylan and Jack Kerouac. It's historically fact that the bohemian centers in any culture give rise to sweeping social changes in art, and social reform, and yes, even spiritual matters. That's no different here than it is in Paris, Berlin or any other major city that hosts an avant-garde community.

"And, frankly, despite the status and fame of all of these people, the movement they generate is more important than their personages. Do you think the people in the Stonewall knew what they were creating? Do you think that the folks in Gerdes Folk City knew how Dylan was going to turn music in America over on its head? Do you really think that Pearl Buck or Marianne Moore or Edward Albee knew how they were going to influence literature the way they did. Hell no. They were all hanging out in Greenwich Village because it was a place where they were comfortable, and they were just doing their thing.

"Like I said, there's a buzz going on around these sacred streets, and sure, it's about you and what's happening at the Thatched Rooster, but it wouldn't be happening if you didn't represent something bigger than just you going on. I need to figure out what that is and tell my readers about it."

Aziza took this in. "Okay, I'll concede that there's something going on with all these people jamming themselves into the Rooster, or even wanting to read what I have to say. Which I need to point out, I didn't post in the first place. A friend of mine decided all that for me, without letting me know about it until it was a done deal. But I don't know how I can help you about all of that. I still can't figure out the why of all this hubbub. I'm sharing my ideas, but why anybody is interested is a mystery and a half, to me."

"Well, maybe that's why you're the guru and I'm the journalist. Let me ask you a bunch of questions, and maybe we'll think this thing out." She looked squarely at Aziza. "What do you say? We could talk here, or if you want, we could do the interview over at my offices, or even at the Thatched Rooster, for that matter."

Aziza thought about it. She wasn't getting anything done, anyway, and getting out of the heat into some air conditioning would sure be welcome. And, some part of her did want to figure out the larger sense of what was going on, why this whole thing was spiraling out into whatever it was. "Okay, give me a minute to put something on. Either your offices or the Rooster. Either is all right."

"Well then, you go change and we'll jump in a cab and go over to my office. We'll probably be more comfortable talking there, and anyway, I've got my camera there."

Almost turning around and changing her mind when she heard "camera," Aziza just nodded and went back to her room. Guess I'll have to put something decent on. This gets more and more interesting. I think.

11

Aziza had changed into a smart man-tailored shirt and a pair of white slacks, prior to coming over to the *Village Voice* offices. White sneaks, not sandals. There could be nothing on her which said "guru." As she sat down in Claire Ethanger's office, she wished she had just thrown on some jeans and a tee. It was a comfortable workplace, more of a comfortable meeting room, than anything else. Looking around, she couldn't help but notice the many awards and plaques for various features articles. Whoa, she's interviewed Mailer! And Capote. No Pulitzer, but impressive.

"So how do we do this?" she asked, as Claire brought in a couple of cups of coffee.

"Well, if you're ready to begin, I'll turn on the recorder, and we can start." When Aziza didn't respond, she started the tape rolling and began her interview. Aziza was surprised that she wanted a lot of background information about family, growing up in Hollis, and the spiritual/religious orientation that had been present in her youth. The woman was intrigued with Aziza's passion for the transcendent, despite having no formal religious instruction in her early years. When Aziza made no mention of a father, the reporter inquired as to her paternal origins. At first, she started to bypass the issue, before reminding herself that there was nothing to be shameful about her conception through rape, and spoke openly about it. The family had never shied away from this discussion. Whenever the issue had come up, Mom had consistently put it right out there, resolved that the dishonor was on the part of the abuser not the victim. She had always made it clear to her daughter, that if her conception had not been an outcome of love, her existence had from the first been met with love, by both herself and her grandparents. Aziza should never believe she had sprung from anything but unconditional affection and devotion. Chen and Aunt Lian, had only deepened the caring support that she felt beneath her. And Grandpa, could there ever be a greater champion or stronger advocate?

Funny how unintended consequences emerge from unexpected conversations. Aziza realized that there was a new perspective to be gained in addressing Claire's questions about her family. She recognized, probably for the first time, how little she had ever questioned her value or worth, compared to most of her peers. How little she needed or sought validation. How strange it was that her mother's acceptance of the outcome of a brutal rape could lead to such a strong and vital love. Love which she was replicating at this point in her life, with Eddie, or her friends, and maybe even with the folks she didn't really know, over at the Rooster.

And no, she had never had any desire to go to Israel and find out any information about her biological father. God, no! Even if that were remotely possible, it wouldn't serve her in any way that she could envision. Was he some instrument of universal intention? An interesting idea, she'd have to think about it, but off the top of her head, probably not. That would imply a higher power with personal intentionality. And no, she didn't have any biologically driven feeling of connection with the Holy Land of the world's religions. If anything, the land of Israel or Palestine was associated by Aziza with organized religion, foolhardy war and conflict. And surely, if Claire had read the pieces she claimed to have read, then she knew that Aziza was no fan of institutional religion.

The conversation drifted into Aziza's aversion to being called a guru, and what did that say about her? And what did it imply about her relationship with those who were clearly holding her in the type of esteem through which they looked toward her for spiritual wisdom?

Again, Aziza had never looked at herself or questioned herself from this perspective, and thought that maybe it was a valid if not valuable area of inquiry. Forget for a minute the word 'guru', and the negative association that came to her mind when people called her that. Why did she recoil from people thinking of her as possessing sagacity, feeling as if she had something vital to offer them? In those times when it was just a conversation, having some talk over a beer or a cup of coffee, then she had no problem asserting what she felt to be true, and felt comfortable while doing it. But when the same people anointed her as some sort of spiritual leader, she wanted to put on her sneakers and run as fast as she could. No, it wasn't fear that her thoughts didn't hold up, that she might be plain wrong. They did hold up or they didn't, and that was all okay. It's about the search, and the search lasts forever. False ideas can only lead to the truth, over time. Henry had taught her that long ago. No one who follows a path of searching for universal truth should expect to find a point of nirvana where truth has been secured and the search ends. The pot of gold beyond the rainbow can only be approached as a limit. Hmmm. She really should write about that. Maybe tomorrow.

What was it then? Some reverse ego thing? I'm not sure I even know what that means. I don't know. The closest I can get to it is that I just don't want to feel responsible for other peoples' lives, their actions, behaviors or beliefs. I'm still just trying to work out a relationship with this universe I exist in for myself. Who am I to claim I have some special insight into the All and Everything, that I can lead others into their own relationship with their Creation? I mean, Grandpa always told me to have chutzpah, but c'mon.

Aziza was surprised at how comfortable she felt in her conversation with this reporter from the *Voice*. It wasn't that Claire had some special journalistic way of drawing stuff out of her, or calming her distrust about how she would be portrayed. It was more that Claire knew how to listen, that she didn't add or subtract or agree or disagree. She provided an opportunity for her interviewee to externally express the threads of their thoughts without fear of judgement or interference. Sometimes this would even generate new thoughts precipitated by the questions. That's a skill, Aziza admired. I wish I could learn that.

The exchange moved on to Aziza's social perspectives. Ethanger was interested in Aziza's take on a wide variety of issues. Crime, poverty, addiction, the women's movement, and on. She seemed to be suggesting that others viewed these matters from a perspective of good vs. evil, and wondered whether a spiritual outlook necessitated the application of moral standards toward social behaviors. Again, not something that Aziza had thought much about, but she found herself saying that it would be difficult to imagine icons like Gandhi or King separating their social and spiritual objectives. That would represent a false dichotomy. And good vs. evil? No, she didn't buy into a theological stance that would have a Prince of Lightness contrasting with a Prince of Darkness, signifying virtue and sin as universal themes that warred forever. In the All and Everything, everything is just what it is. Our conduct here on this planet, that is a very different thing, in which good and evil actions clearly exist in a wide spectrum, as we apply ethical judgement to human behavior.

The women's movement? Gender equality starts with all of us, male or female, experiencing ourselves as being equal. If I know that I am a worthy part of the Creation, an honorable citizen of the Planet and human being who is doing everything I can to be human, then I have no problem asserting myself as equal in value to anyone else, of either gender. First, we women have to overcome our own self-loathing and prejudice born out of a long history in which religious institutions were at the forefront of the perception of the female as inferior. Letting go of any institutions, religious or not, which support and guide this stupidity is an obvious necessity for women. Hmmm, that was a little more strident than I would have expected of myself.

For whatever reasons, Claire didn't delve into any of the postings from the Rooster, although she had a bunch of them on her desk. Toward the end of the interview Aziza asked her about this, and was told "I already have those and have read them. You write well, Aziza, and I'm not confused or unclear about what you are presenting. I needed this interview to learn about who you are and what you represent. I certainly didn't want to restrict our conversation to your spiritual perspective."

She asked if Aziza would be okay with a photographer coming in and taking a couple of head shots, and Aziza agreed, even as her body internally was saying "do we have to?." But it was over in a couple of minutes anyway, and a little later, as she was walking back to the apartment, Aziza laughed at herself for worrying about a picture after she had spent a couple of hours revealing a lot more than her external image. Part of her expected that some editor, Claire's boss, would throw the whole article in the circular file, feeling like his reporter had wasted a lot of time on some still adolescent girl who had some glorified sanctified pretensions. Part of her was worried that she was going to be portrayed as a self-aggrandizing buffoon. But, when she thought about it, she dismissed these thoughts, believing that Claire was genuinely interested in what this all meant, and wasn't into writing a hit-piece. I guess we'll find out pretty soon. Like I said before we left the apartment, life sure is interesting.

12

On A Journey Without Preplanned Destinations

There is that part of us that always seeks a destination in our life's journey. We have become so imbued with a linear model that we only feel secure if we sense that our life is going "somewhere." It feels as if our existence would be meaningless if we didn't get from "here" to "there," here suggesting that our being is insufficient at this point in our life, and there implying that we can progress to a point when our lives will be both improved and validated. Our ship will come in. The destination will make the whole trip worthwhile, no matter that it may have been painful and confusing along the way. If we can reach that special station, we will have won the game of life. Whatever our origins, arriving there will allow us to feel that we have completed our journey and lived a good life in the process.

In secular terms, people set goals for their life. Some wish to amass some level of wealth. Some want to rise to a particular level in their occupational ladder. Others are satisfied with family goals as a significator of the worthiness of their life.

In spiritual terms, people seek either some point in their life's path that offers absolute transcendency whereby they become a cosmic know-it-All, or a point after death in which their life is validated by acceptance into a special only-by-invitation afterlife. Whether in life or after death, these destinations would be marked by a state of bliss and the experience of a love that has no boundaries. There would be no more struggles or hardship. Confusion, shame and disappointment would be in the rearview mirror. And there would somehow still be a self that could be aware that it had succeeded in life by virtue of reaching this special point.

Some people buy into this ultimate spiritual destination because they have not been able to accomplish their secular aspirations. In turning over their lives and choosing a celestial target for living, they can still win in the losers' ladder. Other folks, who think of themselves as pragmatists, are concerned only with obtaining a predefined degree of material or social success. They are confident that their peers, who seek a heavenly success, are missing the boat in a shark filled ocean.

These concepts of the Path are all grounded in a linear paradigm which requires a beginning, middle and end. To perceive the Path through a lens of recurrent waves is either inconceivable or impossible to them. A cyclic path generates anxiety for people who have been conditioned to always seeing life linearly. Without a clearly identified terminus, they would have to be always inquisitive, ever adaptive, and continually willing to redefine themselves and the nature of their universe. It means surrendering to a world of the always unknown, even after moments of transformation or transcendence.

We accept that the All and Everything is infinite. How audacious it would be to imagine that some particular moment of clarity about its make-up would reveal the entire glory of its nature. Yes, there are special moments when it feels as if an entirely new dimension has been added to all that we are, and all that we perceive. But there will be new dimensions after that, and new dimensions after that, as our Path winds its way through time and the totality. Our search is never ending. Each moment of sudden and overwhelming clarity becomes another foothold to move on and reach the next.

When we are freed from notions of satori or nirvana, points of ultimate transcendence, we can travel on our journey without fears that we will miss some ultimate understanding of all understandings, the mother of all insight and connection. Nor will we feel the need to travel some prescribed route in order to attain a predefined loving or joyful state. We must be free to allow our Path to both define who we are and to be defined by who we are. We don't have to fear "missing it" when we know that the infinite universe has infinite Pathways with which to explore the All. While we look up at the sky and connect the dots so as to make constellations, therefore trying to bring order to what we see as total chaos, these constellations are man-made illusions. They may help us to navigate on Earth, but will cause us to get lost when we venture into the infinity of space.

A transformation for me can serve as a touchstone or waypoint for my life's travel. For you, it could be a starting point, or possibly just plain irrelevant. There need be no necessary points of inflection or absolute benchmarks for us to mark on a sanctified map. We can let go of reaching for a point where we merge with the gods and achieve ultimate satori. Instead, we can unwind our Path toward the truths it discovers along the Way, resting from time to time, but not stopping, on our unique and endless journey. Search on!

13

A Conversation With

A Reluctant Guru - Aziza Shapiro

By Claire Ethanger

Whatever preconceptions I had about the woman I was about to meet were blown away when she opened her Alphabet City apartment door. With expectations of ashramic affectation fixed in my mind, I was met instead by an engaging "girl next door," if your next-door neighbor happened to be a take-your-breath-away beauty. Without pretension or artifice, a young but sagacious woman welcomed me into her home, disbelieving that anyone would be interested in reading about her. The next three hours were spent in an enlightening conversation that was the equal to any interview I have had with Village luminaries through the years.

I had set out to meet the cause of all the stir from The Thatched Rooster, a well know watering hole on Avenue B. For weeks I had been hearing about the Rooster, as if it was a new spiritual Mecca. Once a neighborhood hangout for East Village locals, the coffee house/bar was becoming a magnet for all things and folks spiritual. Friday nights found tables full with people of all religious backgrounds and beliefs, avidly sharing and debating the transcendent issues which are usually reserved for seminary classrooms and places of worship. And at the center of it all was this young woman, dubbed The Guru of Alphabet City, whose homilies had been selling like hotcakes. It had become a phenomenon, and I hoped to discern the portents of this new trend, by engaging with the woman who appeared to embody the craze. For the past century and a half, Greenwich Village has been the breeding ground for most of the important movements in American culture, in art, music, literature and social issues. What was this new development, and what did it mean going forward?

Not yet twenty, Aziza Shapiro is exquisitely attractive. Her physicality blends the best of her Palestinian and Ashkenazy heritage. She is without any pretention. What you see is what you get. And what you get is a brilliant mind that appears to have been focused on understanding the universe beyond her vision from her earliest days. Brought up in Queens, she was clearly cradled in a loving home and family. While not directed to any religious orientation, all of the elements needed for serious spiritual inquiry were always present. She was grounded in the importance of ethics, empathy, and a need to speculate on the questions which seem to be unanswerable. Even as a child she sought to see beyond the stars.

Her teachings, and she would be the first to object to categorizing them as such, appear to incorporate a wide array of religious and spiritual views. She is no friend of dogma, and calls out the follies of religion for being self-centered when the task of the spiritual would be better served by practicing institutional humility. She simply seeks to help us all to discover in our lifetime who we really are, what the universe we live in is really all about, and what relationship would be best between the two. No small task, but this is a woman who is mature beyond her years, and willing to take on the cosmic challenge.

But as enthusiastic as she is about deciphering the eternal questions, she is equally reluctant to be identified as a guru, or even teacher. She simply wants to explore and share what she finds along the way.

She blends confidence with humility and openness with privacy. The 70's brashness marked a shift from the subterranean feel of the 60's. While both these decades were addressing the need for a more loving humanity, between the lines, all puns intended, they were slowly giving rise to a culture marked by incredible levels of narcissism. Could this reluctant guru be a forerunner of a counter movement, one marked by humility and concern for a more personal ethic? One can only hope.

We certainly need it. The reluctant Guru of Alphabet City has a needed role to play in this time when too many of us have become stuck in a self-centered universe. Will she be able to find her way to accept such a role?

Will we allow her? Stay tuned.

14

The city was setting records, now in its 13th day of temperatures over 90 degrees. However, Aziza wasn't at her parent's house in Hollis to avoid the scorching weather, although she had to admit that the air conditioning was a welcome respite from the heat wave. Instead, she had left Manhattan on Sunday morning to get away from a different atmosphere, a succession of reporters who were chasing her like paparazzi on the prowl. Following the publication of the piece on the *Village Voice*, every paper in New York, other than the *Times*, wanted in on the story. They jostled and prodded whoever was in their way, calling out for "just a couple of words," or "just a picture of two." On Friday night, over at the Rooster, she and Eddie had to sneak out the back door, with the hounds circling their table, throwing out inane questions, and disturbing the usual Friday night interactions. They stayed Friday night at Eddie's place, which thankfully hadn't been discovered by the press. Aziza went back to her apartment late on Saturday, when it felt relatively safe, and then left for "home" early in the morning.

"Mom, it's so fucking unbelievably weird," she complained. "You'd think I was Princess Diana. What makes these people give themselves permission to insert themselves into every obscure corner of somebody's life?"

"Well, I guess that's what happens when a someone becomes a somebody," Esther responded, with an almost admonishing tone.

"Really? I didn't ask for this," Aziza defended herself. "I mean, Mom, you were there. Alicia took my stuff and posted it, and the whole thing has taken off from there like the Beatles or the Stones coming to America. I feel like I'm locked in some autopilot car, destination unknown."

"Well, you did agree to do the interview for the *Village Voice*. Honey, you opened up the door for this attention, in more ways than one."

"But that's what's so frustrating about all this. I agreed to the interview with Ethanger because she was interested in the larger picture that all this represents, not me. I've got no problem with her, or the article, for that matter. All these other reporters, they come from a very different and, frankly, a sick place. It's like they just want to create some cartoon image in the public eye, and then turn around, smack it around, and knock it down. No thanks."

Shen, cautiously, as was his way, joined in. "Sweetheart, can we look at this for a moment from a different perspective?" He paused leaving time for an objection to his intrusion, and also a moment to gather his thoughts. "You are not, and never have been, someone who seeks attention or notoriety. It seems to me that you care, care deeply, about what you study. Your interest in spiritual matters has been constant ever since I've been a member of this family and a part of your life. And now, there seems to be a conflict between these two aspects of you. On the one hand you want to share your thoughts and interconnect with others and thereby evolve your thinking about theology and the transcendent. On the other, you don't want to assume authorship or notorious attention for your efforts. You strongly believe that people's thoughts and views are private, and, I would add," he stressed, "as long as we keep them inside, they are. But once we put them out there in the world, there are responsibilities and consequences that ensue."

"I don't follow. What responsibilities and consequences?" Neither Esther nor Aziza was clear where he was going with this.

"Okay. If you speak about your thoughts concerning issues that no one cares about, small talk, random ideas, whatever, then there is no particular responsibility attached. But when you broach areas of social or intellectual significance, then you become responsible for shepherding your contemplations, ensuring that they are neither misunderstood nor bastardized, nor that they have a negative effect on others. When we give birth to ideas, they are our children, and they must be protected.

"Similarly, while speech is free and we will hopefully always have the right to speak freely, there are still consequences that arise for us from what we say, in public. We have to be clear whether or not we want to be subject to those consequences before we throw them to either the public square or the wind."

"You're talking about your father, aren't you Shen," Esther clarified, recalling his painful history, and knowing how seminal his father's 'disappearance' had been in all of their lives.

"Yes, my father had to know that his words could have the consequences that they did, and he still felt the responsibility to speak them. But we all have to accept this. You, Esther, speak your truth to families that are at risk on a daily basis, knowing both the responsibilities and the consequences. I do this in business. The areas we address and the bottom lines may be different, but the underlying issues are the same."

Aziza took this all in and was taken aback. In due course she said, "You know, I've probably heard the admonishment to 'take responsibility for your words' a thousand times, but I've always taken that to mean that I should be careful to think things through thoroughly and to avoid saying anything that would hurt somebody needlessly. But what you're saying turns all that upside down. . . . . I've just realized something, and like it or not it's true. I guess there comes a time when young adults have to start taking themselves and their ideas seriously, because . . . .they're not kids anymore. They, no. . . . . ., not they, me, have matured into a whole different context . . . . Whether or not I want to, I can't think of myself as incidental to the 'grownup's' conversation, or even just a college student, anymore. My lord, is that a major revelation for everybody around my age, or am I just late to the table?"

"I think we all are belatedly surprised at the complexities and difficulties of becoming adult," Mom nodded in agreement. "When we're still teenagers, it feels like we have a kind of special cloak of protective invisibility, because the adults don't take what we say seriously. After all, we're still just kids, aren't we? We want to be taken earnestly when it's about getting the perks of adulthood, but still want an available excuse of just being a child when we shout out our ideas. Welcome to the club, oh daughter of mine."

"So, Dad, does all this come down to a choice between adulting my thoughts or choosing to keep them to myself?"

"You could put it like that. But that leaves out reckoning with your sense of mission. You can't make this choice that lies in front of you until you know your sense of purpose. It was my father's mission that caused him to make the choice he did. And I learned many years ago that your mother's dedication to at-risk adolescent girls would always outweigh any concerns I had for her safety."

Aziza synthesized all of the conversation. "This is so damned strange. The frame keeps changing up on me. When I woke up this morning it was all about attention versus privacy. Then, just a minute ago, it was about shepherding versus isolation. Now it's morphing into mission versus self-interest."

Shen heard her, and responded, "Are you sure that not all of those frames are in play? Either fortunately or unfortunately, circumstances are forcing you to define yourself prematurely at barely nineteen years old, when most of us usually have the decade of our twenties to slip into our skin."

"So, the bottom line is that the issue is me, not the reporters, or the handy cash, or even my speculations. It's about deciphering and declaring who I am, ready or not."

Esther put her arm around her daughter's shoulder. "Life certainly compelled me to figure myself out on the spot when I found out I was pregnant with you. And Lian and Shen had to redefine themselves a lot younger than either of us. Maybe there are critical moments in life, that can occur at any age, when situations demand delineation of our identities. Is it ready or not, or sooner or later?"

"Well, sooner or later I guess I'm going to have to face that mob. Maybe I'd better put on my big girl pants and deal with it, ready or not."

"You will, my dear. Of that I have little doubt. You've always been someone who faces up to the challenges." She didn't need or want to tell her daughter what to do, only express her confidence in Aziza's ability to choose her correct path. Esther turned her tone and the conversation in a different direction. "And one more thing. I think you should consider talking this over with Henry. In some ways he could be more helpful to you than Dad and myself. You know, you always have recognized his knowledge and expertise in all things theosophical, but you forget that he has a very pragmatic side to him. He is the administrator of a unique congregation, that has to weave and bob its ways through complex interactions with the larger community."

"You're right. I should give him a ring. Maybe I can stop there on my way back to the city. But for now, there's no way I'm going outside until the sun goes down and it cools off."

15

On The Nature Of Sin

There are those who would divide human behaviors into two opposing categories, those that are moral, and those that are immoral, or sinful. Some would assert that there is a Higher Power, or God, who defines and guides us to know which behaviors lie in which category. To them, we serve God by behaving with goodness, or serve evil by behaving in a sinful manner. Others would assert that the moral division of human behaviors is a social construct, a core foundation piece of civilization, if you will. When behaving well we serve the society or community in which we live. When behaving badly we betray and subvert the society which supports both us and our neighbors.

We reserve these behavioral dichotomies for human beings. We don't, for example, consider the predator animal to be sinful for killing its prey. It is considered to be the natural order of things that a lion should act like a lion. The animal kingdom doesn't have the consciousness to be aware of and consider the implications of its behavior, nor the intelligence to consider and choose from alternatives. It is the consciousness that we humans possess that distinguishes us from the rest of the animal kingdom. We are aware of the implications of our behavior and choose which behaviors to follow. Thus, immoral or sinful behaviors are seen as being the product of either a corrupt or malfunctioning mind. Some see these "disturbances" to be caused by mental or social illness, others identify it as being the product of being possessed by an evil counterpart to their Higher Power's goodness, a Devil or Satan, or Beelzebub.

For those who follow the model of a universe in which the eternal forces of good and evil conflict forever, choosing goodness and forsaking sin allows them to serve their Higher Power in its battle with a "lower" power. Those who don't join in this universal struggle need to be saved from themselves. For those who follow a social construct, it is believed that their responsibility is to serve and preserve the "family of man" by choosing ethical and righteous behaviors that are helpful to all, and to rehabilitate their peers who behave badly.

These two models can be boiled down to two core beliefs. The first would have it that beyond survival and reproduction, the purpose of life is to serve one's Higher Power. The second would have it that the purpose of life is to serve Civilization.

We have asserted elsewhere that we perceive the purpose of life to be learning who we are and our relationship to the All and Everything. Life is a process of discovery, of self, of other, and of the dynamic relationship between the two. We are each of us a finite part of the infinite universe from which we were composed. The time we get to discern our Self is limited to our lifetime, as much as we yearn to know beyond our years. We both learn who we are and discover who we are not. There is a process of shedding a false self along the way, the true self becoming clearer as it is less adulterated. As we realize our unique Self, our behaviors change. Behaviors which were grounded in social conditioning and were not reflective of our true nature are shed with the false selves they reflect.

From this perspective, our human capacity for increased awareness of our true Self requires that we adapt or change our behaviors as we move further down our Path, with greater knowledge as to who we are. Then, sin becomes defined as continuing to behave in ways which were reflective of a false self after learning otherwise. Sin is knowingly acting in ways which contradict our knowledge of who we are. Whatever it may appear externally, the greatest injury of sin is to self.

We have observed a great surge of narcissism within our culture. The narcissists are individuals who devote their life to an adoration of the false self, and are therefore perhaps the most sinful of personality types. Narcissists also are unaccepting of perceiving themselves as part of a larger whole. Consequently, they are also the most sinful when looked at through religious or social lenses. The power and influence they seek serves only their empty shell.

Would we do better to avoid sin or to pursue goodness? Goodness here can be defined as staying true to the lessons we have learned about ourselves while living our lives. Set your direction to goodness. We don't have to fear that our life lessons will turn us toward evil. While we all possess the capacity to harm others, human beings are a social animal that is biologically disposed to be part of communities, complete with their mores and ethos. Our individual welfare is unequivocally bound to our social well-being. Being ourselves includes being an ethical human being. When we devote ourselves to being who we are and that which we love, sin becomes irrelevant. Neither the culture nor the cosmos needs to fear us when we are true to our Selves. When we are thoughtfully true to ourselves, we do not need to fear the retaliation or repugnance of either the cosmos nor the culture.

16

Mom was right. The good Leader Posert had a side to him which Aziza had never thought about, even if it seemed obvious in reflection. It turned out that before his protégé's visit, he hadn't heard about the article in the *Village Voice*, or the bruhaha that ensued after its publication. He listened carefully as she laid out what had happened and her present difficulties, and responded in a different manner than she had anticipated. "Aziza, it seems to me that you are experiencing a situation which many of us "ivory towers lost in the clouds" types fall into all the time.

She looked at him askance. "ivory towers lost in the clouds" types?"

"Well, sure, I know that kind of phrase is usually put out there as a dig by folks who don't appreciate our focus, but that doesn't mean it doesn't have some truth to it. I had to admit to myself many years ago that there were some skills in which I was totally deficient, and these were probably a direct outcome of my concentration on what I prefer to think of as higher issues."

"Like what?"

"Oh, there's a whole range of stuff. Like I'm particularly poor at small talk, even if being the leader of a congregation needs that kind of talent all the time. Thankfully, I have a spouse who has no problem lending her proficiency in that area to our common interest. Aziza, I absolutely suck at parties, local politics are an anathema to me, and, yes, I'm a moron if I have to deal with the press. I may not be the stereotype of the absent-minded professor, but if I'm honest, I have to admit that there are many practical components of life that, let's just say, I suffer at. And truthfully, when this egghead thinks about it, I'm not really inclined to devote a lot of energy to developing a more robust ability in any of these areas."

"Oh Uncle Henry, you're not that much of a social oaf." She laughed at his klutzy portrayal of himself.

"Well, maybe not to you, but that's my whole point. We speak the same language, you and I. Our attitudes and altitudes are alike. So, there's never been anything clumsy or discomforting when we relate to each other. Even when you were a child at the time we met. Honey, I'm not putting either of us down. I'm simply pointing out that despite our abilities, we don't tend to care that much about the social niceties that are what motivates many of our respective peers." He ever so slightly groaned. "Look. Tell me honestly that there's no part of you that feels like you often don't quite fit in. I mean from your side, not about whether other people accept you. Other folks clearly are drawn to you and find you attractive. But their being drawn to you doesn't mean that you feel like you fit in with them." He added, "I know that feeling, even if I don't attract people like you do."

"Uncle Henry," she started, a bit uncomfortable with the personal disidentification, "I don't know what this has to do with my situation. Yeah, okay. I'm not a social butterfly and don't yearn to belong. Never have been, and guess I never will. But these reporters are all over me like white on rice, this guru business is wearing awfully thin, and I feel like I'm drowning in attention, hardly missing it."

"What I'm trying to tell you, Aziza, and I guess not particularly well, is that you should stop trying to handle this situation for yourself. You'll never be very good at it. You need to get someone who knows how to manage these things to handle it for you."

"Granted. But, like who?"

"Like here at the Society. I have both a personal secretary and a public relations firm that can deal with all the situations which I would cope with badly. I wouldn't think of doing their jobs myself. Aziza, of course you don't know how to handle the press. Who would ever expect that you would? That's why mayors have press secretaries and CEO's have publicists."

"And just how am I supposed to hire someone like that? I can see the ad now. Wanted. One experienced public relations expert for a broke college undergraduate. No salary, but lots of spiritual benefits. Apply in person to the Thatched Rooster."

"Very funny. No, I know that you're not in any position to hire some PR firm. But lucky for you, you're speaking to someone who loves you and has someone just like that on retainer. Let me speak to my guy, Carl. I'm pretty sure I can get him to either take care of all the press that are banging on your door, or at least, he can advise you on what to do."

"Could you really? If I could just do what I do and leave this mess in someone else's hands, I'd be the happiest guru in New York City. All kidding aside, Uncle Henry. That would be wonderful, if you could."

"Well, I'll call him later and give him your number. Hopefully he'll contact you tomorrow. Now, how about some lunch? I picked up some bagels and some whitefish this morning. Hey, I'm good for some things!"

"On the contrary, Uncle Henry, you're good for most things."

17

Carl Porcaro, Aziza thought, could have materialized out of a cubistic painting. Square jaw, flat top hair, shoulders clearly molded through daily strenuous workouts, he was all right angles and talking-head speak. His verbiage even had a kind of rectangular rhythm to it, shortish chopped sentences, angular. To the point.

"Ms. Shapiro, after I spoke with Henry last night, I checked you out with some print media connections. You are hot, no doubt about it, you are a hot topic. Don't know if you appreciate it, or not, but it is what it is."

They had met over a cup of coffee in a luncheonette on 2nd Avenue and 6th Street. "Hot? What does that mean, Mr. Porcaro?"

"Well, let's see. At least four major magazines want interviews with you, the *Times* would like to do a piece, and there are some rumblings that a couple of heavy-duty publishers are looking to solicit you for a book. And that's just print media. You can be sure that both of the publishing houses would look to get you on 60 Minutes, if you signed a book deal with them. Like I said, you're hot!"

"I still don't get it. I keep thinking they must be talking about someone else. Why all this interest in me or the spiritual pieces of mine that have been distributed.?"

"It's like this. The timing of your entry into the public space is impeccable. Pretty much anything that can have a New Age label attached to it is going to sell these days. And the story, your story, is just about perfect. Beautiful young girl rises out of New York's East Village, organically mind you, through no effort of her own, and gets to be put on a guru pedestal. How did that *Village Voice* piece put it, The Reluctant Guru of Alphabet City? The most brilliant PR peddler in New York couldn't have created a better persona. Like I said, like it nor not, you're hot. I mean Henry said you've generated a lot of attention, but frankly, this is a phenomenon and a half, way more than I expected when he and I talked." He pointed at her cup. "Want a refill? I'm a coffee fiend myself."

"No thanks. One more cup and I'll just get jittery. As if I wasn't edgy enough" She redirected back to their conversation. "But what do I do with all this? I can't have all these people bugging me every time I turn around. It's intolerable. Reluctant? Hell, it's unwanted and oppressive."

"Well, to tell you the truth, Aziza, may I call you Aziza" she nodded affirmatively, "you keep all these jerks off your back by having someone like me to represent you, be the intermediator between you and the press. People think of public relations agents as just creating an image. However, we also serve to insulate public figures, so they can pay attention to what they do, do their thing, so to speak. But the truth is, I, or anybody else, can only represent you if you know what it is that you do want. Just being left in peace isn't enough."

"Again, I'm not following you."

"So, I'd need some parameters about what you want and what you don't. Like, maybe no newspapers but high-end magazines are okay. Or none of the above, but let's explore a book deal. Keep it about what you're writing, not you, if you know what I mean. Who are you trying to reach with your writings? All that kind of stuff."

"But why would I want any of that 'kind of stuff' as you call it?" Aziza reacted.

"Well, there could be two different reasons. Maybe like Leader Posert, you feel you have some messages you want to get out there, because it's part of your professional objectives or personal calling. You know, something you want to 'broadcast' that you feel is worthy, or maybe even imperative. And, frankly, there's also a financial angle.

I mean you better believe there are dollar signs attached to all that hotness!"

"Dollar signs?"

"Aziza," he began to take on a paternal tone, "Aziza, honey, a book deal would probably be starting around the six-figure mark. When a major publishing house pursues an author, rather than the other way around, you're usually talking significant money. They know that if they hit it right with a spiritual work, then it can be a seller in the moment and also go on for years. I mean, without even mentioning the bible, which is the all-time bestseller, but something like Kahlil Gibran, that's been a bestseller for decade after decade. It sure doesn't surprise me that they want to take a hard look at you and your stuff."

Aziza was beyond astonished. Six figures. Like "The Prophet"? Her stuff? "You'll have to excuse my confusion, Mr. Porcaro, but I'm blown away by all of this. I never had any intention of writing for publication, at least not any time soon, and this is all very overwhelming."

"Yeah, Henry told me that this was something that had just gotten away from you. I mean, that's why he wanted me to spend some time with you and kind of get you up to speed on what's going on. But to tell you the truth, I think this is a bigger deal than he even imagined. And look, I'm not looking to land another client. You just think about it, and if you get clear about what you want, and conversely, what you don't want, just get back to me, and we'll take it from there. You don't need to worry about paying me anything. I'll just take my fees out of any proceeds that come your way because of my efforts, if that's what you want. Does that work for you?"

And a few minutes later Aziza was sitting alone in the luncheonette booth, holding Carl's business card, mouth somewhat agape, wondering where the hell this whole thing was going, and yes, where did she want it to go, if anywhere. The waitress came by and asked how she was doing, and Aziza could only wish she knew how to respond. "I think I need another cup of coffee."

18

The more she thought about it, the more Carl Porcaro's entreaty that Aziza clarify her aspirations made sense to her, despite the fact that she hadn't sought all this hoopla in the first place. Apparently, a return to anonymity wasn't in the cards. She could tantrum all she wanted, but what happened had happened, and the clock couldn't be rewound. This only reinforced Shen's admonishment that she take responsibility for her circumstances.

What did she want? What didn't she not want? Certainly, it was clear that she had an aversion to being in the public eye, having a distaste for the slightest trace of celebratory status. Privacy was very important to her, being left alone to think, to write, to interact with those she loved and to explore both her inner and outer worlds. But when she related this to Eddie, he surprised her by asserting that sometimes the cultivation of a public persona was necessary if leadership was part of one's purpose. He asked her, "When you write, is it purely for the clarification of your own thinking, a working through of your personal mentation, or do you assume the existence of a reader, someone other than yourself, who you wish to influence with your ideas?"

She knew immediately that she needed to reflect before she answered his question. Interestingly, she mused, she found herself more ambivalent than she previously would have thought. Surely, when she had initially begun to write, it was all for herself. She would send pages to Henry for his input, and enjoyed when he wrote back and shared ideas with her, but there had never been an assumed reader or audience in those early adolescent days. Other girls kept diaries to explore their thoughts and visions for themselves and their emotions. She explored her thoughts and visions of the universe. It was meant to be inviolably private.

But she had to admit that somewhere along the way, probably in her senior year in high school, around the same time she had reached out to explore the city and its houses of worship and its temples of art and culture, her motivations had started to change. She had begun to assume an imaginary reader, someone who would take in her observations and imperatives, and, yes, be influenced. As much as she wished that her life stay private, she also felt a sense of mission to move people toward living their lives in harmony with the All and Everything. These were two conflicting, ambivalent themes working within her. To lead a private life, and to help others to lead a spiritual life. She had to admit that there was within her a growing desire to be a change agent, to align herself with those who sought the greater good.

But did that mean she needed to cultivate some public persona, like Eddie was suggesting? Did she need to hawk spiritual principles as if she was Anita Bryant selling orange juice? Did one have to create some oversized façade, like Norman Mailer, for people to pay attention to what you had to say? She wondered if intellectual and transcendent reckoning had devolved to just another area for public relations nonsense. My lord! Was she really considering hiring a PR person herself?

But, these two needs didn't need to be in opposition to each other. Surely, one could wish to have others read in the privacy of their own homes what you had written in your own comfortable isolation. The message was on the page, not the personality, or at least it should be so.

As far as money was concerned, financial desires were hardly at the top of her list, but there was nothing inherently wrong in being compensated by a publisher for her writings. And if publishing meant that she could put funds aside for future use, at a time when she had a clearer idea of the lifestyle that suited her, then that could only be viewed as making some reasonable sense. Aziza had never held a desire to take a vow of poverty. She was certain that she could be honest enough with herself not to let money corrupt her actions. Money was a symbol of value, and if she thought her notions had value, there was no wrongdoing in being compensated, even if the numbers that Carl was talking about seemed more unworldly then her words.

The next day Aziza sat by the phone, stalling, but eventually pulled the trigger and called Carl to share with him her conclusions. "Yes, Mr. Porcaro, I would be grateful if you represented me. As for what I want, I wish to be free to pursue my thoughts and my writings with the same level of privacy that has been my experience up to now. And if being compensated for what I do allows me to further these ends, then that's okay. I don't need to be some Greta Garbo, but I'd like to keep interviews or public appearances down to a minimum. If something comes up and you tell me it's necessary, then it's necessary, as long as we're not chasing any spotlights. I guess it comes down to my saying that I'm entrusting you to keep this whole thing focused on the concepts and ideas that I represent, not some Madison Avenue representation of me, in which I get pumped up like a cartoon balloon at the Macy's parade."

"Okay," he responded. "You want me to protect you from the nonsense, but free you up to promulgate your sense of what's important. It doesn't have to be about you. I may have to flesh out your story more, give folks a feeling that they know the person they're listening to, but the image doesn't have to conflict with who you are. It really doesn't. As a matter of fact, you might be on to something with that Garbo thing. If people think you're something of a recluse, they'll only lean in, and want to know more. We can use that to minimize personal interviews, while at the same time make the ones you do something special, exclusives given only to journalists who are concerned with ideas before ratings."

"You're suggesting a scenario that by letting people know that I'm reluctant to be thrust in the limelight, a story about my need for anonymity can be promoted and that, in turn, will attract people to what I have to say? I guess paradoxes aren't restricted to philosophy. Is that really what you're saying?"

"Sure. Garbo's image as a recluse became as storied as her fame as a movie star. It kept her need of not being in the public eye, constantly in the public eye. I mean, she hung out on 5ᵗʰ Avenue, but wrapped herself up in her scarves. Like she was saying 'look at me trying to avoid you seeing me'. People love that kind of paradox."

"Stop it, Carl. You're going to chase me back into my rabbit hole."

"Okay, okay. Why don't we get together tomorrow? I have to be out at the Brooklyn Ethical Culture Society, and we could meet there. I'll have some papers drawn up, and if you'd like, Henry can look them over for you. Or anybody else, for that matter. Aziza, I think this is going to be worthy endeavor. I know I'm looking forward to it. And I promise you. I won't paint you into any corners, or pictures that you don't want to be in."

19

On Likes, Dislikes and Ethical Perspective

We have all heard of the Serenity Prayer, which advises us to accept the things we cannot change, change the things we cannot accept, and be wise enough to know the difference. The prayer notes that this takes wisdom and courage, which when properly employed will yield serenity, or peace of mind. It addresses essential questions about the relationship between our understanding of who we are and our perception of the phenomenological universe in which we live. In some ways we define ourselves by how we react to the actions and realities of life around us. The way we see ourselves is often dependent on the judgements we make about these same happenings. The serenity prayer properly implies that our acceptance of a happening doesn't necessarily require our approval. We can accept things that go against our sensibilities, that appear to be contrary to our wishes or beliefs about ourselves or the world. Just because we don't like it, we can still accept that what is, is. If the universe rains on our picnic, we are best advised to accept the rainout. Punching wildly at the raindrops is a futile waste of energy, and leaves us in a state of disharmony.

But there remain unanswered questions. Can we implicitly trust our judgements concerning what we have observed, what we think of as comfortable, or justified, or right or moral? Two variables can warp our judgement. The obvious one is the potential for our perception to be faulty. Our observations may have been influenced by a host of problems, such as false expectations or distorted environmental conditions or covert prejudices, and on. Having perceived a situation inaccurately, we may find ourselves in the unenvious position of reacting strongly to what's not really there.

More complex is the situation in which we make a judgement about a happening, without appreciating the multiple phenomenological perspectives through which the situation can be seen. This is often a source of ambivalency or internal dissonance. I love the present my friend gave me for my birthday, and love that she thought enough about me to buy it. However, I hate that the present is not climate friendly and feel ashamed that I'm selfish enough to want to accept it. Here, my relationship perspective is conflicted with my societal perspective. And I may or not be aware of the causes for my ambivalent thoughts or consternation. Knowing what we accept or want to change or modify isn't always as simple as it appears. As a person who was conceived from rape, is it surprising that I have conflicting judgements as to the rightfulness of abortion? Personal, familial, community and planetary perspectives can yield very different judgements, all of which can be felt deeply.

Is there a spiritual perspective which overrides all these perspectives and instructs us when to accept and when to challenge the actions around us? Without such a superseding vista, can we ever trust the judgements, opinions or emotions which feel as if they are the correct response? Do we require some Supreme Authority to advise us of what is right, what is true, or what is moral? Many think so. They think of us as either too unconscious or too confused or, in some cases, too infused with original sin, to be the arbiters of proper judgement of our own or other's behavior. Having a Supreme Authority or ultimate Spiritual Umpire to call the balls and strikes, relieves us of the obligation to constantly examine self and our relationship with the All and Everything. But is there a supreme arbiter, and how would we know of its existence? Should we accede to the perspectives of prophets who claim to have had "Sinai moments," in which they shared communication with an otherworldly consciousness? Personally, I'm too much of a spiritual pragmatist to indulge myself with such fantastic practices. More to the point, following the directions of a Supreme Authority would appear to be a means to avoid doing the hard work which a true spirituality necessitates.

The awareness of being part of wholes that are greater than us is central to living a spiritual life. In this pursuit, while we acknowledge that there are multiple perspectives which we need to examine and coordinate in order to arrive at a position which is authentic for us, we give added weight to the widest of our perspectives. The wider the perspective, the stronger its influence. Thus, what we perceive as a planetary perspective has greater hold than a personal view. An international perspective has greater weight than a local community outlook. Divining a spiritual understanding requires identifying all of our phenomenological vistas, weighting them all from the widest to the narrowest, and allowing a synthesis to take place which then feels internally resonant. By making this effort, we can be reasonably assured that we are not indulging our ego, or childishly demanding what would be the most pleasurable action or outcome.

Too often, spirituality is utilized as an adolescent excuse for rebellion against authority. In the need to differentiate themselves from the personas of their parents, adolescents or young adults can challenge the mores and morals that have been taught to them, often utilizing "rockstar" spiritual systems or incomplete understandings of sound spiritual systems. This represents an immature spirituality in that the only larger whole which the individual surrenders to is their fellow adolescent peer group alliances. They have not reached a level of maturity in which they can appreciate the broad spectrum of perspectives and proceed to the grind of synthesizing who they really are and what they truly stand for.

For those that choose a rigorous spiritual path, a long road unwinds itself. A constant effort must be employed toward knowing our position at any particular point on the path. What we cannot accept at one point on the path, may become perfectly suitable at another point, even if these turnabouts are infrequent. What seemed righteous at one point may become heinous at another, if we are true to our self-examination. We need to be aware that as we experience spiritual growth, our likes, dislikes and ethical standards will correspondingly grow and transform with us.

20

It had been an improbable but incredibly wonderful day. Aziza and Carl had spent the morning at the Alfred A. Knopf midtown offices reviewing, and eventually signing a contract for her writings. An editor had been assigned to help Aziza organize and expand the collected treatises into a book. Initially taken aback by having anyone other than Henry work in this way with her, Aziza found that she felt comfortable with Joan Peabody, the person delegated to assist her. Ms. Peabody was clearly razor sharp, and when introducing herself made it clear that her role was to add an editor's perspective, not have any influence on the substance of what was written. There was an expectation that the entire process would take a couple of months, with an outside chance that the project might be completed for the Fall list. When handed the advance check, Aziza almost fell over backwards. Despite knowing the amount for the past two and a half weeks, it still felt incomprehensible when she held it in her hands. She couldn't help herself from being mindful that her mother's salary for three full years was still less than what the little slip she held in her hand indicated.

Adding to the mind-boggling absurdity, the meeting had been scheduled in the AM because Aziza had a full slate of courses to attend in the afternoon, back at NYU. The segue from author back to sophomoric student wasn't lost on Aziza. She couldn't help but wonder what Professor Niemeyer, a middle-aged scholar who had devoted most of his life to academia would think, if he was aware of what had just happened with her. Who was she to receive all this attention, and platform, and yes, money, when he had been quietly toiling at his discipline for two decades? This girl, and she was still a girl, who had been sitting in his classroom for six weeks, was a pleasure to have in class, but what universe gave her access to a golden ring which he could barely dream about? There was something outlandishly unjust about it all, and Aziza couldn't stop herself from feeling somewhere between contrite and guilty. She knew rationally that this was ridiculous, but still couldn't shake the feeling.

Should she be worried about how her life was going to change?? Was this change in every corner of her circumstances going to warp her into someone she didn't recognize? If she was published, and had money, would others see her differently? Would her relationship with Eddie suffer? She knew that he had more than enough confidence in himself than to be put off by her attainments, but did all this put them into some sort of relationship inequality, by throwing them into separate strata? There had never been any issue about who was going to pay for anything. Whoever had it paid. Simple. Equal opportunity penury. Now what? Was there going to be some weird discomfort in the air every time one of them had to pay the tab at the Rooster or at the movies or at the grocery? Their interests and motives and values had always been complimentary. Was this going to upset their balance? Oh, for God sakes girl, she thought about her thoughts, stop your damned ruminations! The sky is blue, the city is crowded, and Eddie is always happy for your successes. And how about you trust this universe as much as you say you do.

She looked forward to getting home and changing before meeting Eddie at the Rooster. As exciting as it had been to open an account at Chase with all those zeros on the deposit slip, it felt good to anticipate getting together with her guy for a plain old normal Friday evening, hanging out with some friends, being challenged by strangers who were becoming more and more familiar, while having a cheeseburger and a couple of brews. Alex was heading out the door as she came in, heading over to the Rooster himself for a shift. They shared a quick hug and he was on his way. Bill was in the middle of making himself some dinner, but turned off the burner so he and Aziza could sit and schmooze for a few minutes. Yeah, it was normal, sitting around the kitchen with a roommate, comparing classes and the idiots de jour in their respective schools, even if there was some minimal discussion of the morning event at Knopf. She felt reassured that not that much was going to change, and her friends weren't going to hold her at arm's length.

Eventually she threw on some jeans and an old Creedence tee, and was off to meet Eddie. Bill wasn't sure if he would make it over. It all depended on his getting a paper finished, an assignment which he had put off way too long. He envied his roommates' facility with the humanities. Himself, he would be happy if he could just live in a world of numbers and theorems.

Walking in the door at the Rooster, it felt like everything was falling into just the right place. Friday night at the Thatched Rooster! The bar was overflowing, Alex and Alicia stopped a minute from waiting tables to give her a quick hug, and Eddie was at their "usual" table, already engrossed in heated conversation with this week's collection of spiritual groupies. He seemed happy, in his element, engrossed in avid conversation and debate. Aziza knew a few of the folks at the table, and extended a quick greeting as she slid into the seat which Eddie had saved for her. There was Carmelo from the Bronx, a devout Catholic who seemed to be challenging himself to maintain his orthodoxy, ending almost every discussion with an "Okay, but." And Harriet, the Christian Scientist who almost always needed to steer the conversation to a debate about modernism. It felt good to see Pierre, a French exchange student who happened to be in one of her classes, actually Niemeyer's, back at the Rooster again. The assemblage was loud and turbulent, everyone cutting everyone off, smiles and shouts and accidental spittle thrown around the table with passionate vivacity.

She was famished, too busy since a quick breakfast to find time for a meal. She had managed to stuff down a snickers bar on the way to Niemeyer's class, but that had only been good for a quick sugar rush. Sneaking a couple of bites of Eddie's Reuben and a few fries, it hit all the right notes, and she ordered one of her own.

She couldn't help but notice a small man, sitting directly across from her. Overdressed with a sports jacket, on a warm night, in a hot crowded pub, he sat quietly, sweating, through all the debate and interaction, making almost tortured grimaces at various assertions and remarks. His beer sat before him, untouched, the foam fizzled away, the condensation puddling around his glass. He seemed remarkably uncomfortable and eventually Aziza called out to him, "Hey there. You look like you'd like to contribute to our conversation. Is there anything you'd like to say?"

The man almost was trembling as he stood from his seat, and his words were stammered and sporadic as he began. "Yes, there is. . . . , there is a lot I've. . . . , I. . . . got to say." He pivoted and looked squarely at Eddie. "You two, ..., you two horrible people," he waved his hand back and forth from Eddie to Aziza, "You two, ... hideous people, ...you come in here doing the work. . . . . of Satan!" His screeching became shriller. "Somebody, ..., somebody's got to. . . ., got to, ...stop you." Reaching into his jacket and pulling out a small handgun, he aimed his weapon at Eddie, at point blank range. With total disbelief, most everyone at the table jumped back, their chairs, food and drinks thrown askew, falling and flying everywhere. Except for Carmelo, who leapt from his chair and crashed his body into the stranger just as the gun went off, desperately attempting to change the bullets trajectory. The slug just missed Eddie's his head, but slammed into his shoulder, three inches above his heart. The shooter went down in a heap to the floor, with Carmelo on top of him, and others, recovering from their shock, joining him in holding the crazed assailant down, the gun thrown far from his hand toward the bulletin board wall. The shooter continued to scream and cry and kick, but was firmly clamped to the floor by an avalanche of bodies. Somebody by the bar yelled "Shooter! Shooter!" and half the crowd fell to the floor while the other half rushed toward the street. The entire pub was in total chaos, a sea of startled and fearful people trying to navigate the intersection of panic and horror.

Aziza cradled Eddie, joining the chorus of people yelling, "Call 911! Call an ambulance!" looking into his outsized eyes, which were not yet feeling the pain, both of them disbelieving that what had happened had happened. But the blood was real, and it was warm and flowing. Aziza grabbed a handful of napkins and pressed them into Eddie's shoulder to hold back the stream. Miraculously, in what had to be less than a minute, two police were by the table, one securing the shooter, while the other pushed Aziza out of the way to get Eddie on the floor and keep him still, until the paramedics arrived. Aziza stumbled off to the wall, looking back at the terrifying surreal scene which was playing out in front of her, something that happened in movies, not in life, not in her life, watching the police know what to do, when she hadn't a clue what to do herself. She felt more helpless, more powerless, more desperate than she ever could come close to imagine. She found herself mumbling, pleading, praying. "He's going to be alright. He's going to be alright," over and over, not knowing whether to believe it or not, but needing to assert it, needing to demand it.

21

On Escaping The Dark Night Of The Soul

Some of us reach the dark night slowly, hoping and praying that it will be avoided, even when all the while it has become clear that the abyss in inevitable. Others are thrust into these depths of despair in a blazing flash, their world turning black in an instant, caught in the snare of a horror filled truth, where it feels that truth should never reside. Described by some as the times that try men's souls, portrayed by others as the lower limits of hope, these are the moments when it feels as if whatever faith we had that we dwell in a loving universe has been pushed aside and been replaced by a gaping oblivion, a dark hole in our countenance. A trap door has opened beneath our appreciation of the All and Everything, and we have fallen into a state of desolation and disorientation.

It can feel as if there is nothing to grasp hold of, nothing to reach for, nothing to support us. In a world gone wrong, the critical beams of our life have been ripped away, and we are alone, part of nothing larger than ourselves which could yield comfort or familiarity. The horror is never the monster.

The horror is being adrift in the empty wake of the monster, disconnected from the trustable life we had previously inhabited.

The dynamics of these moments of hell can all be boiled down to being alone in an infinite void, existing without the context of a universe, without contact with an other, without a firmament, without anything to be part of, without the existence or potential to join, to unite, or to love. Even death can feel preferable, for in death at least we get to bond with the All and Everything. In the dark night it feels as if the All and Everything has been replaced by the Nothing and Never.

But can the universe disappear? It is axiomatic to all the laws of physics, biology, consciousness and spirituality that no thing can exist without the context of another thing. Only in a dynamic interaction with something or someone else can beingness occur. We talk about the eremite wandering alone in the desert, but wandering alone, without a phenomenological reference, is an impossibility. We were an integral part of the All before we were born, we remain a part of the Everything while we live, and we will return to the All and Everything when we die. Ashes to ashes. These statements go beyond belief or faith. They are axiomatic to existence.

We fall into the dark pit when we experience a loss of someone or something that is an essential structural component in our capability to love, something upon which our facility to love rests, a critical foundation piece, if you will. This can be a person, perhaps a spouse, sibling or parent who has served as a symbol and model for all other loves. With this person gone, it feels as if all other loves are either impossible or insignificant. The loss can be an idea, a formulation which lies under and supports ones' sense of mission, meaning or connectedness, the absence of which causes the whole deck of cards to fall.

When it feels as if we are in a state of Nothing and Never, we still have the ability to challenge what is essentially an illusion. In reality, our loss is limited to what is gone, and there is still much that we are joined with, even if it doesn't seem to matter in the instant. In these moments of despair, we need to reach out and connect, to anything and everything we remember that subsumes us. This is the time to practice a basic principle of love, that we cannot lose what we are joined with, as it has become a part of us. Furthermore, all our loves are interconnected within our heart. And through awareness of this expansive connection we can realize that loss and gain are two sides of a coin. There is loss. There is gain. There is hope. There is despair. There is confidence There is uncertainty. Our path continues on by means of the waves and cycles in which the Everything moves through the All.

The interconnected touchstones of love which surround loss can return us toward a balance, when we allow ourselves the broader view, realizing that despite the loss of what feels like our sun, there is still a galaxy of love. We can fear that the loss will be compounded and avoid touching the touchstones, or we can know that at the moment our nadir of emptiness happens, a personal big bang can occur, connecting us with every loving star that we have experienced in our life. Love is not a metaphor. Love is that which binds the Everything into an All, even when we feel lost in dark caverns of despair.

Part Six

1

Once Aziza was reassured by the attending physician at the hospital that Eddie's condition was serious but not critical, she found her feelings of shock, fear and anxiety being replaced by an overriding sea of anger. The damage from the bullet had torn apart much of the musculature of his upper left torso, but there was no damage done to vital organs or arteries. He would need to be in the hospital for another day or two, and would require intensive physical therapy, but the prognosis for a full recovery was good, although the shoulder would never be as strong and fully functional as it was before the damage.

Curiously most of her anger was not directed toward the shooter, himself. He was, as far as she was concerned, a disturbed man, drawn into the arrogant and self-aggrandizing attitudes of religious institutions which rarely practiced what they preached. At least for now, he was safely in some treatment center, somewhere, and wouldn't be harming anybody else.

Her anger centered on herself, and extended to most all of her intimates. How could she have allowed herself to become immersed in all of this "guru" business? How could she have let herself become some inane symbol of spirituality for others, going against all of her natural instincts? It felt like she had known all the time that this ridiculousness wouldn't lead to anything good. Never in her wildest imagination did she foresee that it could lead to a violent attack, but why, why ,why did she put herself, and Eddie, in the position to be projected upon. It wasn't as if she didn't know that whatever was venerated would also be despised. But she had allowed her ego to be stroked, and pumped up into some distorted cartoon of version of herself. Vanity wasn't what she was all about, and still, she might as well have been some moronic teenager vamping on the street corner, hoping to be seen by a Hollywood producer. How could she have consented to all this?

And Eddie, how could he have talked her into indulging in her musings getting put up on a board and distributed at the Rooster? For a couple of bucks and some insider fame? And obviously Alicia, who had no right to put her stuff out there. And her folks, and Henry, the adults in the room who should have been warning her, not encouraging her to "be responsible" for her thoughts. The whole thing felt like some grand conspiracy, with just about everyone she knew joining in to nurture the worst parts of herself. It didn't matter that they all were thinking that they were there to help assuage her ruminations and obsessive thinking. Like she was some overgrown kid who had to be placated because her OCD was getting in the way of her accepting success.

That was the core of it, wasn't it? She couldn't help herself from verbalizing her infernal internal preoccupations, and that always led others, all the people who loved her, to think they needed to jump in and make it right, help her finally get off the fucking dime and reach a conclusion which would work for her. For her? For them? It was like she sucked them all in and their own egos ended up stroking hers. All in the name of love. Love was supposed to bring out the best of you, not the worst.

Except for Grandpa. He was the only one who had stayed out of the whole mess. Yeah, he was as enabling a codependent as they come, and would tell her constantly how wonderful and special she was, but he was also the only one to stand back and hadn't said a damn thing. Even about the book deal. For the man who had put every scribble she ever wrote on his fridge, to not say anything about her being published, that had to mean something. Didn't it? Well, she couldn't go back to the hospital until tomorrow morning. Maybe she should go out to Hollis and talk to Grandpa.

2

"He's okay? Eddie's okay? Ben needed reassurance that Eddie wasn't seriously wounded. He liked that boy. Not that Aziza should be in any rush to get herself tied up with some fellow for the long term. There would be plenty of time for that. Plenty of time. For now, she should just worry about getting an education, getting that all important degree, and she shouldn't have to do it the hard way like her mother did. I mean, Esther's done just fine, but it shouldn't have to be such a humongous struggle to get there. It shouldn't be so hard.

"And what's all this guru business? Shen shows me this article, from the paper, no less, and I don't understand. Like you're some spiritual Dear Abby for people who don't want to go to church or shul? People need you to tell them what to do about God? I mean, you're a smart girl, as smart as they come, but I don't know, Sweetie, jumping into other people's politics or religion, isn't that kind of asking for trouble."

Aziza began to question whether Grandpa was really the right one to talk to right now. But she took a few minutes to fill him in on all the events that he clearly knew nothing about. He listened patiently, interrupting a few times to make sure he understood. It was hard for him. He still thought of his granddaughter as a smart precocious teenager who would someday become something special. Real special.

But someday, not now. Why were all these people expecting her to solve their all too complicated lives for them, when she had only graduated high school a year ago? Didn't they know that you shouldn't put all that pressure on someone who is just barely a grownup? "These people are selfish," his inner thought slipped out, "These people are selfish, I tell you."

Now it was Aziza's turn to not understand. "Who, Grandpa? Who's selfish?"

"All of them. The whole damned bunch of them. Those people in that Rooster thing, those people in that newspaper who need you to become some super-guru-rabbi for everyone, those people who seem to be grabbing at you and wanting a piece of you. They're selfish, I tell you. Why can't they just give you a little time to grow up some more before they put all their problems on your pretty head. And that includes those book people. They're trying to make themselves a lot of money off all that publicity stuff that you're some big shot guru prodigy. More pressure. It's all too much pressure for any girl your age, even you, as smart as you are, to handle."

"So, what do I do, Grandpa? Are you saying that I should back out of this book deal?"

"No, no, no, Darling. Trust me, when somebody gives you a check for money like that, you don't turn it down. No, believe me, you don't say no thank you to big time money. That's not what I mean. I'm trying to tell you that you shouldn't have to deal with everybody and their needy mother weighing you down with their mishigas. If there's one thing in life that I've learned, and boy have I learned it the hard way, when people make you responsible for running their lives, they're going to turn on you later, and say it's all your fault when it doesn't turn out the way they wanted. First, you're a symbol of who they want to be themselves, and then you become some cockamamie symbol for how people disappoint them, because you can't fix what they need to fix themselves. These people who come to you at that Rooster place, do they try to know you, and care that you're okay, or do they need you to be some Dear Aziza person for them who does the hard thinking about what they should do for themselves?"

Aziza had not ever thought of it from this vantage point. To her it had always been an open discourse in which she and like-minded people shared ideas and perspectives on spiritual matters, in a world where such discussions were neither popular or common. It felt to her like an opportunity to be herself and to feel connected with people who shared a lot of her worldview. "I don't know, Grandpa. I think most of the people who we hang with at the Rooster really care about me and Eddie, and aren't just a bunch of intellectual moochers. I mean, that guy, Carmelo, he probably saved Eddie's life, and maybe mine also. I don't know. It's probably the same as everywhere else. There are takers and givers and a lot of people in between."

"My precious Granddaughter, I should probably do the right thing and make a confession here. Forgive me if I sound selfish myself, but the truth is I don't care about any of them. None of them I tell you. It's you I care about, and you I worry about. And I just want all those bloodsuckers, those leeches, to wait until you're ready to fix this lunatic world of ours."

He paused, a little apprehensive before he continued, with that twinkle in his eye. "I get it. Believe me, I get it. Who says all the messiahs have to be boys? We've probably missed out on a bunch of messiahs because we were always expecting that he should be a he. When you think about it, women always seem to have a less selfish love than us men. They do, and that's the truth. And messiahs need to be for sure loving. But can't you just cool your heels a little bit and wait until maybe you're all grown up before you solve all of humanity's problems?"

She overlooked his sarcasm. "But Grandpa, that's what I'm trying to tell you. I don't want to be some rock star guru or a messiah or some savior of the universe. Wonder Woman and Superman, or maybe the Beatles, they can have at it all they want, because I'm no superhero. All I want is to be able to privately work out for myself where I fit into this universe, and mingle and relate to people like myself." And that's the truth she underscored to herself. The simplicity of her response reverberated within her.

"So then, that's what you should do. Set up your life for those two things, the things that you know you want to do. Make a place for yourself where you can think and write and talk with whoever you want, and not with anybody you don't want. Maybe the only mistake you made was having all these conversations in public. And you know

Darling, with all this money that they're throwing at you, maybe you could even set it all up like you want, and they don't even have to know where you are. Who said you have to do this mingle thing, at that Rooster place? I think that's why we have living rooms and back porches. No?"

He was right! She didn't have to do interviews, or talk shows, or some stupid book tour, or any of that stuff that the publisher wanted. She could put together this book the best she could, and do it in the private manner she liked, even with the editor they wanted her to work with, and if it didn't sell as many copies as it might have with a whole lot of publicity, then that was okay also. All she really needed was to have enough money to get a different place to live, and, as a matter of fact, she did. She could be in control of who was there and who wasn't, wherever there was. The real problem was that the whole thing had been spinning out of control, beyond her control, and maybe she now had the resources needed to get back to controlling her own life. If she wanted to go have a beer with some friends at the Rooster, or anywhere else, she could do it whenever she wanted, not at some time when she was expected. She could put all her best energy into creating a book that reflected her thoughts and ideas, because that's what she loved to do. If people liked that, and thought they benefitted from that, and it seemed like that was the case, then that was all the better. The bottom line was that instead of not liking the way other people were trying to run her life, she could take control and run her life the way she desired.

"Grandpa, I knew you were the right person to talk to. You're always the right person to talk to." She threw her arms around him.

"Well, I don't know about always. It's not like I'm some Dear Grandpa either. But you, I know that you always deserve the best. I tell you, you're the cream of the crop. You deserve the best."

3

Visiting hours at the hospital started at 9 in the morning, but Aziza ignored the signs in the lobby and was next to Eddie's bed well before then. She had been told, and she believed that he was going to be okay, but still required the reassurance of his body next to hers. A gruesome fear that she was going to lose him forever had been embedded in her psyche in that horrid moment of the explosive concussion, and she was overwhelmed with a need to touch him, to hear his voice, to feel him touch her. She experienced a tangible relief just walking through the door and seeing him, free of tubes or any other medical stuff, seeing him seeing her, and breaking into a wide smile.

"Oh Sweetness, it's so good to see your face," he declared. "I probably missed you more last night than I ever could have believed. There was so much swirling around my head and I didn't have my Aziza to bounce it off of. I never realized how much I need you to help me clarify what's going on deep inside of myself."

She held his head and kissed him. "Me too. I'm still shaking from the thought that you could have been taken away from me. Just thinking of that, even here in this moment when I know you're okay, causes my heart to shudder and my hands to tremble. If I lost you, I'd lose me. I can't even begin to separate where I end and you begin."

"I know exactly what you mean. That was one of the most compelling thoughts I had last night. If I had been killed, or if you had been killed, either way, we, this thing of ours, that would have been lost. I can't bear to think of that."

Aziza realized that in all the time since the terror had struck, and the PTSD-like shock that had set in as she saw a gaping hole open up in Eddie's torso, she had never considered, even for a moment, that it could have been her that was killed. Hearing his fear of losing her brought that front and center to her mind. She was dumbstruck by both the thought and that she hadn't thought it..

Eddie went on. "Mom and Dad were here last night until about eight, and after they left, I kept rolling over and over in my mind, all the implications of what has just happened. Even with the painkillers they're giving me, there was no way I could sleep. I probably didn't nod off until two or maybe three."

She grinned. "You must be catching my obsessiveness."

"No, I don't think this was about being obsessive. There was a pervasive realization that this changes everything. No one can watch some crazed gunman unload a bullet into their body, feel their flesh being ripped to pieces, know that their life could be ending in the next few seconds, and not reassess their whole lives, from their actions, to their loves, to their beliefs, to their sense of dedication and mission. Well, maybe some could, but I certainly can't." He paused, letting the impact of what he was saying sink in. "Honey, this feels like a critical inflection point in my life. Nothing will ever be the same again."

"I know exactly what you mean," she responded. "I found myself talking to Grandpa yesterday afternoon, and the realizations just flowed one after the other, all the way through the rest of the day. All the things I have to change. All the ways I need to run my life differently."

"Tell me. Tell me about it."

"No, you first Eddie. You're always listening to me and all my ruminations about everything, and being my sounding board for all my stuff. No Eddie, you're the one that's in this hospital bed. You first."

"Well," he gathered his thoughts, "after a while of babbling to myself in every conceivable direction, it all boiled down to this. There was a person, a man, a real live individual, who wanted me dead, who tried to kill me. This man, filled up to his gills with hate instilled in him by his religion, wanted to eradicate me from this planet because I didn't buy into his belief system." They both shuddered at the straightforward simple but shocking truth of this.

He continued. "And the more I thought about the bare faced truth that this demented person tried to execute me for what he thought were my sins, the more I realized that this was just one small part of what feels like the most overriding conflict of our times. It all comes down to a battle, and I use the word battle very specifically, it all comes down to a battle between spirituality and religion. You and I have talked about this over and over, endlessly, about the difference between being part of everything, or needing everything to be a likeness of you. But we, both of us, we have always talked about this through an intellectual lens. Having a bullet pass through you changes all that for me. It becomes real. It becomes tangible. You realize you are part of a war, a war that you never would choose, a war that makes no sense, but a war that you have no righteous way to avoid. You've helped me realize for a long time, even as I've argued against it, that I can't just live my dad's life. Ministering to a congregation is worthy enough, and a commendable mission, but the point has been irrevocably driven into me that I need to engage in a larger purpose, a wider fight, if you will. I somehow know that I need to devote myself to this struggle between spirituality and religion. I don't know exactly what that means, I don't know where that path will lead me or the steps that I have to take. I don't know yet what specific role I need to play, but I know that there's been a significant change in my sense of purpose and meaning and mission."

Aziza had never heard Eddie speak with such clarity. He was right. His intentionality had undoubtedly taken a right-hand turn. As his words sunk in, she felt herself in two minds. On the one hand she knew that he had never been as filled with certainty as he was in this moment. This guy, her guy, knew in broad terms exactly what he needed to dedicate himself to, and even if it had taken a bullet to clarify it, this was a good thing, a righteous thing. On the other hand, his certainty appeared to fly in the face of most everything she had realized in the aftermath of the same dreadful event. He was dedicating himself to be an active participant in a very public combat for souls, while she was simultaneously committing herself to becoming more private, pledging to herself that she was meant for mentation and meditation, and ultimately for the writing that came from the process, for herself and the greater good, in solitude, away from the maddening crowd. It was as if they had been confronted something ultimately demonic, and were coming away from it, reacting, with totally different conclusions. The potential of this difference caused dread to course through every cell in her body. Could this shooting cause her to lose him after all?

"And you? Where did all this take you?"

She didn't want to answer. She knew that she was frightened to share with him her conclusions, but also knew that not to do so would make her fears a fact. "It seems the same event has pushed us in different directions," she honestly responded, despite her anxiety. "I've realized just how out of control my life has been for the past few months, how much it feels like I'm being pushed and prodded into being someone who is nothing like I know myself to be. I've realized that I can't allow myself to become a stranger to myself and everything I love. The ultimate insult was when that motherfucker tried to kill you, and okay, maybe me, and that event could have shaped my life into a horrible distortion of everything I think I stand for. I can't live like that, Eddie. I can't love like that. And all that scares me, because at exactly the time that you seem to be needing to move outward and face the monster, I seem to be needing to retreat and do my thing where I feel I can be effective and safe, and in control of what's to come of me. That really scares me, Eddie. It scares me for us to be possibly going in separate directions."

He took her hand firmly in his. "I hear you Ziz. I think I understand why you would go in your direction, but that doesn't scare me. It feels to me that our love is stronger and more vital than to fear being different from each other in some particular respect. It isn't that we have conflicting values about it. We just need to approach what we care about differently. That's okay. We love each other both for our differences and our similarities."

She had to agree, even if there was some infernal part inside that tugged at her and wanted her to panic. "All right, Eddie. I'm going to trust you on that one." And she folded over the covers, scrambled into the hospital bed, and held him close. Without words for a change.

4

The trajectory of their disparate paths wasn't immediately apparent as Eddie came out of the hospital and was able to finish up his coursework at St. Johns, while Aziza completed her semester at NYU. They continued to occasionally grab a bite and a beer at the Rooster, but without any regularity. As long as none of the pub's habitues could predict their arrival and be there waiting for them, it felt safe. The hangover from the assault left them unable to sit with any comfort at the tables, so they would hang by the bar and catch up with Arthur, who was still as much in shock from the shooting as either of them. The Rooster had been Arthur's freewheeling rostrum and play house for a decade, and in one ugly night it had all turned dodgy for him. Patrons talked about rumors that he was looking for another job, somewhere out of Alphabet City or the Village. Maybe it was time to devote himself more to his poetry. The bartending gig had started out as a way to support himself while he wrote, but it had quickly overtaken his time and mind as his infamous personage became a "thing."

As soon as her final exams were completed, Aziza started to spend weekends out on Long Island, and in New Jersey, with real estate agents. She wanted to find a secluded home, away from everyone, where she could write, free from all of the influences which seemed to have steered her life in unhealthy directions. The book needed to be completed, and if she could find the right place, she could make it happen in peace, without interruption. Her editor, Joan Peabody, had assured her that most of her authors lived outside the city, and the contemplated move wouldn't present any problem to their collaboration. Aziza let Carl Porcaro know that once she was able to find a place and establish residence, agreed upon interviews, whenever possible, would take place at her new digs. If a trip away from Manhattan wasn't worth it to them, then it had little value to her either. He understood, even if he wasn't thrilled.

Aziza was determined to reconfigure the parameters of her life in the manner she had talked about with her grandfather. She needed to feel in control of her home, her times for social interaction and complementary periods for seclusion. She was requiring herself to be in charge of her comings and goings, while devoting herself to what she felt were the essentials of her purpose, or what was needed to find meaning. She wanted to study, to write, to be living on her own terms. Somehow, the shooting had created her to be firmer, more resolute in her approach to the world, even if her internal process was still hesitant.

Her parents were all in on the idea. Esther realized that her daughter needed time and a place to work through the trauma. How could anyone go thru what Aziza had experienced that night at the Rooster and not be left with a PTSD. She was flooded with memories of her own early trauma, when she had retreated, needing to redirect and reorganize almost every aspect of her life. Aziza was strong, but that didn't mean that she needed to be fighting off a vampiric world, while she licked her wounds.

Shen, always pragmatic, advised that investing in some real estate was the wisest thing she could do with her new found capital. He cautioned her to only put half of the purchase price into the acquisition, as she would need some tax deductions, because the anticipated royalties from the book might inflate her income. Of course, both parents hoped that she would find a home on Long Island, somewhere close to them.

That wasn't to be, as Aziza discovered exactly what she wanted out in Sandyston, N.J. It was a little further out from the city than she had anticipated, but seclusion does come with a price. The listing was a 22-acre property with rolling hills, adjoining a national park, complete with a modern and modest A-frame sitting just off a country road. A pastoral setting, only an hour and change from Manhattan, Aziza loved it immediately. There were two bedrooms, a decent enough kitchen, and a magnificent porch that completely surrounded the home. It had scenic views abounding of the Delaware Water Gap, the Poconos and a deep green deer filled forest bordered by a small stream. While exploring the property with the realtor, and walking around the deck, Aziza found herself associating the ambiance to Walden Pond, her own personal Walden Pond, where she might think, process, write and breathe.

The next day she insisted on dragging Eddie and her folks out to see it. The level of her excitement concerned her a bit, and gaining consensus from them could calm the trepidations that she might be going off half-cocked. What was she missing? What did she really know about houses anyway? Aziza's obsessive nature would never allow her to simply get enthused about anything without worrying that she was being carried away by her emotions in some problematic tangent. They would all collectively hate it, find faults that she should have seen herself, or they might think that she was biting off more than she could chew.

But as it turned out, all three of them loved it. Shen found himself reminiscing about the campsite where he and Esther had first acknowledged the romantic nature of their relationship, which was only a few miles away. It felt karmic to him that she had found the location without knowing any of the history. Esther immediately related to the peacefulness of the setting, and how right-sized the house itself was. Aziza could handle this. Eddie simply smiled and remarked that seeing the property in person confirmed everything he knew about her; it framed her perfectly, it was her. An hour later, back in the realtor's office in Branchville, with Shen jumping in to bargain the best price, the papers were signed. The sellers were looking for a quick closing, and with such a large deposit, a mortgage could be obtained swiftly. Aziza could anticipate occupancy, in a matter of weeks.

Later that evening, back in Eddie's place, they speculated about what changes the Sandyston house would bring with it. Aziza shared what he had already suspected. She was going to take a year off from school. "I just need the time right now, to be away from everybody and everything."

"I hope that doesn't include me," he countered.

"Not a chance. You don't get away from me that easy. And related to that, there's one more purchase I want to make with all the money that's dropped into my lap."

"What's that?"

"Would it be too forward for me to pick up a car for you?" He started to object, but she cut him off. "No, no. Be clear, I'm being very selfish here. It's the surest way I get to see your butt on a regular basis, and I don't want to get one for myself because, well you know that driving's not my favorite thing. I can't expect you to deal with the bus and train all the time. And I'm not talking about some costly new vehicle. Just some decent transportation that can get from Brooklyn to Jersey and back again."

He relented, but then added, "Okay, but I should tell you that I've got some new things going on myself. I'm going to be away a decent amount of time this summer, and probably into the Fall."

"What? What's going to be needing you to be out of town?"

"I've accepted an exciting position with the Brady Campaign. They're trying to build a clergy component in their campaign against guns, and I'll be travelling for the next few months all over the country to speak to and hopefully enlist local clergy to join the campaign."

"Wow! You said you were going to get involved, but I never expected it to be this fast. Eddie, it sounds so perfect for you. Only I'm not the only one who is presumed to have a fall semester in front of her. What are you going to do about school?"

"I'm not sure yet. I'm hoping that by the time the fall semester arrives I'll be able to coordinate the work by telephone. I can handle the schoolwork and this new job in tandem, if I don't have to travel too much."

Her face sunk ever so slightly. "It doesn't sound as if there's going to be a lot of time left for us."

"I know, but it will only be while I get this campaign going. I meant what I said the other day. I feel that it's essential that I play some role in what I see as the iniquitous intersection of religion and violence. It's become personal for me now, and I've got the scars to prove it. And Ziz, I know that you have been scarred, as well. Maybe not on your skin, but scarred nevertheless."

She touched his cheek. "Like you said, we'll be okay. Our need to fulfill these dreams and missions is baked into us now. I know you have to stay true to your purpose. Hey, Tonto, that's the you I love."

5

Most of the work on the book came easy. Reworking and editing each of the separate essays, with Joan's advice and input, was tedious but flowed at a reasonable pace. They had identified seven new pieces that needed to be written. This represented something of a new challenge. Previously, all of her work had been spontanious. The circumstances of life, or sometimes, just a random thought, had demanded her to generate a response that would settle an inner turmoil. But as Aziza toiled with this new material, she found that the process which had served her since her early teens continued to do so. She would often struggle for a day or two, intentionally immersing herself in the conflicts and dualisms that were central to the matter, waiting for the magical moment when words that brought light to the darkness would effortlessly flow from her spiritual center. She often was startled by the righteousness that the words held, because they didn't feel as if they were the product of some logical progression. While rejecting a notion of "channeling," she had learned at an early age to trust that allowing the inconsistencies and contradictions to war within her would eventually lead to resolution. She remembered the first time she read about the dialectical process asking herself, "How on earth did I know this?"

Being alone at Rooster's Rest, as she had begun to call her home, was as peaceful and serene as she had hoped. She established a routine in which she would wake early, have a small breakfast, and hike for an hour in the woodlands that surrounded the house. No two walks were ever the same, either physically through the adjoining terrain, or the wildlife she encountered on the way. She would consistently arrive back at the writing table and single chair she had organized on the side deck vitalized and ready to work. She preferred to initially carve out her words on yellow pad, transcribing them onto the computer in the living room later, in the afternoon, if and when she felt right about them.

It was the Preface that plagued her. There needed to be some introductory piece that tied it all together, that in Joan's words, let the reader know the purpose of the book, why she had written it, what it encompassed, and why they would want to read it. This flew in the face of the part of Aziza that continued to question why anyone would want to read something that she had written. But beyond her self-doubt, more central to the inner strain, was the absence of some overall "why," some specific intention, that had demanded that she put words to page, in the first place. To her, it had always felt that she had no choice. She had always felt compelled to resolve the conflicts, uncertainties, and confusions that were precipitated by one life event or another. It had all started as a kind of adolescent journal. The only way she had ever known to work her way through the weeds was by letting it all unfold on paper. It had been her spiritual therapy, in which she practiced free association and hoped it took her to some place of insight. The freer she was, the more she had felt the issues resolve themselves, calming her, with a wave of tranquility replacing the tension.

Who would want to read somebody else's therapeutic babblings? What was, at the end of the day, thematic about all the separate essays? At this point in her life, what did she really want her reader to come away with? Ultimately, what was the value of her collected words to anyone other than herself? What was her mission in creating this book? Seemingly unanswerable questions upon questions beleaguered her attempts to fashion a preface that would meet Joan's criteria.

Where to start? Okay, I'm not a guru. I'm not, as grandfather had teased, some female messiah who's charged with fixing all the worlds' problems. I'm a woman who inexplicitly has always had an inner passion to know and experience a universal order of spirit, matter and mind. I guess I can say that I've suffered the spiritual ignorance and arrogance of the so-called gurus, messiahs, priests, imams and rabbis of the world. In some ways, I'm just a kid who's in the midst of discovering her purpose. In other ways I feel sure about my life intentions. What is it in my life that brings me here, on the porch of Roosters Rest, putting to paper a treatise on spiritual life?

It started to come together. Maybe, she thought, it was no accident that I was conceived out of violence and hate, in the crucible of humanity's inhumanity. Perhaps it was not incidental that I hold within myself the DNA of millenniums who sustained hope in the face of despair. For sure, I've been irrevocably shaped by an extended family of diversity and adversity. Perhaps even that hideous moment of facing a madman discharging bullets at Eddie, and watching his flesh torn apart, has had a strong influence of bringing me to this moment. Perhaps each and every moment of my life had been leading me to what feels like a new inflection point, a string of pearls creating a life-force with definition, intention and meaning. If that's true, then my preface is the book's preface. Maybe, even the nonsense of being labelled an "alphabet city guru" has some a purpose to it.

She took out the yellow pad from the folder. She was ready to write.

6

Preface to "The Reluctant Guru of Alphabet City"

I was conceived of hate and born of love. Dualism is my birthright. Like you, I find myself having to navigate the mysteries of being a tiny speck of energy in an infinite ocean of energy, with tides pulling and pushing me in every direction, at times threatening to drown my soul in waves of violence and terror, at times cocooning me in its folds of love. Like you, I sometimes feel myself needing to crawl inward, fearfully avoiding the cruelty and madness which threaten me to my core, at other times, needing to reach out and touch others, secure in a circle of trust. At times I am lost. At times I am found. I am you. We travel together on our separate paths, living, loving, fearing, hurting, searching, isolated, connected, alone and always joined. I am you. We are one.

It was never my intention to be a spiritual guide or teacher. My need to gain some understanding of the All and Everything has always been very personal. Perhaps my psyche required some resolution of my disparate origins. I was raised in a home by parents who both overcame early violence and transformed that brutal energy into both a sheltering love for me, and a strident care for their greater community. Perhaps the collective unconscious I absorbed from their struggle, and their parent's struggle, and their parent's parent's struggle, to respond to cruelty with love, has driven me to attempt to understand the universal interplay of creation and destruction. For reasons that often appear to be indecipherable, I have always suffered and sufficed with a need to comprehend the unfathomable, to know beyond my knowing, to see beyond my vision. It feels as if I have been created as a spiritual Icarus, drawn by forces I will probably never comprehend. I have learned to accept these forces, albeit with insufficient knowledge of their nature, as a cornerstone of who I am.

In some ways, spirituality is so simple. It tells us to experience ourselves as part of that which is larger than us, yet includes us. Once we can know ourselves as a fragment of a greater Whole, we have the potential to know what our isolated self is incapable of grasping. As a single neuron cannot hold or comprehend the immeasurable knowledge its parent organ, the brain, possesses, only by accepting ourselves as a miniscule component of a larger consciousness, can we begin to comprehend knowledge of the All and Everything.

In every society since the dawn of civilization there have been spiritual leaders who have helped guide others to the freedom found in being more than one is. In diverse forms, spiritual practices have always been essential to the growth and prosperity of all civilizations. The social groupings of humanity require their constituent members to accept being part of a larger, greater whole. By accepting membership in these communities, large and small, individual humans became safer, healthier, wiser and more moral.

In time, spiritual leadership became institutionalized and eventually evolved into the many and diverse religions of the world. It is ironic that as the baton was passed from single shamans to organized religion, spirituality became diluted. Being a significant cog in these religious communities became more important than being an unsubstantial part of the All and Everything, which the religion was originally created to instill. Religions became competitive. Religions asserted that only their particular vision had value. Religions became arrogant and, not surprisingly, they eventually turned violent. The more a religion refused to recognize being part of the larger spiritual community, the more it lost its spiritual foundation. Religions, unfortunately, can become as lost as the people that administer them and the people they serve.

An individual human who is without acceptance or bond with that which is greater than herself, becomes an arrogant, narcissistic person. She or he becomes all about herself, lacks citizenry, and her spiritual-less soul becomes dangerous. Similarly, an individual religion which is without acceptance or bond with that which is greater than its own institution, fares the same. It may turn aggressive and if powerful enough, can be a potential danger to the planet.

Many have turned away from religion in recent times, having come to experience emptiness and hypocrisy in the institutions which served their forebearers. Some turn to other practices that promote and teach a spiritual experience. More lose desire or need for spiritual experience altogether. Is it any wonder that we are living in a narcissistic age, in which the worship of self has become the prominent religion, soulless, serviced by materialism, suffered by multitudes?

It appears to have become the norm that;

People experience their wants to have greater priority then the safety or security of others, and therefore feel justified in stealing, raping or assaulting whoever they wish;

People experience their right for arms to be more important than the safety or security of others, and therefore utilize weapons of war to bully their way past their hidden insecurities;

People experience their grievances to be more important than the lives of others, and therefore feel justified in shooting, maiming and killing them.

People feel their need to be superior to others as more important than the lives, safety or security of those others, and therefore feel justified in denying others their equal rights;

People feel others' admiration to be more important than moral or ethical behavior, and therefore justify criminal actions as practical necessities;

People feel their freedom to do as more important than other peoples' freedoms to be;

People feel their need to be seen as a special parent more important than parenting their children to find and become what might make them be special;

People paper their personas with more and more coats of false imagery, and in the process create an impenetrable shell that surrounds an empty self, causing addiction and suicide rates to soar.

While it may have never been my intention to be a spiritual teacher or guide, given the dearth of spirituality that abounds, and the rise of narcissism this deficiency creates, I have reached the conclusion that I need to play some part in hopefully reintroducing spirituality as a necessary ingredient in a worthwhile life. Circumstances seem to have pushed me in this direction, although I continue to be reluctant to follow this path. I am not an activist. I am uncomfortable calling attention to myself. I am young and feel myself still needing to tap into other people's wisdom. I do not feel ready for such a monumental task.

But the least I can do is to share with you my musings about spirituality and our relationship with the All and Everything. For that reason, I have organized my thinking and present it to you here, in this volume. Please read what follows not as a sermon, but as the beginning of a dialogue between myself, yourself and us all. It is my hope that in subsequent dialogues, in this and other mediums, you and I will be able to fully explore our exquisite human potential.

7

It wasn't surprising that neither Aziza nor Eddie returned to college when Fall turned to Winter. On Eddie's part, he felt that working with the Brady Campaign was too valuable to walk away from, and he was much too busy to think of adding his studies back into the mix. He found himself traveling to visit a wide array of clergy around the country, for roughly half of every month, interacting, discussing, recruiting, cajoling, doing all he could to enlarge the ecumenical component of Brady. Often, it was an easy sell, to congregational leaders who were already firm in their stance against weapons of war. On other occasions, he met strong opposition, which he found difficult to reconcile with the teachings of the faiths that these preachers and clerics represented. To him, the conflation of second amendment rights with biblical instruction was an unfathomable reach. He would return home either bursting with youthful enthusiasm or sulking in an idealist's despair when confronted with a world whose reality was more malevolent than he ever could have imagined. Generally surrounded by friends and colleagues whose world view matched his own, he was stunned when he encountered societal leaders who were shackled to the past, or worse yet, when they seemed to support an armed dystopia. He wanted to scream out that

"You can't lead while blindfolded and behind!." But he was only screaming at himself.

His father met with him after most homecomings, looking to raise or lower his disposition, depending on what the outcome of the latest excursion had been. "Eddie, you're not ready for this. Finish school, and then seminary. Get a congregation. Then you'll have the resources, internal and external, to support you while you're taking on the demons and dragons of this world." But the son wasn't ready to take his father's advice. "Dad, I can't do that. At least not yet. I promise you the time will come when I will return to St. Johns, but not right now. Frankly, I'm learning more in my dialogues with the clergy that I visit then I could ever learn in a classroom at college. I don't always like what I learn, but it's valuable knowledge all the same. Give me some time, Dad. Yes, I know I come back at times discouraged by responses that I never could have even imagined, from people who supposedly represent Christian teachings and morality. But even in those cases, I'm learning something about the intersection of religion, community and politics, and the folks who are supposedly shepherds." His father would hear him out, eventually accepting what he ultimately had no control over. Muttering about youth and their idealism, internally he would still be proud of his son's labors.

Eddie began to spend more and more of the time he wasn't travelling at Rooster's Rest. For her part, Aziza had taken a leave of absence from NYU for a full year. While she had presumed that things would calm down after the book was published, just the reverse came about. Carl was calling three or four times a week with various requests for interviews that met her criteria, invitations to join in spiritually pertinent colloquiums, and sometimes, absurd proposals that he knew she would reject, but were too bizarre not to enjoy passing on. One Hollywood producer was desperate for her to audition for the lead in a new Joan of Arc epic he was planning to shoot, in Australia. He thought her perfect for the role and was confident that a lengthy acting career would be sure to follow.

Book sales had far exceeded Knopf's expectations, and within one month of the release of the Fall list, a second printing had been necessary. A translator for a French edition had been engaged, and there was talk of an Arabic translation. Aziza was more than pleased about her decision to move to her still clandestine retreat in Jersey, where she could avoid most of the clamor. Away from the circus most of the time, she was still able to stay at the apartment on 10th Street with her friends when she accepted one of Carl's requests for an event in the city, or sometimes, just because she wanted. Continuing to pay for her fourth of the rent was not an issue at this point, even if she was only there occasionally. They were always glad to see her, and she felt warm and secure in their company.

Many of the interviews that Aziza consented to participate in were tedious and repetitive, but she needed to agree to some, if for nothing else, to appease the folks at Knopf. She found herself comparing these interviews to her initial meeting with Claire Ethanger. With her, she had felt both known and stimulated. That was the not the case now, more often than not. Carl had worked out an agreement with Knoph that if the interviews were restricted to those that appeared essential to sales, and were also relevant to the substance of the book, she would agree to participate. More often the reporters would be required to drive out to Rooster's Rest. They would sit and chat outside with Aziza, relaxing on lawn chairs for a couple of hours. For the most part, the journalists were decent enough, and sometimes were sufficiently incisive for Aziza to enjoy the conversation, gaining some take-a-way for herself. The few interviews that she agreed to do back in the city she experienced as mind-numbing. She wondered if that was really the case, or if her negative impression was essentially a product of her feeling out of control, on their turf. Either way, she still did her best to be cooperative and revealing. Invariably, she found herself stressing to them that her celebrity status was more a reflection of a societal need for connection with all things spiritual, than any special attributes that she possessed. As long as the interviewers focused on her thoughts and her writings and not her personal information, then the exchange went well. She struggled, but tried not to be rude, when it seemed that they just wanted to do a personality piece on her.

Other than the days when she and Eddie could be alone together in Sandyston, her most enjoyable times found her alone, thinking, writing and corresponding. People began to write her, with responses and reactions to having read The Reluctant Guru. Aziza read most of these letters, and often wrote back, when she felt there was a worthwhile exchange of ideas to be pursued. She had meant what she had written in the Preface. She hoped for a dialogue, and corresponding with her readers felt confirming. It reminded her of Fridays at the Thatched Rooster, but in a different form. She most appreciated the letters from folks who were engaged but found fault with her reasoning, or suggested a different take on an idea. In a short while, a full hour and a half of most afternoons needed to be devoted to correspondence.

On the day of the Columbine massacre, Aziza was home, preparing for a colloquium at the 92nd Street YMHA, scheduled for the next day. Ironically, the topic for discussion was American Youth, Religion and Alienation. She had initially been averse to joining the panel, but ultimately agreed when Carl advised her that the other two panelists were Professor Niemeyer, who she had not seen since the day Eddie had been shot, and Nityaneeta Naropabhava, a siddha yoga guru, whose books Henry had recommended in the summer after high school. She had come to admire the Guru's terse but sagacious insights into material that others would ponderously bloat into massive page counts. Aziza considered that this was a woman who was worthy of being seen and accepted as a guru, as a saint! To be put herself into such a category was ludicrous.

As she sat in front of her television, glued to CNN's coverage of the barbarism in Colorado, all the hideous memories of the Thatched Rooster assault returned and flooded her mind. She came close to slipping into a debilitating panic attack, heart beating out of her chest, thoughts and images rushing too fast to be followed. Her hands, shaking and sweaty, were eventually able to turn off the assaulting news programming on the TV, getting away from the repellant memory of her worst nightmare. She sat and settled her breath into an easy rolling wave, and felt her composure slowly begin to return. After she calmed, she immediately tried to call Eddie, filled with an image of him having a PTSD-like reaction himself. It would probably be even stronger than hers. But he wasn't at the Brady Campaign offices, where it sounded like everything was going completely haywire, and their phones were ringing off the hook. She was relieved when two minutes later he reached out to her, from a telephone booth in Brooklyn.

No, he hadn't had a panic attack, although he understood and could identify with the mindset that could cause her to fall into such a chasm. Unlike Aziza, his reaction had been pure anger. He was enraged. "Twenty years ago, these kids would have acted out by setting off fire alarms, or they would have broken into the school at night and pointlessly broken shit, or they would have crashed the senior prom and made nuisances of themselves by hurling paint on some prom queen's dress. Now they've been given weapons of war, assault rifles, and they kill and maim indiscriminately! For God's sake, we all know that kids act out their anger and angst. It's been like that forever, since biblical times. Only now we give them the power of assault rifles to kill each other. How idiotic can we be? How stupid can we collectively get?"

She let him rant. He needed to discharge the heat in his veins, to release his rage. But as she listened to him, it was also undeniable to her that the availability of weapons was only half the root of this ongoing social catastrophe. In a world without spirituality, perfectly normal adolescent anomie intensifies to a whole new plane of aloneness. These kids don't feel identified with any teen-age group, and they don't even feel like they fit in their family. They plain and simply don't fit anywhere. They don't experience that there is a future for them in society. Rage rises to another level when anyone, especially a teenager, lacks grounding, and doesn't belong to some greater scheme, to some universal purpose, to some God's design.

"Please, come home, Eddie. Come be with me. I need you, and we need to talk all of this through. It feels overwhelming to both of us. Listen, I have to be in the city tomorrow for a colloquium at the 92nd Street Y. Please. It feels important that we be together and process all this abhorrent destruction. Can we meet up downtown when I'm done with the workshop and travel back to Roosters Rest together?"

His response was immediate. "Of course." There was nothing he could want more.

8

The colloquium had, unsurprisingly, focused on Columbine. The nation was in shock, again, at man's inhumanity to man, but as Professor Niemeyer pointed out, "None of us here are surprised. Appalled, yes. Outraged, yes. But how could we be surprised when outcomes are predictable. If we create a narcissistic society that cares only for self-imagery, should we be dumbfounded when personal grievances are sufficient to induce mass murder?"

Aziza had directed her remarks more specifically at the scarcity of spirituality in the culture. The relationship between this paucity and violence had consumed her in the hours since hearing of the Columbine carnage and feeling the horror terrorize her all over again.

In her contemplative way, Nityaneeta echoed this when she noted that "There will always exist the complements of creation and destruction, of goodness and evil. But when we lack a vessel to hold them together, their interdependence disintegrates, and that is when the universe goes askew." Aziza marveled at the guru's facility to express powerful complex truths with a modicum of words, words that seemed to flow elegantly from her centered being.

"I am so honored to meet you," she shared with the Guru as they walked toward the exit. "Your writings constantly bring new light to my darkness, even when I have read them many times before."

"I have recently read yours," Nityaneeta responded, "and what you have written has been a welcome addition to my knowing." She stopped momentarily and looked at Aziza with what seemed amusement. "I am intrigued, I must add, at your reluctance to accept the title of Guru. I have a car waiting for me outside. Would you like to sit with me for a few minutes and ride around the block? It would give us an opportunity, even if just for a few minutes, to get to know each other."

How could she not accept such an invitation? Eddie was waiting for her at the 10th Street apartment, but he would understand if she was a little late. "I am honored again," she said as they got into the waiting limousine.

Aziza waited for the guru to initiate conversation, feeling Nityaneeta had some purpose in wanting to interact. But the woman just sat in silence for a few minutes, minutes that seemed like an eternity, bemused by Aziza's building puzzlement. Eventually she said, "Please excuse my enjoying myself in this moment of embarrassment and confusion. I am remembering when I first initially my Master, for the first time. I was about your age, and had no idea why this holy man, this great man would want to talk with me, a nothing. It was mystifying, to say the least." Her facial expression transitioned from amusement to contemplation. "Tell me. Why is it that you decline the assertion that you are a guru?"

Aziza thought about how to answer. She was directly being asked the question that had in some ways dominated her self-appraisal for the past year. "With all respect to you and your sense of purpose, Nityaneeta, I've never aspired to any leadership roles, much less being a guru. While I feel compelled to grasp the universal understandings that connect us to the All, it's never been my intention to inflate my position and tell others what they should be and how to live their lives. Admittedly, I have a sense that I can help others to move toward a more spiritual life, but I have never been comfortable with being highly visible, being an object that other people project upon. You, of all people, must know what I mean."

The guru's face and tone became stern. "What I know is that you are a very spoiled girl! All you talk about is what you want or have always wanted. Do you really think that this is all about what you aspire to, what your intentions are, as if you were deciding whether you want to be a banker, baker or a candlestick maker? Who ever said that being a guru is something that anyone would want, or choose, or plan to be?"

Taken aback, Aziza felt slapped in the face. "I don't understand. Maybe I just don't appreciate the difference between a cleric and a guru."

"Stop defending yourself, child! You are sophisticated enough to know the difference between doing a job and being in service. We can choose to do this or that, to pick from a list of things that we can do. We don't choose who we are. You have twice said you honor me. Is that for what I do, or who I am? I assume the latter. When my Master revealed his vision to me about who I was, do you think I had choice?"

"Is that what is happening here?"

"No. In my culture there is lineage. Not necessarily of birthright. When we know a saint's vision for us, it is not ours to question. In your culture there are no saints, there is only consensus. And the consensus about who you are is very clear." The guru's tone had begun to soften. The limo had arrived back at the steps to the Y. "Now, please leave me. I will see you again when it begins." She gently touched Aziza on her knee, as if showing her the way out of the limo.

When it begins? Aziza found herself abruptly on the sidewalk again, her thoughts absolutely everywhere and nowhere, lost, but on the cusp of being found. It was a full minute or two later, although it felt like an hour, when a few passersby bumped into her, throwing her momentarily off balance, and she regained her sense of time and place. Stupefied, she moved toward the subway. She felt strange. On the one hand she had a sense of fatigue, as if she had just run five miles. On the other hand, she was as exhilarated as she could ever remember. It was a blur and a blaze at one and the same time. When what begins?

9

On The Journey to Enlightenment

When I am being me, there is a rightness of fit, a physical sensation of my energy being centered, flowing freely, balanced and intact.

When I fall into being other than me, my energy feels blocked and obstructed, creating tension and instability. When my body feels cramped and constricted, it is a message for me to search for the ways and manners in which I am being untrue to myself.

I am always me, even in those times when I don't accept that I am who I am. False ego attachments can alter my self-perceptions, but who I am just is. Acting in ways that are inconsistent with who I am doesn't change me. It only hides me behind its costume and camouflage.

I am the path with which I travel through the universe. I am both me and my interface with the All and Everything. If I were set apart from Everything else, I would cease to exist. My insipient mission existed when my path was first unfolding, despite my being unaware of the destinations which would ensue along the way. The changes, inflections points, transmutations and transformations in my journey were set in motion long before they occurred.

I engage the mystery of who I am and how I interact with the All and Everything as a choice to constantly reaffirm my life. It is senseless to fear whatever I might discover about being me, because I will continue to be those parts that I seek to discard, no matter if I foolishly work to reject them. Only the false me can be removed. The true self remains and always has the potential to be revealed.

My path travels through a world which is itself always changing. Expectations that my life will remain static can only lead to conflict with what is. I will continue to evolve in a synchronized relationship with the evolving world around me. The path to my destiny is infinite, complex and synergistic.

As I evolve, I have the opportunity for the balance between the side of me which is centered in me and the side of me that is grounded in the All and Everything to shift toward the direction of universal identification. At the point that the All-inclusive me grows to exceed the me-alone, I become freed from the tethering to ego-anchors, and can explore the farther reaches of my illuminated Spirit. Enlightenment happens when we unify with this light, and is often experienced with the release of enormous energy, as the individual Soul joins with the All. The opportunity for Enlightenment is present in everyone's journey.

Upon reaching Enlightenment, life goes on. Life's choices still exist, but become simplified, as our knowing reaches beyond immediate circumstance. Uncertainty, self-doubt and anxiety about decision-making evaporate. Obsessive indecision vanishes. Life becomes a dance, allowing yourself to flow with the music of the All.

Come, dance with me. Shall we dance together? Can you hear the music?

10

Eddie and Aziza were in absolutely opposite emotional states as they drove toward Sandyston. As he sat behind the steering wheel, he was sullen, mostly silent, doing his best to contain the frustration, rage and resentment which filled him. He strained to check himself, so as not to project his malcontent toward Aziza, whose attitude and disposition were clearly dissimilar. She was equally uncommunicative, but with a tranquil air about her. She seemed as comfortable with their scant verbal exchange, as he was on edge because of it. In the past, he had often expressed the idea that couples shouldn't have expectations that they would always feel the same about mutually shared experiences; but in this moment, it turned out that he craved validation of his distress. She had expressed it just yesterday. Where was it today? What had changed? There was something different about her, and he couldn't put his finger on it.

Eventually, as they were nearing Roosters Rest, she reached out her hand to soothe his thigh and said, "It's all right, Eddie. It's going to be okay. I promise you." Just that, and nothing more.

He was feeling the fury that young idealists encounter when they relentlessly come up against the hard realities of a world resistant to change. It was incomprehensible that smart people could be so stupid! It was inconceivable that ethical leaders could bend so far toward the immoral! His devotion to being part of a movement with hopes and dreams for a more peaceful world was being challenged by an unexpected social entrenchment in violence, hate and prejudice. Some of his core beliefs about his purpose and mission in life were being tested, and he was coming up to that confounding point where some part of him wanted to fight violence with violence. It was all he could do to keep his hands from balling into fists. And here she was, calmly leading him out of the car, and suggesting that they should have some tea.

In some ways, he felt like a little boy, needing to be comforted by his mom. But, in truth, he resented this regressive need, not the woman who was tending to it. He rhythmically stirred a teaspoon of sugar into his cup, hoping the swirling motion itself would lessen his tension.

"Eddie, let me talk for a little while. I know that you feel like you're bursting at the seams right now, and I know that you can't understand why my outlook right now doesn't match yours, but if you could just sit back and bear with me for a while, I'd really appreciate it. A lot of things have fallen into place in the past few hours, and I'm experiencing a sense of peace that I never thought I was capable of knowing. I want to, I need to, share that with you, because I love you, more in this moment than ever before. Yes, even in this moment of disequilibrium.

"You know, it occurs to me that I've never fully understood why clerics, and gurus, and spiritual leaders so often avoid partnering up or getting married, seeming to lead a lonely, if worthy, life. Perhaps it is because of times like this, when they can't expect their partner to be grounded in the same sensibility they are experiencing. But I believe we can do this. I think our love is built on a trust that we don't have to see through the same eyes or listen with the same ears. We can learn and grow and become stronger through our disparity. I don't love you because you are me, but because you are dissimilar, even as we share being part of a unity." He nodded agreement, without disturbing her train of thought.

"Everything has changed for me today, although nothing has really changed. It all seems to have happened when I was leaving the colloquium up at the 92nd Street Y, and Nityaneeta asked me to ride around the block with her in her car. So help me, Eddie, a five minute ride around the block! She chided me. She was harsh with me, but in a loving manner. The way a caring mother might chastise their child. She pointed out how utterly selfish I have been, more concerned about what I wanted for my life, than actualizing who I am meant to be. She caused me to face a fundamental question. While we have free will about what we do, do we have free will about who we ae?

"It's impossible for me to express how freeing it has been to fully allow myself to settle into myself. Sure, I've been advocating forever that we need to be who we are, but when directed at myself that was a whole lot of intellectual crap! Personally, emotionally, I've been fighting myself every step of the way, and when I think about it, it was so obvious, so right in front of my face, that it is almost embarrassing to admit it now. I've bought into the craziest, most narcissistic component of our culture, that you can choose to be who you want, that you should choose who you want to be as if you were selecting your life from a Sears catalogue. I didn't want to be some gurulike spiritual leader. So, what! I didn't want to ever be the center of attraction. I didn't want to put myself out there where people could criticize me. So, what! It's like I've known who I am basically since I was twelve years old, but it always seemed audacious, or scary, or presumptuous for me to admit it, so I've played this ridiculous halfway game where I accept me for myself privately, but do my best to hide it from others.

"In the moments after Nityneeta left me, I stood on the sidewalk and it seemed as if every moment of my life was flashing before me, every step of my path, every juncture of my journey, and it felt complete! Eddie, I felt complete! Nothing was missing, nothing needed to be done, I had become exactly who I was always intended to be, and I no longer had any fears about being who I was. The fears were gone! I don't know what she did, or if it was just her words, but I was freed from being afraid of me! "

"And who is that?" he interjected, with some hesitancy.

"Well, I know I'm not a guru in the sense that Nityneeta is. I'm a product of the American culture and for me to pretend to be some maharishi-like figure would just be another fabrication. I don't chant mantas in foreign tongues or advocate others to do so or not to do so. I don't sit cross-legged in front of mandalas wearing a sari. I'm comfortable in jeans, torn jeans at that. I like to eat meat, and have been known to overeat at bar-b-ques. All of that stuff, Eastern or Western, is just cultural norms and mores, and irrelevant to spirituality. You and I have always known that esoteric mysticism is just an exotic or trendy justification for being more special than everybody else.

In truth, what I am, inside and out, with every cell of my body, is a Spiritual Leader, someone who is devoted to humanity's understanding that we are each of us a part of the All and Everything. At the foundation of my being there has always been the Shema, that bold and beautiful exclamation of Oneness, an expression that all universal energy is comprised of that godlike Oneness and we can know and experience being a part of it All. I have a life-long history of obsessively searching and studying to comprehend and best articulate the infinite applications of this seemingly simple statement. For sure, my joining with you has been a further confirmation of the spiritual nature of my being. And now, our world seems to be faced with a new rise of violence and hatred and inhumanity, all the demons that our parents' generation were so confident that they could, and would, eliminate. My path has been leading me to this intersection of violence and spirituality from the very beginnings of my life, and I am crystal clear about who I am and how I need to respond. And I don't mean being someone who perfunctorily echoes age-old expressions of horror and dismay, allowing myself to become a stereotyped protestor, playing out a typecast role against the corrupt political process. Rather, I need to be the spiritual leader that I am."

"So, you think that what I have been doing is just some empty articulation of distress, and not an effective tactic for being a change agent?" Eddie started to get defensive.

"No, I think the role that you have been playing is a necessary and principled political action, but I question if you are the one to play it."

"I don't understand. Don't the teachings of the Reverend King advise us that politics can't be separated from religion, and that an activist clerical community can help to move society toward a more moral and ethical stance?"

"Of course. Don't get me wrong, my love. I can only applaud you for bringing your brilliant energy and person to the Brady

Organization. But I think you could be more effective and be truer to yourself by joining with me, in something new, right here at Roosters Rest." Realizing she was way ahead of herself, she smiled, and continued. "I guess it would make more sense if I explained the vision I have for me, for us, for this place. It all fell into place for me, when I accepted my being who I am."

What was he to say? This was not the tentative, questioning, need to be sure she had it just right, Aziza. She had an air of certainty about her, and he instinctively wanted to hear her out. "I'm all ears, Ziz." All of his rage had been replaced with needing to hear her out.

"On the ride down from 92nd Street, a clear visual picture of a transformed Roosters Rest come into my mind. It was extraordinary how detailed the visualization was. About seventy-five feet east of this house there was a segmented courtyard with four statues set in the corner of each respective quadrant. Three marble benches were placed by each statue, with intricate garden beds between the benches and the statues. Oh Eddie, they were beautiful. Each were sculpted with a shining stainless-steel finish. As I looked at them more closely, I realized that each of them represented a religious theme. Toward the house, there was the hand of Fatima, opposite to a Buddha, a happy smiling, laughing Buddha. On the side of the courtyard away from the house, there was a Star of David, opposite to a large cross. Each of them seemed to reflect ambient light toward a magnificent fountain, that stood between them all in the center of the courtyard, also constructed of the same steel. A second later, I became totally thunderstruck, when I intuited somehow that each of these statues, and also the fountain, were cast from guns that had been melted down to be reused, or perhaps I should say, reformed. Stretching out from the courtyard there was an extended statue garden, filling maybe half of our land, all that land which is now forest, that slopes down toward the stream. The statues that filled the garden were each forged from smelted weapons, rifles and guns which might otherwise have been utilized to kill and maim. The evil had been joined with good, and together they helped to create a sculpture garden for people to walk through, and have a direct spiritual experience of being part of a vibrant, powerful call for peace. It felt like the embodiment of everything we have always hoped for but couldn't divine.

"And it was you who had procured all the weapons, from everywhere across the country, from gun buy-out programs, from law enforcement seizures, and from congregations whose clerics implored their congregants who would listen to donate. You were using all the contacts you have made while with the Brandy group. And back on the western portion of our land, hidden in the forest, was a large forge, part of a workplace and studio where the statuary was created by artists who were attracted to the project. I saw myself strolling through the garden, teaching, talking, being who I am, imparting some grounding in Spirituality for anyone who was moved by the art, and called to fathom its meaning. We were together, being who we are and doing what we do."

"Talk about beating swords into ploughshares." Eddie, captivated by all the implications of her words, had now forgotten his frustration and rage. He was transfixed with the possibilities, and before even communicating to her how extraordinary her vision was, found himself leaping into a rush of organizational procedures and practical steps that would need to be taken. A board would have to be formed, and a non-profit status would have to be procured by the right legal team. The board of directors would have to at one and the same time represent the spiritual nature of the organization but also be composed of individuals who could raise capital and engage a hopefully receptive political system. This immense project was not going to be inexpensive or fast or easy. It astonished him when he realized that there were people, already part of their personal network, who were perfect fits for necessary functions. Could there be anyone better than Bill to supervise what would clearly be major engineering issues in the design and running of the foundry? Shen's leadership abilities and drive could be invaluable if he agreed to be a member of the board. Carl already had the perfect resume for handling the public relations of a spiritual enterprise. And Henry, Henry was the most obvious of fits, someone who could organize and institute an advisory group of artists and artisans and spiritualists and clergy. Perhaps his own father would join.

Eddie had become so immersed in the fastmoving internal flood of practical applications that he had to find paper and begin to write out all the thoughts and notions and imperatives before he lost them. He mumbled something about excusing himself for a second and went to get some legal pad and a writing utensil. Aziza was left to watch him from a distance, patiently waiting for his anticipated return to her, probably in about a half hour.

11

The ride out to the Rest gave Esther and Shen ample time to talk through the parental issues in which they felt confounded and mired. Aziza had requested they participate in an organizational meeting for what seemed, at first glance, like an undertaking of beyond mammoth proportions, by a couple of kids who hadn't even completed their undergraduate degrees. Nothing had followed any of their expected sequences over the past two years. You anticipate your child going to college, picking a major, finding a social identity and network, gaining a foothold on an individuated worldview, and eventually graduating, whereupon the next series of crossroads would await. Of course, as Shen quickly pointed out, neither he nor Esther had followed such a customary course themselves, yet here they were, expecting that their daughter would.

How do you reconcile the world certifying your child as a mature personage of sagacity, while you couldn't help but see her as your little girl, barely out of her teens, not yet fully formed? She was supposed to be just getting over dealing with sex, drugs and rock'n'roll, and moving into a sophomoric prescience, not unraveling the issues for which government leaders and the intellectual elite were unable to find meaningful solutions. She was supposed to be reading the classics and seminal books, not writing them, finding herself on the *NY Times* bestseller list. Parents imagine that they will need to continue to guide their children at this age through the complex business of crafting their foundations for an adult life. They had anticipated this as a time when they would need to balance how often to directly offer advice and counsel, and when to display confidence, by standing back and watching, albeit with anxious fingers crossed behind their back.

Esther and Shen were equally preoccupied with the issue of Aziza completing her degree. Both of them had been required by their unusual circumstances to put immense effort into completing their undergraduate and graduate coursework. They had been motivated by a belief that a foothold of formal education was a necessity, and their success had born this out. First you gain the necessary credentials, then you step out and take on the world. Even if Aziza had some modicum of fame and unexpected financial security, having a degree in her pocket would always safekeep her life in the event that her fortunes changed. Esther had to admit to herself that for some people degrees are totally unnecessary. She remarked, "Lincoln, Ben Franklin and Einstein come to mind. But, Shen, as much as every parent fantasizes their kid as a genius, accepting real exceptionalism is a totally different matter. I'm okay with confessing that I was one of those parents that wanted my kid to be counterculture, to go against the conventional social grain. It's probably true that I vicariously wanted her to fulfill some early agenda of my own, which needed to be put aside when I had her. Be careful, you might get what you wish for."

How much of their consternation came down to accepting that their role of parenting seemed to be ending, a least as far as Aziza was concerned? Were their egos having a hard time letting go of what they had hoped would be an ego-syntonic undertaking? Did all this come down to a commonplace struggle of accepting that your child was an adult? Roulan would inevitably be next, and then empty nest? Another waypoint on the road to mortality?

Eventually, Esther settled the matter. "This is absurd. We are obviously overthinking. Shen, we can throw this back and forth forever, but at the end of the day, the reality is very simple. Our daughter is asking us for our support. Whether or not we think she is ready to take on this challenge, is ultimately immaterial. Whether or not we are ready for her to do it is ultimately immaterial. She thinks we can make some helpful contribution to an undertaking that she is about have a go at, with or without our permission or approval. Why would we even contemplate doing anything other than supporting her to the best of our abilities?"

12

Eddie met his father in the driveway. The Reverend Ricardo Huertas had driven out alone, although Aziza's parents had invited him to accompany them. Like them, he had welcomed some travel time to think through how he would respond to Eddie's request. He and his wife quarreled just before he left Corona. On hearing her husband carp about Eduardo being way over his head and totally unprepared for the task he was about to undertake, she reminded him that a lot of his family said the same thing when he started his church in Corona. Now look at it! Your congregation is almost as strong as that catholic church, two blocks over. "It's different," he barked back. "I wasn't taking on national issues. There wasn't a powerful NRA and a thousand politicians hostile to my meagre efforts." She disregarded his words, striding over and stroking his cheek. "He reminds me of you more and more as the days go by. You've done a good job, Ricardo." And how do you argue with that?

"Hijo," he asked his son, "is this you or Aziza? You know I love that girl, but are you getting tied to her desires instead of your own?"

"I assure you, Dad, I want this even more than Aziza does. Having had a bullet shot through my body, this is something that I can't let go of. It's as personal as it gets. Dad, can you see that as long as the right to arms issue is portrayed as a political dispute, there will never be any progress? What we're planning here is to frame the issue properly, as a spiritual matter, as a moral and ethical matter. And you, of all people, know this to be true. How many of your congregants have been shot to death on the streets of Corona because of lunatic machismo? And what is machismo other than a lack of godliness in one's masculinity? I've tried for the last year to speak to clergy all over this country, and most of them don't get that it's a spiritual, not political issue, even when they want restrictions on weapons. And that's why I have to see this done, Dad. And that's why I want you by my side."

For the second time that day, Ricardo found himself saying, "And how do you argue with that?"

When they went inside, Ricardo knew most all of the other invitees. Aziza's parents, of course, and the kid's friend Bill, who he remembered from high school as Moose. He and Leader Posert had known of each other for years, but had finally met socially at Aziza's graduation party, and again at a birthday party for Aziza's little sister, Roulan. Was that last Spring? Posert was a good man. Eddie had spoken well of the other two gentlemen present, Carl Porcaro and James Wellsworth, his son's boss at the Brady Organization. From what he had heard from Eduardo, the two men were skilled at what they did, and would add some seasoned experience, if this ambitious project was to get off the ground. There were also two women that he might have met at that birthday party, someone whose name he thought he remembered as Betania, and another, Lian, who he seemed to remember was Shen's sister. Lian was sitting with her husband Marty, the guy who was a set designer and had given them four tickets for that wonderful Broadway play. What a wonderful night that had been, Felicia and himself, out with the kids. Maybe he should have brought Felicia along today.

Aziza asked everyone to settle down, and began the meeting. "I want to thank everyone for coming today. I think of most of the people gathered here today as family. We, all of us, look to our families for support, and again, how lucky am I that all of you bear this out. Eddie is going to manage the bulk of this meeting, but I wanted to say a few things first.

"As much as I appreciate your personal support, and the majority of you have been there with me since I was a young child, I need to note that with regard to this matter, I'm not seeking encouragement or reassurance or validation. We are talking about what will hopefully be a significant, although incremental, step toward a more peaceful world. I am aware how pretentious this may sound, but isn't that true of every effort that was ever made toward achieving a more honorable society? If this dream is to be transformed into a reality, it will require a collaboration of people who are devoted to a shared belief. We will all need to agree that asserting 2nd amendment rights as having a higher priority than the right to life of others is a direct contradiction of any form of righteous spiritual conviction. Through this project, we seek to promote a basic spiritual mentality and ethos which will bring this principle to light. I deeply hope that all of you share this vision, and wish to join us in its creation.

"Eddie and I will need you to challenge and refute us when we are off base, and pull no punches when we are being naïve or gullible. I recognize that both of us, while having whatever talents we have, and being as committed as we are, still lack the life experience most of you have. When the inspiration of the young is fused with the learned proficiencies of their elders, their collaboration will most likely be able to meet its objective. It's not a secret to either one of us that some of you question the advisability of the two of us embarking on this ambitious journey. You may think of us as Quixotes tilting our lances at an impermeable windmill. But our cause, our mission, is not only ethically and morally correct, it is also achievable. I would add that I believe the vision is divine.

"This small group will have to be multiplied many times over for us to be successful and bring the vision to completion. Some folks have taken to calling me a guru, a seer. Usually, I recoil from such a title. However, with regard to the creation of this sculpture garden, I accept the designation. I will do my best to honor that mantle. I see us, no, I know us, establishing a foothold for spiritual sanity in a world gone mad with murderous narcissism. I know this to be doable. I have total certainty that it will come to pass."

She took a few breaths, before continuing. "I'm sorry. You need particulars, not just my celestial aspirations. Eddie, it's time for me to step back, and give you the floor, to address the necessary pragmatic ways and means of accomplishing this complex mission."

In the first few sentences, during which he only partially heard Eduardo's words, Ricardo found himself taking a new pride at his son's ability to command a room. Successful fathers often are the last to recognize their offspring's realization of leadership skills. When had this happened? His boy had clearly grown during the past year with the Brady group. ". . . . . and I have taken the liberty of dividing our efforts into four stages. In the initial stage we will have to ensure that we will be able to, in fact, secure the guns, mostly from American police departments. Until we are confident of this, nothing else can proceed. Jim, you have been a mentor and friend over this past year at Brady, and I hope you will be able to assist me in securing the weaponry, giving us the ability to put the steel to a higher purpose. In addition, during this first phase, I hope we can convince many black and Spanish-speaking inner-city ministries to conduct buy-back programs, increasing our supply chain of weapons to be melted down. It's my understanding that Brady can bring funding to these programs, if we can enroll local churches in the effort. It is my hope that my father, yes you, Dad, who has a voice in these communities, will lead these efforts.

"Hopefully we will learn quickly that we can procure the weapons, and Phase Two, the detailed planning stage, would follow. Marty, we were hoping that you and Lian would create and lead a group to design the sculpture garden. For once, Marty, your elegant art would last beyond a season or two on Broadway. Like the sets you create for theatre productions, your design would be the heart and soul of the venture. Hopefully you and Aziza might be able to secure an audience with Frederick Franck, whose home is only half an hour or so from here, and who has created a sculpture garden on the land surrounding his abode. He calls it *Pacem In Terris*. If you were able to convince him to join an advisory board, it would be an extraordinary addition, given his renowned relationship with both spirituality and the arts. There is also a small artist's colony, just a few miles from here, Peters Valley, and perhaps you could be persuasive in enlisting their presence on the board. Henry, the other half of this advisory board will require a wide range of clergy and others with a strong spiritual sensibility. If you could locate willing members, and then chair this board, it would be a godsend.

"Shen, this is obviously going to require a major fundraising drive, and I know of no one better suited to head up that area than you. No monies can be raised until a non-profit corporation is legally achieved, and Aziza and I hoped that you, Esther, who have worked for and with so many non-profits, could find the right lawyers who might donate their time, and work with them to help us become a legal entity. I would add that there will be a slew of other local and state legal requirements which will need to be identified, permits obtained, licenses secured, and on.

"Betania, there is another component of these gardens which we were hoping you could lead. We want to create a library of sorts, collecting newspaper and periodical articles that report on every armed homicide in this country, starting with Columbine. We know that many of these tragedies don't receive the type of attention that mass murders do, and if nothing else, we hope to be able to demonstrate the sheer accumulated volume of death and destruction that is the direct outcome on our national obsession with guns. As much as we might hope that Columbine would be a stand-alone horror, it is inevitable that many more will follow, given the easy access to arms and the epidemic proportions of aggrieved narcissists.

"Phase Three is, of course, the actual construction of the park, from the gardens, to the forge, to the sculpture, to the library, each and every component of it all. It's going to take an exceptional person to coordinate all the intellectual, artistic and brick and mortar components of this production, and we believe that you, Bill, would be perfect for the job. If I'm not mistaken, you're finishing up at Cooper Union in another six months, and how about a super complex humongous job, right out of the box? Obviously, we would all have to supervise our respective components throughout all of the construction. And, my guess is, that this is right around the time that you, Carl, would need to begin your work, letting the general public know who we are, and preparing them for the fourth phase, the actual opening. Beyond that Carl, we were hoping that you would be able to join with James and take over the ongoing administration of the gardens, after the opening.

"There have to be a million and a half questions we should get into. And I don't want to pressure any of you to respond to our requests for your assistance publicly How about we break out of this formal presentation and spend the rest of the afternoon in more easy-going conversation?"

Later that evening, after everyone had left, and it was just Eddie and herself remaining at Rooster's Rest, Aziza decided that she needed to send a quick note to Guru Nityaneeta.

My Most Honored Friend,

I thought you should know, it has begun. It strikes me that you probably somehow know this already, as you precipitated all these events when you allowed me darshan in your car.

Your Devoted Guruette

(Am I permitted some humor in this otherwise serious matter?)

Aziza

13

On Work

There can be a trap for folks who are drawn to the transcendent. Not surprisingly, many of the people who are attracted to spirituality tend to devote the best of their energy to contemplative thinking. When viewing a common landscape of people and places and things, their third eye searches for a higher order of import, a deeper sense of purpose, reaching away from the immediate toward the farther reaches of our universe. Some may go so far as to make a judgement that the stars are superior to the soil, and that understanding the architecture of the heavens has more consequence than the cleaning and maintenance of their immediate shelter. A senseless divide often is established between doing the "ordinary" work of managing one's life and the extraordinary alternative of searching for the esoteric, the exotic and the extreme in their "work beyond the stars." Such searchers end up trying to balance themselves on a single foot, perched on a wobbly stone, with both hemispheres tied above their head. And when they rudely fall back to the soil, they disdain the ground that saves them from falling further.

Life instructs us daily about balance and cycles. The light of day is balanced with the dark of night. Our breath is balanced between intake and outflow. Our hearts pump out and the blood flows inward. We toil, we rest. Our solar system maintains its balance with a complex set of cycles within cycles, modelling the galaxy, which models the universe.

To be spiritual, we must experience our self as a part of that which is larger than ourselves. Spirituality gives us the opportunity to know and feel our existence as an integral component of the All and Everything. Yet, here too, there must be balance and cycles. Without an everyday self-encapsulated self, there would be no one present to experience the larger Self. We need to nurture and administrate our physical, social and phenomenological natures, as they are the ground on which we stand when we reach for the heavens. Only a strong ego can allow itself to disappear.

There are no shortcuts. We must do the work. Part of the work is establishing an equilibrium between earthly and celestial pursuits, with a basic understanding that the perception of them as segmented elements is a disabling illusion. No one meditates well with a grumbling and rumbling stomach. We need to do the work of caring for our activities of daily living, as a foundation for our work to merge with the divine. Roughing our hands and exhausting our muscles while building the brick and mortar of our cathedrals precedes their lofty dedications.

Too often those who represent institutionalized spirituality think of themselves as elite. They disjoin themselves from ordinary work, assigning it to others, thinking they can devote themselves to some higher purpose. Having lost their balance, their work becomes disconnected from both the ground and the sky, cocooned in a judgmental miasma. Whatever purpose they originally pursued becomes lost in the higher altitude mist, and they turn to power, protecting themselves from becoming aware of their spiritual insolvency.

It requires discipline to maintain the balances. Work must be balanced with play. The ordinary must be balanced with the extraordinary. The earthly must be balanced with the ethereal. The intellectual must be balanced with the emotional. The ego must be balanced with the absence of ego. The serious must be balanced with the lighthearted. The disciplined work of the seeker is to cyclically juggle all these factors into a cohesive virtuous life. The righteous work is in the discipline and the righteous discipline is in the work.

It is not lost on me that the great prophets of humanity have all had occupations. Jesus was a carpenter, as was Noah. Joseph was an agricultural administrator. Mohammed was a businessman, Buddha a teacher, Abraham a shepherd. Each of them had a discipline of maintaining a homeostatic balance between their immediate tasks-at-hand and their ultimate visions. By directing their energy to both sides of life's equation, they achieved both the pleasure of their need's well met and the ecstasy of uniting with All and Everything.

Once we develop the capacity to balance and discipline our energies and intentions, we become ready to recognize and pursue our larger mission. That is the point when our purpose unifies with universal consciousness.

14

A few days before the opening of Rooster's Retreat, Ben asked Aziza if she would mind him strolling around by himself. "It's like every time Morty would design some new and fancy coat, me, I had to try it on myself, you know, see how it fits, see how it feels. Lots of things look great on some drawing board, but until you've got your arms through the sleeves, who knows? Who knows, for sure?"

"Grandpa, of course you can take a walk-through. Would you like me to walk with you?"

"No, Darling. I think I want to go by my lonesome. This walk I want to do alone." The real truth was, Ben intended to be with Rose, to talk to his wife as he explored. "You know, Rosie, once upon a time, before we had Esther, we used to walk a lot in Cunningham Park, just the two of us it was. It felt so good to stroll along the footpath with you, to kind of promenade, I think that's the word, to promenade. The pride, it filled me up when you held my arm, and I got to show you off, to show everybody how lucky I was to have the prettiest girl on my arm. And I think, maybe, that you were proud too, Rosie. That you were proud of me. It was good, a good thing to be out and walking in the park.

"And then you went and died in the back yard, in our garden. Ever since then, I've looked forward to kibbitzing with you in the back yard, by that bush I planted right in the spot where you left me. That's why I never want to sell the house, even if Shen and Esther want me to live with them. You know, Rose, I never was much of a cemetery person. I mean, I think the plot I got is a nice enough place to rest in peace, like they say, but I can't talk to you there. It doesn't really feel like you're there. Sure, I want myself, that I should be buried next to you in that spot, but then, it's not like we're going to be doing any schmoozing. In the backyard I can talk to you. Here, in Aziza's garden, maybe I can talk to you here also."

He entered the courtyard, inspected all four of the central sculptures, and sat down on the bench opposite the Buddha. "You know what I always liked about Buddhas, Rosie, I always liked that he was depicted as fat. Yeah, I know that you didn't like anybody being chubby, and you were always wanting to go on this diet or that diet, but did you ever notice that whenever any of the other religions, including ours Rosie, including ours, whenever they show their hero's, or prophets or any of the special people, they always show them off like they're fit and trim and ready to be a halfback for the Giants, you know, like Gifford. I mean, Moses always looks like he's ready to go and do some decathlon Olympics event, throw the javelin thing or run a bunch of miles. And the Christians, they always make Jesus out to be some handsome white guy who's ready to wear a 42 long suit with a little bit taken in around the waist. I mean, sure, we always sold plenty of those suits, but you know Rosie, most people weren't ready for the magazine cover of GQ. The trick was always to make the ordinary guy look good because he was wearing that suit. It just seems right that when some religion wants you to make yourself out to be like some hallowed person, maybe he should look like the rest of us schlubs.

"And you know what else, Rosie? I really like the way that Buddha is laughing and laughing. I don't know if he just really had a ball in life, or maybe he's laughing a little bit at us, like he's mocking the way we make such a big deal about all the things that don't really count. Maybe I'm wrong, Rosie, but it feels like most of the rabbis and priests and all those people, they spend so much time on all the petty stuff, all the little things that don't really matter for much in the long run, that they miss out on the important things. I think that's why I like that Posert guy. He cares about the big picture stuff, and doesn't seem to waste everybody's time on baloney. And he's been such a good influence on our Aziza. He's been good for her, Rosie.

"You know, this granddaughter of ours, our Aziza, she's a very special person, a very special person. And as smart as she is, and as famous as she is, she still comes to her grandfather every once in a while, because she knows that she doesn't know everything. Our granddaughter is a big shot, but she's not some know-it-all. Like Goldsheid, that ganiff. Does he have even a bissel of humility in that short little body of his? But Aziza, the smartest thing about her is she knows all she doesn't know, and that's why she knows so much. We did good, Rosie. We did good, for us, for our families, and maybe we also did good for the world. Our Aziza, she's a blessing, a blessing I tell you."

He rose, and stopped for a minute in front of the cross, which stretched out a little higher than the other three in the courtyard. "And you know, Rosie, you know what else I really like about this granddaughter of ours? She doesn't have that chosen people lunacy filling up her brain. And, she doesn't hold it against all the Christians for what they did to our ancestors for the past couple of thousand years, or maybe even our parents' generation. I mean, you and me Rosie, we were brought up with all that stuff about the goyim, like dividing everybody up into us and them, the Jews and the gentiles. None of that stuff's good Rosie. It's meshuggeneh. All of this 'us and them' stuff, Rose, it's not good, it's a bad thing, I tell you.

"That's why all this horrible shooting happens, Rosie, all these ignorant people killing and thinking it's okay to do such a thing. That's why it's important, like Aziza and Eddie say, to get rid of all those guns that the 'them and us' people feel like they have to have. Do we have to always have this group and that group setting themselves off from all the other groups, and then they start thinking that all the troubles they have is because of the 'them'? It's always Cowboys and Indians and cops and robbers and good guys and bad guys, and you know what the funny thing is, Rosie, everybody thinks they're the good guy and those other guys are the bad guys. The kids are right, we have to get rid of all these stupid killing machines, but we also have to figure out a way that all this 'us and them' stuff gets lost It's so farblundjet, crazy I tell you.

"You know, Rose, it's not like I remember, that I pretend, like we were always cozy-shmoozy, all the time. There were lots of time you thought I was being a jerk, and other times I wished you paid better attention to what really mattered, to what you really wanted. But you know, Rosie, we never had in in our heads that it was 'him and me' or 'her and me'. I think that's how we got through our hard times. I think that's how Esther and Aziza turned out so good, I tell you. Maybe that's why Esther helps so many girls, and why Aziza can create this beautiful garden for the whole world to see and learn from. Maybe it's all about remembering that we're completely 'us'. And you know what, Rosie, we're still us, even now, even after all this time since you've been gone from me."

15

On the morning of the opening, after two years of construction, nobody knew quite what to expect. Carl had, of course, sent out the press releases, and arranged for both Aziza and Eddie to do TV and radio interviews with local stations, but as he told Henry, "I don't expect, or even want, some big crowd when we open. We don't want searchlights, and clowns and guest appearances of baseball stars to bring in a swarm of people looking for a fair. We're not opening a 24-hour carwash. What we can hope for is maybe a hundred people the first weekend, mostly some neighborhood folks who are curious about what it's all about, maybe some who have read Aziza's book, maybe a carful or two that were just driving by. This is the kind of attraction that grows slowly, mostly by word of mouth, people telling their friends about how moved they were as they walked around the garden. Journalists who have been here telling others about the feeling that came over them when they experienced the beauty that had been created out of ugliness. I think of this like the Cloisters, just a few miles away from Yankee Stadium, always having a steady stream of people who are drawn to art and religion, not the roar and excitement of thousands in the baseball stands."

"I totally agree," replied Henry "This isn't about being a splashy show. It's about planting a seed, a seed of hope, in a world which has become long on suffering, and short on faith. And the seeds will not only grow in the hearts of people who visit, but the sculpture garden itself will become a symbol of the contrast between man's capacity for righteousness and the impiety of weapons of war being spread throughout the civilian population. And don't forget the relationship between this park and Aziza. I expect her charisma and status as a Guru who represents the broad scope of spirituality will grow proportionately on these stunning grounds. This isn't meant to be an esoteric spiritual platform. Some will be attracted to the Arts. Some will be attracted to the blooms. Some will even be attracted by the politics. But it seems to me that most everyone will find Aziza's words and presence reaching a part of themselves which they may have not known was there."

Abruptly, there seemed to be some commotion from the direction of the parking area. Henry looked out, and was distressed to see a half dozen protestors putting together a score of placards and voicing some indiscernible grumblings into the air, although there wasn't anyone else there, as yet, to listen. A youngish man, thirtyish, dressed in camo's, appeared to be the leader, organizing them into a circle, barking out orders as if they were all part of a military troop.

"I don't believe this," remarked Bill, the well experienced protestor. "What rock did these yahoos crawl out from?"

"It's not really unexpected," answered Carl. "When you communicate with people you believe will respond well to your message, there will always be some others who are offended by what you have to say. Who knows? There's still an hour before the time we officially open. Maybe they'll talk themselves out and be gone by then."

Aziza gazed out the window and said, "I think I want to go out there and talk to them." She started toward the door.

"Wait up, Ziz," Eddie called out. "There's no need to focus on whatever negative dribble they're spouting. Just let themselves tire themselves out and feel silly when no one listens to them. There's nobody here right now to hear them anyway."

"That's not the point, Ed. They've come to Rooster's Retreat, for whatever reasons they have, and I have to think of it as an opportunity to interconnect, and to share whatever insights might be helpful. Isn't our intention to hopefully diminish fears about the 'other'?

Aziza left the house, and then the deck, and approached the protesting strangers in the parking lot. Eddie and Shen followed protectively behind her. As she approached, all the picketer's eyes were directed to the man in the camouflage suit, confirming him as the leader. She stepped straight to him, and smiled. The two were a study in contrasts, his glower confronting her serenity, his stark military outfit facing her flowing white and lilac organdy dress.

"Hello, my friend, I'm Aziza. Can I help you?"

"Oh, so you must be that guru who set up shop here."

"There are people who call me a guru. Yes, and we have built this sculpture garden. Would you like to see it, to walk around?"

He seemed to be put off by her welcoming tone. "Look lady, we're here to give you a simple message." He pointed toward a sign which read, **Don't Mess With Our Guns Unless You Want Our Guns To Mess With You.** Another broadcast, **My Guns, My Rights.** "Like I said, it's simple, we have our constitutional rights to bear arms, and we don't appreciate folks who want to take our rights away."

"So, do you believe that our using the metal from other people's guns to make statues of beauty, that honor the great spiritual concepts of the world, is going to deprive you of your weapons? I'm not clear how it is that what we are doing here threatens you."

He was quick to retort. "Believe me lady, you guys don't threaten me. And we don't have anything against any of your religious or spiritual stuff either. I mean, that's protected in the constitution too. We just don't get what your spiritual opinions have to do with guns."

"Many people don't see what spirituality and gun control have to do with each other. Would you like me to explain the connection? I would be glad to share that with you."

"Knock yourself out. It's not like you're going to convince us to throw our guns away."

"Okay. I see by your clothing that you believe in teams, in people banding together. All for one, and one for all. That's sort of what spirituality is all about, being a part of something that includes you, but is larger than you. Sometimes your team is made up of brothers that you know, sometimes it's composed of zillions and zillions of people or energies that we can hardly comprehend. But even if we can't identify all of the members or all of the energies, we still know we're part of the group. Like humanity, we all know we're part of humanity, even if we don't know the billions of people who inhabit our planet.

"And that's where the all-for-one and one-for-all phrase comes into play. On a team, each and every one of us has to stand for and protect all our brothers. You see, if you're spiritual you need to protect the other people on your humanity team from getting hurt, and they need to protect your right to bear arms. The spirituality is in the teamwork. You with me?"

"I can hear that, but I still don't get what that has to do with our right to bear arms."

"It's not about your right to bear arms. It's about the particular arms that you want to bear. As a part of a team, you want to protect your teammates from wicked people who would use weapons of war to kill them, without generals or captains or sergeants to ensure that they follow the rules of war. Guns and rifles that are made for civilian use, for hunting and the like, or just for their own protection, that's another thing. All of us should protect your right to have them. As you say, that's in the constitution. But weapons of war should only be used in a justifiable war by a team that we call an army, made up of honorable citizens with an authoritative line of command. That's all this park is trying to communicate about spirituality and weapons. I am sure that you must be just as horrified as we are by mass shootings like Columbine, and all the others."

"So, you guys think we should keep our guns as long as we make sure that military arms only end up in military hands?"

"And do what we can to keep guns away from civilians that have made it clear that they want to hurt or threaten others, people who you wouldn't want on your team. I think you would agree that people who are unstable or somehow not together enough to handle the responsibility shouldn't be put in a position to make horrible mistakes." Aziza observed some accord beginning to bloom in his face. "Maybe you would reconsider taking a walk with me through the garden. I think you might appreciate how our handling of guns has been good for our team, you know, the larger team."

Over the next few minutes, Eddie and Shen relaxed, realizing that this man, who Aziza was about to introduce to them, was probably the best first visitor that they could have hoped for. As she had said, it was all about diminishing peoples' fears about the 'other'. Including their own.

16

It was approaching midafternoon, and it had been a long day. Myra Kellogg sat on the bench facing the "Sending Our Prayers Aloft" sculpture, her 7-year-old twins cuddling with her on either side. Her husband, Matt, walked in a semi-circle behind them, holding his camera aloft, as he looked for the best angle to capture the full image. This statue, by an Alaskan artist, Hollister Bream, was far and away the largest in the park, measuring a full 18 feet in diameter. It depicted a Native American shaman, a Roman Catholic priest and a Buddhist practitioner, all transforming the air around them with vapors. The shaman held his smudge pot toward a solemn young woman, cleansing her with the smoldering sage. The priest's thurible swayed back and forth, releasing the myrrh, carrying his congregants' prayers to heaven. The Buddhist lit three incense sticks, and placed them on an altar, to honor Buddha. Centered between the three men, a three-sided vessel released a pungent waft of frankincense into the air, the fragrance carrying on the wind toward the stream.

The Kellogg's, who lived in the Tribeca neighborhood in Manhattan, often took daytrips out of the city on weekends. They were devoted parents, whose family activities were most always designed with the education of the children in mind. Matt was emphatic in his strong belief that it was crucial to the kid's upbringing that they partake in both rural and urban culture. "Sure, we are fortunate to have

378

MOMA and The Met and all the other treasures of the city in our back yard, but we can't rule out how equally important it is for the twins to see some hamlet's small historical museum or ride a 19th century railroad from one small town to another. American culture resides with both the city and the country mouse, and our girls shouldn't get a distorted view of who we are."

They had decided to visit Roosters Retreat after Myra had read an article about its opening in The New Yorker, and were glad they had made the trip. The children were getting to see sculptures in a natural setting, unlike their visits to Manhattan museums or city squares. Perhaps they would develop a broader appreciation for art, in an environment where they could run and laugh and breathe. The atmosphere in a museum was oppressive to pre-pubescent kids, with all the necessary restrictions on noise and movement and play.

"Art shouldn't be stuffy," Matt pronounced in his own stuffy way, as the twins ran off, chasing the drifting smoke and aroma in the breeze. The photo in his mind captured them as part of the sculpture, as if they were an integral part of a live animated statue. "It should be fun and freeing. It should feel as if they are in a playground"

"But it should also be instructive," added Myra. "I don't mean in some heavy-handed Soviet style drill-the-point-home manner, but doesn't art need to tell us something? Like a simple still life often reminds us to see the beauty in everyday objects, or a landscape instructs us to go beyond the immediate and observe the broad panorama. Part of what I love here is that the twins are getting a life lesson in ecumenicism and religious tolerance, without any words or diatribes boring them to death."

"But how about the other message, intended by the folks who built this garden. Does the symbolism of melting deadly gun metal into art mean anything to them? I'm afraid that's over their head."

"Not if we buy one of the miniature sculptures that we saw in that combination Library and Gift Shop. I'll bet they'll be telling every friend that comes into our house about how it used to be a gun, and now it's been turned into a statue. Have you ever seen a kid that didn't love transformers?"

Betania had fought for the gift shop to be included in the library, despite the opinion of others that the idea was too commercial. To be totally honest, she hadn't been keen on moving out to God-knows-where in the first place. Never in her wildest dreams had she considered living in the boonies. But at the end of the day, she had a sense of debt to the Shapiro's, and if it would help Aziza, then she was all-in. Her son, Bobby, had recently moved out, for college, and it couldn't hurt to do something new.

Her insistence on a gift store, had nothing to do with bringing in more capital, although that in itself wasn't a bad thing. More than anyone else associated with the project, well, maybe not Shen, she knew that money counts. It had more to do with Betania's belief that if the visitors to the garden were to bring the meaning of the park home with them, they would do better to actually bring some actual thing home with them. She loved Aziza, and Eddie was a good dude, but the two of them, as for as she was concerned, lived up in cloud city. Didn't they get that ordinary folk needed reminders, reinforcements, if they were going to hold onto an idea or concept. It's not like this was a religion where you bring home a bible and show up every week for another dose of the Kool-Aid. There needs to be something concrete that they can take with them, whether it's a replica of one of the statues, or some pictures, or postcards, or whatever. Most folks need to hold it, to feel it, to taste it, to see it, if they are going to get it. And keep it.

17

Abagail White, had travelled from Chicago to be part of the opening day at Roosters Retreat. She was a small woman, barely five feet tall, whose 34 years had been marked by unending tragedy. Brought up by a single mother who died from a brain hemorrhage when Abby was 9, she was brought to live at the Mercy Home, a Roman Catholic orphanage that traced back to the late nineteenth century. She married young, at seventeen, in part because she fell in love with a bus driver, Paul, whose smile was as engaging as his heart was devoted, in part to be free of institutional life. It wasn't that the priests and staff at Mercy weren't kind and giving. They truly cared. But she craved for someone to love her when it wasn't their job. And Paul sure did just that. She was his "little brown muffin" that he wanted for breakfast, lunch and supper day in and day out, which he never tired of telling her.

Their fifteen years together brought a ton of bliss, and one baby boy, Paul Jr., into her life. Until it all came apart when her two guys were shot down on their way back from the pizzeria, two more victims of ignorant boys shooting at other ignorant boys, and wildly missing their intended targets. Another day in Chicago. Two more statistics thrown into the homicide hopper. It served as a confirmation that anything that life gave to Abby would just be a tease, to be taken away by God's whim on the wind.

Abagail was on a pilgrimage, of sorts. For two years she had been just plain broken. She went to work, cleaning other peoples' homes, only to come home again to her own messy house, which she was too depressed to tidy. Unsuccessful at trying to get a decent night's sleep, she would repeat the cycle the next day, holding back her rage and pain every waking moment. Only in her early thirties, she was consciously living out an empty life, waiting to be spared by death, shunning any attempt to give life another chance to taunt her again. The nuns had said it all, a long time ago. God giveth, and God taketh away. Don't give that sucker another opportunity to play "now you see it, now you don't." It just hurt too much.

On the second anniversary of the loss of her husband and son, Abby went to the church, back at the Mercy Home. While she had no use for the religion and only went through these doors this once a year, it was the only way she knew to remember her loves, to celebrate her lost happiness. She would light two candles, one for each, remember their faces, and the touch of their cheeks, try to remember their smell, and then get on her way. But as she watched the flickering of the twin flames, a command voice called out to her, spoke clearly to her. It said, "Get the guns. Steal the guns."

For a week or two she could think of nothing else. What was the meaning of this? Was God really speaking to her, and if so, what was she supposed to do? And then one weekday night, when she was watching, although not really paying attention, when she was watching the news on TV, she heard about this guru who was opening up some sculpture garden in New Jersey, and all the statues were going to be cast out of melted down guns. There it was! It was clear. She was supposed to steal guns and bring them down to that Aziza person. With every gun she stole, somebody else's son, somebody else's husband, maybe she could save them from some stupid meaningless death. Maybe there was something she could do with her life. And if she got shot herself, in trying to steal the guns, that was okay too. Who knows? Maybe better. She could be with her guys.

The first two guns were easy. One was in the closet of the house she cleaned Tuesday mornings, the other a handgun in the nightstand on her Wednesday afternoon job. Just grab them and put them in trunk of her car. But the real guns she wanted to rob were from the gangbangers, from those ignorant kids in the neighborhood who thought they were tough but were just little boys who played dangerous shoot 'em up games, and killed themselves and strangers in the process. She decided that she could act crazy, dress like some crazy ho, and seduce these stupid boys into doing her, and that would give her some opportunity to snatch up their gun when they weren't looking. Some of the time it worked. Some of the time it didn't. She could wash off their filth with a quick shower, and that was that. But over two weeks' time, laying down with a different kid each day, she was able to steal three more guns. And that meant five. Four handguns and one shotgun. She could bring all of these five guns to New Jersey.

All the way there, she was smiling, for the first time in a long time. Maybe, just maybe, she had saved some other person's loved one. The guns were in a big old duffle bag that Paul Sr. had brought home from the army. She was walking around that quadrant area, the place where there was this great big cross, like the one on the steeple back at the Mercy Home. That's when she saw the Guru. Somehow, Abby immediately knew it was Guru Aziza. Was it that beautiful white and lilac dress, or the serene look on her face? Who knows? She just knew it was her.

"Excuse me, are you the guru person?"

"There are people who call me that." The lady extended a hand. "Glad to meet you. I'm Aziza."

"Well, I'm Abagail, and I just drove here from Chicago. And I got something for you." Abby held out the duffel, indicating that she wanted Aziza to take it. Aziza unzipped the bag, and was a bit startled by its contents. "Abagail, where did you get these weapons?"

"I'd rather not talk about that. Let's just say that they weren't any place good, and I was able to bring them here. Now, they're someplace good. The way I heard it was you could take them and melt them down and make a better purpose for them. Do I have that right?"

"I have a feeling that there is a larger story here than you're comfortable with sharing right now. Would you like to come inside, and maybe we can talk about some of what's going on with you and these guns? Yes, we will find a purpose for them, but I'd like to find a good way of thanking you."

Abagail knew she had done the right thing.

18

It had been a long and strenuous day, physically and emotionally. As dusk settled over Rooster's Retreat, Aziza sat in the kitchen, quieting her body and mind. It had all gone well, even if there were shaky moments at the start. Enough visitors not to be disappointed, not so many as to overwhelm the needed learning curve. It had been a good start. Most importantly, there had been many memorable moments interacting with the people who had found their way to the garden. All these conversations had felt natural, organic. Aziza reflected that the park and the sculptures were the attraction, but the human dialogue was the purpose of it all. Hadn't this always been the case? For her and Eddie, starting with the table at the Thatched Rooster. It was always about the interchange of insight, vision and energy. Souls touching souls.

Family members and staff had mostly left for the day, save the few who were staying over, and Eddie had volunteered to show that wonderous woman from Chicago a room where she could spend the night. What an amazing odyssey that woman had travelled! There were two bedrooms in the foundry building, built for visitors, on occasions such as this. Finally, Aziza was alone, for the first moment in over eleven hours. She appreciated the time to look back at the day and catch up with herself.

As she sipped on a cup of tea, Aziza realized, with a start, that unconsciously, somewhere in the back reaches of her head, she had been expecting Guru Nityaneeta to put in an appearance. I will see you again when it begins. Was today not the beginning? She hoped her silly "guruette" remark hadn't annoyed the guru? Her thoughts swung back the other way. How egocentric was she being herself to expect that Nityaneeta had nothing better to do than come and recognize her efforts? Obviously, if she had intended to come, she would have sent a message or had someone make a call. She reproached herself. Don't lose the exhilaration of the day in useless rumination about the one person who didn't grace us with her presence. You advise others to focus on what is present, not what is absent.

Ed was returning from his errand. As always, hearing his footsteps on the deck was a welcome and reassuring sound. But she thought she heard him in conversation with someone. Did Abagail find the bedroom in the foundry unsuitable? Had a staff member returned for some reason?

Instead, Eddie escorted Guru Nityaneeta into the kitchen. The broad smile he had been sporting all day had only widened. "Ziz, it appears that we have one more guest."

Aziza started to rise from her seat at the table, but Nityaneeta motioned for her to stay seated, and picked a chair for herself to sit. "Please remain seated, Aziza. You have undoubtedly had a long and strenuous day."

Aziza began to ramble. "I can't believe that you arrived, just as I was thinking about you. I felt so foolish being disappointed about your absence. Your words, I don't know, was it your words or your energy, either way, it was you that precipitated the vision that led to this garden, and this day. I was so focused on your saying that you would be here 'when it begins', when the vision was brought to reality. And now, today, that has happened. Your being here, it confirms to me that our efforts weren't being wasted, and that this project is spiritually authentic. As much as I have been sure that creating this sculpture garden was righteous, some part of me has been worried that the blending of the political and the spiritual was incongruous, that the two parts didn't really fit together."

Eddie excused himself and started to leave, to allow Aziza and the Guru to be alone. But Nityaneeta stopped him. "I think you should remain. From what I gather, you are probably the best person in Aziza's life to remind her of what I am going to say, and in the coming days she will require that counsel from time to time." He moved toward the sink and leaned on the counter, to be there, but not to be in between the women.

She turned toward Aziza. "My dear, you have been mistaken when you believed that when I said I would be here where it started, I was referring to the inauguration of this wonderful, and yes righteous, righteous is the right word, vision of yours. I am here today not because you have opened what amounts to a sanctuary, but because you have begun to be the Guru that you are. That is what has started.

"As you know, gurus are necessarily part of a lineage. For thousands of years there has been a passage of wisdom from saint to saint, from guru to guru, and in such a manner we do not lose the indispensable sagacity from one generation to the next. It has always been an essential part of a guru's function to recognize those who are destined to be gurus themselves, when they come across them on their path. The Master and the Novice encounter each other, a conveyance of mind and energy ensues, and the process moves on in time. The baton is passed, the lineage is regenerated. In my culture, this passage has always been, and will always continue to be.

"The novice never thinks that she is worthy of wearing the mantle of the guru. If he or she did, their egoism would itself be an indication that they could only be a false prophet. You think of your self-doubt and obsessive nature as a personality fault. In fact, it is the fountainhead and foundry of your clarity, and the certainty that is yet to come.

"The priest and the guru are very different roles. The priest is a cleric, someone who chooses a worthy vocation, a job, if you will, of serving the spiritual needs of their community. A guru has no choice. They do not select the role. The role selects them. In my culture there are both clerics and gurus.

"When I experienced the calling to be here in America, I naturally responded in the affirmative. It is my belief that my being here has been a benefit to the spiritual life of your country and its people. Through the building of our ashram and our outreach to those that reach out to us, goodness, love and awakening have been achieved. But I have also recognized from the beginning that there were limitations to what my presence could achieve here. Some people are drawn to me due to their disaffection with their religious upbringing, not their affection for what we represent. Others are attracted by what they feel to be different, foreign, exotic or cool. Sometimes it can become difficult to determine whether devotes are devoted to the trappings or the heart. In short, as a guru, I will always be perceived as something of an outsider while I am here, and this will always present some limitations on my service.

"I became aware a number of years ago that I would need to be vigilant for an American who was meant to be another link in the lineage, and that this searcher would look very different from what I was, when I first encountered my Master. Some years passed, and I felt it unfortunate that my path never crossed such a person. And then, I was given an article about you, about a reluctant guru. I was intrigued. When your book was published, I read it immediately, and what I read confirmed the feeling I had that you might be a worthy person to continue the lineage. It was not an accident that we spoke together at the 92nd Street YMHA. While I am often asked to participate in such public discussions, I rarely do. That day, it was me that initiated my participation. I needed to experience you in person.

"Reluctant as you are, Aziza, you are what you are, and you will need to find your way as a guru who is reflective of an American society. Clearly, you will not be required to dress in a sari or walk barefoot from village to village, or follow any of the various practices that are part of the traditions, and come naturally to me. I don't believe that you will need to forsake all other roles as a woman, as it is natural in America for women to serve many functions and responsibilities, certainly many more than men. You will have to find your way as a guru, allowing your path to teach you what the external manifestations of being a guru in America are. But I know that you already possess the heart of a guru, the vision of the prophet, and a sacred communal energy. I will not reach out to you again. But I will always make it a priority to respond to you whenever you require me, whether here in America, or at the ashram in India."

She took a scarf from within her sari, and tied it around Aziza's collar. As the scarf was tied, Aziza felt a surge of energy burst through her head and flow down her spine. She was surrounded by a blazing white light that held her still. After what seemed like forever but was only a minute, the flood of energy began to subside, Aziza started to physically respond, but once again the guru held up her hand, motioning her to stay still. She turned to Eddie and said "Take good care of her. That is your responsibility. We will meet again." And left.

19

Copernicus Day Address 2023
    February 19, 2023
    Eduardo Huertas, CEO, The Rooster's Retreat

As has been our practice for over a decade, Guru Aziza and I address the state of Rooster's Retreat on the date of Copernicus's birthdate. We choose this day because it was Copernicus who first challenged the ego-centric perspective of most of the world's religions, and in doing so, advanced a new potential for spiritual insight. Paradigms matter. Discarding the belief that we were the center of it all made a huge leap from ignorance and arrogance to spiritual humility at this critical point in history. While it is natural for our bi-cameral minds to compartmentalize knowledge into truncated segments, all of our understandings of the universe are essentially interlocked facets of the All and Everything. There are no conflicts between Science, Art and Spirituality. They are all the same.

It has been a good year for Rooster's Retreat. We have added two new sculptures to the garden. One, a towering piece, titled *Insight,* by Rashad Albaneeze, has recently been installed on the clearing by the stream. The other is a statue of Henry Posert, one of our Guru's early teachers, who passed away a year ago last December. This statue has been placed near the Guru's residence, near the statue of Ben Shapiro, the Guru's grandfather, and, like Henry Posert, an original board member.

The new apartments for visiting students are approaching completion. It is anticipated that by June of this year they will be occupied by 16 students, and 4 families. This will double our capacity to house individuals who wish to study with the Guru. If you know of particularly deserving individuals, let them know that there are grants available for those who do not have the financial ability but wish to be part of the Retreat.

I am pleased to share with all of you in our community that our week-long conference in Brady Hall, of Clergy Dedicated to The De-weaponization of America (CDDA) was a great success. CDDA is now over 2300 strong, with clerics of every faith, in every state in this country. The message is getting across. Gun violence is, at heart, a spiritual issue, a measure of the faulty character of the culture, and the narcissistic nature of our society must be challenged. We cannot claim to be a land of faith and a land of armed brutality at the same time. These are irreconcilable attributes.

The Guns For Art (GFA) campaign continues in 47 cities, removing over 23,000 handguns, and rifles from the streets of America in the last year alone. Just over 5000 of these weapons were assault rifles. This effort, centered in our offices on K Street in Washington, D.C., has helped to create works of art in all 47 cities, beautifying their parks, while decreasing the potential for death and destruction on their streets. While we are aware that these numbers reflect only a miniscule amount of the weapons currently held by civilians, there is a growing recognition that the weaponized consciousness of our nation must change. As we move away from an extreme and perverted interpretation of rugged individualism, we are confident that our populous will move to disarm itself. This will not happen overnight.

In the coming year, we are planning to campaign for each state to require all gun owners to carry liability insurance on all of their weapons. The dangers of death and destruction from weapons and from automobiles are similar, and this is a step toward compelling those who own guns to be responsible for them and the consequences of their usage. The greater the lethality of the gun, the cost of the insurance would proportionately rise. Our good friend, Carl Porcaro, will once again take the lead on this very important endeavor.

On a more personal note, Ben and Rosalita, the Guru's and my children, continue to grow strong, in body, mind and spirit. Ben is moving on to middle school this year, while Rosie, dispirited by his absence, remains in primary school, in the 3rd grade. As a family we were privileged last August to visit with Guru Nityaneeta, at her ashram in India.

Wishing us all a world without violence,

I remain,

Rev. Eduardo Huertas

20

Copernicus Day Message 2023
    February 19, 2023
    Guru Aziza

May this be the year your consciousness dances
with the stars.

Once,
Before an undifferentiated All and Everything,
    A compressed seed of an infinite garden,
Explosively burst,
There was only consciousness,
    Too ponderous to be aware
                Of awareness,
    Too dense for energy
                To stream,
    Too packed for existence
                To be.
Consciousness without existence is unthinkable
    Lamented a lonely depressed Gardener,
Boring itself with its singular plaything.

Then,
As the big bang boomed and revealed the All,
Everything swirling and coming to being,
Galactic dust fathering stars,
Infinite consciousness broke into pieces.
Energies mothered life forms
Each capable of beholding the All.
What is the worth of a universe,
Without eyes to see it,
Ears to hear it,
Or physical forms to dance to
its rhythms?
Awareness verifies existence,
Love authenticates life.

Now,
With consciousness implanted as your birth-day
gift,
Mindful of your mind,
Sentient of your world,
Do you mimic the pre-bang gardener,
Condensing life to a trough filled with presets,
Limiting vision to a decelerated life?
Or do you join with the Everything,
And dance with the All,
Choosing the Universe as your
dancehall?
Can we be dance partners who hear the music,
That symphony of spark and sound,
And dare to tango with the orbs?

May this be the year your consciousness dances
with the stars.

Thank you for reading.

Please review this book. Reviews
help others find Absolutely Amazing eBooks and
inspire us to keep providing these marvelous tales.
If you would like to be put on our email list
to receive updates on new releases,
contests, and promotions, please go to
AbsolutelyAmazingEbooks.com and sign up.

About the Author

Larry Lentchner, Ph.D. is a practicing psychologist. His concern for the spiritual well-being of our population grew out of a half-century of tending to patients in psychotherapy, observing and experiencing their pain and suffering, seeing them turning to drugs to avoid the emptiness within, unable to connect their larger selves. Dr. Lentchner presently snowbirds between New Jersey and Florida, maintaining a small practice of psychotherapy, to allow himself time to write. He has four children and five grandchildren.

For sales, editorial information, subsidiary rights information
or a catalog, please write or phone or e-mail
AbsolutelyAmazingEbooks
Manhanset House
Shelter Island Hts., New York 11965-0342, US
Tel: 212-427-7139
www.AbsolutelyAmazingEbooks.com
bricktower@aol.com
www.IngramContent.com

For sales in the UK and Europe please contact our distributor,
Gazelle Book Services
White Cross Mills
Lancaster, LA1 4XS, UK
Tel: (01524) 68765 Fax: (01524) 63232
email: jacky@gazellebooks.co.uk

AbsolutelyAmazingeBooks.com
or AA-eBooks.com

www.ingramcontent.com/pod-product-compliance
Lightning Source LLC
Chambersburg PA
CBHW050303030726
47505CB00003B/545